Between a Rock and a Hard Place

A Dutch Policeman under Nazi Occupation

Johanna van Zanten

Between a Rock and a Hard Place

A Dutch Policeman under Nazi Occupation

Addison & Highsmith

Addison & Highsmith Publishers

Las Vegas ◊ Chicago ◊ Palm Beach

Published in the United States of America by
Histria Books
7181 N. Hualapai Way, Ste. 130-86
Las Vegas, NV 89166 USA
HistriaBooks.com

Addison & Highsmith is an imprint of Histria Books. Titles published under the imprints of Histria Books are distributed worldwide.

Library of Congress Control Number: 2021940694

ISBN 978-1-59211-102-2 (hardcover)
ISBN 978-1-59211-281-4 (softbound)
ISBN 978-1-59211-283-8 (eBook)

"There's no doubt fiction makes a better job of the truth."

— Doris Lessing

Chapter 1

Jacob Van Noorden slipped into the police compound at four o'clock on a chilly spring morning in 1940. The village of Overdam was dark, its streets completely deserted with a wet sheen on the pavers, the air damp from the nearby river. No need for a guard at the Mounted Royal Marechaussee at this hour. He stole into his house and climbed the stairs avoiding the creak of its sixth tread. In the bedroom, he slowly undressed to his underwear and crawled into bed beside his sleeping wife. He coddled up to Margaret's warm, soft backside. She didn't move.

Exhausted, he was about to surrender to sleep when he heard the faint, but by then familiar, noise. Tempted to ignore the world, he sat up anyway, swung his legs sideways, and placed his bare feet on the cold linoleum-covered floor in one smooth movement and got out of bed. He shivered.

"Wake up, Margaret," he said quietly as he jumped back into his pants. She didn't stir. He gently shook her shoulder. Louder now, he said, "Sweetheart, do you hear that?"

She sat upright and rubbed her eyes. "What? Oh, you're finally home. I waited up for you. When you didn't come, I went to bed. I don't hear anything, dear."

"I'm going to check." He ran up the stairs to the attic and pushed open the blacked-out attic window, right by the landing, extending its forged-iron sash bar out as far as his arm would reach. Yes, there it was, a low buzzing sound, like a giant radio, warming up. He pulled away from the tiny window, hurried down the narrow stairs to the bedroom, and put on more clothes. With a low voice, he shook Margaret's shoulder once more.

She had fallen asleep but responded to his nudge by slowly lifting her head off the pillow.

With urgency, he said, "Get dressed Margaret, please, you must get up, I think the Krauts are attacking us."

She put her head down on the pillow and sighed: "Really?"

He didn't wait for her and stomped down the stairs without a thought for the sleeping children; breath quickened, thoughts racing. In the corridor, he stepped into his rubber boots and grabbed his jacket on the way out the door.

In the yard, he looked up. A large cloud of dark, flying objects was visible against the slightly-lighter, violet-black velvet of the sky above. He focused his gaze and could see many tiny lights moving westwards. This fleet was much larger than any he'd seen traversing the airspace before. He listened, alert, and heard the distant buzzing, but nothing else, no gun or artillery fire, and his heartbeat slowed somewhat.

So far, the only visible signs of the war between Britain and Germany had been smaller fleets of British planes, moving east early in the morning and flying home later in the day. The German Heinkels flew on the opposite schedule, southwards and westwards. It was all to little effect; some called it a ghost war. He didn't notice Margaret beside him until she touched his arm. She wore her coat slung around her shoulders. "Do you see them, dear?" he asked.

"I am so glad you're home, Jan. We missed you very much." She held on to his arm.

"Me too, *lieverd* [darling], but it was a busy week. I'm exhausted, and now this. You see those planes?" His voice was quiet as if he feared somebody listening in on their conversation.

"Yes, I do. Are you certain those are German planes?" She was wide awake now.

Her voice had the quality of a child's, soft and questioning, something he hadn't noticed before. It must have been her week alone that made her insecure. He put an arm around her and pulled her close. She leaned into him.

"I think they are, from their direction. Are you cold? Did you really miss me?" He scanned her face, then gave her a quick kiss on her lips.

She smiled at him. "No, it's not that but those planes scare me — there are so many this time. Don't worry about me. I feel better living in the compound with neighbors close by, but we did miss you. The boys kept asking for you."

Jacob squeezed her tighter, smiled, and looked up again.

She glanced briefly in the direction of the planes and wondered, "Where might they be going?"

The earthy fragrance of spring mixed with sweetness permeated the air, and a faint mist hung between the blossoming fruit trees in the backyard. Without any moonlight, the night was dark, although many stars seemed randomly thrown against the velvet sky, the reason it took a while to spot the twinkling lights of the planes. Jacob located the North Star and the panhandle of the Little Dipper, Ursa Minor. After a few minutes of silence, he spoke again.

"I might be wrong. This fleet is flying at almost-invisible altitude. Like before, it might be headed for England, only this time a few hours early and with more planes than usual. England will be ready for them. On the other hand, it just might be a diversion tactic; I'm going to check the radio. You shouldn't have waited up for me. Why don't you go back to bed, dear?"

He turned her away from the spectacle high up above. With his hand in the small of her back, he guided her to the house. Walking with her, he was lost in his own thoughts. What if the target wasn't Britain? He had just returned from a long week of covert operations. He longed to punish the Nazis for their international law violations, for walking into sovereign nations — Austria, Poland, Denmark, and Norway — as if a border didn't mean anything. The Dutch leadership had cowardly signed more peace treaties, but if an attack on Holland were to occur, a war would be the only response to defend the nation's honor.

"If these *moffen* are after us, I'm ready to show them what we're made of, teach them a lesson," he suddenly growled. He used the pejorative word for German soldiers, shorthand for effeminate fighters, carrying *moffen* [hand warmers] before being able to load and fire a rifle in winter.

Startled by his tone, Margaret turned to face him.

"What are you saying? That's foolish, dear. Only short-sighted people would say such a thing. Nobody wants a war. You just came back from a week away, and you tell me you want to leave us again?" She realized she sounded like a nagging housewife and stopped talking as she resumed walking.

Her words had an effect. A sense of contrition crept up, but Jacob didn't like her tone of voice. "Just go back to bed, you're tired," he answered curtly.

She walked into the house and hung her coat on the rack by the front door. He followed her. To his surprise, instead of going upstairs, she walked into the living room. Her question hung in the air between them.

"Of course, I don't want a war," he said quietly. "Sweetheart, forget what I said. I just want to check the radio; you go on ahead upstairs."

She ignored his suggestion and sat down on the chaise longue — the divan. "If you stay up, I'm going to stay up too, I want to be with you. You don't need to protect me from what's happening. I want to know. And I want you to stop saying that ugly word. It hurts my feelings when you say it. Would you just say Germans, please?"

He sat down by the radio in the corner and considered her request for a few seconds. Although Margaret was German-born, she had no personal reason to feel German anymore. She arrived as a child with her whole family, and all of them had been Dutch citizens for almost two decades. Of course, she still had uncles and an aunt in Germany. He had visited Margret's aunt in Hildesheim once with her before the boys' births.

"Oh, you're too sensitive. Don't take it personally, *lieve vrouw* [dear wife]. I'm talking about enemy soldiers and generals. Everybody calls them that. I don't mean civilians. I don't consider your family members *moffen*." He laughed half-heartedly and looked at her for its effect.

She didn't laugh. She just tightened her jaw and looked down at the floor when she commented, "My uncle is in the Wehrmacht, didn't I tell you?"

He took a few seconds before answering and softly said, "Margaret."

She looked up.

"I forgot, sorry."

She smiled and brightly said, "That's alright. Uncle Klaus might be retired by now."

He wondered how her sympathy for the Heimat would play out if the German army indeed invaded Holland. The thought of it hit home. Fear made his heart race, and sweat formed on his brow, anticipating.

Bending over in his chair next to the radio, he fiddled with the dials in the dark living room. The radio's cat-eye took a minute or two to change to chartreuse, indicating the tubes were heating up. He turned the dial to fine-tune the bandwidth until the now green indicator slimmed to a narrow, vertical pupil. The crackling noise from interference became an ear-splitting-loud voice, speaking clear sentences through the loudspeaker — obviously Jaap's handiwork. His one-year-old son liked playing with the dials.

"Turn it down! The kids will wake up," Margaret called out over the noise.

He already turned the volume down and muttered: "Sorry, sorry."

The voice continued: "This is a repeat of the message. This is a special broadcast from the Central Air Observation Center. Large numbers of unidentified aircraft have crossed the Dutch border in the northern provinces and are moving westwards across Dutch territory at an altitude of about 2000 meters."

"Goddammit!" The rare blasphemy escaped his mouth before he could repress it. He crouched closer to the radio, uncertain what to do next as the airborne army advanced to its destination without any barriers in its way. It called up a biblical scene on his mind: the proverbial plague of grasshoppers chewing through anything alive at the end of times in the book of Exodus. He had startled Margaret.

"Jan, what is it?" She used his common, abbreviated nickname instead of the formal Jacob, something she occasionally did for emphasis or when she was worried.

As he considered how to interpret the radio message for her and explain the significance of the fleet's size, a little voice cut through his thoughts.

"I heard the radio. Papa, you're home!"

Four-year-old Hendrik stood by the door, rubbing his sleepy face, then ran towards him and wrapped his skinny arms around his shoulders.

"Hi, little man. Did you wake up?" Jacob sat the boy on his knee and gave him a kiss on his head as he looked at Margaret: "That's all we need," he mouthed. To his son, he spoke kindly: "We're just listening to the radio, son. It's too early to get up. Go back to bed, Hendrik. Mama will take you upstairs."

As soon as he had finished the sentence, little Jaap also stumbled into the room, sobbing:

"Mama, Mama." When he saw his dad, he stopped crying. On unsteady legs, he moved to his dad. The boy laid both his tiny hands on Jacob's knees for support and looked up. "Papa, Papa."

Jacob lifted him onto his other knee and kissed him. "Hello, my baby boy," he whispered.

Hendrik demanded his attention again and pushed Jaap away, defending his spot. "Papa, you were gone so long."

Both boys clung to him, arms tightly wrapped around his neck as if he had been gone for a year. Jacob got up from his chair with both boys in his arms. He hugged them, kissed each on the cheek, and set them down on the floor. "Yes, boys, I'm back. Mama told me you missed me. I missed you too." He gave them his order in a gentle voice: "Go back to bed now. I promise I'll come up and tuck you in."

While Margaret pulled the boys by their hands out of the room, the children looked back at their dad, but Jacob's mind was already elsewhere as he smiled at them and waved goodbye. He returned to listening; the radio repeated its message.

His phone rang: "Van Noorden, go to the office and stand by. The Krauts are attacking us and I heard the bridge was already taken. I'll keep you informed. Talk soon," said his department head Den Toom.

Jacob exhaled sharply and then used an internal line to his deputy, Sergeant Van Houten, who lived in the adjacent residence within the compound. "I think we are on the verge of action, Van Houten," he breathed into the phone. "Meet me in ten minutes." Then he ran upstairs, his mind racing, his blood pumping.

Chapter 2

Margaret sat with Jaap on his bed; Hendrik was wide awake in his bed across when Jacob entered the boys' bedroom. Excited from the anticipation of any action, although he didn't know what to expect, he was all business now.

"Go back to sleep, boys. Papa will stay home for a long time. Margaret, best you stay upstairs with the boys, at least until they're asleep. I have to go to work. You better just stay at home today."

"I wasn't planning on going anywhere," she said, sounding offended. "I want to see you at lunch today."

He sighed, and forcing his voice to sound patient, he said, "Sweetheart, I'm just worried about you and the boys. I don't know what will happen today, but I have the feeling that something will. If I'm not back by evening, go to your mother with the kids, as we talked about before." He tucked in the boys, kissed them, then whispered in her ear: "Germans crossed the border, and our bridge was taken."

She looked up, startled. With distaste in her voice, she responded: "I love my mother, but I'll only go to her as a last resort. I don't want Mutter's reputation to rub off on me in this town, where people know nothing about us. Anyway, I'd just fight with her about her crazy adoration for that awful man. You be careful now; I wouldn't want anything to happen to you, *schat* [darling]." Her face was pale. Her hair had slipped from underneath the hairnet, and she wiped it out of her face.

"I know you love her, and she loves you, and you'll be safe there," he said in a soothing tone. He gave her a quick peck on the lips, stroked her hair and left. He wondered what sort of role lay ahead for him in the nation's defense. He tried to pretend he was worried but knew he hadn't fooled Margaret. His voice had barely contained his excitement. This change of pace was exactly what he'd been waiting for. Although the director's news caused him some concern, at least something was happening after the years of increasing hostilities in other countries.

Walking down the stairs, he considered his options. As a thirty-five-year-old policeman with two boys under five, he didn't long to go to war, but he would never shrink from his military duty in the face of intimidation and injustice. No, surrendering wasn't his style, but no sane man in his position would choose outright combat at the front. He would find a meaningful role behind the scenes. His family's safety would come first.

Margaret's mother, Johanna, lived with Juergen, Margaret's twin brother, in a duplex farmhouse only an hour's bike-ride from Overdam, closer to the border. If the Germans were coming through, probably on their way to France or England, Margaret surely would be safe there because Johanna was a staunch admirer of Hitler, and Juergen had signed up for the Dutch Nazi Party. Jacob hated their allegiance to the Germans and couldn't imagine how that might play out with a German invasion. He would have to wait and see.

Chapter 3

Jacob and Van Houten stood outside in the compound yard, both dressed in uniform, and searched for the waves of tiny, buzzing lights up high in the sky, virtually beyond observation. They heard faint explosions in the distance, maybe twenty or thirty kilometers away — about the distance to the border.

Van Houten pointed out to Jacob the inconsistency of the sounds with what they observed. His voice trembled with excitement, maybe also fear; Jacob couldn't be sure. "If the planes are attacking us to the west, Opper, I think the only plausible reason for explosions would be that our border defense is destroying the bridges."

His crew members called Jacob Opper [Gov] short for opperwachtmeester, his rank. Jacob didn't reply right away and breathed a few times deeply to calm himself down. His heart was beating one hundred clicks an hour.

"I wonder what's happening on the ground. How much time would a well-equipped army need to defeat the border troops, you'd think? It wouldn't be longer than a few hours. I'm calling the department head now. Come inside too," he told his sergeant. After all, the Marechaussee Corps was military police, and in such dire times, the unit might be assigned a particular task beyond policing.

Jacob returned to the building and sat down at his desk in his private office. He considered his intent for a moment and then decided to call the mayor instead. On announcing his new assignment, his commander had instructed him to make sure that, as the chief, Jacob must show courtesy to the civilian leader of Overdam in this rural posting, where everybody knew each other and relationships counted. He only had met Mayor Van Voorst tot Voorst once. Good, the telephone operators were still on duty. She put him through.

"Van Noorden, do you think I'm deaf and dumb?" the man shouted in his ear, then softened and grumbled, "Of course, I know about it. The whole damn country has heard about what's happening."

Taken aback by the response, Jacob nevertheless was glad he remembered to call the man first, and he politely replied: "Sorry to call you so early, Mayor."

"Never mind. I've been up for days with the radio on. I sent the Air Defense earlier to blow up the bridges across the Vecht, but they failed. German soldiers already controlled the bridge into town with the help of some Dutch civilians, can you believe it? Damn it. The Germans took charge of the access road into town, too. My unarmed auxiliaries were useless and were still in bed at that time. What about your men, did you have anybody on the graveyard shift? I guess not. Get a few of your men to the bridge anyway to see what's happening."

That wasn't what Jacob had in mind. "That's a tall order, Mister Mayor. My brigade is only seven men strong, and I have to get my orders from my superior in Zwolle yet but I'll see what I can do. Got to go now."

After he disconnected, the phone rang immediately. The operator had his boss on the line, the regional director of the Royal Mounted Marechaussee Corps. He took a deep breath. "Yes, Commissioner. Van Noorden here."

The commissioner's voice was matter-of-fact as if reading from a bulletin. "The Wehrmacht crossed our eastern border at the exact moment the Luftwaffe began bombing all Dutch airports in the west. Our men are in battle. It doesn't look good for us."

"That explains it," Jacob exclaimed.

"What do you mean?" the commissioner demanded to know.

"Oh, sorry, Commissioner. I meant we heard explosions here in Overdam and wondered what was going on at the border. You know about the bridges then, Sir?"

The commissioner ignored his question and went on. "I'm calling all brigades in my region to remind them. You remember the government guidelines for a hostile invasion?"

Jacob didn't have to think about it. He had instructed the crew in the weeks before about it. He promptly answered, "To stay in our positions as long as the citizens are served and the enemy respects the international laws. Sir, the mayor has told me German scouts have already secured the bridge over the Vecht. My department head Den Toom knows about it."

"Exactly. There's nothing for you to do. I wouldn't want your crew to get in over your head. Your unit is designated police, not combat. I'm waiting to hear more updates. Glad you're back, Van Noorden. Mobilize your crew and wait for further orders. I expect the attacks of the Wehrmacht won't last long; those damned Krauts will be stopped. Good luck to us." The commissioner disconnected without waiting for a reply.

Jacob shivered; his heart rate slowed down, and his arms showed goosebumps. He pushed hard to get his muscle through some massive resistance as he got up from his desk chair. His eyesight seemed to fail; everything was fuzzy. When he realized this was the moment he had been waiting for, adrenaline kicked in, and blood flowed to his brain. He went to the squad room and told his sergeant to get going on the telephone and mobilize the crew.

Whereas he became quiet when stressed, his deputy became chatty.

"What do you think, Opper, will the mayor distribute his stash of weapons to the auxiliaries? I think he should. Don't you think it a good idea?" Van Houten looked at him, apparently expecting an answer.

Jacob didn't respond, only vaguely aware of what Van Houten talked about.

"Remember, a couple of weeks ago, when the mayor ordered the local hunters to hand in their hunting rifles and ammo?"

He remembered. "Ah, Sergeant, yes. We don't need a bloodbath here, don't you agree?" he said and then updated his deputy chief on the bad news about losing the bridge to German scouts.

Chapter 4

"Didn't anybody hear those damn planes? The crew should've been here already," Jacob said. He didn't get an answer. The sergeant was still on the phone with the operator, requesting to be connected to a succession of numbers. Deputy Van Houten had turned on the radio and the portable short-wave wireless; the crackling sound of interference hung in the background.

Jacob decided he'd better fill him in immediately and interrupted him. "Sergeant, hold on. The mayor wants some men to go to the bridge to check it out, but the commissioner wants us to sit on our hands."

Van Houten put his other hand over the speaker and looked up. "I agree with the mayor. Do you want me at the bridge, Opper?" Van Houten got up from his chair, the black phone in his hands. Besides being a chatterbox, he was a bit of a hot-head, eager for action.

"Alright, when the others arrive you, can take three of them with you, with the horses. I hate to ignore our boss but what the Mayor wants is important too. I want to know what's happening."

It took them only a few minutes to mobilize the rest of the unit. Within fifteen minutes, the five other marechaussees had arrived on their bicycles: corporals De Wit, Peters, and Dijk, and constables Leversma and Dikkers.

All of the men were younger than Jacob, although Peters and Dijk were not that far behind him. He stood in front of his men, hands in his pockets, jacket unbuttoned — confident. The age advantage over his men gave him more authority, but not that much more. This assignment as group commander was a challenge. He had to project confidence he may not feel in the moment. As the youngest in his family, he only knew about older brothers. He hadn't liked his position as the litter's runt then, so at least he was slowly climbing up to a better place. He grabbed the back of his neck, extremely itchy, and he wondered whether flees had found him and rubbed it briefly. He gave his orders.

"Before going out, listen carefully. No shooting. Stay calm until you get new instructions. We're no combat unit, and we'll just stick to observing and policing. Everybody clear? Regroup in an hour back here."

The sergeant left immediately for the stables with Dikkers, Dijk, and Peters, all of them excitedly talking battle strategy. Jacob sent De Wit and Leversma on patrol to the two access roads at either end of town. Sitting by the radio in the squad room, he listened to the updates.

The mayor called and demanded an update, with a hoarse voice this time, and he added his thoughts on Germans. "Just so you'll know, I'm not planning to provide the Krauts with a welcoming committee. You can tell them where they can find me. Are your men watching those soldiers on the bridge?"

Jacob rolled his eyes but replied in a polite tone. "I sent a patrol, Mr. Mayor. If they're not back soon, I'll go and check myself. Got to go now." He disconnected, disappointed that he hadn't been able to completely keep his irritation from his voice. Oh, well. He stepped outside to listen.

Overdam was quiet without any traffic this early, except for the farmers, busy delivering the milk to the dairy cooperative in the grey dawn. Once in a while, the heavy sound of an explosion was audible somewhere, not that far away, but not close enough for it to be the local bridge into town. Away from observing eyes, he slowly inhaled and exhaled the fresh morning air, inspected the skies, saw no planes.

He realized the hard lump inside him was his guts, cramped up from fear, and only then did he allow the enormity of the moment to sink in. War. He had been too young for the previous war, and good fortune had kept the country neutral anyway. Everybody had been aware of the heavy toll on all countries involved, its shadow still casting dread into the present. This time, he wouldn't be that lucky. He went back inside to face with great trepidation whatever may come.

Chapter 5

Jacob stroked his thinning, dark hair back and exhaled and then got back to business. After the two men had returned from their patrol, he instructed de Wit and Leversma to stay put at the station, took his motorbike from the back, and went on patrol himself, worried about his men. He knew enough about people to see that Van Houten was a young buck with a temper who could cause trouble for him and others.

Jacob rode his bike on the main exit road towards the bridge over the river Vecht. After five minutes, he spotted the Air Defense team's uniformed members standing around and talking, several hundred yards before the bridge out of range of any gun.

He geared down and noticed closer to the bridge his group of four mounted police officers standing within shooting-distance of about a dozen German uniformed soldiers. Six Nazi soldiers occupied each end of the bridge with their machine guns at the ready, barrels downward. A camouflaged Opel truck parked on the far side showed a mounted heavy gun protruding from its open back. The Wehrmacht scouts had successfully secured the bridge over the Vecht in the night without firing a shot. Damn them to hell.

Jacob loudly accelerated the engine to make sure he got the soldiers' attention until he heard the pop of a shot, and a bullet whistled over his head, dislodging his cap. He squeezed the break. With screeching tires, he threw the bike in a lateral move to a halt. His hands were shaking when he bent to retrieve his cap from the ground but managed to keep his voice steady when he called out,

"Hold your fire. I want to talk. What's your mission?"

A man dressed in a dirty woolen jacket over clean coveralls and with a brand-new farmer's toque stepped forward. He walked the distance between the group of Wehrmacht soldiers and Jacob's motorcycle in ten steps, stopped in front of him, and replied:

"If you can't see for yourself, these German scouts are holding the bridge free for traffic. I'm the interpreter."

The speaker's outfit was obviously fake, and the guy wore bright-new wooden shoes. Jacob compared the new equipment of the soldiers to the pistols and old-fashioned carbines of his own men. He got off his motorbike, put it on its stand, and, with his usual cop's entitlement for asking questions, demanded: "What's your name?"

"That's none of your business, old man. You've got no authority anymore," said the traitor with a broad smile.

A flash of anger delayed Jacob's response as he swallowed hard to regain control of his voice.

"We have a non-aggression alliance with Germany. Aren't you the least bit embarrassed about helping these invaders? You're nothing but a traitor. I'll remember your face, even if you're too much of coward to give me your name."

The man was still grinning, turned to the Wehrmacht soldiers and spoke loudly, translating what Jacob had said, calling him a *dummkopf* [an idiot]. They laughed together.

The heat rising in his neck, Jacob took a step forward on an impulse, and as the Dutchman looked back at the leader of the soldiers, he hit the jerk square on the jaw with a solid left punch.

The man just grabbed at his jaw. "Ouch."

The German smiled at him and called out:

"*Sie haben nicht gewonnen. Sie sind ein sauere Verlierer.*" You didn't win. You're a sore loser, Jacob could make out. "*Kommen Sie mahl hier. Fürchten Sie sich nicht.*"

Come closer. Don't be afraid. He understood that. Humiliated, Jacob nevertheless was not prepared to admit defeat. He walked up to the Wehrmacht boss and glared at him. He slowly and loudly said: "Your Wehrmacht was not invited," and the Dutchman translated. "Crossing our border is a violation of international law. I have no doubt you will be defeated, like before."

The Wehrmacht representative kept smiling and told Jacob the first lie, translated by the fake farmer. "We'll see about that, Dutchie. Our army will protect your people. We will make yours a better country. Your job is done here. Go home and take your men with you. Goodbye." After his Heil Hitler salute, the uniformed man turned his back to Jacob, as the interpreter was still speaking.

Without a word, Jacob got on his bike. Driving past his crew members, he called out, his face all frown: "Back to base."

While completing a quick trip around town in the rising sun, he cursed at the absent Dutch army. A minute later, he saw the object of his grief — army trucks with soldiers — in the distance on the highway to Zwolle, moving westwards, away from the border. Deflated, his left-hand sore, he suddenly shivered on his bike and returned to the Marechaussee brigade with the premonition that this day, the tenth of May 1940, would end badly.

Chapter 6

These last few days, Jacob had thought often about the inevitability of war. Back in August of the previous year, the government had taken steps to put the army on high alert and had gradually mobilized the career military — just in case. Everybody hoped and prayed its stance of neutrality would hold, and Jacob had prayed on that, too. In 1914, the Netherlands had escaped that dance by not engaging in overtures when the Germans had started the great war to end all wars. Jacob was just ten years old when that war broke out, at an age when boys want to be soldiers.

When on September 3, 1939, the German army invaded Poland, the British Prime Minister of England declared war on Germany. So did France. They requested the three BENELUX countries — Belgium, Netherlands, and Luxembourg — to join their alliance. Jacob expected the Dutch government this time to agree and join the war, but the cabinet refused again. He had not agreed with that. Two months went by before Prime Minister De Geer finally ordered the conscripts' mobilization, and all 150,000 of them flooded the system for training.

Just last April, less than a month ago, the Germans had taken Denmark; its king and cabinet capitulated within six hours. In Norway, the king and his ministers escaped to Britain, but a politician called Quisling grabbed the power and formed a new government that willingly cooperated with the occupier — a traitor. Jacob had no words for that kind of blind ambition.

Only three days ago, General Winkelman had ordered the immediate mobilization and suspended all furloughs. Jacob's six-day-long undercover assignment in preparation of hostilities was tricky, and he'd completed the last arrest early this morning. Like everybody else, Jacob knew war with Germany was imminent. His deputy had taken the reigns in his absence.

When the sergeant and his crew returned from the bridge, Jacob had shaken off his impotent exchange with the insolent German commander. As if nothing had happened, he got back to business and asked Van Houten in the squad room: "Sergeant, did anything happen while I was away?"

The deputy perked up. "Not really. What about you, Opper? How many traitors did you arrest?"

Jacob stuck his thumbs in his waistband and said, "Although it's none of your business, I'll share this much: we got about all of the NSB elite, except Mussert. That snake slithered away. We got some members of the civil service and some German expats suspected of spying, and some suspected VIPs." Realizing the removal of those dangerous elements might have been too late, he couldn't help but sigh and added, "I hope it'll make a difference."

Van Houten looked at him with open curiosity. "What does your wife say about it all, her being German and all?"

Jacob glared at the younger officer and empathically told him: "You're wrong. Margaret hasn't been German since she became an adult. She's Dutch now and, for your information, she doesn't want to be associated with Nazi ideas."

"Oh, sorry, Opper. I just know her brother, Juergen." The young man looked chastised.

Hearing the name, Jacob's temper flared up, angry with himself as much as with his sergeant. He had failed to connect the dots: Juergen was part of the community and a peer of Van Houten. "Damn well think before you speak, Sergeant. I don't share confidential information with my wife or her relatives. They'll just have to accept what I do."

He thought about those early days when he was stationed in the town of Margaret's mother. Within a couple of days, he had bumped into the Zondervan family's reputation when somebody asked him if he was related to that fascist family. He didn't want a repeat of that in Overdam.

Van Houten — and everybody else in the squad room — got the message. In a timid voice, the sergeant replied. "I see. Sorry, boss. Didn't mean to imply anything. Can't be easy for the both of you then. Good thing you moved away — "

Jacob raised a hand and cut him off. "That's enough. For heaven's sake, where are those Krauts? I'm tired of this."

The crew should never know how inept he felt in this first job as the commander. Being in charge wasn't a familiar situation. His life at home with his older brothers hadn't been comfortable, but he had made some friends in military training — equals, men of the same vintage with similar experiences. The experience had lessened his wariness, but the leader's role was still a stretch.

He reminded himself he should soon place a call to his bud in the capital, The Hague — the center of it all — to get the rumors about what's going on, whether the ministers were convening to declare war. Knowledge was everything.

Chapter 7

Less than an hour later, the mayor called him again and told him verbatim what the Air Defense commander had reported to him, some minutes earlier. The German scouts had left the bridge, and a division of German cavalry was coming down the main road, easily avoiding the asparagus in the pavement. The man meant the foot-high spike bands, dug in between the street's pavers.

"I see, thanks. Gotta go," Jacob said breathlessly and threw the horn on its cradle. He could just imagine the animals gingerly stepping through the shallow water of the drainage ditches beside the road instead of staying on the pavement. With a shout to Van Houten to join him as he passed the squad room, Jacob rushed out of the brigade building. Dressed in his full uniform, he carried his loaded service weapon in its holster at his right hip, and his carbine slung over his left shoulder.

Standing in front of the brigade building, he saw the cavalry already coming down the street. They galloped past him without so much as a glance in his direction on their way out of town. If these hadn't been Krauts, he would have admired the tableau of the horses gleaming in the bright, early morning sun, and the dapper men in their grey-green uniforms, skillfully driving them on. As the horse smell reached him, he recalled his training days and his delight in getting close to the powerful but sensitive animals. His own horses in their stables neighed, moving about in their stalls, and one animal kicked the boards repeatedly. The animals were nervous too.

Van Houten hadn't come outside yet. Jacob quickly walked to the stables in the back of the compound to check on the horses. He spoke to Susie in a calm voice — his favorite charger and the most-ornery of the bunch — until she had settled. Susie dislodged his cap but he caught it in time, then returned to the road, expecting the Wehrmacht in their tanks to show up any minute. He paced back and forth in front of the building. His legs trembled, and his stomach hadn't returned yet to his usual, soft belly.

His head felt wet. Jacob got out his handkerchief, took off his high cap, wiped his bold spot, replaced the uniform cap, and pushed the cotton cloth back into his pant pocket. He didn't have enough air. He forced his breathing to become deeper and slower. He wondered where his deputy was and considered getting him, but that would seem weak, so he didn't.

A minute later, Van Houten appeared, finally remembering where the chief would be, when he wasn't in his private office. They waited together, standing within touching distance from each other.

Jacob was grateful for his chatty deputy keeping his mouth shut, for once. No more than five minutes later, a low vibration under his feet got stronger as he heard a fast-increasing rumbling sound. A cloud of dust appeared in the distance on the elevated highway. It rolled rapidly closer through the flat landscape and metamorphosed into a large number of armored Panzer vehicles. The caravan of metal and dust soon veered off the highway onto the road into the village. The tanks wouldn't have any trouble driving over the spikes. His brain had a life of its own and focused on details: what's the use of asparagus, it wondered.

A shiver ran over his back. He was all fired up. His hearing was exquisite and he thought he could hear German words spoken. His sense of smell distinguished diesel oil, metal, dust, earth, even dew. Making up for his 1.70 m. frame, he took the posture of someone in charge, hands clasped at his back, chest forward, wide stance. After all, he was the legitimate commander of this Marechaussee unit.

The earth vibrated in a long shudder as the vehicles rumbled past on their mission to the center. The two men stood frozen in front of the building. Jacob held his breath without realizing it and only exhaled, when his lungs ran out of oxygen. His legs mirrored the vibrations underneath him as he inspected the enemy troops in their tanks. He heard his sergeant whistle through his teeth and whisper, "Jeez."

Suddenly, one of the Panzers' cannons swiftly changed its direction and pointed at the two policemen. Jacob's first instinct was to duck, but he resisted the urge and instead drew his pistol. The porthole in the turret revealed the driver's head. He aimed, and as if in a trance, fired three shots in the head's direction. The bullets ricocheted off the armor. The tanks' caterpillar tracks kept on grinding forward under the loud squeals of metal-on-metal.

"What are you doing?" shouted Van Houten and threw his hands up in the air.

The tank's gears rotated the turret on the hull, and the cannon resumed its forward position as the Panzer continued its planned route. All of it had taken no more than fifteen seconds. The crack of his pistol and the smell of powder, sharp in his nose, brought Jacob back to reality. After holstering his gun, he grabbed his head with both hands for a few seconds, then dropped his arms. He stared blindly after the disappearing cloud of noise and dust.

"I'm not sure. He …he was aiming at us," he stammered. Then in a more decisive tone: "You saw it too, admit it." He knew it sounded like a weak excuse. "Goddamn nerves; don't mind me. Sorry." He looked at Van Houten with a helpless expression, wondering if he had now lost all credibility as commander.

The sergeant roared. "Haw, haw, that Kraut was toying with us." Seeing the chief's face change into a deep frown, Van Houten quickly stopped himself but had one more comment. "You're defying your own command of no shooting, Opper."

"Shut up. It might happen to you too." Jacob said under his breath.

"We'll see, sir," Van Houten said mildly, and his smile was still there, just the tiniest tremor around the corners of his mouth.

Jacob looked at his deputy with a stern face, willing him to shut up. He took a deep, slow breath and the tension broke inside him. He couldn't help it; a laugh broke loose from his throat, haw, haw, haw, then he recovered.

"Those damn Krauts. I didn't think they had a sense of humor," Jacob said, and Van Houten laughed again. Now he had a Sergeant who had seen him succumb to pressure. Oh well, nothing he could change now, he'll have to live with that. At least Van Houten seemed like a half-decent chap, much younger, and probably somebody he could manage.

Chapter 8

Van Houten went inside the brigade, but Jacob waited outside a while longer to allow his body sensations to return to normal. He was strangely disappointed; the invasion was a let-down. After the last tank had disappeared from sight, Corporal Peters returned from the stables. The man seemed lost and looked inquisitively at his boss before finally asking: "Who was shooting? I heard shots fired." That damn Peters was a curious man.

"One of the gunners aimed at us. I lost my nerve and took a few shots at him. The sergeant thought it was funny," Jacob said and looked back at Peters with a stern expression. "Don't you dare trumpet that around," he added in a threatening voice.

Peters didn't laugh out loud, like Van Houten. "You're lucky he didn't fire back," he commented.

Jacob frowned. "Peters, wipe that grin off your face. What do you have to report?"

While the corporal continued his report, Peters' big grin turned into a slight smirk.

"Opper, I got some interesting information from some local farmers. At midnight, they'd seen some out-of-towners loitering by the bridge. Looks like our own people helped the Germans to secure the bridges for the tanks. What were we supposed to do, anyway? Arrest our own people?"

"Yup, we would've, if we'd heard about it earlier," Jacob grumbled. "Those scouts must've entered the country the day before and met up with the traitors. We'll just have to wait for further orders."

"Where are those planes headed, you think?" Peters pointed to the sky.

"My guess is as good as yours," he said slowly.

They both looked up, shielding their eyes with their hands from the bright, early morning sun. The heavy droning sound of military planes had resumed, clearly visible now and flying lower than last night, when he had first noticed the buzzing, out of reach of any Dutch artillery.

Jacob realized he would have to forward a report on firing his weapon to the department head, and he softly mumbled a curse, hoping Peters and Van Houten wouldn't blabber about his response to the rest of the crew. Peters still looked like he was having fun, a glimmer dancing in his eyes when Jacob looked at him.

Jacob quickly replied, sounding more confident than he felt. His bravery of earlier hours had left him. "They're probably heading south to Belgium, or possibly to the west, hoping to catch the Queen and the cabinet. Looks like that's all we got for Krauts today." He was proud of his voice; it sounded indifferent, in control.

The two men turned their gaze away from the sky. They were about to enter the building when a camouflaged motorbike with a sidecar stopped at the entrance. An officer in drab-green got out and greeted them with the full Heil Hitler stretched-arm salute. Jacob responded with a half-hearted salute with a hand up and the elbow bent, like the universal hello gesture, and he mumbled a soft Heil Hitler. As he expected, Peters copied him but with his arm stretched appropriately.

"Verzeihen Sie mir," the officer asked. "Sind Sie der Polizei Kommandant?" Are you the police commander?

Not ready yet to try his German, Jacob confirmed it with a nod and gave his rank: "Groepscommandant, Opperwachtmeester." Group Commander, Warrant Officer.

The man looked at him with an evaluating eye before he continued.

"*Gibt es ein Problem? Ich habe einen Bericht über Schüsse abgefeiert, ich werde zu Untersuchung geschickt* [Is there a problem? I received a report about a shots fired. I'm sent to investigate]."

Taken aback, refusing to speak German, Jacob stammered: "Yes, yes, ah, those shots. A hasty mistake of a nervous officer. My apologies." He recovered, and more firmly, added in German that didn't sound right: "*Aber we werden das Feuer zuruck-geben wenn wir unter Feuer kommen* [But we'll return fire when we're shot at]. His face turned beet-red as he glared at the German]."

The officer in his perfect uniform stared back at him, then astounded Jacob by clearly speaking Dutch in a calm and polite tone of voice with only a slight accent.

"I assure you we're not here to fight the police authorities or fire at civilians. The Reich's authorities are now in charge of this village, but we want to collaborate with the local police. I hope you want that too." The German now set his eyes on Peters and studied him for a minute.

Jacob measured himself against the German and concluded that the man was larger and better dressed, like all of them. He searched for words, not wanting to be submissive but not willing to antagonize him either.

The German was done with Peters and stared at him now, waiting for an answer. Relieved he didn't have to speak German again, he replied. "Indeed, my instructions are to collaborate, keep order, and stay on my post as commander of my crew."

The German calmly held his gaze. "Not to worry about being fired at without provocation. Where is the mayor, *bitte?*"

Jacob wanted to say a whole lot more, swallowed a few times but nothing helpful popped up in his mind. "Three buildings down, that way, in the town hall."

"Thank you, Commander."

The Nazi clicked his heels, turned around, and got back into the sidecar.

This time, Jacob didn't bother with returning any formal salute and just watched the motorbike leave as he exhaled and let his shoulders drop. He wondered what would come next. Like frozen to the spot, he watched the duo. The driver stopped a hundred meters down the road in front of the town hall. The officer got off and walked with gusto into the building.

Chapter 9

Jacob and Peters joined the other officers in the squad room. Everybody was soon talking over one another, the main topic the chance of the nation surviving the German attack. Work wasn't on their mind. De Wit said the Germans had only seven divisions compared to the Dutch with ten, but the Germans had a mighty airborne force, as they all had noticed. Dikkers interrupted De Wit saying the Dutch had an impossibly long front to defend from the north to the south along its shared border. Peters suggested the south was a problem. Its loosely-defined border with Luxembourg and Belgium made it hard for any army to take the Ardennes, with its mountains and dense forests throughout. Leversma said the Dutch neutrality in the last war was a mistake: without battle experience and proper equipment, the soldiers were at a disadvantage.

The crew spent most of the morning speculating, and Jacob let them. He knew he would turn his men into enemies if he tried to pull rank to make them do routine work. From his own experience, he learned that the tension of not knowing the future and feeling vulnerable could make one talk, and talk, and talk. The phone lines were down, but radio updates were broadcast every half-hour. The men huddled around their only link to the outside world.

By 11:00 a.m. that day, they learned the attacks on the ground took place simultaneously with the German airdrops of paratroops on the airfields around the capital, The Hague. After they had landed, the massive shelling had begun, and the German army had taken the airports soon after. Nobody went home for lunch, not even Jacob, against his custom, but he stopped in at home to update Margaret. At the end of that day, Jacob pulled Van Houten into his office. He invited his opinion, and they deliberated what to do for the night.

The sergeant suggested taking precautions against NSB agitators, who might feel courageous now that their heroes invaded the country. "Like everywhere else, it might come to street fights between loyalists and national-socialists."

"Good suggestion, Sergeant. I'll put two men on duty to deal with unforeseen events. Thanks for keeping your mouth shut about that accidental firing. Appreciated.

We'll make it all work here in the brigade, you and me, trust me." Jacob got up and came around the desk to shake hands with his deputy.

Back in the squad room, he gave his orders for the night and ended with: "Call me if anything at all happens tonight. You all, stay calm, and we'll meet in the morning."

***

Religion was the organizing principle in Dutch society, and also in Overdam. It was common knowledge that local Jewish organizations had already established refugee camps. German Jews stayed there, and some had arrived from further east, all before the Dutch government closed the border. One such establishment was located an hour's ride away. Jacob didn't expect any trouble on that front. As Jews began to leave their countries all over Europe, Jacob knew that they could expect little protection as refugees from the Christian denominations in Overdam, as anti-Semitism had infected the general population wholesale. Damn those Nazis. It was not right, but he was at a loss as to what to do about it all.

He was aware that several austere denominations of Calvinists had settled in the community of Overdam, its members with strange beliefs and a narrow range of accepting people, intolerant to those who were different from them. Most were dressed in black, and the women wore white caps and black woolen stockings, giving the church the name of the black stocking church. The town also had a Catholic congregation.

Jacob was a member of one of the Calvinist congregations with moderate convictions. Before joining him, Margaret had been a member of the Dutch Reformed church, substantially more lenient than his own Calvinist church. Overdam also contained a basecamp of the Anthroposophical movement, in a forested section nearby with cabins. Its adherents exclusively visited in the summer and had no representation in Overdam. They kept to themselves.

***

When Jacob had stopped in at lunchtime earlier that day, Margaret stood in the kitchen at the counter, preparing a meal. Jacob gave her a loving tap on her behind, then put his arm around her shoulder and kissed her on the lips. She kissed him back.

"How was your morning? Were the boys good?"

She nodded and sounded unperturbed when she asked, "What happened? Tell me. I heard shots and the tanks."

She had the boys quietly eating a sandwich at the table. He let go of her and sat down at the kitchen table with his sons. He said hi to the boys who were too busy to talk. For a second, he envied them for having their meal as the most essential task.

"It looks like we'll have no fighting here. The German troops have passed through already. Those shots were nothing, and I met with the first German." He glanced briefly at her, and she seemed fine. "Are you scared?"

"No, I'm not scared. There's a sandwich for you." She pointed to the end of the table.

"I've no idea what'll happen next," he said. "But don't worry, it'll be fine. The brigade will be safe." He got up, gave her a quick peck on the cheek, grabbed the sandwich sitting ready for him on the table, and went back to the office. His left hand was swollen, and he kept it hidden in his pocket.

***

At the end of that day, Jacob and Margaret sat at the dinner table. The boys were already in bed, their dinner over. Jacob couldn't stop thinking about that shameful moment of today. Why the hell did he have to return the Heil Hitler salute to the first blasted German officer he'd met on this Friday, the day to remember for the rest of his life, but he didn't tell Margaret about it. Ashamed and quiet, he just sat there.

In Overdam, it was all over. The enemy had just invaded his country, and he hadn't done anything to stop them. In this town of mostly conservative farmers and other God-fearing, Christian citizens, it was bound to stay quiet. He was not needed.

That night, with his head in the radio, he heard that the battle continued elsewhere, and his anxiety levels rose. The radio reported the frantic defense of the country taking place on various fronts. He told Margaret — who listened with him for part of the broadcast — not to worry too much.

Jacob was exhausted. His week of undercover work with little chance for resting had left him already sleep-deprived. The news of the invasion, the endless wait for a battle, the letdown of watching the German army moving unchallenged through his town, and then meeting the Kraut officers while still trying to determine what his attitude should be — all this left him whiplashed and short of breath. The sense of doom from this morning had disappeared but now returned and settled in his stomach.

Chapter 10

On Sunday, the German troops penetrated Rotterdam's outskirts while the bulk of the Dutch defense concentrated north of the river Maas. The Dutch army was in deep trouble. It was Jacob's turn for church, but because the radio news was more important to him than a pastoral sermon, he let Margaret attend the service while he stayed at home with the boys. After the move to Overdam, Margaret agreed with Jacob's decision to change from her family's Dutch Reformed church to this one. She didn't think much of it.

Jacob wasn't sure of his reasons. Maybe he needed to create distance from the in-laws for his young family, or he needed divine inspiration in this time of immorality and chaos. Perhaps his membership of the largest congregation in this town might help his relationships with the community. After his marriage to Margaret, he acknowledged his yearning for more boundaries and a stricter code of conduct for him and Margaret to raise their children, and do it differently from his parents' poor example. Their church was too rigid, stifling even.

When she returned home, she told Jacob about the minister's prayer for peace.

"He should've prayed for a victory," he grumbled, kicking the divan, spilling his coffee which Margaret had just handed him. "Druthers," he said under his breath.

Margaret ran off to the kitchen to grab a cloth.

"Sorry, dearest, that wasn't meant for you," he said softly when she returned and dabbed the spilled coffee.

"That's alright, husband, you had a few hard days," she said as she caressed his balding head.

After an early dinner, he decided to go for a bicycle ride in the forest on this lovely spring day. He wanted some quiet time to think and didn't ask Margaret to come, but Hendrik always was an excellent companion, and Margaret might need the break from him. Hendrik always wanted to come. Jacob pulled the safety bar upright over the rear wheel for Hendrik's back, lifted his eldest son, and put him on the carrier.

"Hendrik, remember to hold your legs out wide, so your feet won't get mangled by the spokes." He promised himself he'd have the bike shop mount foot supports on the wheel for his son someday soon. He wasn't much of a handyman.

"Yes, Papa."

The four-year-old boy was an active kind of kid who drove Margaret bonkers at times but sitting behind his dad watching the world go by was a treat for him.

Jacob liked to teach his boys about the types of trees and plants, the weather, the stars, and the wildlife, making a conscious effort to have a better relationship with his sons than his own dad had with his seven boys. To peer into the eyes of his own children taught him to understand what his parents went through. If he could repair the break with his dad, he now would, but it was too late. His mother had died of pneumonia and his dad of a heart attack in the last decade.

Today, he pointed out anything he could name, such as the hawk in the air hunting for mice on the moor. Hendrik stayed pretty quiet during the ride, but Jacob knew the boy looked around, taking in every detail. He felt his little hands excitedly tugging at his coat as his little body turned left and right to see everything.

He rode along the edge of the forest on the trail — not more than a cow path — where the adjacent moor with the peat bogs had just started blooming and was covered with sweet-smelling purple heather. He stopped the bike. With both feet on the ground, he turned to lift Hendrik off the bike first, set him down on the path, then swung his leg over to the other side of the horizontal bar.

The two looked at the sky from the moor's edge, where planes were still flying westwards. The roar of a low-flying plane coming out of nowhere startled them. Jacob resisted the impulse to throw the bike into the heather and drop to the ground, and he stayed standing, tightly holding on to the handlebar. He grabbed Hendrik's hand and told his son to stay close to him.

When the plane had passed, Hendrik asked, "Why are there so many planes, Papa?"

"These are German planes, son," he told the boy, weighing what he could say to a four-year-old. Hendrik's head still seemed so large compared to his immature frame. In contrast, his questions let him know the boy was growing up. He hoped that Hendrik would grow up into a more significant body than his own, so older and bigger boys wouldn't be tempted to bully him.

"We're at war now."

"What's war, Papa?"

Just as he was about to answer, a smoke plume rose in the distance, where the plane had disappeared. Two seconds later, the boom reached them, air pressure vibrating their eardrums. "Holy smokes," he shouted.

Hendrik looked around him, scanning the moor and looking back at him.

As he held Hendrik's warm, small fist and felt protective, wanting to shield his boy from the hardships of life, but knew he would not be able to. He pointed to the distant column of dark smoke and let Hendrik's hand go. "That was the plane we just saw flying over, there, where the smoke is."

Hendrik stared at him.

"War, it's like when you fight with Jaap. You're not to hit each other, you know that, huh? In war, people are not listening to each other anymore or the rules, and they really fight with all they've got, guns and tanks, and fighter planes, trying to hurt each other to win. That bang? The plane was shot down, is now broken, and it's burning. The men flying the plane might be injured, or even dead. That's war."

The boy still looked up to him, eager to get it, and nodded yes with vigor, as if he knew what "dead" meant. Maybe he did.

"Is it wrong to fight, Papa?"

Good question. Now how to answer that? "It's not good, but sometimes it's better than letting someone beat you to a pulp. You have to defend yourself. Not all fighting is bad, son."

Hendrik got restless, pulled his hand free, ran a short distance into the heather, and then returned. "Who are fighting, Papa?"

Jacob thought for a few seconds before replying.

"Our country is attacked by Germany, where Oma and Mama were born, and two other countries are helping us against Germany. Those friends of ours are England and France. Did Mama show you the tanks?"

"No, Mama said we weren't allowed to go outside, but I heard them, and it sounded like thunder."

"Good boy, for listening to Mama. Yes, those were German tanks rolling through the streets on their way to where they're fighting now." He gave Hendrik a quick pat on his thin shoulder. The boy again ran a few yards into the purple heather and quickly returned to stand by his side.

"Will we win, Papa?" He stood still and stared at him. "Are you going to fight too?"

Jacob exhaled slowly. "We don't know yet, son. We'll pray to God we'll win and fighting won't be necessary. If not, I probably won't join the battle and will stay here in my job. Somebody has to look after you and Jaap, and Mama, right?"

With his head down and in a soft voice, Hendrik asked: "You're not going to chase the German soldiers away?" He threw a sideways glance at his dad, waiting for the answer.

"Good question, son. I don't know what exactly I'll do. Better get going, Mama will be wondering where we are." He put his hand on his son's shoulder and kept it there, guiding him back to the bicycle, disappointment still visible on his son's face.

On the way home, Hendrik's question lingered in Jacob's mind. Do not kill, the Bible said, but defending one's country should be the exception. He was no evangelizing fundamentalist but a member of the silent majority of protestants with much hesitation to declare his religion the only true one. He was a convinced believer, though, and always spoke a prayer before and after each meal. Both boys knew enough to remain silent. When Papa said the prayer, Jaap sat usually on his mom's lap after dinner, thumb in his mouth and happy as a clam. He knew Margaret had her battles trying to stick to any routine with two small children, and the eldest was not always complying with the strict boundaries. Jacob chalked it up to Hendrik's young age and her leniency.

He and Margaret talked about the looming war, but always when the boys were in bed. The burden of telling his son weighed heavily, mainly because he knew he had disappointed Hendrik. The echo of his own father's voice floated through his mind: Can't you do anything right?

That night, the family had their supper with the radio off. Margaret and Jacob both carefully avoided the subject of a potential stay with Johanna and Juergen. Under the circumstances, Margaret's ties to former Germans who love Nazis wasn't a pleasant topic. When Jacob and Margaret tucked in the boys, they hugged each child one extra-long. Jacob stayed upstairs for a while longer and read the children a story from Grimm's book of fairy tales — the chat about the reality of the day, not an option.

Chapter 11

The next day, General Winkelman surrendered to the German high command on behalf of the Dutch government-in-exile to understand the Wehrmacht wouldn't carry out its threat to bomb the cities Rotterdam and Utrecht. Despite the verbal agreement, thirty German planes bombed Rotterdam. With smoke rising over the city, the parties signed the capitulation agreement in a suburb near the destroyed international harbor. At the brigade, Jacob's crew gathered to discuss the news of the surrender. Van Houten was often the first to offer an opinion, which he spat out as soon as he got the chance.

"The bastards, killing nine-hundred civilians for no reason." He choked back his rage and shared his concerns in a flat voice. "I heard eighty-thousand people became homeless. And the whole harbor was flattened. All those workers unemployed, what are they going to live on? What a lousy trick. And Middelburg bombed as well, even after the verbal agreement. They should've given them time to catch up to reality. The Krauts are not fighting fair. Killing civilians is unethical."

Jacob nodded.

"You said it, man, damn right devious," Leversma agreed in a shaky voice. "I doubt the harbor's bombing really was an accident. To me, it sounded planned, a deliberate action to destroy the seaport's capacity for future battle."

"But the Germans had to make it clear they've won," Peters argued. "How else were they getting us to stop from fighting? The war is over."

Although Van Houten and the others could afford to be outspoken, the chief had to hold back his views, but he had to say something in response to Peters. "Do you mean to defend the Nazis, Constable Peters?" Jacob said slowly.

"No, I'm not, but, hey, why continue to fight, when the battle is lost? Our army doesn't require suicide."

Some officers in the squad room shifted uncomfortably, turned away from the conversation to go back to work, or tapped their fingers on a desk. Van Houten stood up first and squared himself in front of Peters; his face was one big frown. "Might be the battle's lost, but the war is not over yet. Don't you forget it!"

Most men vigorously nodded.

Van Houten sat down again. "I heard the troops in Rotterdam refused to surrender and are still fighting," he added.

"I heard that in our southern provinces, the French Allied soldiers with their Moroccan troops are still fighting," De Wit said.

"Luckily, the Queen and her family left the country in time. Let's hope they'll be safe in England," Jacob added.

"The Krauts will never get to England, but in the meantime, what are we supposed to do now?" Leversma asked.

"Don't you worry," Jacob replied. "We'll find out soon enough. I'll get more instructions from our department head today. I suspect the Germans will also send someone."

"How bad is it going to get?" Van Houten wondered.

Jacob had the same thought and had fretted for days about his future. "Good question, we'll have to wait and see," he said and turned to go to his own office.

Was he going to be fired, or should he quit? Were the Germans going to imprison the members of the military? And who would pay his salary if he was allowed to stay on as police? Unlike his own father, money was of lesser interest to him. His main goal was Margaret and his boys' well-being first, although he recognized the need for an income. How to best take care of his family under German occupation confounded him. In an emergency, he'd steal, as he had done before — feeling guilty ever since — but this time for a good cause. The dread that stirred inside him like a tapeworm since the invasion hadn't left him.

Chapter 12

The closest neighbors outside the compound along the street were Ruth and Bram Groenheim. Margaret had found out they happened to be Jewish and that Bram operated the butcher store in the village, although it wasn't just a kosher shop. All burghers from this side of town shopped there. After the move to the brigade quarters, Margaret had asked Ruth a couple of times to keep an eye on the boys when she had to bike out to the store or go out on an urgent errand. Margaret told Jacob Ruth was lovely, and the boys had liked her. Ruth's older children, Rosanna and Peter, were sweet kids as well. Margaret hoped Rosanna, the eldest child, could be a babysitter for their boys.

Jacob still hadn't met the family. One evening at dinner, he brought it up.

"Maybe you should invite them over for coffee and a chat sometime soon. I'd like to meet the butcher, see if he plays chess. I could use more chess mates."

"I will do that next time I see Ruth. Do you think ten years old is too young to babysit our boys, dear?"

"Not sure, Hendrik is a handful. It might be an option for a short while after Jaap has already gone to sleep. If we're ever invited somewhere, we could try that, but you know best. Whatever you decide, lieverd." They hadn't made any friends yet since the move to Overdam.

***

A couple of days after the capitulation, new neighbors moved in down the road from the brigade. In his cultivated voice, the mayor told Jacob about it, as if he was keeping his jaws clenched.

"Van Noorden, if you take a few steps out of your driveway, you'll see the Wehrmacht HQ. They've moved into the White Swan Hotel. By the grace of God, the commander let me keep the town hall. I should be grateful, but I resent it. Their HQ is only a couple of doors down. I'm being watched."

In an attempt to form a connection, Jacob shared his thoughts; the mayor supervised a couple of municipal constables, who might come in handy. Even if his ideas turned out not feasible, the mayor surely would appreciate being asked for his input.

"Sorry to hear it. I can imagine how you feel, Mayor. That's too close for comfort. We'll also be under the microscope," Jacob replied. "I wonder how soon the German boss will order me to report for further orders."

"Why wait, man?" The mayor sounded angry. "As the chief of police, you should assert yourself and send one of your crew to scout out the Germans, see how they're settling in, and please, keep me in the loop."

As if he wished he could be in Jacob's shoes. He wondered what kind of relationship the mayor had with the previous police commander. For an elderly man, close to retirement age and raised in the nobility's comfortable circumstances, the man sounded competent enough. Jacob wondered how he would hold up under the looming ordeal of occupation by a foreign power.

The German in charge of them all surely would be ignorant of the stratification oddities and the class differences of Dutch society; not just anybody could become mayor. The Austrian-German governor, Seyss-Inquart, had promised to treat the Dutch well and not make any changes but Jacob doubted it.

"I'll think about that, Mr. Mayor," Jacob replied politely but wasn't convinced.

***

The following day after lunch, a Wehrmacht soldier stopped by the brigade and asked for the police commander. The soldier stood to attention, greeted Jacob with a "Heil Hitler" and a raised arm. This time, Jacob returned the greeting with a quick touch to the hat, staying silent.

"*Sie sollen mit mir zum Wehrmachtstation kommen um den Chef zu sehen* [You are to come with me to the Wehrmacht station to report to the Group Leader]." The messenger provided no alternative options.

Jacob wasn't unfamiliar with the German language, as his mother-in-law exclusively spoke German. He did alright for an untrained German speaker, understood everything, but couldn't get his tongue around the pronunciations. He took his time strapping on his belt with the holster and his service weapon, a 9 mm Browning-Belgian-made modification, the M25.

Chapter 13

When Jacob arrived at the commander's office — the hotel's converted dining room — the Wehrmacht boss had been waiting for him and stood up from his desk chair, heel-clicked and barked "*Heil-Hitler.*" He introduced himself as Fritz Heusden in the rank of *Hauptfeldwebel* — a petty officer's title.

Jacob greeted the German with a fingertip to his uniform cap. He intended to observe rather than speak. His heart pounded as after a 400-meter sprint, and he unobtrusively wiped his hands on his pants, grateful he didn't have to shake hands.

Heusden was a relatively short man of Jacob's age with a stocky build and a full head of dirty-blonde hair, an emperor's handlebar mustache, and kind, brown eyes. His riding pants ballooned excessively from the knee up, narrowing around the calves tucked inside tall, impeccably polished leather riding boots, which were quite a difference with Jacob's own worn-down, ten-year-old boots of cracked leather and about to rip.

The heavy-set man moved deliberately to his seat, his comportment steady with a rigid body reminding Jacob of a teddy bear but lacking the potential to all of a sudden catapult himself into a fast run, like real bears. The German sat down behind his desk but left Jacob standing at attention. Heusden asked whether Jacob needed an interpreter.

Jacob didn't consider accepting the offer as needing an interpreter made him look weak. He intended on staying on equal footing with his opponent. Not expecting an intricate strategy session with the German just yet, he planned to keep the conversation superficial and pleasant. During the coming weeks — maybe even months — this enemy was to be his keeper, his overseer for the Germans. Dread overtook his mood.

He recalled the image of his father hovering over him in the office of his store, criticizing Jacob's attempts at bookkeeping, breathing down his neck. It hadn't ended well. Back then, he couldn't find the words to defend himself. It was better not to get involved and play it cool, although he couldn't put off speaking that coarse language any longer.

"*Nein, danke* [No, thank you]," he said coolly, with a nod for emphasis.

Heusden chatted about his cultural heritage, including birthplace — Niedersachsen — and invited Jacob to do the same. So, Jacob told them he came from Gravezande.

The commander then said that the Dutch government had abandoned the country, obviously the party line. Heusden then presented his circular argument that the Dutch ministers and the Queen were not needed anyway. The German State — *das Reich* — was in charge now.

Hearing this spin on the truth, Jacob's first impulse was to punch the man in the face, but his arms and back were getting tired, and his legs gave signs of circulation difficulties. After the first flood of anger subsided, he recovered his resolve and decided he'd had enough of this. He interrupted the German.

"*Verzeihe mich* [Excuse me], Oberfeldwebel Heusden, I'm taking this chair, if that's alright with you."

The commander quickly got up half-way off his chair and gestured with an open hand to the other chair across his desk before he lowered his substantial behind again. "Of course, *verzeihe mich* [forgive me]. How inconsiderate of me. Please sit down."

Jacob sat down on the only other chair in this large room, fit for fifteen dining tables, and spoke slowly with long pauses for finding the correct German words.

"Thank you. I must strongly object to your characterization of the situation. Our government did not invite the German State to take over our territory. Your army invaded our country and breached the non-aggression treaty. Our government left to avoid imprisonment. I suggest your government would do the same in that situation."

Although he had to search for some German words and substituted a Dutch word here and there, all in all, his statement proved satisfactory. By the looks of Heusden's twitching left eyelid, the officer was paying attention and understood him.

"Alright, I'll accept it," the German said quietly, took a deep breath, and continued. "I'm not here for a political discussion with a local policeman. The German State has taken over, and it gives us the right to set the laws. You and I are on different sides, but we'll have to work together, nevertheless."

Heusden then assured Commander Van Noorden — whose name he quickly bastardized into the German Von Norden — that the Dutch police would not be involved in the investigation and arrest of German-hostile elements.

To Jacob's relief, Heusden assured him that the local marechaussee unit was expected to strictly keep the order among Dutch civilians. "That's alright with me. I've got my own superiors to answer to," he reminded Heusden.

A shadow of annoyance appeared on Heusden's face for just a second and disappeared again as quickly while the man continued explaining.

"As you can imagine, a German army official will supervise also your superiors. That will be Herr Hans Rauter, SS-*Obergruppenführer*, commander of the Security Services, SD for short. He also heads the Security Police, Sipo for short, and the Secret State Police, also known as the Gestapo, and of the *Schützstaffel*, the SS. As you can see, Rauter is an important leader. His direct superior is SS commander Heinrich Himmler."

"Hitler's right-hand man," Jacob gasped.

"Indeed," Heusden said, nodding in approval of the quick learner across from him.

Aware that hierarchy, rank, and status in the military were most important to Germans, Jacob stashed the names away in his memory. He knew he ought to get it right in his future dealings with the Nazis. Feeling his neck hairs rise in fear, he still found his courage and spoke up.

"My commander instructed me to collaborate, but I am not allowed to take direct orders from any German commander. And by the way, I do know about the SS and what they did in Poland." The words rolled off his tongue before his brain could evaluate them. His heart immediately protested and returned to an after-sprint rhythm. He knew that was the adrenaline preparing him to take off in flight, but he couldn't flee.

Heusden stared at Jacob. "Pardon? What?"

Jacob took a deep breath and blurted out what he had on his mind.

"Well, to be blunt, you know as well as I do that the SS was responsible for the deportation of the Polish Jews, who your leaders call enemies of the German state for no good reason. To be clear, the enemies of das Reich are not the enemies of the

Dutch. If I receive an order to arrest a Dutch citizen without a criminal offence committed or suspected, I cannot in good conscience, follow through with it."

As soon as Jacob had started speaking, Commander Heusden shot up from his chair.

While speaking, Jacob stood up as well, standing straight as a ramrod, mirroring the German's body language as he finished his sentence. Only after Heusden sat down, Jacob followed his example.

Heusden visibly swallowed a couple of times before replying in an icy and controlled voice, his brown eyes not so friendly anymore.

"I won't deny the truth of your accusation, but I want to make it clear to you we have won the war, and you'd better settle for cooperation with us." He rubbed his hand over his face, then continued speaking. "Von Norden, I would really like to collaborate with the local authorities and keep *Obergruppenführer* Rauter and his SS out of our mutual affairs."

Jacob nodded as the German spoke, then replied. "I also have no desire to get your Commander Rauter involved with anything." With his legs and feet vibrating underneath him, he kept his gaze steadfast on Heusden's face.

The German officer continued in a much softer tone of voice:

"I want to remind you that technically, I'm in charge of Overdam, but not to be concerned. For you and the villagers, life will go on as before, as long as you, Dutchmen, are cooperative. You are now under the protection of das Reich."

Protection? Jacob wanted to argue with a whole slew of objections, but his lack of language skills and his capacity to only speak like a half-wit in German positioned him at a disadvantage. For something to do, just to keep his wits about him, he eyed the man across from him and studied his appearance.

Heusden was wearing a too-tight tunic of that drab Wehrmacht color with five buttons at the front — all tightly closed, even the top one — with a two-inch-wide belt over the waist, visible over the desk's rim. With the looks of a six months' pregnancy, Heusden's pewter buckle held his protruding belly in check. The clip sported an eagle in relief, grasping the ancient Asian symbol for good luck — a swastika. And, of course, a big Gluck gun rested on the German's hip. The man must be hot, dressed like that on this balmy spring day.

Jacob startled when Heusden barked at him.

"*Verstehen Sie* [Do you understand], Group Commander Von Norden?"

Jacob barked back: "In *ordnung*, [agreed]!" Only then did he look Heusden again in the eye, and noticed the man across from him with beads of moisture collecting on his brow, also eager to end it.

"Could you come back to discuss the future tasks? I have more."

Calm and seemingly confident — his legs still now — Jacob replied: "Certainly if I have time. When?"

After it was all arranged, they parted ways.

Jacob ignored Heusden's extended hand, then each stepped back and saluted in their own way. Jacob felt strange doing it, stripped from his military rank a few days earlier, foremost on his mind since the bastard had so clearly rubbed it in. He'd like to pull his gun and put a bullet in his enemy's head, to get it really over with, once and for all. If he had the guts, he would punch the man comatose right this minute when Heusden didn't expect it. The moment passed.

On his way back to the brigade with nausea tugging inside his stomach, Jacob assessed his opponent as a man who likes his conveniences — his food and drink — and pushed into a leading position. As he calmed down somewhat, he assessed the German as lacking ambition or intelligence and not the SS-officer type. He might just be workable for his own purposes, might even be a half-decent man, his rank and life similar to Jacob's, besides having enlisted in the Kraut army under Hitler, of course.

But why for the devil had the commander treated him as one of his subordinates? Of course, aggrandizing themselves was a typically-German trait. It shouldn't be a surprise to him. Good thing the German had restrained himself. Jacob would have been pleased to balance any soreness in his left hand with a hard, right punch on the Nazi's face.

Chapter 14

A few days after the capitulation, Margaret and Jacob listened to the eight o'clock news. Instead of Margaret washing dishes or doing some other chore, she now spent evenings listening to the radio with him, seated across from each other at the dining room table. Margaret usually had some knitting in her lap or was busy repairing socks. This was becoming a new ritual.

"I said before I wanted our government to go to war before the invasion, and you asked me if I had lost my mind, remember that, love?" Jacob said. "I now know that PM De Geer was right in not wanting to go to battle. We just don't have the military capacity. How stupid of me to think a war is the answer. I wanted our men to win so badly, but I was in dreamland."

She nodded. "Yes, dear man. I knew you'd come to your senses." She put her knitting down and reached for his hand to pat it.

Jacob held her hand for a few seconds and pressed a kiss on her palm before he let go. "We could have kept up a decent army over the last decade, and then we'd have a chance against the Germans, but we didn't. The pacifists were wrong, Germany didn't want peace."

"What do you think Germany wants?" She was paying attention and waited for the answer, her hands still.

"They want to regain the territories they lost in the peace treaty of Versailles, and grab more than before. *Lebensraum*, they call it. Restoration of the old German Holy Roman Empire they want. Like Hitler promised. He said it all in his book, *Mein Kampf*." He looked at her and stroked his pate.

They sat in their living room in silence, looking at each other. Margaret just stared at Jacob, who had never been in a war. She had experienced war when she was only five — too young to really remember much — and near the end of it, her family moved to Holland. How does one behave as an adult under such circumstances? What would a family need to survive?

Margaret vaguely remembered the time before the move, having nothing, often being hungry as her family traveled in a wagon, following behind the railroad construction, when Mutter, right there at pay time, sold goods and prepared food to the men. All five children went to primary schools along the way if there was any close enough, except the last few years. Vater came home every day at dusk, tired and dirty, too tired to spend time with her or her siblings.

Back in Germany, it seemed normal to suffer deprivation. She heard people talking about the war, and she saw many soldiers on the road. Then Vater took them back to his hometown and his family: two brothers left and a sister — her uncles and aunt. She had to get used to a new country and a new school, where she had to speak in a completely new language when only nine years old. At least, they got more food then. Margaret was happy with the chores feeding the animals. She learned to milk their cow and tackle up the horse. They had a real house with a stable and a yard. Would this new war mean they'd have to go through all of that again? Numb, with the idea, she could only look at Jacob, wondering what he was thinking.

Jacob followed his own thoughts about his very last assignment — arresting Dutch Nazis, members of the NSB. The German occupiers indeed had released those traitors. All these long hours of work, wasted. He wanted to ask Margaret a question and searched for the least offensive words he could find. Slowly and in a neutral tone, he proceeded.

"Margaret, *lieve vrouw* [dear wife], do you happen to know whether Juergen actually signed up with the NSB? It becomes a bit more urgent for me to know now."

She looked at him with surprise. "Well, no. I'm not sure. You could ask him if you really want to know. But I thought you didn't want to know what goes on with him? That's what you said before."

Margaret's response got his attention; she knew everything about her twin brother. She was close to her relatives, something that he'd been envious of since he'd met her. He didn't get to see his sisters, closest in age, as much as he would like. They lived in the west of the country. He didn't bother to visit his brothers, his childhood bullies, although the two eldest were much older and had left home before he really knew them.

He missed their couple's custom after dinner: he would be leaning back on the divan, legs stretched, and Margaret would sit beside him in a fauteuil. It was their time to talk without the children. He sat up and straightened his chest, crossed his legs, and turned away, not looking at her. Speaking into space, he said with irritation in his voice: "Never mind what I said before. Things have changed from before. If he's a Nazi, I need to know what he and his comrades are up to and keep an eye on him. Perhaps you could ask your mother?"

She picked up the knitting from her lap and avoided looking at him as well. "You sound angry. Why would you need to know? He doesn't even live in the same town."

In a voice full of self-importance, he told her. "I'm in charge of keeping order and I'm taking my job seriously. Especially with the Krauts, sorry, with the German occupiers taking over, I must know which way the wind blows, as I'm still responsible for the locals. I don't trust Juergen and his buddies of the NSB to stay out of trouble. That much is clear from what's going on in the street fights in the cities. They beat up and harass Jews and anybody else who looks at them the wrong way."

"Juergen wouldn't do that."

From her hurt glance, he knew he had spoken more harshly than intended. In a much softer tone, he continued. "No, you're right, *schat* [dear]. I should ask Juergen myself. I get that you're close to your family. I won't put you in the position of having to rat on your own twin brother. But it is an issue. If things get off the rails, I might get fired, or maybe taken prisoner, who knows what might happen."

When she looked up from her knitting, he smiled warmly at her.

She didn't smile back. "I wouldn't tell on him. It wouldn't be necessary, because Juergen isn't doing anything bad," Margaret said empathically.

"Of course not," Jacob replied in a soothing voice. "I hope you won't tell him whatever you might hear from me either. Promise? How's your mother doing, by the way? Are you making plans to go up for a visit soon?"

Margaret frowned, and her eyes stared back at him. Maybe some tears started forming; Jacob couldn't be sure.

"I would never pass on whatever you say to anybody. How could you even say that? What do you think of me? I'm no traitor. If you'd ever got arrested, I'd be putting our boys in danger."

"No, of course, you wouldn't." He spoke softly, taken aback by her fierceness, and walked up to where she sat at the table, squatted down on his haunches beside her, and put an arm around her waist.

"I'm your wife," she said, eyes full of tears.

Jacob squeezed her tightly against him, lost his balance when he let her go, and rolled over onto the floor. She laughed through her tears as he lay stretched out on the floor. He got on his knees before her, grabbed her hands, and said, "Oh, I know, my dear, I'm a monster. I didn't mean to imply anything. Sorry, I even mentioned it."

She became serious again and thought for a few seconds, then said, "Why would you be arrested? Will they replace all Dutch police with Germans?"

"I don't know yet. Heusden told me nothing would happen if we cooperate with them. I've got no crystal ball. But I do know I can't operate under a Nazi regime. It goes *linea recta* against my beliefs."

Margaret's face turned red, and her voice became higher as she spoke.

"You'll have to find a way. What about the children and me?" She was close to breaking out in tears. She pulled her hands free and got up, turned away from Jacob, and started rummaging around the room, cleaning up the boys' clothes and toys.

Jacob sighed as he got up from the floor and wiped a hand over his head, realizing he hadn't found the right tone if there even was a proper tone in all of this. The catastrophic proportions of their situation slowly sank in. Fighting over small things didn't make the big ones disappear.

Chapter 15

Jacob acknowledged Margaret was close to her family, maybe too close. Her relatives had always helped one another out in many practical ways. He remembered things she had told him about her life after immigration. The xenophobic locals had looked at these foreign newcomers with critical eyes. Margaret had been called *vuile mof* [dirty Kraut] more than once. Luckily, she had grown up with their father's Dutch name, or else her life would've been much worse, and now she had Jacob's name.

He walked over to her and led her by the hand to the divan, where they sat down together. He put an arm around her. She didn't resist him. In an upbeat tone, he asked: "How would you feel if I stopped working, and you go back to nursing? I know you liked working."

Exasperated, she turned towards him and told him what she thought about that. "I'm telling you, being married to you isn't easy. You expect so much."

Jacob's mouth turned down, he crossed his knees, and his leg hanging free, started swinging up and down. "Now that's just not true. You're exaggerating."

She pressed her hands together and looked at her lap as if surprised there wasn't any piece of knitting.

"Yes, it is. All those moves in the force every couple of years or so and having to get settled again — it's just too hard. We're still strangers in town, and we're still scraping by financially. We haven't made any friends here."

He looked at her with interest, scrutinizing her expressions. To be able to lean back against the backrest, he had to let his arm slide off her shoulders. He tried the light-hearted way and smiled at her. "Really? I didn't know you had it so bad. Why didn't you tell me?"

She sat ramrod straight on the edge of the divan and looked down at him, stretched out beside her. With a jerk of her head, she replied: "I'm telling you now. Be honest, Jacob. You would've been angry with me if I had been permitted to stay on with the asylum. And with the children now, it's impossible to go to work. What are you trying to say?"

After Margaret had a few years of advanced education and completed her nursing training, she had worked in the Sanatorium in Santpoort. It was close to her hometown, and she lived in the nurses' dorm. Sometimes, she still wore a cap on her hair and was dressed in her blue uniform with a white apron, meeting Jacob at the dorm door for a quick conversation to set up their next date. She'd told him that she'd seen unending streams of injured and insane people roaming the roads in Germany, survivors of the war and fugitives from all parts of Europe. She had wanted to help, and becoming a nurse had seemed a natural career path.

Remembering that, Jacob shrugged and tried to grab her hand, but she pulled it away from his touch. "That's too bad," he said. "Nursing is a desirable job for a woman."

"Jacob, if you really want to know, I hated quitting my job, and I blamed you. I really liked working at the Asylum, but the management wouldn't keep me on as a married woman. I would've preferred to stay working, but you know very well that returning to work is now no option for me."

"Oh, I didn't realize that then," he replied sheepishly.

She was on a roll. A rich vein of total honesty had been laid bare.

"My dear husband, could you really be a house-husband and fulltime father? You wouldn't last a day at home with the boys. You're just saying you'll quit. Besides, you aren't the easiest man to get along with, and you always want to be right," she added as an after-thought.

He was struck by the truth. Only now did he fully understand. For him, Margaret had given up all her ambitions, quit her career. Her years of continued education and her training as a nurse — all gone to waste. Margaret's life hadn't been the rosy life he thought it was.

Solely to convince her he had no other options than to stay on in his career, he'd brought up the subject of quitting his job, but he really hadn't thought it through. He didn't want to be unfair and force Margaret to mediate between him and her relatives either.

As if she'd read his mind, she ended the conversation in a firm voice with her own demand.

"In any case, stop criticizing my mother's opinions or my brother's political views, please. If you need to know, go ask Juergen yourself." She glared at him, bent down and picked up her knitting from the floor, and got up from the divan, thus ending their little spiel of close combat.

Jacob had no desire to turn her against him, but adjusting to reality was also tricky. His world had drastically changed within a few days with no options left. He felt sorry for himself and wanted to change the subject. He started verbalizing his discontent as Margaret walked to the kitchen. He got up and followed her.

Standing in the doorway, he said, "I am sorry we are in this mess. I apologize for not realizing your predicament. I just wanted you to be on board with what I do. Why does it have to be this way? Those damned Germans broke all international agreements with this war. Their word isn't worth the paper it's written on. Germany took the country within five days. What a humiliation." He had gone off on a tangent.

Margaret looked at him with something that looked like pity and left the kitchen.

Without his audience, he sat back down and started a cigar, something he reserved for Sundays only, but today had been a hard day. He deserved some slack. Cigars were expensive and, like everything else, available only through government coupons or on the black market. He had to save up and trade coupons with colleagues to get any cigars at all.

He wasn't enjoying his stogie as much as he had hoped. He turned the cigar around with both hands and took its little, colorful band off, carefully pushing it from the cigar, and laid it on the side table for the boys. In frustration, he chewed on his cigar as he reflected on the way the newscaster had described the German army's strategic skills.

The German troops had passed through Overdam — and many other eastern towns — reaching the center of the nation within two hours. It had been a walk-in. The humiliation of the army had been complete — his army. It was simply too much to bear.

***

Margaret came back into the room and sat down at the dining table to fold the laundry.

Jacob couldn't leave well enough alone and pushed her some more, seeking to lay bare the truth, no more cover-up, no more tiptoeing to keep everybody happy. He needed to know who Margaret was. If that led to more disasters, so be it. Now was the time to be brutally honest, to show true colors. The honeymoon was over; real life had begun.

"Tell me Margaret, was your mother always the one to wear the pants in your family?"

She shook her head in disbelief and stared at him.

"Good God, what a dufus you can be. Just because she earned an income with running the concession at a time when nobody made any money, that didn't mean she lorded it over my dad. She just was smarter than him. Maybe not smarter, Vater was just worn out from hard labor on the railroad. It killed him before his time; his heart gave up, I bet from too many worries. If he would've known in advance that Germany would get into a war, he probably had not bothered emigrating to Germany. He'd become a shopkeeper, just like his father, living off little bits of money coming in. I'm sure he'd rather be hungry and unmarried, instead of working his butt off for his family in a foreign country, but he was eighteen when he made that decision. What does anybody know at that age? What were you doing at that age? Why did you ask anyway? You aren't afraid of Mutter's sharp mind, are you?"

Throughout her speech, Jacob had looked at her, taking it all in. He was beginning to understand her better, now all this misery is coming down on them. He got up, stuffed his hands in his pockets, and stomped through the room as he replied to her questions.

"Of course not. My parents with twelve children were struggling too. Nobody had any money after the crash and the depression. My brothers had to work in the fields to help earn. I helped in the shop, like my sisters, and delivered groceries on a bicycle with a cart behind it. After my mother taught me at age ten how to keep the ledger up to date, I did that too. I hated being at home and left at fifteen, still wet behind the ears. My father was the boss at home, and he was a nasty boss. I was just wondering how your home life was."

He didn't tell her about stealing the money from the till, and fudging the ledger afterward, and how angry he'd been, able to kill his dad, but hadn't. He quickly pushed those thoughts away and said, "By the way, she can't be that sharp, if she likes

Hitler. But your dad — he must have left the children's care to his wife, didn't he?" He stood still to watch her face.

She avoided looking at him and kept folding the laundry. With a voice devoid of any emotion, she replied. "Ah, yes, he did, mostly, but don't you worry about it, my dear husband. You can too."

She didn't tell him about her struggles with Juergen, pressed into mothering duty over her twin brother as early as four years old — the age Hendrik was now — while her sister and brothers were playing and enjoying all the freedom they wanted.

Jacob continued his pacing and — oblivious to the signs of getting angry in Margaret — his yapping, and told her how he the youngest, and the puniest, didn't get any good attention, and left home early because he couldn't stand it any longer. "At least you don't have as many kids as my parents had, so you can do a better job giving them the attention they need."

She didn't hesitate one second. "They're yours too, by the way. Maybe not now, but we're not done having children yet. Have you considered that we may have to sleep separately, or else you may do what the minister of my mother's church told you, in our pre-marriage counselling, and get some of those rubbers." She blushed as she said it, but Jacob didn't see that. On a roll, she continued. "Jacob, I don't want twelve kids anyway, just to let you know. My mom had five children within three years, and it was too much. I have a lot of respect for her and so should you."

"I do, I do, I really respect her," he protested feebly. "Your parents were very resourceful and admirable in scraping money together in Germany during that horrendous time. They even were able to buy land in Hardenberg, very smart."

From his self-study — reading books borrowed from the library and the minister — he recalled that more than sixty million people were on the move after those devastating four war years ended in 1918. Ill and desperate, thousands and thousands of displaced and homeless people clogged the roads and sought shelter in sanctuary churches of Europe.

Ashamed about his callous response to the hardship of his wife's family, he shut up. His own father had married into a wealthy family to get out of difficulties, and then the store his parents bought, didn't thrive. His dad wouldn't even visit with his in-laws, a sore point between his parents — another reason to hold his tongue.

Margaret threw her laundry in the basket without neatly folding the pieces, as she used to.

"I don't know what's wrong with you, Jacob, but you are being horrible, quarrelling like this. I will spell it out for you: if you do quit your job, we'd both have to find a job elsewhere, and still find somebody else to look after the kids, or would you do that, really? And who'll do the laundry then? You tell me that. What do you want from me, anyway?"

Jacob, chastised, sighed, then said, "I'm being horrible, aren't I? I'm sorry Margaret, forgive me. I had a hard day, and I surely will get more of those. *Lieverd*, I only want to make sure we have no secrets between us," he said. "I need to know that you are on my side. That you'll defend me in front of your family, always, and not only once in a while."

He should let Margaret be in peace. It wasn't her fault the Germans had taken the country within a week, that her brother might have turned into a member of the NSB, or that her mother loved Hitler. He got the picture: being married to him wasn't easy. A small adder slithered around in the grass, and with his ear close to the ground, Jacob heard it whisper. Margaret had bossed her brother around; she could've stopped him from joining the Dutch Nazi Party. He shook his head to clear his head.

The quarrel with Margaret had at least given him new energy. He realized he wouldn't know what to do without her. She knew hardship, she was strong, and she got him. He walked up to her and tried to kiss her, but she resisted him.

"Margaret, do you regret marrying me?" he asked in a soft voice and stroked her cheek. She didn't answer, and he tried it on a different tack. "I am a jerk, I know. I don't mean to criticize your parents. I apologize. Forgive me, please." He kissed her again.

This time she kissed him back, and said, "I forgive you."

Chapter 16

Eight days into the occupation, a group of Wehrmacht cavalry soldiers traveled east through Overdam on their way back from their victory in the west. They demanded to be billeted, including their horses. A German courier on a motorbike arrived the day before to inform the mayor of the need for accommodation. Mayor Van Voorst tot Voorst called Jacob.

"I think the Marechaussee paddock might be a good spot for the horses. What do you think? It's just for one night, and the gesture would create goodwill with the Wehrmacht."

Jacob didn't want any Germans in his brigade but couldn't afford to rebuke the mayor.

"It depends on how many. We only have five stalls and four are taken, but more animals could stay in the paddock if the weather holds. If it rains, we'd have a mud pit."

He instructed Corporal Peters — who seemed to like the German soldiers — to prepare the backyard for the animals. Although it was spring with usually lots of rain, the weather held. The soldiers arrived at the end of the day, and under Jacob's supervision, the five strange horses were stabled or led into the paddock. He completely ignored the soldiers, silently wishing them to hell. They disappeared as fast as they could. The horses neighed and kicked for a while until they all finally settled in their respective spots.

Jacob observed that the German horses were well-fed and beautiful, at least as good-looking as — if not superior to — his own animals. He spent some time with them tenderly stroking their noses while softly talking, feeding each a carrot. These blameless animals reawakened his love for this part of the job, and he decided it was time to take Susie out for a run before dusk would set in.

The invasion had interrupted his usual routines, and the animal needed the exercise. In normal times, the hired hands conducted the daily hour of walking on the lead in the paddock or the brigade crew, if they had the time. Beyond that minimum, a mounted policeman had to commit to riding a horse three times a week, not just for the horses' exercise, but also to maintain the riders' mastery.

Jacob saddled ten-year-old Susie, his large, black mare who liked to nuzzle his head and push his cap off with her velvet lips. He put his left foot in the stirrup, hoisted his body in the saddle, and swung his other leg over as he promised her, "We're going to have a fast run today, Susie." She pranced out of the brigade compound. Jacob guided her along the berm beside the road towards the forest, a ten-minute trot from the brigade. After the warm-up, they reached the packed dirt of the wooded lane along the moor, where Jacob nudged Susie's flanks with his knees, and away they went, galloping along.

It was a lovely run. As the clumps of dirt flew from Susie's pounding hoofs, the rider and the horse working up a sweat, Jacob's worries took flight. He melted into the thousand-pound bundle of muscle power. Under his control, they became as one. This was heaven, the only place in his life where he felt unencumbered — even empowered — the way he was meant to be: strong and free.

Two hours later, Jacob looked at her, safe and sound in the brigade compound, washed down, watered, fed, and cooling off. He was satisfied, happy even, and savored his job. No, he wouldn't give it up voluntarily. He gave Susie another carrot for a treat and went back to his office. Regardless of whatever else may happen, from now on, he would resume his usual horse routines. The following day, the German horses departed, leaving their messes behind for the marechaussees and stable hands and a chief who was newly committed to his job.

Chapter 17

Ten days after the invasion, a special courier delivered a written brief for the Marechaussee unit with new instructions, straight from the Deputy Minister of Defense's office, Mr. Ringeling. Most of Jacob's men were in the brigade's squad room when the messenger entered. Jacob took the package, went back to his office, read the documents, and called for Van Houten through the open door. They discussed the new instructions, then returned to the crew together.

"Gather 'round, men. I've got an announcement," Jacob said in a loud voice.

The staff room was an ample open space off the main corridor with linoleum flooring, wooden desks with some typewriters, a couple of filing cabinets, and a tall weapons vault. Everybody was there already, but Jacob's formal announcement made it all the more official. Contrary to his true feelings of worry, he tried to project confidence. He assumed his typical stance with feet comfortably separated, his knees locked, hands in his pockets, and his uniform jacket unbuttoned.

In training, he had learned to address a crowd confidently as the first step in crowd control, and a stint as a law instructor of recruits helped him develop some presentation skills. He cleared his throat and was set to project his voice through the room:

"As you know, the Queen and the Cabinet have left for England. I suggest you don't listen to the Nazi-inspired backstabbing with the aim of destroying your loyalty for the Queen and the Cabinet and ignore their suggestion that our government abandoned the country. They made the right decision."

"Right you are," said Van Houten. Others murmured their agreement, and he heard several men use the word bastards.

"I'm sorry to announce the fact we're not operating under Defense anymore." He then explained that with the disbanding of the military, the crew had lost their military status. Ringeling resigned but would supervise the army's dissolution. Jacob ended in a hoarse voice full of suppressed emotion, surprising himself. "From now on, we're just a plain police force."

The men looked worried, and Jacob heard more curses.

"Men, we're instructed to stay on our post. You know the conditions. One: the execution of our work will still be in the nation's interest, and two: as long as the Germans will allow us to serve the public properly, and I emphasize the word properly. In case of any doubt, you're to consult with me. So, we still have a job, for now. No vigilante actions are tolerated. Understood?"

Everybody fell silent.

He looked at Van Houten for his help but then remembered his laugh and felt a blush creeping up in his face. He quickly continued speaking and divided the work among the men. Corporals Dijk and Peters were to make the list of suitable civilians to form a crew for the new Air Defense Services under the new authority, whichever that was. With the military's dismantling, the old crew members had lost their jobs. Jacob made it clear that he didn't care how, as long as those on the roster agreed. His last instruction was: "You can do it during work hours. When you have a list, run it by the mayor." Unsure on how to proceed but prepared for anything, he waited.

Constable Leversma, who had five kids to feed, lifted his hand to ask a question. Jacob nodded.

"Opper, can we put ourselves on that list and does it pay overtime? We could do a shift, of course after first completing our own work at the brigade."

He replied. Promptly. "I know times are tough, but, no. I hope it'll be a temporary job only."

Leversma grimaced.

Jacob noticed the display of displeasure, and he responded, alert to attempts to undermine his authority. He was taught to deal with that possible dynamic at the earliest occasion. It might as well be now.

"Leversma, don't sulk. You must have learned in training that a marechaussee brigade is not a democracy. Dijk and Peters, you'll make a list, is all. You can hire back the same people if they still want the job. The blackout's been going on for months and checks should've been done, but let's just go with it and pretend it's a new service. It's up to the new boss to make a schedule. Peters, you are on night watch so you can start on it tonight. If any trouble comes up, let me know immediately. I don't know yet how things will change, but change they will."

He fell quiet. All stayed silent. He looked at his hands, then threw a furtive glance to Van Houten to see if he'd get any support for the orders, but the young fellow just stood to the side, listening. Peters, on the other hand, stepped eagerly forward and stopped in front of him, raring to go. "Yes, sir."

Jacob resumed speaking in a calm voice. "Good. Men, we are in trouble. Prepare yourselves for it. I just want to say this. Our soldiers have battled hard, but we lost. Let's make the best of a bad situation. The Krauts' eyes are set on conquering England, as we all know, so the Wehrmacht might soon be moving on. I'll let you know of further directions when I get them. All dismissed."

Jacob had already moved towards the exit when Van Houten spoke, raising his voice over the desk chairs' scraping sounds and the shuffling feet. Jacob turned around in the doorway.

"Opper, it's damned disappointing to see the fall of our government. Now the military has disappeared, the crew would want to know what ministry we fall under."

"Good question, Sergeant. You are correct to assume we have a new department leader. With the cabinet gone, the deputy ministers became the highest-ranking public servants to administer things, keep everything going. We're lumped in with the police now under the Department of Justice, which falls under Deputy Minister Jan Tenkink."

"Oh, so no more special missions for the Marechaussee?"

Jacob assumed he referred to his absence before the invasion. "Right. I won't be going anywhere and you won't have to cover for me. We'd all just be on police duty, and for now, we'll be paid at regular pay. Just do your work as always. If you're needed after hours and it isn't your night shift, I'll have to approve the overtime. I won't be too difficult about it."

Van Houten threw up his hands in exasperation. "So, we've just become plain coppers. Bugger. With the Wehrmacht here, who'll be in charge then? Are we also to become collaborators? And what laws are we to follow?"

Van Houten didn't give any signs of backing off and had moved to stand right before him, too close for comfort.

Jacob resisted the urge to step back and frowned.

"Are you being difficult? What are you getting at, Sergeant? No, you do not take orders from any German soldier or officer, just from me, or the department head. Stand down and don't make my job any harder, or we'll be butting heads. You're supposed to be my second in command, my back-up, and that means backing me."

The others had retreated to their desks or to whatever they were doing, but Van Houten didn't leave.

Granted, Van Houten's voice was polite, but Jacob had expected him to support his commander, and instead, the jerk challenged him, and his patience began to seep away.

"Just making sure I understand, Opper. One more question, if I may."

Jacob took his hands out of his pocket, half-turned to leave, and growled: "Yes?"

"What about the NSB? Our home-grown Nazis are acting out all over the country. How should we deal with them?"

Van Houten seemed genuinely concerned and needed an answer. Jacob tightened his fists and stuck them back into his pockets, and kept his voice neutral when he replied.

"I haven't seen many of them in Overdam. Anyway, I wouldn't hazard to guess how important they'll become under the Krauts, but I would strongly advise you not to let them bait you into actions you might regret later. Either when you're in town as a civilian, or on the job. Just turn around and leave. Any more questions?"

"But, Opper, if they disturb the peace, why shouldn't we arrest them? Isn't keeping the order still our job?"

Jacob sensed that his efforts to stay patient and his failure to do so were evident to al. He pulled his hands out of his pockets and put his fists on his hips.

"Yes, of course we'll arrest the ones causing a disturbance, if and when it happens here in Overdam. We'll just have to roll with it. So far, it's been quiet here. Any more questions?"

He figured that everybody had questions for which no answers existed. He wouldn't be able to satisfy anyone under the circumstances, although not just anybody would challenge him. What to do with this rebel, Van Houten? He was starting to sweat, changed from one foot to the other, and decided to terminate the Q &A game. He reached for the doorknob and was about to leave to his office when Peters took up the ball:

"Can we now officially join the NSB and SS?"

A sudden heat got Jacob hot under the collar, and he tried to loosen it with his index finger. Angry, he blurted out: "What the hell would you want to do that for?"

Peters stammered his reply. "Um, sorry, but no offence, Opper, but well, uh, uh, now we've become part of Germany, I just thought it might be a good career move."

Jacob held himself back with great difficulty, grabbed his elbow behind his back with his opposite hand, and held on tight as he looked down at the floor, gathering his words. Finally, he found some. He turned to Peters, looked him straight in the eye, and replied with a cold voice.

"I didn't think such a treacherous thing would ever be said by a Dutchman inside a Marechaussee brigade." As his fiery eyes held Peters' gaze, he finished what he really should have said in the first place. "The regulation for public servants forbids joining a prohibited party, such as the communist party. As policemen, we have political freedoms, but it doesn't include joining a foreign army, including the SS. It's considered treason."

He spat out that word, paused a few seconds, and finished his thought. "What you asked may become an option in the future, but I would have a problem with it. All dismissed."

He didn't want any more questions, as he had no answers. Peters' eyes shot daggers at him. So be it. He turned around and grabbed the doorknob again. On leaving the squad room, his words to Peters were less benevolent: "You should be glad I didn't punch you in the face, like the other traitor on the bridge."

In his office, Jacob had lots of paperwork to deal with and many detailed directions, now coming at him in a steady stream from head-office. He couldn't focus, and his mind wandered to Peters, the opportunist, and that mouthy Van Houten. Jacob intended to be helpful but felt his competency sorely lacking in this brand-new situation with these rural, passive-aggressive people he couldn't read at all.

He had charged his men with what were clear and simple orders, but maybe he hadn't been direct enough. His mind was far from transparent. He worried about how long the occupational forces would stay and whether the Germans would continue to behave. Up to now, he had been confident he could rely on his crew. He would have to rethink that hasty, overconfident assumption.

Chapter 18

As the Nazi leadership promised, the German soldiers were polite and went about their business for months after the invasion. The population had settled into a new situation after the first disappointment faded that the Germans hadn't left.

Heusden asked Jacob along to inspection the — now empty — vacation camp of the anthroposophical organization dedicated to Krishnamurti. Heusden's boss had confiscated the property in the Nazi's quest to dismantle all non-Germanic and non-Christian organizations in the Dutch nation. The place was in good shape, and Jacob had to agree it'd be ideal for a future, temporary prison camp. The higher echelons in the DOJ agreed with the corrections branch to create more spaces for relief of the regular prisons, filled to bursting with offenders of the new German laws.

In their follow-up meeting, Jacob had shared with Heusden that Margaret's birth-place was in Germany, the same region in the north-west Commander Heusden was from, called Niedersachsen. The German sounded pleased. In turn, he then shared with Jacob the news that the captured Dutch soldiers would all be released soon. The German State Office was confident the Dutch soldiers wouldn't cause any trouble and offered the POWs the option to join the German army if they had the right attitude. Heusden promised that Governor Seyss-Inquart was to announce it on the radio in the next couple of days.

"I don't think you'll get many volunteers," Jacob stiffly replied.

***

To Margaret, he used different words later at home.

"The gall! Does he think we're all traitors?"

She didn't comment.

They heard the latest news, announcing that every political and religious broad-casting association from now on was to submit their scheduled programs to the SD to screen for anti-German information. The Reich's Security Services Division — SD for short — was assigned to censor the government run-news, the ANP, and all other radio programs. Governor Seyss-Inquart had studied Dutch society. According to the newsreader, Hitler's deputy would patiently help his Germanic brothers with acclimatizing to the new rules. Elections were scrapped.

The Dutch were proud of their religious freedom and their history of offering sanctuary to the persecuted throughout the ages. Successive Dutch governments consisted typically of representatives from the religion-based political parties together with non-religious parties. The party Jacob voted for had a significant influence on Dutch politics.

"What? You must be kidding me. We're going to be governed by decree without input of any of the parties?" Jacob cried out, then continued to listen.

Reichsführer Seyss-Inquart made all foreign senders illegal, except, of course, the German stations. The SD announced that listening to any other stations posed a danger to the country's security. Anyone tuning listening to the anti-German Radio Orange, would face additional, severe repercussions — possibly incarceration.

"Jesus, help us. It starts now with one swing of the Nazi ax," he said to Margaret.

"What starts?" She looked at him with a blank expression on her face.

He put his hand up. "Shhh, I want to hear this."

The newsreader listed many items no longer permitted on radio and in periodicals: any photos and information connected with the government-in-exile, Queen Wilhelmina and members of the House of Orange. Hanging the red-white-blue Dutch flag was prohibited, along with the Orange banner and mentioning the names of the Dutch royalty in public. Any state photos of the Queen and her relatives were to be removed immediately from public buildings and private homes.

"That'll be the day. If they want Wilhelmina's portrait removed, they'll have to do it themselves, for goodness sakes," Jacob grumbled. As he uncrossed his legs, his feet stamped loudly on the floor. "Your mother won't like that either; she loves our royal family. I think she likes all royals and celebrities in those German magazines she gets from your aunt in Hanover, what's it called, *Filmwelt*?"

Margaret smiled. "Yeah, she loves those. It makes her dream she could've been Sisi, princess of Hungary, empress of love. You know, Elizabeth, who married Emperor Franz Joseph?"

Jacob laughed. "Oh, my lord, is that what women dream of? You'll be short-changed if you dream like your mother." He smiled broadly at her.

"I'm not my mother, Jan, and you're right, you're no prince," she said decidedly but smiled at him anyway.

He returned to his dark thoughts. "Hmm, yeah, gossip magazines, if you ask me. Would be alright if we weren't reading that trash anymore, but it is German trash, so we still can. But you asked, what has started? The mind control, that's what," he bristled and got up from his comfy chair to turn off the radio.

Still sitting at the dining table, Margaret sweetly asked, "I thought your meeting with the army chief went alright?"

"Yeah, it went, but having to listen to the twerp is always humiliating. What I meant, is: this German interference in our affairs is going much farther than anyone anticipated. We can no longer rely on the radio news for accurate information. The Germans are brainwashing us with Nazification through fabricated facts. And we are already governed by Seyss-Inquart's idiotic decrees, never mind our own laws and the elections. It is beginning to look like a real occupation."

He saw Margaret's face cloud over. He suspected she was taking his complaints as personal attacks, and quickly added, "Never mind, *vrouwtje*. It'll be alright. I'll just have to learn to pretend better. Apparently, the Germans will arrest a lot more people." He exhaled, exhausted, went to the divan, lowered his body on it, and put his feet up in anticipation of a small nap before dinner would arrive on the table.

Most days, Jacob came home late and Margaret would have already fed the children; they were in bed. She got up from the table to go to the kitchen as she kept talking. "Oh. So, what does that have to do with you?"

"Our crew will have to help guard the prisoners during the walk from the train station to the camp. Right through town for all to see, darn it."

Margaret didn't show signs of having heard him, or she ignored him; he wasn't sure which. She called out from the kitchen, "Since we're talking about my mother, she asked if we'd come for a visit, as long as the weather is good. If we come within in the next week, she'll let us have some part of the pig she will have slaughtered."

Jacob got up from the couch and joined her in the kitchen as she was getting a plate ready for him. He took it from her and returned to the table to eat it. He wanted to have an early night, needed some love, and gobbled up the food without tasting it, as Margaret stood watching.

"That sounds great, you make arrangements with her then. What I really want is an early night. Are you coming to bed?" He got up and put his hands on her hips, standing behind her, and nuzzled her neck.

She giggled. "Agreed," she whispered.

*****

That night and that whole month, and even the next month, everything stayed quiet in Overdam, as the new decrees and regulations became the new reality and worked their way through the systems and the communities.

Chapter 19

The following day, Jacob planned to tell Margaret about Heusden's connection to her German family, but decided not to. Might as well start now with practicing keeping quiet about a lot of things. To Margaret, he said, "I wonder how I would get hold of Radio Orange's bandwidth. We should stay aware of what really goes on, but I suppose we'd better not listen to the BBC at home anymore."

"No, maybe not," she replied as she put his breakfast of two slices of bread with cheese and a slice of almost black roggebrood — dark rye bread — and a cup of tea in front of him. "Maybe Mutter and Juergen can help here. They might be able to get a license for listening." She waited by the kitchen door, all helpful and willing to form a bridge between her and her relatives.

Jacob ignored her remark, not sure where things were heading with Margaret, Juergen, and Johanna. He must steel himself against any sentimentalities and still hadn't told her about punching the traitor on that first day. Never mind his urge to hit Peters. He could think of many more subjects to avoid from now on. He looked at her as she exhaled, tightened her shoulders and disappeared through the kitchen door. It was time to go to work. He got up and left.

Chapter 20

The following Saturday, the family rode to Hardenberg on their bicycles. The weather was great, although unseasonably warm. Too hot in their fall coats, Margaret and Jacob threw off the coats, as soon as they arrived at Johanna's place.

Johanna greeted them warmly and said she was delighted with the visit. She lifted Jaap from his mother's carrier hanging off the front and walked with him to the back. Hendrik followed her, as soon as Jacob had set him down. Johanna always kept some treats for the children, and Hendrik was well aware of it.

Johanna had set up the backyard with a table and chairs and a blanket for the children. A few minutes later, both boys sat peacefully together on the horse blanket, spread out on the dried, brown grass. They seemed content to chew on the sweet licorice Johanna had given them. The adults relaxed in their rattan chairs around the iron garden table with their cold, orange-flavored syrup diluted with water, called *ranja*. Jacob lit a cigar, put his matches on the table, and drew hard on the stogie to get it going, blowing smoke rings for the children.

Johanna told Margaret and Jacob what was happening inside the house. The butcher had arrived earlier this morning and was cutting up the pig, away from children's curious eyes. She thought the kids would get in the way. "Juergen is helping the butcher and will join us later. I got permission to slaughter this one last pig for my family."

The Reich had ordered that butchering required a mandatory inspection, with a share of the meat confiscated for the Wehrmacht. Puffing on his cigar, Jacob squinted through the smoke and asked, "Are you going to have more pigs this year, Johanna?"

She didn't hesitate and brightly answered him. "No, this is the last one, for now. I'll get new piglets in the early spring, so the pigsty is empty now. My cow is still out in the pasture. It's time for her to come in; the nights are already cold. Juergen will get her later. I won't ask you to do that, Margaret," she chuckled.

Margaret ignored her comment.

"Nice cake, Mother," Jacob commented.

It didn't take long for the children to get bored with sitting and being polite. Hendrik was already trying to get the late-season pears out of the tree in the orchard. Jaap, now almost two years old, had scampered off to look at the chickens in the coop, deeper into the backyard, and the boy stood before the chicken-wire fence, pushing bits of dry grass through the holes.

The adults were chatting while enjoying their drink and Johanna's fluffy sponge cake. The conversation went to the politics of the moment. Johanna and Jacob both became more animated. At one point, Jacob forgot himself and accused Johanna in a rather loud voice that, if she thought that Hitler would really make things better, she deluded herself.

Margaret listened to them argue and became annoyed with Jacob. He had promised not to get into that. She heard the sound of trickling water or a waterfall and wondered what that sound was.

Suddenly, Juergen came running out of the backdoor, screaming like a pig to the slaughter. "Fire, fire, help me!" He startled them into standing, their heads turned, throwing over the chairs as he swung an empty, galvanized pail by its handle and pushed it into Jacob's chest. "Quick, help me pump more water, in the back, but hurry, the pump is close to the fire." To his mother, he called out: "Mutter, call the fire department, tell them there's a fire in the back of the house, I think it's the pigsty." He ran straight back into the house. Jacob ran after him.

"*Ach, Herr Gott,*" Johanna exclaimed, and as quickly as her rheumatic limbs would carry her, she disappeared to the front of the house around the corner, to the front door.

Margaret saw flames of a meter high through the roof from the part where the pigsty was. "Where are the kids," she shrieked, looking around, her face distorted in agony. A second later, she ran through the backyard, frantic, loudly calling their names, "Hendrik, Jaap, where are you, Jaap, Hendrik."

She found Jaap, still standing in front of the chicken coop, and snatched him up into her arms. She had to find Hendrik. Where could that rascal be? She had seen him last by the backdoor, playing with the rocks in the drive next to the ditch with the tall brown grass, separating their parcel from the neighbors' land. She ran into the tall grass, pushing her way through with her body sideways, holding Jaap tightly in her arms.

"Ouch, ouch, Mama, Mama, ouch," he cried. Something stung on her legs, and another, and again, as if an army of ants was climbing her legs. She was walking through stinging nettles, and Jaap felt them too. She lifted him higher and kept walking.

"It's alright, just a little longer, dear, we're almost there," she told Jaap, half-crying herself, pushing on through the weeds until she stood in the neighbors' yard. She shouted again, "Hendrik, where are you?" She looked up at the house and saw the one big flame had multiplied. She pushed the thought away that those flames would incinerate anybody in it.

Then she heard Hendrik's voice nearby, calm and clear, "Mama, I'm here." She looked around her. There he was, crawling from underneath an upturned wheelbarrow on the path in the neighbor's vegetable garden, a few steps away. Hendrik's face was dirty, streaks of soot on his cheeks and stalks of straw stuck in his hair.

She put Jaap on the ground, grabbed Hendrik, lifted him up, and squeezed him in her arms. "Thank God," she whispered and held him and kissed him on his cheeks. Then she abruptly set him down again, grabbed him by one skinny arm and pulled him back and forth twice, as if to shake some sense into him, holding on tightly. "What have you done, *deugniet* [rascal]," she said in an angry voice, bent over, her face with a big frown almost touching his.

"Mama, you're hurting me," Hendrik cried. She let him go and righted herself.

"Where were you?" she demanded, more controlled now.

His face was distorted into a grimace and a tear rolling down his cheek; he answered: "I was in the pigsty and was afraid for the fire and then I ran away through the weeds."

***

At that moment, the fire wagon with six men hanging off it rolled into the drive, all bells clanging, drove up to the backdoor, where the men jumped off and unrolled the hoses. The commander yelled at Margaret, the only adult person around, until then. "Is there a ditch with water here?" She didn't know what to say and stayed silent as she looked around her, thinking hard, frozen to the spot by the neighbor's vegetable garden.

Three people came running and stopped by the property line. The woman yelled back, "Yes, over there, the well at the back of my property." Two firemen grabbed a hose from the cart to unwind it and ran with it to the back of the yard, past where Margaret stood, holding hands with the boys. Two other men directed a stream of water to the roof into the flames within a few minutes. A loud sizzling sound erupted, followed by a cloud of steam and soot flying up into the sky.

A man Margaret assumed was the butcher came stumbling over the threshold, coughing hard. A few seconds later, Juergen and Jacob ran out of the backdoor, full of soot and now dripping wet. The three men stood, side-by-side in the driveway, and looked up, watching the effect of the water on the fire. The smell of charred wood and burning straw engulfed the watchers, and the sizzling sound emanated from the roof for a while longer, much like bacon sizzling in twenty frying pans.

Jacob looked around him, searching for Margaret and the boys. He found them, still standing in the neighbor's yard. He hurried to them, lifted Jaap up in his arm, pushed Hendrik with his other hand against his knees, and kissed Margaret on her cheek. His eyes red-rimmed and breathing hard, he asked, "Are you alright, wife?"

Margaret broke down in tears. With faltering breath, she softly said, "Yes, we are."

Jacob put Jaap down, pulled Margaret into his arms, and briefly hugged her. "It's all over now, don't worry anymore. We're all safe."

***

The whole disaster with the fire in the pigsty on top of everything else had completely exhausted Margaret. She feared Jacob would give Hendrik a good spanking after finding out the fire's origin but he hadn't. He had just sighed when she told him. Quite dirty himself, he had said, "Let's go home." He probably remembered leaving his matches on the table.

At home before dinner, when she was with Jaap in the kitchen, she heard Jacob call Hendrik. She watched from the doorframe and saw him lift Hendrik up onto a chair. Jacob sat down across from him on another chair. With a quiet voice he talked to his Hendrik. "Were you scared, son?" Hendrik nodded.

"You like to do what Papa does, right?" Hendrik nodded again.

"Hendrik, you are too young for smoking cigars and for burning the trash. You have to wait a few years yet before you can do that safely. I'll teach you when the time comes. Playing with matches can be dangerous. You have learned that now, didn't you?"

Hendrik nodded, wriggled off his chair, and as the boy tried to climb on Jacob's lap, he lifted his son on his knees. They hugged. Softly, he told him: "I am not mad at you, Hendrik, just grateful we were all safe. Don't forget to say thank you in your prayer when you go to bed."

The pigsty inside had burned down to the dirt floor, and the roof had a hole, but it could be repaired before the winter. Mutter commented that the most important thing was that nobody got hurt. Jacob offered to help pay for the materials, but she declined the offer.

***

That night, Margaret was cleaning up in the kitchen, alone. She was left with a sense of doom. She understood Jacob's growing doubts about his role as a policeman. She had absorbed his increasing distrust of her relatives. She was going to prove it to him that she could be useful and trustworthy, before he did something irreversible, like quitting his job.

Today wasn't the right day, but soon she would talk to Johanna about the radio station. Nobody would suspect an openly pro-Nazi German farmer-housewife of listening to Radio Orange, which made her place perfect for a bit of illegal radio entertainment. She finished up her dishes and went to bed early. She was more tired in her third pregnancy than before; she still hadn't told Jacob about it. These last few weeks, she and Jacob went to bed at different times, all fine with her.

Margaret laid in bed, wide awake, thinking of her mother, when they still lived in Germany, and about the railcar full of children, parked beside a stream at the railroad construction site. She remembered seeing many people traveling on the road. They looked hungry. Her twin brother was always afraid back then; he quickly cried, like Jaap. Mutti told her she was so much more mature than her brother and should look after Juergen and to always stay close to the wagon, where she could see them. They must have been no older than four or five.

While Mutti prepared the tea and sandwiches for the railroad workers, Elfriede and her eldest brothers were allowed to play further away from the carriage. She would heat the large kettle for tea on an iron stove under the make-shift canvas roof. When

Vati would come home around dusk, he was always dead-tired. After his meal of potatoes and onions, he climbed in the back part of the car with the beds, and went to sleep. She only had some vague recollection of that time.

When it was time for a move, with everything loaded onto their railcar, the children sat on top of things in the overfull space, until the whole construction enterprise had moved down the newly-laid track. Mutter was always busy, too busy to look after them. Margaret realized they had practically raised themselves until they moved to Zeeven, and Mutti didn't have to work for the railroad. They stayed in a real house, and Vati joined them at the end of the week. A few years later, they moved to Vati's village, where there was no war. She had heard the people in uniform ask questions as they checked the papers, and Vati called himself *Holländer*.

Their life got much better in one respect, with more to eat and a roof over their heads, but harder in other ways in this new country with a different language that she didn't speak yet and another new school. Soon after, she started to call Mutti with the grown-up name of Moeder to be more Dutch, but sometimes she reverted back to the German Mutti or Mutter. Juergen, a timid boy, was especially so in the new country. She couldn't remember a day she hadn't looked after him.

Mother always said Margaret had mothering skills and had been right: the nurses' training suited her. During her work in the asylum, she saw adults anxious like Juergen, like eternal children, scared of their own shadow and crying like babies in a corner, rolled up in a ball. With her light chatter and a mug of tea, she had a knack for getting most of them off the floor and into bed, and so sparing the poor sods the water treatment with the hoses in the bathhouse, meant to shock them out of their anguish. The strong streams of water coming from two directions at the patient were a violent method. Margaret wished they wouldn't do that, and when it was her shift during treatment, she always cried afterward.

She liked being needed. Secretly proud that Mother had called her help when Father had his heart attack, she had rushed home from work, but he already had found his peace without her. The only honor left for her was to lay him out on his bed together with Mother and Juergen and wash his worn-out body. Her own heart ached. Closest to him, she enjoyed his quiet love, undemanding and generous. Juergen took after him while her own temperament was a happy mix between Father and Mother.

After the others had gone off into the world, she had Father for herself, living close by.

One of the joys in life on her days off was helping him with the harvest, together with Juergen. Her short but muscular frame of 1.60 m functioned as a reliable machine, and she worked as hard as a man. This kind of work on the field offered her the fundamental, physical release of uncomplicated, hard work, followed by quiet camaraderie, as she rested with her companions in the fragrant fresh hay for their sandwich and tea. She still missed Father today.

Although she didn't want the twelve children Jacob's parents had, caring for others gave her purpose. Jacob couldn't give her the love and attention she so craved like her father had — undemanding, tender. Perhaps being one of many hadn't taught him how to give love. He had dated Elfriede for a short time before he asked her out, and she had resented that then. At times his motives look suspicious, and she tried to look behind the obvious into his soul, his emotions, but he kept those a secret. On the other hand, he could be very charming, and that's how he got her to fall for him — her first serious boyfriend after a string of unsuitable admirers, mostly farm boys, and a baker's son.

Their quarrel about Jacob giving up his job and her return to work confused her, his proposal unreal, even farfetched. She hadn't heard of any man staying at home and his wife working on the job past marriage. She wouldn't trust him looking after the boys properly anyway; he'd be too impatient. Without decent work, Jacob would be bored to death and blame her for it.

When Hendrik was born, she found a new purpose, and she reconciled to giving up her job. She hadn't been alone with Jacob long before she got pregnant, and she wondered then how long his infatuation with her would last. Twenty-eight years old was already late for a woman to become pregnant. Raised in Germany, she didn't know the Dutch children's world, so she taught her children German nursery songs, and Jacob sang the Dutch songs to them. Another difference between them: as immigrants, her family members stuck together, while she knew few of his relatives.

Jacob still seemed content in their marriage and clearly loved his children, although he rejected her other talents. Father had taught her to be self-sufficient, and she certainly was not a dainty, fragile woman and applied that around the house on jobs the man of the house usually did, but on the sly. A shoe was magically fixed with a new sole, or the cabinet hinge was repaired, a chair painted. The thought occurred to her. Many women settled for a mediocre mate. Had she likewise simply been a means to an end for Jacob — a family of his own? Maybe not Jacob, but her children needed her. As long as his eyes were open, Hendrik surely warranted her attention. As her eyelids closed over her scratchy eyes, exhaustion settled in her body. She dreamed of many disheveled people on the road begging for food.

Chapter 21

After he arrived at the office, Jacob would first inspect the brigade compound and the horses — he was a stickler for a clean and tidy brigade. That day, everything was in excellent shape, and the horses had been taken care of. He expected a call later in the morning from his direct superior, the regional department head of his marechaussee crew, with news about Lieutenant-Colonel Pieter Versteegh. He was eager to debrief his own concerns with his boss.

He left the stables and walked around to the brigade's front entrance. About to enter, he heard the sound of a two-stroke engine and looked into the street. He saw his brother-in-law rounding the corner on his motorcycle, drive by the brigade, and stop in front of the Wehrmacht HQ. Simultaneously to Juergen parking the bike, Johanna stepped out of the HQ entrance. What the devil were they doing there? Jacob hadn't expected them to be so blatant about their love for the Nazis. How naive could he have been? His heart beat faster, and he inhaled deeply and then caught a whiff of wood smoke.

A horse-and-wagon was parked in the hotel's driveway. It looked familiar. Yes, it was Johanna's horse, and he realized his instincts were intact, thrilled he hadn't told Margaret anything important. Johanna must have been delivering goods, indeed chopped wood for heating, by the smell of it. The nights already were rather chilly this fall, and even though everything was still rationed, the Nazis' needs for heat were beyond the grasp of the law.

Hidden from view around the corner, he watched the scene. After exchanging a few words with his mother, Juergen walked into the building. Johanna left with the empty wagon.

Jacob wished he was a flea on the cat Heusden kept in his office, a long-haired, completely white creature that lounged on the Wehrmacht's desk sometimes and entered or left the building as it pleased. Jacob adored dogs. The situation was odd. What else could Juergen have to offer Heusden?

Only one way to find out, so he marched up to the hotel entrance and straight into Heusden's office. As he suspected, Juergen sat across from the commander who got up when Jacob entered. The German clicked his heels — second nature for the guy. "*Guten Morgen* [Good morning], Commander Von Norden. Did we schedule a meeting?"

Jacob ignored formality and stayed by the door.

"*Morgen*, Commander Heusden. No, we didn't. *Entschuldige* [Forgive me]." He continued in Dutch. "My apologies for bursting in, but I thought I'd catch my brother-in-law before he leaves town again." He turned to Juergen. "Morning Juergen. Before you go home, could I get you to drop by my office?" To his satisfaction, Juergen's eyes just about bulged out of his head. It reminded him of a horse in distress.

Juergen's response came slowly as he looked down at his hands. "Oh, sure, I could, if you really want me to."

Putting warmth into his voice, Jacob said, "That's great. See you soon." To the commander, as he saluted, he said, "Again, my apologies, Commander. *Guten Tag* [Good-day]."

He quickly left the office and marched back to his own building. He spoke with his night officer and, after the night report was completed, dismissed him. Not much was happening around town. The old Air Defense Services staff had been replaced. Any non-compliance with the black-out would be in the hands of the Mayor anyway. The city weekenders had returned to walk the moors and camp out, enjoying the beautiful wooded areas surrounding Overdam, with the occasional drunken bash at a cafe in town. Traffic accidents and small thefts, instances of hoarding goods, domestic and other disputes, and common assaults, the usual police work — nothing to worry about.

Relaxed, Jacob sat back in his chair to explore the potential for future problems with Juergen. He wasn't sure what he wanted to say to his brother-in-law, who wasn't breaking any laws, as far as he knew. He couldn't think of any formal charges to follow up on. Juergen's problem was all attitude, an ethical problem.

Dutch Nazi parties had been popping up since 1934, the biggest of them the NSB led by Anton Mussert, with five percent of the electorate vote in the last elections. After the invasion, most Dutch people loved to hate the leader, Mussert, and his party, and the NSB became the symbol of treason. Jacob recalled his week of arresting potentially dangerous individuals. Mussert — the sly fox — had escaped his arrest. Jacob's colleagues from The Hague had arrested Mussert's vice-president, Rost van Tongeren, but alas, the slime-ball was now a rising star in the Nazi world and had the ear of the Nazi Governor Seyss-Inquart. He even rose to President of the Central Bank.

Jacob had seen how Nazi demagoguery turned people's heads. Hell, even the deputy ministers, the DMs, clearly fell in line before ordered to comply, and not to forget some of his own crew members, in awe over Hitler's Blitzkrieg methods. A knock on the door sounded, and Juergen appeared.

"You want to speak to me?"

"Yeah, come in, have a seat."

Juergen stepped in and carefully closed the door but stayed standing.

"I'll come right out with it: I saw you enter the enemy's headquarters and thought I'd ask you directly. What are you doing there?"

Juergen was quick: "How's that your concern? I can do business with whomever I want. You can't stop me. Mutter and I are doing legitimate business. We have to survive, and I don't have a job right now."

"Don't you have any reservations about helping the enemy?"

Juergen looked at him with an arrogant smile on his face, raising Jacob's blood pressure. "No, why should I? You might as well know, I'm a party member, and there's nothing wrong with it either. We like what the German Nazis are doing, I mean reducing unemployment and all of that. We're all part of the Germanic tribe anyway. This is a new day, and the people will rule. Hitler is all for the people, he's a socialist."

Aggravated by the man's shameless attitude, Jacob started speaking louder.

"Thanks for owning up to your membership in the NSB. That's exactly what I wanted to confirm. I believe that everybody has a right to vote for the party of their choice, but I draw the line at parties, that play on fear and intend to stir up hate against certain citizens." He reminded Juergen of the Nazi assaults on Jews in the streets of Germany and Poland, that their stores and their money were taken for no reason, and the owners arrested. His conclusion was succinct. "That is the opposite of love for the people. How do you feel about those things, heh?"

The duty officer peeked around the door and said, "The department head is on the line," and closed the door again.

Jacob quickly finished his thought: "Get this through your head, man. You're betting on the wrong horse. I'm warning you not to get out of line with your NSB buddies, because we'll arrest you for breach of the order, or assault. Sorry, I'll have to take this call. Say hello to Mother for me."

He picked up the receiver and covered the mouthpiece while watching his brother-in-law. Juergen looked at him with a blank face, his mouth slowly forming the word asshole, and then stepped out of the office.

After his long call with the department head, Jacob was in a better mood. Like his boss said, it was only natural that the staff's perspectives on the front lines differed from those bureaucrats at the top, the managers. It was nothing to worry about. He had let himself be caught up in the speculation and paranoia of the occupation, like most people in the nation. Grateful for the guidance, he leaned back in his chair.

Margaret came to mind, who looked so glowing of late. He loved her and always thought she loved him too. He sometimes asked himself what she really, down deep, thought about him. She seemed like a mystery to him sometimes. Could she, would she ever take a lover? No, that was impossible. She'd been quite shy and still a virgin when they married, although he wasn't.

His thoughts landed on the woman of his bachelor days. She'd been his landlady, who so generously looked after him throughout his assignment, there at the border. They had been matched wonderfully, their passions mutually heightened in each other's company. He shook his head and stretched his body in the desk chair. He should go home earlier today, see what's going on with Margaret.

***

Jacob didn't mention to Margaret having seen Juergen and Johanna at the Wehrmacht HQ. He decided to back off on her relatives and try to be more helpful to his wife. Margaret was more affectionate to him in return. Things were alright between them, and life was good. After an early dinner, the family went for a walk before sundown.

The heather smelled good, sweet, and Margaret looked radiant. She told him after dinner that she was pregnant. His reaction had been non-committal. Considering the circumstances, he instead wished she wasn't, but that's life. For a change, it was a warm summer night. They were without coats and enjoyed the soft, fragrant breeze gently brushing their faces.

The boys were running ahead, chasing each other in obvious delight. Jaap loved to improve his running skills. These were the family times memories were made of. It reminded him of the happy days after he had asked Margaret to marry him, the excitement of the wedding, with all of Margaret's relatives, her aunt from Germany, and even both of his own sisters, Sientje and Adriana attending.

He recalled his intense joy during the wedding day, his pride when the honor guard of marechaussees formed an arc in the air with their sabers for the newly-wed to walk under, and how beautiful and sophisticated Margaret had looked in her white, sleek gown and the mysterious veil. With fondness, he recalled his gratitude that night for the woman, who had taught him the game of love, the reason he could be a perfect lover for Margaret, a virgin on their wedding night.

Chapter 22

Jacob had promised to share as much information as possible in the weekly staff briefings with his crew. He started with bringing up the unemployed military — he still considered himself part of the military. Jacob's crew didn't expect the occupation to last much longer after the twenty thousand POWs were released. With the disbandment of the army, all other soldiers had also become unemployed. Those men needed jobs.

"The Deputy of Employment and Welfare has the responsibility for 300,000 unemployed ex-soldiers. I heard that Internal Affairs wants them to work on their new baby: Rebuilding Services. Which means they'll be clearing rubble. That's a tough dive to take for an officer."

"But not a bad idea now that they're civilians," De Wit replied, "especially in Rotterdam, where people live now with relatives, sometimes 20 to a house. They need new housing and those men could help restore the damage."

"At least they'll get paid," Peters chipped in. "Most soldiers would like it. Better than sitting at home doing nothing."

Van Houten had the long view, scoffed, and added: "It's also in the Kraut's interest. Good roads and bridges for their troops to quickly get to where the Dutch rebellion will happen, right? I bet Seyss-Inquart will approve the plan."

"You think we'll have a rebellion? I can't see it. We have nothing to fight with," army buff Leversma said, perking right up with excitement.

"I heard the police recruiters are looking at hiring ex-military men." Jacob threw that in.

"Great idea. Those men would be useful when we start a rebellion ourselves!" Van Houten, of course, said this, the born rebel. Most of the brigade crew agreed. At least soldiers knew what to do with a gun.

Jacob wasn't sure how to react to the sounds of resistance from his crew, and instead of focusing on his insecurities, shared some of the unofficial department news.

"I heard our second-in-command resigned, you know, Lieutenant-Colonel Versteegh."

"No way. I wonder what brought that on," De Wit said, who had been on the job for some time and knew of him.

Jacob liked Versteegh too. "Good question. I'll find out. I got a mate in The Hague. Versteegh must've had a serious motive for him to abandon us to the Nazis."

***

Over the following days, Jacob noticed that his crew seemed more appreciative of their jobs. He didn't have to remind them to work with the horses, or clean up the brigade. His last promotion to commander was his reward from the police brass for a successful spying mission at the border. Before that, he had a stint as a law instructor at the training facility. He had connections and should use them.

He picked up the phone and asked the operator for Hansen at HQ in The Hague and got his mate on the line. Hansen was part of the police recruiting staff. Jacob's questions about Versteegh's departure led to more disclosures. Hansen confessed he had been astonished by the top brass' instructions to the recruiting teams, and he was eager to spill the beans.

"What specific instructions are you talking about, Hansen?"

"Listen to this: my superiors ordered us to exclude all Jewish applicants. We were told to just take their applications, put them in a drawer, and forget about them. Strangely, this instruction came from the Deputy Ministers of both Justice and Internal Affairs, and not, as might be expected, from the German Reich's Office."

Jacob nearly fell off his chair. "Unconscionable. Once you start anticipating what the Nazis might want, you're on a slippery slope."

Hansen was on the same wavelength.

"When the Nazis force us into it, maybe, but taking the initiative ourselves is unheard of. That must be the reason why the Council of Deputies kept their decision from the general public. Especially Jewish applicants would've liked to know about it. Who knows whatever else they're concocting. Those Deputies are cowards. I bet Versteegh didn't agree with it."

"Sounds about right," Jacob agreed. "Not that I want to be stirring up trouble. I'm a member of the anti-revolutionary party after all, but we still have our religious freedoms in the country to defend against the Nazis. I'd like to keep the Jews in the force. I liked Versteegh. Too bad he's gone now." The various religious and political parties were notoriously at odds with one another about what to do with the nation's anti-Jewish sentiments. He heard a chortle on the line.

"You're not usually so forthcoming with your political views, Van Noorden," Hansen jested.

"These are exceptional times," Jacob slowly replied.

"Yeah, sure are," Hansen said, just as seriously. "You've got a way of bringing someone back to reality, but you're right. The deputies sidestepped our constitution, and acted as if our hard-won religious freedoms didn't exist. Had the public known of their decision, the Council would've heard plenty of protest from the great un-washed. I'm disgusted with them." Hansen snorted.

"For sure. Same here. Thanks, and please, keep me in the know, Hansen." Jacob laid the receiver very carefully down on the cradle of the black console, lost in thought. He realized he needed to share, and it was high time to make his deputy his primary support on his crew. He had been told Van Houten was technically minded and a ham radio enthusiast.

***

In their weekly briefing meeting with his deputy chief, Jacob shared what he had found out about the Council of Deputy Ministers. He carefully studied Sergeant Van Houten's reactions.

The sergeant looked uneasy, shifting his butt in his seat back and forth before he spoke up. "That's disgusting. It's damn well the opposite of our national beliefs."

Jacob nodded. "Yes, I agree. Van Houten. Say, you've lived all of your life in Overdam, right?"

Van Houten leaned back in his chair. "Except my time in training."

Jacob leaned back as well, glad the man across from him showed signs of relaxing in his presence. "So, tell me. Do we have any Jewish policemen?"

"With all due respect, sir, I've never asked my colleagues about their religion." Van Houten raised his eyebrows, repositioned his feet and stared back at him.

Jacob raised a hand in a gesture of peace. "Yes, of course, you're correct not to, Sergeant, I know the constitution guarantees equal access to the civil service, regardless of one's religion. I want you to know there's something fishy going on. I wonder if the DMs have any system for keeping in touch with the cabinet. Short wave radio contact, telegrams, or couriers, phone, whatever. I think they're making some bad decisions."

Van Houten responded as he had hoped. "That wouldn't go. I'm sure the Krauts are keeping tabs on all radio senders. And an illegal operator would have to move the installation every few hours, and not be on the air more than ten minutes to avoid discovery. The telephone lines will be monitored too. We're not sure how operators will respond. They're supposed to keep all calls confidential, but under pressure from the SD, will they?"

Jacob bent forward in his chair and lowered his voice. "What about secret agents, spies?"

Van Houten, still leaning back, sat motionless in his seat and paused. After a few seconds, he responded with caution. "An agent might be dropped off here at night, and then meet with the DMs somewhere secret. The problem lies in sending them back to the English coast under cover, all after that, their trips back and forth over occupied terrain. Sharing their information with the cabinet-in-exile sounds impossible. If they're caught, it will all turn into a nightmare."

Jacob leaned back and crossed his legs. "You might be correct, Van Houten. Besides the Nazis, our yellow Council is another problem we'll have to face."

He had sparked Van Houten's interest. The man's dark brown eyes were holding anger, but his voice gave it away when he hissed: "If their stupid strategies are what we can look forward to, God help us. The Council's Chair, Snouck-Hurgronje, turns out to be a real Nazi-lover. It's just unbelievable he is the DM of Foreign Affairs. He's offering our country to the Nazis on a silver platter, the bastard." He paused and recovered his calm, then asked in an eager tone of voice, "Opper, what trump card do you have up your sleeve?"

Jacob smiled. "Yes, I do. I wonder why we didn't get to hear about this instruction to the recruiters from our own department head. How much does he know, and more importantly, can we rely on him?"

Van Houten sat up and leaned forward, shifted in his chair and looked intently at Jacob, as if trying to convey something, and finally replied. "Maybe he didn't know about it. But that's not right either. If the cowards high up on the ladder are excluding the Jewish applicants, we all need to know about it."

He realized his deputy hadn't directly answered his question about how many Jewish were in his unit. He promised his deputy: "I'll find out from my man in The Hague what he knows about our Jewish colleagues and their job security. The department heads just might start firing them without our knowledge."

"We ought to do something. This is going to be a disaster. Our government was already corrupt, but this is worse than corruption. It's outright treason."

Jacob could see that Van Houten's creative mind was already working and sure to come up with a way to harness the crew against any future disasters. He didn't think it would come to firing all Jewish policemen just yet but didn't rule out some kind of government action. He was beginning to like his deputy.

"That's good. I'll just watch over you, so you won't get in over your head, Sergeant."

Chapter 23

It was Prince Bernard's birthday. The radio news reported crowds gathered in front of the city halls in The Hague, Rotterdam, Amsterdam, and most cities in the nation, and surprisingly, in Overdam. The demonstrators carried carnations — the flower dandy Prince Bernard usually dressed in his lapel's buttonhole.

Jacob was unaware of the happening until Heusden called him, screaming in his ear. He imagined the spit flying from Heusden's fat lips.

"Immediately disperse the crowd in front of my HQ. This is an order. If the demonstrators haven't disappeared within ten minutes, they'll be arrested."

He told Van Houten and Peters to saddle up their horses and meet him at the town hall. Together with Leversma and Dikkers, he marched towards the small group, gathered a few hundred yards farther down the road, next door to the Wehrmacht HQ.

He climbed the few steps to the town hall's front porch, about a meter higher than the crowd at street level, and faced the villagers. His constables, ready to grab their batons, took their positions on opposite sides of the gathering. Six Wehrmacht soldiers stood watching the spectacle from the hotel-annex Nazi HQ next door, holding their machine guns, barrels pointing down. A sudden thought came to him that took him completely off-guard: he wondered if Margaret's uncles had been deployed and, if so, where. He wouldn't recognize them, never met them, but knew that two of Johanna's brothers had fought in the Wehrmacht during 1914-1918. No, stop thinking about that.

Looking over the crowd, Jacob estimated it at fifty, primarily women, and all wore a carnation on their clothes or carried a bunch in their hands. Some waved a small orange banner, not full out over their heads, but at chest height. Jacob wondered where the Mayor was hiding. His police cap felt tight around his head and his collar was too small as anxiety threatened to overwhelm him. A whiff of the sweet fragrance of carnations hit his nose. Just then, his two mounted officers came down the road in a trot. He waited until they had taken their positions at the front of the crowd and then spoke. In a loud voice, he projected his words as far as possible, planning to keep his tone of voice devoid of emotion.

"Citizens of Overdam. We all respect and love the house of Orange and the member you are celebrating. Be that as it may, I request you go home and celebrate in private, as your actions are placing you at risk of arrest. It wouldn't be the Prince's wish, or of the Queen for you to be arrested."

He wanted to say a whole lot more but didn't want to dilute the message. How could he let them know that he merely spoke on behalf of the government, ordering him to abide by the German occupiers' rules, at least for now? That the Wehrmacht authority had informed him the demonstration was seen as an act of defiance against their law, and he'd arrest them if the crowd did not leave within five minutes? So, all he could do was ask. "Please, respect the lives of your own families and return to your homes in a calm and orderly manner. Thank you." Facing the crowd, Jacob gave a quick, formal salute.

While he spoke, the mounted men had already forced the demonstrators a few steps back by their presence and prepared for any order he would give them. The Wehrmacht soldiers watched. The crowd didn't move. Someone yelled at the top of his voice "*Oranje Boven* [Orange Rules], hip, hip, hooray!" Then nothing happened, except the soft shuffling of feet.

Another long minute of silence passed before individuals at the fringes started leaving, slowly at first, followed by others, quietly talking to one another. Within five minutes, the street was completely empty, except for a few carnations left behind on the pavement. Jacob then noticed the Nazi soldiers had disappeared from the roadside. He gave his men the command: "Withdraw."

The crew returned to the brigade, looking somber and responsible. Once inside the squad room, the men let go.

"That was a good speech, Chief!" said his right-hand man, as if he had heard all Jacob hadn't said but had wanted to. "Subtle enough to give our people some gratification without pissing off the Kraut, but serious enough to give them food for thought. The salute was the icing on the cake."

The man's grin was contagious, but Jacob kept his demeanor neutral. He didn't feel so good, his stomach still churning. After a few moments of silence, he responded to Van Houten's enthusiasm.

"I was thinking how much actual time Heusden would give us to disperse the crowd. I didn't like those machine guns. So far so good. I hope the next time the crowd, or the Nazis, won't be any harder on us."

"That's for sure, Opper," said Van Houten.

Jacob drew in his gut and left for his own office, where he took off his jacket and his cap, wiped his face, and balding head with his handkerchief. He didn't sit down to do more work. Instead, he went to the stables and got Susie out for a ride. It was the perfect release for the built-up rigidity of his body. At the end of the day, he went home, relieved, one hell of a workday over with.

Chapter 24

That evening, the ANP news reported on the day of riots and protest demonstrations in all major cities. The newsreader quoted Seyss-Inquart's quip verbatim to a journalist that the Dutch just love a flower parade, its sarcasm lost on the censor. The German Reich's Office had pinpointed the Air Defense Services' Jewish personnel as having played a leading role in the demonstrations' organization.

Just after the newscast, Henk called Jacob out of the blue. He was Margaret's older brother, the one born between the two sets of twins. The operator putting him through used a different name, so Jacob didn't know at first who the caller was. Henk used his father's name to remain unidentified, he said, and wanted him to be aware of a few items, so Jacob could take his measures as he deemed fit. First, The Hague's city council had sent their mayor home for having allowed this act of open defiance. Second, the Reich's Office had arrested General Winkelman, now a private citizen, and he was on his way to a POW camp.

"He had been walking up front in the parade. But something else. The SD is going to arrest the instigators of every participating town. Guess who? The Jews of course. They said they'll take measures, but they mean arrest, in particular against those in the Air Defense Service staff."

Standing in the corridor with the phone in his hand, Jacob said, "Why the Air Defense? Why them?"

"I guess they're in easy-identifiable public positions. I'm sure they won't be the last ones to go."

Hearing this, Jacob quickly thanked Henk and ended the call abruptly. The house phone was attached to the wall in the corridor. He carefully closed the living room door and dialed the operator. He had recommended a local Jewish man for a job with the Air Defense in Overdam. The operator put him through. When Simons answered, Jacob asked if he had heard the news.

The man sounded almost reticent. "Yes, I have. Why are you calling me?"

Pressured, his speech was more like ordering, when he said, "Simons, listen up, it has to do with your job. The Germans are on a mission, looking for an opportunity to set an example. Through my connections, I got word that the SD will arrest all Jews with the Air Defense today or tomorrow. They'll readily break their agreement not to touch the Dutch Jews."

Simons argued he hadn't even been at the demonstration.

Jacob insisted. "I'm telling you: leave town at once, this minute. It's only a matter of hours before the SD will arrest you. Keep your mouth shut about who tipped you off. I've got to go now. Good luck." He hung up.

As he returned to the living room, he looked at Margaret and wondered if she had heard his conversation.

"It's not right," Margaret said.

"What's not right, dear?" He straightened his back and cracked his knuckles, bending the fingers back until the joints audibly popped, and then sat down in his armchair.

"What the radio said. The radio blames people just because they're Jewish." Margaret was folding laundry, standing at the dining table, and glanced back at Jacob.

"Yes, I agree one hundred percent with you," Jacob replied. "Losing their job is bad enough, but even worse, they'll be arrested and put in a camp. You know what the SS did to the Polish Jews, don't you?"

She stopped folding and turned to face him, leaning against the table, disbelief on her face.

He continued talking in a calm, matter-of-fact voice. "That started just like how those protest marches today happened. Hitler blamed the Jews for everything that went wrong in the last war, so his Nazis are going to solve the problem forever by getting rid of all Jews."

"You don't really believe it. No really, that's just propaganda." Margaret looked at him with skepticism. "Bfffft," came from her mouth, "Too farfetched."

He got his pocket knife out and cleaned his nails while talking.

"Well, dear, you believe whatever you want to believe. Time will tell." When he looked at her, she had already turned around and continued to fold, making him look like the angel of doom. She was reluctant to face the truth and needed more time, Jacob concluded. He had to ask her about her uncles yet. Better not now.

She changed the subject. "Jacob, I wanted to ask you, would you mind if Mother came for dinner tomorrow? She's in town on business and wants to drop by. I haven't seen her in a while."

"Sure, whatever you want, dear. Has she recovered from the fire?"

"Yes, Juergen fixed the roof so the rain and snow won't come in. She can rebuild the sty when she gets closer to ordering more piglets."

Jacob had some idea what that business might be. He'd play it smart, keep things under control and play along. More flies caught with honey than with vinegar.

In a neutral tone, he asked, "Did Mother put Juergen on the title of the property, or is he just her renter?"

Margaret looked surprised, seaweed green eyes drawing him in. "I never asked her, but Juergen was the one who took Father's place after he died, so I think nobody would mind it if he got the house, eventually. He worked hard for her, the place might as well go to his family. Why are you asking?"

"No reason, I just thought maybe we should pitch in for repairs, since it was our son that caused the damage."

He got up, put on a cardigan in the corridor, and went outside to the stables: the only place where he found uncomplicated happiness.

Chapter 25

The next night, dinner was on the table at six o'clock. Margaret had made pea soup and large pancakes, as large as a plate, thin ones with plenty of eggs in the batter and bacon pieces sprinkled on each one. The boys were allowed to have a small clump of butter on their pancake that Johanna had contributed. The boys were well-behaved, happy to see their Oma, who always brought something she knew they liked. This time it was dried fruit.

Johanna was in a good mood and happily chatted with Margaret. She said she was planning to participate in the Winterhelp's fundraising action and asked Margaret if she would volunteer for the unfortunate. Margaret sat silent, looking down at her plate. The boys stopped their play with each other, curious about the sudden silence.

"Boys, you can leave the table, go play now in the other room," Margaret said quickly. She got up, took Jaap out of the high chair and set him down. As the boys left for the front room, she sat down, expecting Jacob's reply.

Hearing Johanna's question, Jacob just had to jump into the silence that followed the boys' departure, despite his promise to Margaret to be nice to Johanna and not to bother her with his politics. "The program falls under the NSB. So, tell me, Johanna, was that the reason you and Juergen visited the Wehrmacht boss the other day? I saw you there with the horse and cart, and I spoke with Juergen."

Johanna had put down her fork and knife and faced Jacob, sitting on her chair with a straight back and lifted chin. She looked him squarely in the eye and spoke in her heavily accented Dutch in a patient manner as if he were a child.

"Well, Jacob, I can't see it's any business of yours. We have to make a living. With all comestibles on coupons and all supplies registered, we can't sell our products as well as before the regulations came in. I offered my services and the horse and buggy to the Wehrmacht. I hope to keep my horse by making him useful to the army. Juergen has some other connections, which will help us too, and he'll be involved with Winterhelp. So there. Satisfied?"

"You're correct, Johanna, it's none of my business, yet," he admitted and added, "But I wonder, don't you feel any reluctance? Consider what the Nazis did in Germany and Poland, and how they invaded our country. Don't you have the slightest fear they might start taking the Jews here away as well? And about charity: I heard the Jewish poor are excluded from Winterhelp benefits, which should tip you off about their intentions, no?"

In contrast to his biting criticism, Johanna was still friendly, and she replied softly in German, "*Ich habe das nicht gewusst* [I didn't know that]."

Emboldened, he continued: "Alright, so now you know, Mother. Closer to home, you must have heard what happened in front of the townhall on Prince Bernhard's birthday."

As Margaret was kicking Jacob hard against the shin under the table, Johanna just nodded.

Ignoring Margaret's attempts to stop him, Jacob persisted with his confrontation as if something else took control of him. He just had to do it. He didn't look at Margaret, who was shaking her head no.

"By the way, the Prince also was a German at birth, like Margaret, but since he married a Dutch woman, he decided to be loyal to the Dutch. You could do the same, you know. You married a Dutchman and live in Holland, raised your children here, you even converted to our citizenship."

She didn't take the bait but said with a kind voice, "I heard about the carnation day. Too bad. I like Prince Bernhard, a handsome man."

"And, to answer your earlier question: no, I won't allow Margaret to help you with the door-to-door Winterhelp collection. It's not who we are. We give through our church charities."

Margaret cut in and leaned over to her mother: "Don't listen to him, Mutter." She turned to Jacob and used his nickname: "Jan Van Noorden, stop bothering my mother. She's had enough suffering in the first war, and besides, I'm completely able to make my own decisions. If I would like to go with my mother door-to-door, it's up to me. You cannot tell me not to. I'm a grown woman, not your child. I'm not saying I will, but I might. It's charity for the poor, regardless who collects." Her chin out, her back straight, she looked at him defiantly.

He stood up, angry now, and barked at her. "In my house my rules apply." He willed her with his fiery, dark eyes to comply, but it didn't work.

Margaret stood up too, chin in the air, the mirror image of her mother. "It's my house too and I have a right to make up my own mind."

To Jacob's surprise, Johanna intervened in her German-sounding Dutch. With a soothing voice, as if they were children, she said, "*Kinder, Kinder*, no reason to get into a fight. Margaret is a strong woman, Jacob, and she can make up her own mind. I raised her that way. Winterhelp is a good cause. It's really about helping people. Mayors and ministers are patrons and they ask people to step up, and help out."

Jacob wasn't ready to give up his fight. "It's true, but those mayors probably are Nazi members themselves, part of the NSB in-crowd, so to speak." He scoffed, not sure of its veracity, but it sounded truthful.

Johanna didn't give up easily either, and ever so politely, she pressed on.

"The NSB has many members now, I heard over hundred-thousand. Even your town has a division. You must know that, Jacob. Juergen is helping with organizing the meetings. He thinks we should join the modern times and accept the new reality. I think he's right."

His blood pressure was rising. "The new reality? Well, not my reality, Mother." Less secure of himself than he had been a few minutes ago, he glared at Johanna.

As an elderly woman with a lifetime of standing up for her family, she spoke with a kind voice, berating him like he was a youth of twelve.

"But Jacob, you're one to talk. You work together with the Wehrmacht, so what's the big deal? We all have to make the best of life under the Germanic rule. And the soldiers behave well, no? You can't deny it." Johanna looked to Margaret, then to Jacob with a satisfied, big smile.

He leaned back against his chair with a tiny smile on his face and studied his mother-in-law. Johanna's little speech had given him pause. Margaret sat with a thin stripe for a mouth, apparent determination on her face, and sat looking at him with an expression of what he thought was an accusation. He had to admit it. In the eyes of the world, Johanna would be right. There was no difference between what he was doing and what she did. Damnation to the day the Nazis invaded the country. He stayed silent throughout the rest of the meal.

When Juergen arrived to drive Johanna home after dinner, Jacob had one more thing to say to both, but mostly meant for Johanna. Standing in the compound holding the horse by his halter and Margaret watching from the doorway, he shared his final position.

"We're not on the same side. The Nazis will prove the wrong horse to bet on. They're ruthless fascists with one goal: to conquer all of Europe. They will destroy it. Mark my words. You both will be sorry then, and I cannot help you. I think it's better, if you do not visit our home for a while."

Margaret shrieked and left the doorway: "Jan. No."

"Be quiet, woman," he commanded.

Margaret stood in front of him and looked at him, wide-eyed.

Johanna left with her head up with the same triumphant smile from after her last statement at the table. As if she delighted in causing trouble.

Margaret and Jacob didn't discuss the Winterhelp, or anything else that night, or any other night that month. The deep freeze between them had set in. Neither felt like trying to put some heat into their relationship. Fighting the nearest demon was so much easier.

Chapter 26

Things started to change. The police commissioner and the regional department head both had been replaced by collaborative types. After the shuffle, Den Toom emphasized to Jacob that the Council of Deputy Ministers determined what happened in the nation, not the cabinet-in-exile. Nazi police boss, Rauter, had ordered the justice ministry to reorganize the police and combine the various Dutch police forces into one State Police. Den Toom told Jacob that the upper echelon was happy to oblige, and he liked that idea as well. Jacob knew the top brass had always wanted this centralization to improve control over the ragtag collection of policing branches. Up to now, the various denominational unions opposed centralization.

"How did they get the unions to agree?" Jacob wondered out loud.

Den Toom was proud to say it: "Easily. The Reich's Office simply made the unions illegal and went ahead with the centralization. That's doing effective business."

Jacob was shocked. Ending the unions was blasphemy and went against everything the nation stood for. He had to swallow, and in spite of his rising heat and heartbeat, he contained his anger and politely said, "Oh, really? We lost our representation. Is that a good thing, Chef?"

The arrogant jerk typically replied from a manager's point of view.

"Well, Van Noorden, the reorganization was to our benefit. The Corps Marechaussee finally received the personnel we need as the biggest rural police force in the country. We have doubled our numbers. And another thing: Rauter also established a new training school for police recruits to standardize training. This school will open up soon in the town of Schalkhaar, close to Overdam, another advantage to you people at the front line."

Jacob saw no benefits. He knew the Nazi model would soon push out the old-model policemen, and the robots of the Nazis would take over the force. He already knew that Rauter — firmly in control of the police — would take care of it, but he stayed silent. Who could fight that kind of collaborative attitude? The management is always correct. Without unions, he and his crew could do nothing to fight that presumption. As soon as he could, he got off the phone. A heavy cloud of powerlessness settled over him.

***

A few days later, Jacob received a package of forms to fill out for each member of his crew, with the order to return the completed forms to the police regional headquarters in Zwolle within two days. Its heading read: Aryan Declaration. It looked like a census form with questions about parents, grandparents and great-parents, religion and race the person belonged to, place of birth, and all of that for the spouse. Jacob immediately understood its purpose to separate the Jewish from the rest — three generations back. It also would identify the degree of Jewishness. He sent up a silent prayer for God to give him direction. All day, he sat thinking about it.

He got home early. After dinner with the kids and putting them to bed, he asked Margaret how she would answer the questions, if she had to fill in the form. He asked against his better judgment, but he desperately needed someone to share his conundrum with, even an outsider. He showed her a sample of the form.

Margaret reluctantly took the form in her hands, read it, and slowly commented. Her face was showing her hesitation and she wouldn't look at him.

"I wouldn't know. Can you just not fill it out? What's the worst that could happen?" She glanced at him uneasily and looked down immediately, fiddling with some kind of knitting on her lap.

"I could be fired," Jacob simply said.

He sat quietly and looked at Margaret, whose face moved from a frown to a profound sense of alarm, eyes wide, hand before her mouth, crossing and uncrossing her feet.

Then she said: "Oh no, that cannot happen. What would we do then? What would you do?"

"I don't know. I could work for your mother on the farm in exchange for food, and maybe a bit of cash, if she has any?" He looked at the floor, humiliated, shifting uncomfortably in his easy chair — not so easy now.

Her alarm was gone, and she became practical. "You? Really? You hate to get your hands dirty. You'd never survive it. And if she has any cash, it probably comes from the Wehrmacht, so you'd be working for them. And you'll have to make up with her. You can't quit. Fill out the darned form."

He looked at Margaret, unsure if he should pay more attention to what she said or to his conscience, shifting from believing to not believing her. It was quiet. After several minutes, he asked, using her more intimate nickname, just to make sure she got its significance.

"Dear Greta, you understand it means identifying our Jewish policemen, right?"

She shrugged, and she continued knitting.

"Dear man, it's only a form. It's not like you have to arrest any Jews. You said you wouldn't do that. Anyway, that's a job for the German police, not your men. Do it. This is an easy thing. You worry too much. You can't save the world all by yourself."

Jacob wanted to believe her. He knew the Aryan Declaration meant another step in co-opting the civil service to work for the Nazi State. The first form he had signed, like all other policemen after the capitulation. It was for obedience to the German State Office. Just a formality which would guarantee their jobs, according to the old police commissioner, whose judgment he trusted. This was different. The Aryan Declaration would change the fate of the Jewish policemen only.

At least Margaret was talking to him again, and he was grateful for that change. It had been lonely these last weeks without her. He had been afraid she had begun to resent him. He had inadvertently shoved her on the side of her mother with his confrontation. At least that was behind him. Family attachment was something he didn't get. He hadn't seen his sisters for years, the only relatives he still had a bond with. Maybe it was time to visit them soon. Traveling to the west of the country would be a problem under the circumstances. He felt so tired that he went to bed early.

Chapter 27

The following morning, Jacob called his men together and handed out the forms without explaining anything. He requested their return by next morning, blank or filled out, which was up to each man, he said. He couldn't look anybody in the eyes that day and for a long time to come afterward. Whenever Jews came up in the conversation, guilt gnawed inside his gut. At his core, he knew the Aryan Declaration wasn't just a matter of formality. Something else was bound to follow.

***

A fortnight later, with the identification process completed, the news quickly spread mouth to mouth and via the illegal Radio Orange that several thousand public servants had been fired across all government branches. Valuable, if not brilliant professors and administrators, judges, department managers, and regular front-line workers were let go. It became quickly known these were all Jewish public servants.

No unions existed anymore to protest the move. The Deputy Ministers were silent. The Reich's office remained silent. Due to the imposed censuring decree, the newspapers and reporters were impotent. The only protest came from students of two universities. The students of the Leiden and Delft universities loudly protested the Dutch government's decision and announced a strike.

After the first day of the student strike, the Nazi Security Branch SD closed the Delft Technical Institute. The next day, the SD closed the Leiden university on the day of the announced strike. After these two days, all other universities complied.

When Jacob heard that bad news, he confessed his despair to Margaret about having truthfully filled out the form and for not intervening with instructions to his crew on how to lie. She tried to console him. It was futile. She withdrew, although he hadn't blamed her.

His face a pale mask from lack of sleep, Jacob faced his crew in the morning. The men were stunned by this side effect of filling in a stupid form. In his briefing meeting with his deputy, Jacob recalled their conversation some weeks earlier about the over-compliant Deputy Ministers at the helm. Their fear that those men in charge of the country would lead it into an unavoidable, impending disaster had come through. They hadn't anticipated this slick manipulation. Nothing could be done now.

"I knew the Aryan Declaration wasn't innocent. How could it be? Nothing the Nazis do is without a goal in mind. I shouldn't have passed out the form. I could've sent them back blank. I let you all down."

Van Houten looked more furious than shocked with a deep frown and eyes dark glints.

"Not your fault, boss. We can think for ourselves. But a terrible shame it is."

They sat silently. Jacob didn't have the mind to bring up any other business. His usual chatty deputy stayed numb as well, slumped in his chair with his fists in his pockets. It was the shortest meeting ever that morning.

***

A couple of days after the purge, Peters came into Jacob's office, pale-faced. He lingered by the door and entered only when the boss explicitly invited him to come in. Stammering and turning red in the face, he disclosed his request.

"I have to confess something, Opper. I want you to know, but you must swear to keep it confidential."

"Of course, Peters. What's the matter?"

"I'm not sure it's even relevant, but my family is originally from south-eastern Germany what used to be Hungary, way back when. My grandmother was Jewish, but converted to Christianity when she married. I've known it for a while, but didn't know what to fill out on the Aryan Declaration. I know the Jewish trace themselves mainly through the mother, but I don't know what the Germans think is Jewish, so I thought I'd be fine with how I see it: since she converted, she wasn't a Jew anymore."

"Alright, Corporal, thanks for telling me. I don't understand the Nazi obsession with the Jewish religion. To me, it's a strange, irrelevant phenomenon. I hope the awareness of your own vulnerability will instill in you some compassion and you won't eye the SS for a career move. What makes people good or bad is not whose blood runs through their veins or what religion they choose. Don't you agree?" He leaned back and observed the man wriggle in his chair across from him.

Peters smiled at him, leaving the impression of subservience. "Yes, Chief, like you said. Thanks, I'm feeling better."

Jacob picked up some paper from his desk and dismissed Peters with, "Alright then, do your work."

After the corporal left, Jacob sat back, pondering what he had just learned. He realized he should take his own advice and find some compassion for Peters. The moron was just like a boy, in awe of the Nazi forces, and ironically, unable to join that elitist body if the truth were to come out about a Jewish grandmother. Peters' overwrought admiration for Nazis struck him as pathetic. The lies had already poisoned the man to the point of denying his own Jewish heritage. He sighed, remembering Christ's admonition: let he without sin cast the first stone. He just couldn't like or respect Peters, so yes, he was unable to follow the Lord's example in this.

In the following weeks, Jacob didn't hear any crew members talk about the firing of their Jewish colleagues anymore. He suspected they were preoccupied — like him — and in fear over the Nazis' next move, wondering when it would hit them personally.

Chapter 28

During the first few months of the new year, the orders came rolling in like thunder at the end of a summer's day. On the same day that Rauter's SD headquarters date-stamped them, the commissioner of the regional office passed on the new decrees with lighting speed to the departments. Jacob had known this new commander in Zwolle from a previous job, this Major Feenstra — an ambitious man. His own department head in Hardenberg, Adjutant Den Toom, passed the orders on from Feenstra by special courier to Jacob, as if the death penalty were attached for failure to deliver those on the same day. The pace of new directions made every policeman dizzy. Den Toom called Jacob and requested his presence for an in-person briefing. The next afternoon, Jacob got on his motorbike and cruised to Hardenberg's office for his supervision.

Den Toom demanded strict adherence to the new decrees. "I expect your men to frequently check civilians for their ID, regardless of a suspicion. And I want strictly enforced curfew starting at midnight and nobody stops checking before four in the morning, and put extra men on night shifts. You must arrest offenders on the spot, but leave the political elements to the German police. The Ordnungspolizei will take care of them, or in more severe cases, the security services SD."

Jacob sat across from this overweight, pale-faced man, knowing that his deputy, Van Houten, and most other crew members were already pissed off about the purge. As unit chief, he needed to keep the brigade crew calm and avoid attracting negative attention from his superiors, so he must stay polite. With utmost care, he asked for his supervisor's input.

"Any ideas where are can we put those arrested? Double up in our two cells, maybe?"

The fat man with a billiard ball for a head shrugged, which made his belly fat wiggle.

"Don't be facetious. Of course not. They'll be transferred to a holding location, probably in Amersfoort, or Arnhem, and processed later by a German judge."

Offering him a cigarette from a silver holder, Den Toom bent forward with difficulty. Jacob politely accepted and offered up a match. They lit up, and clouds of smoke floated between them.

"Hum, they'll see a judge then," Jacob replied, satisfied. "That's good. Another question if I may. With the unions gone, with whom do I discuss any disputes about our new job descriptions? You, sir?"

"Correct."

Jacob doubted the veracity of Den Toom's answer. The man was too busy with implementing Rauter's orders and pleasing Commissioner Major Feenstra. There wouldn't be room to listen to him — a lowly unit *opperwachtmeester* [chief guard]. He waited a few beats, took a drag on his smoke, but the adjutant had nothing to add.

"I regret the Reich's move to abandon the professional organizations. I liked reading The Christian Police Servant," he told the fat man.

"You'll be too busy to read, Van Noorden. Werner Schwier's prison project will soon be operational. If you do well, you might get a promotion."

Den Toom referred to the campground located in the forest, close to where Jacob frequently took Susie and went for bike rides with his family. He'd better shut up. Nothing was to be gained from this boss. The meeting dragged on for another half-hour before Den Toom released him, and he could ride home.

Drizzle from a gray sky enveloped him all the way home. He drove slowly. Some of the roads were slick. His mind wandered. So, he had a supervisor who exclusively seemed focused on enforcing the Nazi rules. There went his independence — out the window.

Chapter 29

As the government news radio, the ANP (Public Dutch Press) had become the mouth-piece for the German governor, colloquially known as Adolf's Newest Parrot. Nazi SS boss Rauter used it to lay down the new rules for Jewish citizens' segregation. Among them was one incredibly obnoxious order: Jews were to wear a gold star on their outer clothing in public. Department head Den Toom sent Jacob additional directives for instating a separate unit for the political suspects. Jacob dealt with those instructions in his weekly staff briefing.

"Our brigade is just too small, and even just a dedicated officer won't have enough work. My position remains that the German SD is the designated body to deal with anything of that nature. Better brace yourselves for the future: Den Toom might not agree with me. You are under no circumstances to start acting on your own in those cases. Talk to me if you run into a problem with a political suspect."

The crew accepted his instructions without comment this time. With the Germans next door and only half the formalized authority he used to have, he was now grateful for his crew's compliance.

At the end of the day, Wehrmacht boss Fritz Heusden called Jacob out of the blue and requested police assistance with a particular assignment. Jacob tried to get more information about the nature of this job, but Heusden was hell-bent on keeping it a secret.

"Just show up at the Wehrmacht headquarters with all the men you can spare." Heusden's secrecy made him feel uneasy. Before leaving the brigade, Jacob made sure he had his M25 in its holster and told the men assigned to accompany him to carry their weapons. Jacob arrived at the hotel-annex-HQ with Peters, Dijk, and Leversma, and his righthand man, Van Houten.

Heusden rubbed his chin incessantly. He looked at Jacob, although clearly meaning to address all the men gathered in the lobby of his HQ when he said: "Von Nor-den, this job falls under Oberst Rauter's decree for police assistance. I have nine po-litical suspects on my list for immediate arrest, and we'll put them on the train. Your men will assist with guarding them. Tell me how you want to do it. Then let's go and arrest those criminals."

A big knot settled in Jacob's stomach, which made him speak with extreme care. He didn't take his eyes off the chunky man in front of him. "May I please know their names and what their alleged crimes are, Ortzkommandant?"

Heusden seemed amenable to his question.

"*Ja, sicher.* These men engaged in activities considered hostile to the German state. They are getting a chance for retribution providing labor for *das Reich*. They will rehabilitate themselves at the labor camp at Saint Johannesga. After paying their debt to the German State, they may be released. So, let's proceed."

"Their names, *bitte*?"

"You will learn in time."

Just before dark, as most families had dinner at home, the group entered the street. Four German soldiers with their commander and four Dutch Marechaussee policemen plus their chief marched in formation through Overdam. At the first address, Heusden and another Wehrmacht soldier went in to arrest the man named on the list, according to plan.

As the man walked down the path with Wehrmacht on each side of him, Jacob and his men saw the Star of David on his coat's lapel. Goddamn. They were arresting the Jewish males in town, as he already had suspected. With the evidence in front of him, Jacob called out to Heusden.

"Stop! Halt! Excuse me, Ortzkommandant Heusden."

Heusden hurried from the door towards Jacob in the street and growled: "What's your problem?"

Haughty with righteousness, his hands on his hips, Jacob demanded: "These men on your list — are they all Jewish? Why didn't you tell me?"

Heusden put his hand up to stop Jacob and snapped, ""Damn you. You don't have to touch the Jews. My men will arrest them. Your job is only to accompany the prisoners to the train and make sure they get on. What difference would it make for you to know? You're to collaborate. Wasn't it made clear to you?"

All men watched the scene with great interest.

Jacob's right hand had crept up to his holster and rested on the leather, his elbow bent. As soon as he had touched his weapon, he saw his men tensing up from the corner of his eyes. He kept his hand where it was on the gun. He cleared his throat. With a firm voice and extra beats in his heart, he declared his position.

"No. We cannot help you. It's against regulations for Dutch police to arrest any politicals. Besides, Governor Seyss-Inquart promised the Jewish Dutch were not going to be touched. May I ask who gave this order?"

The Wehrmacht commander's face was beet-red, and his voice rose to a screeching pitch.

"Don't you get it, *Käsekopf* [cheese-head]? All rules are off. We're at war and you're under occupation. We do this job on order of my superior, Kommandant Schwier. His boss gave the command to start dealing with the Dutch Jews. You really want to fight SS-boss Rauter? Stand down, man."

He contravened Heusden's command. "*Nee* [no]. I'm so sorry, Heusden, I apologize. You'll have to ask your Security Services SD or the SS, or wait till your own Ordnungspolizei are back. I cannot comply. *Nee*." He turned to Peters, who was loosely holding the just-arrested man by his upper arm. "Let the man go. We're leaving now."

With a face distorted from anger, Heusden took a step forward as he got his gun from its holster. With his arm stretched, he aimed it at Jacob's heart and screamed: "Stop the nonsense, damn you!" The Nazi soldier looked like a raving madman, eyes wide and mouth wide open, his cap shoved to the back of his head, his big head about to explode.

Jacob also stepped forward, his heart beating twice as fast, as it pumped adrenaline through his system. The two of them stood a hand-width apart from each other, Heusden's gun touching his chest, his arm bent at the elbow. In one smooth movement, Jacob drew his M25 and pushed it hard against Heusden's ribs.

Heusden yelled, his face a couple of inches from Jacob's, his pistol pressing hard against Jacob's chest. "Lower your weapon, you fool, you're under arrest."

With his knees shaking under him, Jacob spoke in a soft and patient voice.

"You know I can't take direct commands from a German authority. I will not arrest Jewish citizens without a criminal offence. At least let me authorize the job with my department head, before I do anything else, just to be sure. Please, Heusden, lower your gun."

He heard noises from his crew members and Heusden's crew, noises he recognized as shuffling feet. They were closing in, but he didn't look — he focused on Heusden.

Jacob's calm speech seemed to have relaxed Heusden a tad, who now looked around him. When he saw the other policemen with their guns aimed at him, Heusden slowly backed off several paces, his gun still aimed at Jacob's chest.

Jacob's gun was still aimed at the German's ribcage, but he raised his weapon and aimed it at the captain's head. He was calm, and he almost dared the man to kill him. If he killed Heusden now, that would be that — the end of all misery, for himself as well.

Heusden's men had positioned themselves beside their boss with their machine guns raised, aiming at the police officers. Jacob's own men had taken several steps forward and stood next to Jacob, guns in hand but with firepower clearly inferior to the Germans.

"I bloody well can give you an order," Heusden spat.

Jacob felt a drop of his spittle on his face as Heusden growled, "I'll have you arrested for refusing to follow an order." The smell of the foreigner's sweat reached his nose.

Everybody clearly noticed that the army commandant humiliated himself with his threats: if the guns didn't impress Jacob, the words surely wouldn't either. He was aware of it, and it boosted his resolve.

The stand-off suddenly ended when Heusden lowered his gun with a groan.

Jacob lowered his weapon and barely controlled the urge to hit the soldier's face hard with his pistol before he put it back in its holster. He tasted bile in his mouth and stepped back a few more steps.

Heusden growled, his voice low and angry: "I will not forget this."

The four police officers had followed Jacob's example, but the Wehrmacht soldiers didn't lower their Mausers.

Calm and self-assured, Jacob replied. "You drew your gun first. I was defending myself. So, that's it then. My apologies, Commander, but you're on your own with this lousy job." He turned away, soaked through with sweat.

"Let's go." His crew followed him. Jacob was ready for another nasty reply, or a shot in the back, the hairs in his neck raised, but instead of the crack of a gun, he heard Heusden yell:

"By God! Ja, I didn't sign up for this either. I'm just a soldier. *Verdammt noch mal* [Bloody hell]."

Nobody had observed the Jewish captive slipping away into the shadows ten minutes earlier.

Chapter 30

Arrived back at the compound, Jacob quickly dropped in at home. Frantic, he urged Margaret to go next door to let Ruth know of her husband's imminent arrest. He requested the operator to be put through Den Toom's office in Hardenberg.

It was a difficult conversation. Jacob argued in vain about the governor's promise, just like few minutes earlier with Heusden. Den Toom's reply was predictable: "Van Noorden, verdomme! You need to collaborate. Seyss-Inquart changed his mind on the Jews. Go out there and do as the Wehrmacht tells you. If this comes back to us, you'll be the one wearing it."

Exasperated, Jacob yelled into the phone: "The Ortzkommandant pulled a gun on me and threatened me with arrest. Why should I collaborate?"

Den Toom simply hung up.

Jacob threw the phone on his desk and kicked his chair, which toppled over with a loud crash. Damn him to hell and back. A loud *Godsamme* escaped his mouth. He stomped to the squad room and told his men the bad news. "It didn't work. Be ready to go in three minutes."

***

Once again, the four marechaussees and their chief went on their way to join Heusden's crew. After a quick search for them in a couple of nearby streets, Jacob saw an out. "We're going back to base. They're gone, probably finished the job already," he theorized, completely happy to sidestep his boss' order for the arrests he thought weren't justified. They marched back through the street, direction brigade.

As the crew neared their building, the event that metamorphosed in front of them was exactly what Jacob had feared and tried to escape. Next-door, a group of soldiers and their captives stood waiting on the road in front of the butcher's home. Margaret came running on the road. When she arrived at the house and stood in front of Ruth's door, she told the four German soldiers in perfect German what she thought of them.

"These people are no criminals. Go away, leave them alone. You should be ashamed of yourselves. Is arresting innocent civilians what you go to war for?"

Ruth turned to the soldiers in front of her, ignoring Margaret.

"My husband will be with you shortly." Then she turned to Margaret. "Thank you for trying, Margaret, but you can't save us."

The young Wehrmacht soldiers were no SS officers, so the two at the door quietly waited, with Margaret standing beside them. Soon after, Bram arrived at the doorway in his long, gray overcoat with the golden star on his lapel and a small suitcase in his hand. There was no wailing, no crying, and no long goodbye. Ruth gave Bram a package with hastily gathered food and retreated in the house, softly closing the front door. The soldiers stepped up, took hold of Bram by his upper arms, pushed past Margaret on the walkway, and handed the captive off to the two soldiers standing by the gate with Heusden.

Jacob and his men had arrived and stood watching a short distance, away, unsure what to do. The crew waited for Jacob's command, but he stayed silent.

As she came down the walkway, Margaret shouted: "Do something, I beg you, for God's sake, this is not right. Jacob, you know this is wrong. Bram hasn't done anything wrong."

She stood still in front of Jacob and demanded in an urgent voice: "Ruth needs her husband. She's my best friend. Please, let them stop this." She took a step to one of the soldiers holding Bram and frantically pulled at his arm.

Jacob swallowed hard. He spoke to her quietly. "I'm so sorry, but we can't help Bram. Go home to the kids, please. You're causing problems for me, Margaret." He put his hand on Margaret's arm and looked at her, pleading, but she pulled away from him and glared at him with an expression that made it clear she had no love for him. She didn't say anything else, turned around, and headed for home.

Chapter 31

Jacob wished he was dead. All his anger had left him. Without defense and without back-up from his superiors, he was highly vulnerable. He wasn't sure what would happen to him but didn't want to think about it anymore. He faced Heusden and lied, "*Verzeihen Sie mich* [My apologies], Overfeldwebel, my chief stood me down. I cannot help you."

The Orzkommandant, the local representative of das Reich, sneered at him. "Too much of a coward, is he? And you follow his orders — also a coward."

As Jacob quietly spoke to Heusden with his crew members standing to the side, some Overdam citizens rushing home in the streets looked at them with interest. One man got off his bicycle and yelled *moffenvrienden* [Kraut lovers], but the German soldiers ignored him. They had bigger fish to fry.

Jacob heard it, loud and clear: it hit him in the gut. His trouble with breathing increased. He got his hankie out and wiped his face and head, replacing his cap quickly as he stared at Heusden, who was accusing him of cowardice. With desperation in his voice, hoping Van Houten wouldn't say anything, he commanded his own men in his loudest voice, relieved he had found the courage to go against Den Toom's orders at the very last moment.

"Back to the brigade."

***

At the brigade with his men gathered in the squad room, a lump was stuck in Jacob's throat and wouldn't go away despite his swallowing. He bit on his lower lip to get a different sensation, then broke the silence.

"I apologize for making you go through this disaster, I am sorry if you feel misled. Den Toom's order was indeed to assist the Wehrmacht, but that was not the right thing to do. He was wrong. I didn't decide till just a couple of minutes ago. It's on me if Den Toom retaliates for my insubordination."

Nobody commented. Jacob had lowered his vibrating body in an office chair across from his sergeant's empty chair. The crew sat scattered throughout the room. Van Houten stood by the window, staring into the street, his back to the team.

After five minutes of deep silence, Corporal Peters lifted his head, never shy to offer himself up for punishment. With the man's admiration for the Germans audible in his voice, he asked: "Opper, how did the Wehrmacht know exactly who was Jewish and where they lived? All any Jew needed to do was just not register their status. Did they all register, then?"

Jacob saw his question as evidence that Peters wasn't the brightest of the bunch, but he knew that already. Beside himself with anger, mixed with fear for the potential consequences of his actions, he perfunctorily offered Peters from tight jaws in clipped words what he knew.

"Skipping registration wouldn't help them, but yes, the Overdam Jews registered with the local Wehrmacht. Thirty-one members. A number of students remain at Eerde's international school on the estate of the baron. They haven't sunk to arresting children yet, but the Nazis are on a mission to eradicate all Dutch Jews."

"Is that so?" Disbelief in his voice, Peters sounded unperturbed, nevertheless.

Jacob couldn't hold back his frustration any longer, and he raised his voice.

"But not only that, our own Central Statistics records every birth and knows the location of each citizen, including all their moves. They obviously handed over the files to the SD without a second thought. It's a piece of cake for the Nazis to hunt anyone down as they see fit." He got up and violently stomped on the ground with each step as he paced the room.

"Jeez, I never thought of that." Peters looked at Jacob with curiosity.

"It must've been divine intervention, when a bomb exploded at the Central Statistics' office in The Hague, the other day. The building was completely wiped out, together with all of its documentation. According to Rauter, it was a terrorist attack by partisans."

"Oh, and was it?" Peters wondered.

When Jacob replied to Peters in a low tone of contempt for so much stupidity, bitterness spilled over in his voice and was visible in the scowl on his face.

"Goddamn, Peters. Don't like them so much for their tricks. Anybody can scour membership and registration lists. Before you know it, you'll become their target too. And the SD will look for people to betray their fellow countrymen. God save the rest of us."

Jacob didn't look at anybody in particular but assumed the others would know he was warning them that anyone among them could be a potential traitor. He knew his monologue made nobody feel any better, including him, and he sighed. He needed to take a leak.

"I'm sorry I couldn't manage to stop Heusden. It's his word against mine. The way it happened and how I am going to report it to Den Toom is that we couldn't find Heusden and missed it all. I hope you all will back me up. I apologize from the bottom of my heart to put you all in this position. I'd best just shut up now." He practically ran to the privy.

Chapter 32

When Jacob got home, the boys were already in bed. As she sat still at the dinner table, he read in Margaret's sorrowful face that she judged him a failure, a loser. He needed a bath as his shirt reeked sour. He went to his wife and tried to put an arm around her, but she wouldn't look at him and got up from the table. As he said what he had to say, she stood still next to him and looked at the floor.

"Dear wife, I'm so, so sorry. I can't tell you how sorry. I want you to know I left Heusden standing, contrary to what that bastard Den Toom ordered me to do: collaborate with Heusden. I am asking you to keep what you saw to yourself, please. I'm going to report something different, that I searched for the group and missed them going back, and that we never witnessed the arrests. That policy of not touching our Jews? All changed. We're going the way of Poland, this is just the start of it. I'm heartbroken we couldn't stop Bram's arrest, and of the others. I'll be praying for his safety every day. Please talk to me. I feel terrible about it."

After a pause that seemed to last ten minutes, Margaret finally spoke in a low, quiet voice. "The boys are in bed. Your meal is on the stove."

He took a step towards her and took her elbow, forcing her to look at him as he pleaded, "I don't care about that, please say something."

She pulled her elbow free, looked him in the eyes and spat out the words that hit him in his heart. "I hate you and your job,"

"Sweetheart, you don't mean that," he pleaded.

"Yes, I do. Jacob, Ruth's my only friend and she doesn't have any other friends either. She'll hate me for being your wife. And what about Bram, and those other poor men, carted off just like that? What about their families? What are they going to live on with their husbands in a camp? What's Ruth going to live on? Poor Ruth. It's so awful. How could you let this happen?"

"I agree, it's truly awful, but I was powerless. Let's hope it is only a temporary incarceration."

She left him to heat up his food in the kitchen, while he sat at the table in the adjacent room. He told her through the open kitchen door some of what he'd told his men.

"It's terrible what the Nazis are doing, but there's nothing we can do about it now. I had to ask my men to lie to Den Toom if he ever asks them about the raid. If it comes out, I surely will lose my job." He was defeated. His efforts had been in vain. He kept brushing his head with his right hand, looking at Margaret through the open kitchen door.

She was stirring vigorously in a pot on the stove and shouted into to the boiling mass on the stove. "But you could've stopped them, Jacob. You had four men there, they had four men, plus Heusden. You said he was friendly. Why didn't you have the guts to do anything, protect those men, chase off the soldiers, shoot them, anything?"

He scoffed. "Don't be ridiculous, Margaret. You know I couldn't have done that. The Wehrmacht would've shot us, if not today, then tomorrow. We've got only seven men against an army." He went on in a conciliatory tone. "Come on, let's not argue. I feel bad about it. Let me give you a kiss."

He got up, went into the kitchen, and took his plate from her hands, but she shirked from his attempt to kiss her. She walked away from him, went through the dining room to the living room. He followed her, put the plate on the dining table, and into the living room, where he sat down beside her on the divan. He took her cold hand in his, but she pulled her hand back and left the living room. "Greta, love, please, stay," he used her nickname, but she went upstairs without speaking.

There was nothing he could say. He was cold and shivered. His body had changed from hot to ice-cold; his feet felt like lumps of ice. His breathing had returned to normal. He knew he should've been smart enough for finding a solution, a way to protect the citizens — his main job. He went to the dining table, ate his lukewarm dinner, and returned to the living room. Margaret was right. Sitting back in his easy chair, he closed his eyes and gave in to his sense of failure.

Chapter 33

Groups of uniformed Dutch Nazis — WA for short — regularly marched through cities in central and western Holland, asserting their newfound status in obnoxious ways, annoying everybody else. The WA louts intimidated café patrons and harassed shoppers and random pedestrians in the streets with impunity — an accepted social phenomenon that the local authorities failed to address. Soon, it all escalated into physical assaults, and got truly out of hand completely when the Dutch Nazis penetrated the old Jewish neighborhoods and destroyed property and shop windows with bats and other street weapons. They put roughly fabricated signs up that read *Geen Joden Toegestaan* [No Jews Allowed].

Riots broke out in all major cities as non-Jews joined their Jewish friends and formed their own fight groups. Rapidly, Amsterdam, with the largest Jewish population in the country, became Street Fight Central. Typical civilian life downtown was utterly disrupted.

The Overdam crew had the radio on all day but got their essential information through the grapevine — much more reliable than the ANP news, which consistently supported the WA louts and faulted the Jews and their comrades for the riots. Until the day a seriously injured WA member died in the hospital, the Germans didn't act.

"The city marechaussee weren't allowed to arrest anybody," Dijk said, who had an uncle in that city.

Jacob underscored what Dijk had said.

"Exactly, it's how it should be: nobody, or everybody gets arrested. If it's about anti-German behavior, we will leave it strictly for the German police to deal with. You and I know the Germans and the ANP news lie, so we don't know what really happened, although we know enough about the WA louts to make an educated guess."

He went into his office to escape the loud radio. A few minutes later, Van Houten stormed into his office, throwing the door open with force, so it slammed against the wall.

"Listen to this: the whole Waterloo Square neighborhood is closed off. Wehrmacht soldiers with machine guns are standing at the barriers threatening to shoot at anybody who wants to go in, or get out. They say it's for their own good, to protect the residents. The Krauts have gone too far this time." He stood in front of Jacob's desk, steaming mad.

Jacob sat back in his desk chair and pointed at the chair across from him and observed the Sergeant as he sat down. "Sounds like the Weimar Republic in the days before Hitler's takeover, and the cancer has spread," he said. "I'm afraid this is the beginning of the true German takeover of our society. Better be alert for more actions outside of Amsterdam. What do you suggest we'd do, Sergeant?"

The younger man sat upright, his body alert, ready for action.

"I'm not going to arrest any demonstrators, no way! They have the right to say what they want about the government and defend themselves. If we can't say what we think anymore, I'd rather go into hiding. Or go on a strike. I heard there's talk about striking. Van Houten had calmed down somewhat and leaned back in his chair. "What about you, boss?" The Sergeant said, awaiting Jacob's answer, curiosity in his eyes.

"Me? I'm not sure. I wouldn't know where to go, and then, I have a family to look after, two children and one on the way. Not that I haven't thought about it a lot, but I haven't found a solution so far. The arrest of our neighbors really affected Margaret, and me too, to be honest. We feel so helpless. Margaret wouldn't speak to me for a week, but we're good now. She eventually understood I already put my job on the line with refusing our assistance to Heusden, and armed resistance is no option at this time. But she lost her only friend, Ruth. It's a hard time for everybody." Jacob nodded at his Sergeant.

"Good point. I just have my wife. I'm surprised Rauter has let the WA escalate. He hates the obvious lack of discipline from those NSB bastards, and besides, he must know street riots can lead to something else, like a revolt. How will he know it'll go his way, and not the other way? Imagine that: I'd join the rebellion in a heart-beat. We should've taken a stronger stand against the Krauts earlier, Chief, when Heusden tried to make us do their dirty work." His fiery eyes said the rest.

Jacob heard in his deputy's comment an accusation of lack of courage. His own sense of guilt surfaced. "I agree with you, but, how could we? After the first demonstrations on Carnation day, I expected for the Jews to be blamed. With the SD arresting only the Jewish participants and their supporters, we know the pogroms have started. Letting the fascists off the hook will make it escalate, exactly Seyss-Inquart's plan. He's looking for a reason to send in the troops. I heard that Wehrmacht soldiers in uniform fought in the streets on the side of the WA gangs. That tells you the whole story. God help us."

Chapter 34

The day after his conversation with Van Houten, Jacob was cleaning his pistol on an old newspaper. Margaret was resting on the divan, feet stretched out to reduce the swelling in her feet. Jacob told her about his day. He was already upset but tried to be calm.

"Terrible things are happening in the cities. I'm waiting for the eight o'clock news to hear what ANP got to say about it. By the way, what about your uncles in Germany, are they still on active duty? I don't want to run into a Wehrmacht soldier and find out I shot your uncle, although the chance would be small, but still. It looks like the Wehrmacht is out to subdue us."

"I'm not sure, Jacob. I would have to ask Mutter. After we came to Holland, I seem to remember Father didn't want her to stay in touch with them, with the war still going on and all. They were both rather old anyway back then. They might be retired."

So, they were a bit older than Johanna, who was sixty. He hoped these relatives might stay out of the picture. He didn't need any more relatives on the wrong side.

At eight o'clock, they listened to the radio news announcing the wildcat strikes. Jacob expected biased reporting, but what they heard took the cake:

"In a foolish and redundant protest of the justified SD actions against the criminal Jews to restore law and order, some limited numbers of workers of a number of industries in Amsterdam had walked out. The companies that were damaged by their behavior were the shipbuilding industry and the Fokker airplane companies, while public transit had been affected, ferries had delayed sailings, and the busses and trams weren't running as per schedule."

Turning the volume dial down, Jacob repeated what he had heard from a colleague that had raised his anxiety to alarm throughout the day.

"They are lying and distorted the truth. Those were many companies, and the industry was utterly out of commission." He told her about the many stranded workers couldn't get to work and went on strike as well. Nothing was working properly, and many other travelers joined the strikers, who were marching in the streets, and singing. To force the end to their illegal actions, German soldiers from the SD and the SS shot at groups of strikers.

Margaret covered her mouth with her right hand. "Oh, how terrible," she cried out.

It was time to be direct, and he told her what he had heard from somebody in the know.

"They killed nine and arrested a few hundred strikers. The *Reichsführer* let those WA bastards start riots to give the SD the excuse to restore the order, as they called it, just like in other countries. Rauter and Seyss-Inquart then blame the Jews for everything. My colleague in The Hague told me the SD had already arrested 425 young Jewish men this week. They beat them severely, and then put them on a train to Mauthausen, a concentration camp in Austria."

Not understanding, eyes wide, sitting upright on the divan, the tips of her fingers at her chin, she looked at him. "What's a concentration camp?"

With a grim face and a quiet voice, he said, "We know it's a place to collect people that they want to get rid of, but they won't say that, and they call it a holding camp."

"Oh, how *vreselijk* [awful]. What are they going to do with them then, those people in the camps?" She had gotten off the couch and sat down at the table, still in her lab coat, looking confused, her hair disheveled, her hands resting in her lap. She preferred a lab coat as it covered her well and it made her look somewhat like a doctor, but she would never admit that.

Jacob could've shut up to protect her, but strangely enough, he didn't want to spare her any longer from the mayhem going on around them. She was his mate, and he needed somebody on his side who knew what was going on if only, so he didn't have to pretend anymore that all is well when coming home.

"They probably will disappear, killed, used as slave labor, what have you. That's what they do with the Jews." He shook his head slowly.

Margaret exclaimed, "Terrible. The poor wretches." She sighed and had tears in her eyes.

Jacob had noticed that she teared up really quickly lately, and he felt slightly guilty.

"Yeah, brave men from the Communist Party. After De Geer had made them illegal, they had nothing to lose anymore and everything to gain from organizing the resistance against the Nazis. The success of the strike shows us the workers were just waiting for a leader. Too bad those leaders were arrested."

"But you said the Germans weren't going to arrest the Jews in our country. When they arrested Bram and the others, do they take just the men then?" Margaret's voice was higher than usual, her face wrinkled up and she massaged a small handkerchief in her hand.

"I know. The governor lied. Those strikers aren't necessarily Jews or communists, but their whole goal was to justify their actions. It is irrational and also illegal under our laws to kill strikers." He explained that the Nazis needed scapegoats to get the people on their side, and they found the proper stick to beat the dog with, as they say. He had concluded that most people were already not fond of Jews. With the people sidetracked, the governor can do whatever Hitler wants, spend tons of money on arms and wars, and conquer the world.

"I heard the SS leadership have already taken all the artworks and other treasures owned by German Jewish collectors, worth millions, if not billions. With the owners in ghettos and camps there was no pushback."

"But why? Tell me, you think Mutter is an anti-Semitist?"

"I'm not sure what your mother thinks. Does she hate Jews? Or does she just admire Hitler, like one of the celebrities in those stupid rags she reads. I don't know what the Nazis have against the religion. It's just how they get the Germans behind them. Hitler made the Germans believe the owners of the big companies are all Jews, who are getting filthy rich, while everybody else is poor. But that's all bunk."

"What do you believe, Jacob? I would like to know." She felt for her hairnet and found it in place. She leaned back against the backrest with an exhausted face.

"The way I understand it goes like this. The Nazis think that all Jews are communists and allies of the Russians. The communist and the Jews don't buy the Nazis' divide-and-conquer crap." He had educated himself long ago, and he knew quite a bit. He explained that in Judaism, study and research are an integral part of the religion, so the Jews often know more than the average Joe in the street and don't fall in line with the Nazis, like the rest of the Germans. He checked if Margaret was still listening.

She had her eyes closed, and when he stopped talking, she opened them. "I'm still listening, dear man, just resting my eyes," she said quietly and smiled at him, then closed her eyes again.

"Alright, you must be tired. I want to say for the Jewish beliefs — I think they are right to make study so important. That's why I read myself silly when my father wasn't willing to pay for advanced schooling, not even for one of his children. Out of fairness, he said, because he couldn't pay for all of them. Without education, anyone could be easily fooled."

Margaret didn't reply.

He turned up the volume on the radio. He continued to listen to the SS boss Rauter, his voice overlaid by an interpreter, instructing the Jewish congregation in Amsterdam to form a country-wide Jewish Council to help restore order, as he put it on the radio.

"That Jewish Council is going to be held responsible. He's looking for an excuse to deport all Jews, even if he has to manufacture lies to make it happen," Jacob said, not altogether accepting that hypothesis himself.

Margaret, who usually had no interest in the day's political problems, but this involved people she knew. Her eyes flew open. "Would you arrest strikers, if you were ordered to?" she asked him. "Would you go on strike?"

She had a knack for going to the heart of the matter. He clenched his jaw for a moment before he slowly answered. "As a public servant in essential services I'm not supposed to go on strike, and if it comes to that, we'd have to follow whatever Den Toom authorized."

"Just like guarding the Jewish breadwinners," she said in a calm voice.

He looked at her as he replied, "That depends on the situation. I'm still glad I didn't follow through with that order, and nobody has ratted us out, yet."

Margaret stayed quiet but looked at him with a weird, inquisitive look as if she was trying to decide something.

That night, both stayed awake for a long time, each adding up all that had happened in the last couple of years. Margaret hoped Jacob wouldn't strike and leave her in the lurch after his arrest. Jacob attempted to derive meaning from the actions of the Nazis on the strike and predict what disaster would come next. Nothing was certain. It was daybreak, and the birds performed their daily concert when both fell into a fitful few hours of sleep in each other's arms.

Chapter 35

The February strike's fallout had a far-reaching effect: the governor prohibited all radio societies and political broadcasts. Only the censored ANP news and the Nazi programs were allowed.

Margaret had convinced her mother that the real news was much different from the Nazi news. Johanna had applied and got her exemptions for just about every Nazi restriction from the Wehrmacht, her status as former German and pro-Nazi well established. At the farm, Johanna and Margaret had listened to Radio Orange at each chance they got.

But even though the women could safely ignore the radio prohibition, they kept their sessions a secret from everyone, especially Jacob. They would be hard-pressed to give a good reason for their secrecy, other than perhaps not wanting to draw attention to themselves.

Margaret made the regular air-raid warnings of the rooftop sirens into a hide-and-seek game with the children, although the reason for the siren wasn't apparent to the boys. Cause and effect, a hard thing to grasp. One evening, when the boys were still up, they heard a plane fly over low, followed by an explosion nearby. The unexpected single plane had surprised the Air Defense watch.

"Why's that plane just flying around dropping bombs, when the alarm hasn't even gone off?" Hendrik asked.

Margaret answered him with a lighthearted comment. "The pilot must be a happy Harry with a few too many beers in him, honey. He forgot the rules."

***

When Margaret and Johanna were alone, they discussed in German the plight of the Jewish people. They talked freely while Juergen entertained the boys in the yard. Johanna disagreed with the deportations — the only flaw she had detected in the Nazi doctrines. After the last Radio Orange broadcast, Johanna shared some family history with Margaret she had never talked about before.

"My ancestors on father's side were rumored to be Jewish from Belarusian-Lithuania and were Menshevik socialists under Russian occupation. They fled west to Germany in a time of political unrest long before I was born, maybe my great grandfather, I'm not sure. To sound less Slavic, I think it was my grandfather who changed his name to Munzke. My dad hinted at it but was never serious about it."

Margaret looked with curiosity at her mother, as if she saw her for the first time. "Mutter, how interesting. Is that why you like the national-socialists?"

Johanna smiled. "Not really, dear. You know I'm not interested in politics and I don't exactly know what National-Socialists stand for."

Margaret wasn't convinced and pushed her mother, "But why did you keep this a secret?"

"Vater had told us not to talk about it. I wasn't sure I should tell. That's not a reputation you want to advertise on arrival in a new country. I just like Hitler, because he has a lot of charisma, and he is making history. I like a strong man. I think he does a lot of good for the country."

The answer irked Margaret, and she said forcefully, "Which country, Mutter? Not our country. Hitler puts my family in danger with all those crazy rules that the Nazis want Jacob to carry out. The days of your lovely Holy German Reich are over, and even Kaiser Wilhelm is dead now. There's no going back to that time. You might as well accept it, Mutter, that Hitler and his Nazis have wrecked Germany, and now ours."

Even so, Johanna wouldn't budge on Hitler, but Margaret continued to challenge her. "You're stubborn. Prove to me you don't really believe Hitler is good for us."

Johanna turned around to pour boiling water into the teapot. "How can I? You're silly. You're listening too much to your husband."

"*Nein, Mutter*," Margaret bristled, "on the contrary. I've got a real problem for you to solve. You've heard the real news on Radio Orange. You can believe that news, but not the ANP. You now know that the Nazis are hell-bent on destroying the Jews."

She told Johanna about Bram's arrest, her Jewish neighbor, who was deported to a camp, the husband of her only friend, Ruth, and they had two children. "I fear Ruth and her kids are going to be deported too at some point. Would you hide them on the farm? Somebody must have hidden your Minsky family members at some point when they escaped their country."

Margaret had a determined look on her face.

Johanna turned to her and brought the teapot to the table. She seemed to ignore the look on her daughter's face and said, "Don't use that against me. You're crazy. I couldn't do that. Where? And how would I keep this a secret from Juergen and Liz?" Johanna shook her head at such insanity.

But Margaret wouldn't let up. She took a sip of her hot tea and resumed her battle.

"You could put the horse in back of the house, next to the cow. Ruth and her kids could hide, way in the back of the yard, in the horse shed. We could convert the stable for the horse into a living and sleeping space. There's lots of hay and straw, and we could make some adjustments for isolation. It isn't a castle, but good enough for a temporary measure, and better than a concentration camp."

"What about Juergen and Liz?"

Johanna's home shared a wall with her housemates on the other side of the duplex, with a shared corridor between them and a door at the end leading to the utility area behind the living quarters. The cow stable, the pigsty, and the privy occupied the back of the house. The occupants also shared the large backyard.

"It's up to you. They do whatever you tell them to do anyway. You'll have to tell them some story. They'll have to help you by bringing them food, and someone will have to stand on guard, when Ruth and the kids are outside for some air, but you should only let them out at night after dark."

At the end of their discussion, Margaret had convinced Johanna; the plan was solid. She would have Ruth visit Johanna just once, so she could meet her, and they'd become friends. When Margaret left for home, she again felt again as close to her mother as before the invasion.

Chapter 36

Margaret was now visibly pregnant. She turned more into herself, was lost in thought more often. To make sure the unborn child would grow strong and healthy, Johanna and Juergen made sure she lacked nothing, especially milk.

Jacob told her, "I appreciate your relatives' loyalty to you."

She looked at him and brightly said, "Are you going to join me again to visits at Johanna's, then?"

"Do you think it wise for me to visit a pro-Nazi? You tell me. I need to keep the reputation of the police intact as a neutral service." He looked at her and rubbed hands, kneading them as if he had poor circulation.

She seemed unperturbed, her sad mood about his failure to save Bram lifted. "Well, why not? They're family. You're allowed to have family. You should at least be honest and tell them yourself what you feel about them. Next time I go for a visit with the kids you should come." She gave him a sad smile and added, "I think your reputation is tarnished anyway."

He could no longer judge her relatives harshly for their sympathies for the devil — as he saw Hitler. Their good deeds for his family counteracted their words of support for the occupying regime. And so, he went along.

As soon as they arrived, Johanna opened the front door. Jacob shook her hand, kissed her cheek, and decided to get it over with. "Thank you so much for keeping us in food. I appreciate it more than I could ever express."

"Nice of you to say. You're welcome," Johanna answered brightly.

He might have imagined it, but Jacob thought he saw the corners of her mouth turn up and her lips purse tightly as if she was going to laugh. From the corridor, he spotted Juergen in the back. He went over to him and repeated the same thank you.

Juergen said nothing, just looked at him, skepticism evident on his face.

Although it wasn't easy for Jacob, and he found himself unusually subdued, the visit went well. After dinner, Jacob and Margaret went home on their bicycles, the boys strapped in securely on the carriers behind their parents' backs. The day spent in peace had put some balm on the bruises from the insults and divisions between them.

Chapter 37

The citizens who were still using their brains wondered why Hirschfeldt, the Deputy Minister of Economy, hadn't been fired together with all the other Jewish public servants. This gifted and exceptionally collaborative man, who kept the economy afloat, had become the star of the Dutch economy and Nazi governor Seyss-Inquart's favorite Dutchman. Hirschfeldt approved the general collection of civilian copper, zinc, and metal-ware for the Wehrmacht.

Before leaving for his office in the morning, there was no question in his mind when Jacob said to his wife, "Margaret, we will not contribute, even if we had anything to give."

"Of course not," she replied. "We don't have anything extra. But Mutter gave them the lovely antique copper kettle and the red copper woodbin. Juergen dropped them off. I can't believe she did that. What a waste, turning those beautiful things into bullets."

Jacob shook his head in astonishment. "What's wrong with her? If she wanted to contribute, she could've given away the zinc stuff. The rules are ridiculous and require no effort to deliberately misinterpret. Did you tell her about Ruth's husband? By now she must understand how terrible the Nazis are."

"I told her. She was shocked. She disagrees with what's happening to the Jews. I know, some people just won't acknowledge the truth. Give her time, please, she's my mother, she keeps us supplied with food."

He shook his head again and frowned. "I can't condone her behavior. What else is she given them?"

Margaret shrugged. "I don't know."

Jacob kissed her and noticed she had a glow on her face, making her look radiant. "Well," he said, "You know I'm trying but I wouldn't mind visiting them as little as possible."

In the end, only the members of the Dutch Nazi parties handed in their metal-ware, a mere five percent, a minute percentage of the population. Most households claimed they had no surplus to give.

Chapter 38

Jacob's first test of wills with Heusden had left him with a visceral memory, like a deep scratch in the surface of a vinyl record, impossible to wipe off with a soft cloth. Whenever he agreed to meet with Fritz Heusden over a beer at the hotel bar — they were collegial enough — he used the memory to shield him from liking the man as if his life depended on this protection. Nevertheless, they arrived at the point of first name basis when alone. To create some sort of détente and to keep a channel open, Jacob had seen to it that his crew started to have some social contact with the soldiers. It was an armistice of sorts, each side carefully observing the other.

One fine spring morning before the household metal collection deadline, Jacob got another call from Fritz Heusden. This time it wasn't social, and Heusden addressed him formally.

"Chief Von Norden, I'm informing you that tomorrow SD agents will arrest the students and teachers of the Jewish school. You'll be called on behalf of the local police to see that everything goes as intended. I'll call you when I know the exact time of the arrival of the SD."

Jacob's mind went into a tailspin; he went silent. Five seconds later, he smiled. Heusden was calling him because he regretted the previous raid, and was giving him an out. "Thanks for letting me know, Fritz, I appreciate it. See you tomorrow."

The following day around 10 a.m., the call from Heusden came. Five minutes later, four SD agents had arrived from Zwolle in two sedans and were waiting in front of the brigade building. Jacob and three of his men met with the SD delegation. The security men looked smart in their grey uniforms and red diamonds with the letters SD on their sleeves. Jacob and his men got in and rode with the SD officers in their sedans to the school.

On their arrival, the school secretary took the group to the principal's office. The officer in charge barked to the elderly man he took for the principal, "Gather the students and teachers, right now."

The elderly man's face turned white, and he stammered in German, "*Die sind nicht da* [they're not here]."

The SD officers didn't believe him and marched him through the rooms, even the gym, looked in every closet, and even made a mess in the storage sheds in the back yard. They didn't find a single student, and only one other teacher who stammered in poor German, "*Ich bin no Jude* [I'm no Jew]. I am a Catholic."

"Lies," the SD officer yelled, his face pushed into the middle-aged man's face, and he stopped at a millimeter distance from nose-to-nose contact.

"I'm close to retirement. Please let me go, *bitte, bitte*. I haven't done anything wrong."

It didn't help him; he was arrested, as well as the frightened elderly man, who wasn't the actual principal.

The SD commander turned to Jacob. "What do you know about this? Can you explain this? Was it your doing that they're all absent?" The officer grabbed Jacob's arm and held on tight, breathing his foul onion breath all over him.

Jacob noticed Van Houten touching his gun, and the three men moved in closer. Jacob slowly, almost imperceptibly, shook his head as he looked at his sergeant.

"No, of course not," he responded. "The police are collaborating. You can see that: we're here, aren't we? But I've noticed many Jews have disappeared lately. After the arrests in Amsterdam they have become shy." He kept his voice light and watched for humor in his opponent. There wasn't any.

"Nonsense. I'm arresting you instead of these old men. They're of no use. If the investigation shows you people had anything to do with this, you'll regret it. That's treason. You get shot for that. I'll make sure of it." He dismissed the other three marechaussees but marched Jacob to the other SD agents' waiting sedan. From the corner of his eye, Jacob saw Van Houten cross in front of the other two marechaussees, his gun drawn. Jacob slowly shook his head again willing him to stand down with his eyes.

The SD officers pushed Jacob into the car. They got in themselves without so much of a glance in the direction of Jacob's men. The sedan drove off, leaving the three crew members behind.

***

At the Wehrmacht station, the SD boss told his men to guard the Dutch cheese-head cop and marched straight into Heusden's office. Jacob had the sensation as if a cold hand rested on his chest, although he was sweating. His legs wouldn't be still. He realized the SD officer was no idiot.

After about fifteen minutes of what he imagined were intense negotiations, Heusden appeared with the SD chief. "Let him go," the SD officer told his men, then shook Heusden's hand, saluted, and clicked his heels. The four SD officers left in their sedans.

Heusden shook his head and looked at Jacob with a tight little smile. "*Schlimmes Geschäft* [Nasty business]."

"Thank you, Oberfeldwebel Heusden. I owe you." Jacob wiped his forehead with his hanky and smiled big at the Wehrmacht leader.

"Enjoy your freedom while it lasts. Good bye." Heusden returned to his office, leaving Jacob standing in the lobby.

A heavy burden fell of his shoulders, and he just about skipped his way back to the brigade. He stepped into the squad room and announced his good luck.

"Good Lord, am I ever happy this raid had such a good outcome. It could've turned nasty. Thank God for friends in the right places."

"Goddamn Nazis. I thought we'd lost you, Chief." Van Houten grabbed his hand and pumped it for what felt like ten minutes.

"Alright, Sergeant. I got lucky. Thanks for your back-up. Glad you didn't start firing. Why on earth would those two teachers make the choice to stay after having received the warning? I guess they sacrificed themselves, for nothing. Anyway, we don't have to feel responsible for them."

Still, he was worried. He hoped the raid wouldn't have a nasty follow-up, like everything else lately.

***

That evening, Jacob took the motorbike out of the shed after supper and rode out alone. He needed time to think. Why didn't he want to talk to Margaret about today — to protect her? No, to defend himself if he was honest about it. She would have a lot to say. He stopped on the sandy path meandering along the edge of the forest and put the bike on its stand on a small rock. He hadn't paid attention selecting the rock. It was slowly sinking in the moisture-softened dirt as he stared out over the moor without seeing anything. The stand slid off the rock and the bike fell to the ground with a dull bang, its front wheel spinning freely without a power source. He yelled a curse across the expanse of beautiful, wet nature.

In spite of the balmy evening, he tightened his jacket and shivered. The heather was still wet from an earlier shower, but he didn't notice, until a whiff of mold fleetingly entered his consciousness. He took out his handkerchief and blew his nose, then tucked the cloth away. Even if he got an advance warning this time, he couldn't trust Heusden forever. Should his own neck be on the line surely Heusden wouldn't protect him. After all, the man was a soldier on the other side.

He prayed for guidance from above for the next ordeal. He mentioned Margaret and the boys in his request to God. When they entered his mind, a smile came to his face and he felt relieved. He opened his eyes. He had needed this temporary reprieve from the demands of life and from all the people wanting something from him. He returned home grateful, determined to read the boys a story before bedtime.

Chapter 39

A fortnight later, Jacob received a telephone call from regional police headquarters in Zwolle. When the operator mentioned whom she tried to connect him to, he expected some sort of complaint. Without a preamble in an irritated voice, Major Feenstra demanded to know if Jacob intended to get fired. If yes, he would be willing to oblige his wish.

Jacob was too stunned to reply, which was a good thing, as the question obviously had been rhetorical. The commissioner told him that two hundred policemen, including several chiefs, had been fired due to the wildcat strikes. He expected more heads would roll, including Jacob's, should he receive further reports of non-compliance. The man's voice rose in pitch and volume until he was screaming in Jacob's ear.

"The SD complained about interference from the police. You caused the arrests at a school to fail. You, you, son of a bitch. Damn you Van Noorden. I expected your full cooperation with the Germans. Didn't Den Toom order you so?"

"But Sir, we cooperated fully."

"It's not what I heard. I wouldn't hesitate one second to send you packing. For all I care, you can join the other two hundred. You clear? Twenty others are willing to take your job and fall in line." Without giving Jacob a chance to reply, the commissioner disconnected.

Completely blindsided by his superior's mistreatment, Jacob took off his uniform jacket and paced the office. His heart was thumping as much now as when he had been face-to-face with Heusden. How dare that police director to address him like that. He had known the man from before he had met Margaret. Back then, he seemed alright as a commander. What for the devil had happened to that man?

He missed his former boss, always professional and respectful to him. Maybe Hitler himself was getting impatient with Seyss-Inquart's slow conversion of the Dutch. After the strike, the governor had promised the end of the Dutch rebellion. For us, or against us, there's no middle ground, he said.

With two members on his own force already looking to join the SS and with the SD and Heusden stepping up their demands, he was left little room for escape. With the Nazi servants Feenstra and Den Toom on his back, he was pretty well in the Nazi's pocket himself.

The chief of nothing rolled up his sleeves and paced his office back and forth, deep in thought. He landed on Henk, Margaret's elder brother, a man on the right side in this war and uncorrupted, at least as far as he knew. Henk could be helpful. Henk had enjoyed higher education; he must get his opinion. The idea of a future ally beside him calmed him down. He pulled his shirt straight and put on his jacket but left it unbuttoned. Using both hands, he wiped his head from his brow over his fast-retreating hairline to his neck, straightened his back, and left his office to call his men together for a briefing on the latest directions. This was the easy part of the job.

In the squad room, he called out: "Listen up, you all."

He waited a couple of seconds until the men had stopped in their tracks. Van Houten said Peters was cleaning the now-empty stables. "Go get him. We'll wait for him."

When all had gathered, Jacob continued. "I just got a call from Major Feenstra and he was pissed off with us, actually, with me. The SD had complained about the Overdam brigade in regard to the situation at the Jewish grade school. As far as I'm concerned, it wasn't our fault and I'd advise you to not worry about it. Just wanted to alert you of HQ's impression of our brigade. They don't like us much. We continue as we have been. Any questions?"

Leversma spoke up. "That's no news. We all are forced into collaborating now. The Major confirmed it. So, what?"

Jacob sighed and inhaled deeply. He had hoped to create some cohesion and loyalty in his crew. "Alright, Leversma, thanks for your observation, always so helpful. Excuse me for clueing you in. I must be the only one who was hoping to keep some integrity. All dismissed."

His crew members looked surprised at his sarcasm that belied the boss' relaxed posture. He saw Peters whispering something to Van Houten, who didn't respond.

Jacob turned away to his office.

**

He picked up the phone and gave Henk's number to the operator.

"Hello, Jacob. Haven't seen you in a while. How are things?"

"*Goeiemiddag* [Good afternoon] Henk. I wondered if perhaps we could meet soon."

After some chitchat, they arranged a meeting for that same night. Jacob felt better already. He had no choice but to manage the rest of this war, hopefully with a buddy. Were things bad enough to leave his job over? Always an option too. He was looking forward to having an honest talk with Henk without the rest of the family present.

Chapter 40

After Germany invaded the USSR, Jacob's crew told jokes reflecting the national spirit. With the increased Russian manpower of the Allies the prevailing mood was predominantly buoyant and cause for levity. Jacob weighed whether he could afford to laugh with his crew. Before retreating into his office, he listened to the first joke.

"One Russian soldier kills three Krauts. The Kraut kills three Russian soldiers. What's the score?" Van Houten, sprawled out in a chair among his crewmates, waited for a second or two before providing the answer. "Six-nil for England." The men roared, including Jacob, before he disappeared into his office, still smiling.

***

A week later, an advertisement from SS boss Rauter upset the whole police force throughout the country. The police magazine published the news that Rauter was planning to send a contingent of six hundred police members to Russia by June 22. The item caused an uproar throughout the nation including in the Overdam squad room.

As soon as Jacob sat behind his desk the morning after receiving the magazine, Van Houten stepped into the office. He bent over Jacob's desk, leaning both hands on its surface looking intently at his boss. "What's the truth, Chief?"

Jacob sat back and crossed his legs. "Calm down, Sergeant. It's just wishful thinking on Rauter's part. I've heard nothing official about it, but I'll call my colleague in The Hague to find out."

***

Hansen, Jacob's connection at HQ, gave him the low-down.

"The whole affair had started when Nazi boss Rauter bypassed the Council of Deputy Ministers. He did away with all formalities and had gone straight to Boellaard, the new inspector of police of the Justice Department. He ordered Boellaard to implement his latest pet project: utilizing the cops in occupied territories in Russia, and place that announcement in the magazine. When Boellaard told the council, deputy

Tenkink of Justice refused to approve Rauter's plans. Tenkink told the council in the following meeting that Rauter's proposal was unlawful. He found out then that he stood alone and resigned on the spot. The council then quickly appointed a temporary replacement as Deputy of Justice, a guy called Hooijkaas. This good man stood firm with Tenkink on his position that joining a foreign army contradicts the oath to the Queen."

"Yeah, sure, that's the law."

"Hold on, there's more. Hooijkaas had to explain the consequences before the ignorant sods changed their minds. They have no idea what goes on at the front — always a fluid situation."

Hansen went through the ins and out of warfare. On one day, Dutch police could be put in charge of Russian civilians after the Germans occupied that area. That situation could quickly reverse the following day when Russian troops re-take the lost territory. Dutch police would have to defend themselves together with the German soldiers against the Russian forces.

"We'd be in combat against our Allies."

"I, I… I really had no idea things were this complex," Jacob stammered, but Hansen wasn't finished talking.

"Leave it to the nimble DMs to come up with a solution. The council indeed approved a legion of cops for the eastern front, but strictly on a voluntary basis. What do you say about that, hey? Gutsy Tenkink, you got to give it to him. Too bad he's gone now too. We had a leader in Justice with a spine, once."

Jacob scratched his head and exhaled. "Whoa, its despicable what's going on with our wretched politicians. I don't think the Russian voluntary legion will attract many volunteers. Who wants to get killed for the Nazis? Thanks anyway for the info."

At coffee break, Jacob stepped into the squad room to share his findings. The reaction was universal.

"What a crazy thing," Leversma said.

Even Peters didn't like it. "I surely wouldn't want to work in Russia. Who would?"

"You must be suicidal to want that job," De Wit concluded.

Chapter 41

Two days later, Hans Hansen called Jacob with news about several high-ranking police officials who simply refused to stay on their posts and quit. Hansen brought him up to speed about who was fired and replaced with Nazi-friendly officials, such as his new boss, Sybren Tulp, Chef de Corps of Amsterdam.

"That bastard Seyss-Inquart didn't get his way with the nation yet. He's trying another strategy: more soldiers. Didn't you hear it on the news?"

"Yes, I'm aware about the new troops," Jacob sighed. The ANP had announced the arrival of the third division of Wehrmacht troops in the country to assist the more than six million citizens to understand and accept the Reich's goals. "Should I assume the new assignment in our leadership are no fluke, then?"

"God, no," Hansen scoffed. "The son of a bitch is nothing but a corrupt collaborator to give Seyss-Inquart authority over us. The willingness of the leadership to step up to the Nazi's dance tune is assured. What favor had gotten Tulp got his new job, you ask? It was his brilliant proposal to establish a special riot detachment."

"What for?" Jacob asked, "To beat down the next strike?" His stomach rebelled. While listening to his colleague, he crumbled a random document on his desk into a ball.

"Exactly. Sybren Tulp had his whole new battalion of a hundred men outfitted with special riot equipment. We'll have the first riot squad in history now. I'm not proud of it," Hansen said with a subdued voice.

With one hand, he tried to wipe the wrinkled sheet flat as he replied, "You'd think Tulp is an undercover German. Maybe it's just his blind ambition, wanting to get ahead. In my squad, I've got some of those, without a conscience and no loyalty to anybody but themselves. I can't fathom why our leaders would go that far in pleasing the Krauts. Would they really think it morally justified?"

Hansen continued his newsy tale in a higher octave. "But wait, there's more. You know what Tulp did this week? You won't believe it. His riot detachment closed down all the shops owned by Jewish merchants, took possession of the goods, and stored the shops' inventories in warehouses."

Jacob shot up from his chair but couldn't pace the room to calm down with the limiting phone cord. "That's outrageous. How could the Deputy of Justice allow it?"

"Easy," Hansen snorted. "He's only implementing the new anti-Jewish measures. Haven't you heard about those yet, up there in the boonies?" Sarcasm dripping from his voice.

Jacob didn't appreciate the ribbing and stayed silent. He was too angry and would've cursed a blue streak had he opened his mouth.

Hansen continued in an upbeat tone. "I'm just joking with you, got to laugh, Van Noorden, or you'd cry. Rauter's plan for Tulp's special squad is to send it at the end of the year to the new Nazi police academy for retraining in your province, modeling the squad on the SS force." His tone changed when he continued. "Three long-time serving officers already refused to go and were promptly fired."

Jacob gasped. "I can't believe it."

Hansen exhaled sharply. In a flat voice he continued his diatribe: "Yeah. Better get used to it. There's nobody with a spine left in the force. We might have to develop one ourselves — a spine, I mean. What's new in your neck of the woods?"

"Not much, only a new prison camp in our area..." his voice trailed off without finishing the sentence.

Hansen whistled. "Hope for you no guard duties for your crew are on the horizon."

Jacob answered too quickly to completely cover his own suspicions. "No, it'll probably be in the hands of the Germans." He kicked the metal garbage can under his desk. With a dull plonk, it rolled across the floor.

"Good luck with it then. I'm not sure how long I'll be in my post, just to let you know. I might throw in the towel. Talk later." The man sounded tired.

Jacob knew just how he felt. "I will be thinking hard as well. Take care."

As if frozen behind his desk, Jacob held the phone in his hand for several minutes more, before he disconnected. He didn't thaw out that night and couldn't get his jaws apart to share his misery with Margaret.

Chapter 42

Soon after the call with Hansen, Jacob received new, devastating directives from his department head, Den Toom. After the end of the conversation, he had one of the men put in an order with the baker for the next day for *heertjes* [little sirs]: a typical Dutch coffee treat, baked with much butter and filled with almond paste. The baker likely had to scramble to find the ingredients. If he had to re-allocate some of it from his supplies destined for the Wehrmacht, so much the better.

The next day at coffee break, Jacob gathered his men, including those on night watch, and had them sit down. He watched his men in the squad room devouring the treats and making small talk, but he couldn't participate, as his stomach hadn't stopped rebelling since the previous night. As they ate, Jacob informed the crew of the German police commander's newest stunt. He couldn't help but sneer.

"Chief Rauter has generously opened up the German army, specifically the SS, for all of our policemen to join. The Dutch SS force would be distinct from the general German SS force, and would not be called the Dutch SS, as one would expect, but the Germanic SS. You know, as in: we're all part of the Germanic tribe."

Nobody responded, so he continued.

"Governor Seyss-Inquart's order specifies that anyone joining the German army is eligible for German citizenship. He guarantees that they can keep their Dutch citizenship." He emphasized the word keep. "Any questions or comments? Come on now, nobody has any comments?"

Still, nobody dared say anything. Some were looking at each other; others stared at Jacob.

Compelled to say more, he was winging it, when he continued.

"I'd like to give you my own opinion, for all it's worth, and you're free to discard it without prejudice on my part."

Jacob explained that from the point of view of Dutch law, a citizen forfeits citizenship for two reasons. One, signing on with a foreign army, and two, accepting foreign citizenship. He pointed out that Deputy of Justice Tenkink had made the point-in-law when Rauter threatened to send police to Russia. That Tenkink had quit over the principle.

Jacob looked around and suggested that others in the force might disagree with Tenkink. He paused for half a minute to let what he had said sink in as he saw some crew members whisper to each other. He ended his brief speech by putting the question before his crew.

"Keeping in mind how your actions during the occupation might be considered after the war, I need to know: who wants to join the SS?"

All stayed quiet. The men looked at each other and back at Jacob. Finally, Corporal Peters spoke up.

"What would happen if I did join the SS, because I wouldn't mind more career options and financial benefits."

Then Dijk joined in. "I'd like to pursue it as well, but would it affect my job here at the brigade, or would I get different duties, or how's it to work, Chief?"

Jacob thought he'd been clear. Obviously, he'd been wrong, so he carefully made his voice sound patient and neutral.

"I can't stop you, but I'd ask you this. How can you serve two masters, at war with each other? Remember, the war is not over. If you swear allegiance to the German leader, how do you think it would jive with your allegiance to the Queen and our government? Even when the cabinet and the Queen are in exile, they still are our government. Right?"

Some men shouted, "right".

Peters demonstrated he didn't have enough grasp of the subject of loyalty and piped up: "With all due respect, we don't know what is going to happen in the future, Chief. We may end up as an official territory within greater Germany. We're to implement all their measures anyway. What's the difference? We're all working for the Germans now." He looked around to see if he had any supporters for his ideas.

Jacob had to avert his gaze away from Peters to stay calm. Finally, he controlled his voice enough to carry on.

"You'll have to follow your conscience. Personally, I don't know how we could work with German soldiers in our midst. If you did join the SS, I wouldn't be able to trust you any longer. I ask you, what would our working climate be like as a split

German-Dutch force? How would we implement our code of confidentially then? Can anybody repeat that code for Peters?"

"What you hear, read, and see here cannot be repeated outside of this office."

"Excellent, Leversma," he called out with false optimism. His face contorted into a sneer. He eyed Peters, then looked at each man separately as she spoke, trying to pierce their souls with his eyes. "Would the SS soldiers in our midst keep our code? And another point: as an SS member, you'd be isolated from the rest of the crew, because you can't be trusted."

He saw Van Houten turning red. De Wit shifted perpetually from one foot to the other as if he was dancing.

About to burst himself, he needed to return to the quietude of his office, and he hurried through his last sentences.

"Anyway, Peters and Dijk, thanks for giving me the advance warning. I cannot stop you, but frankly, I'm appalled any policeman would even consider it. You'd be fools to join, but it's just my opinion. Thanks for attending. All dismissed." He ran out of the squad room, leaving the men unusually quiet as they turned to their jobs at hand.

The realization hit him full on: his brigade would completely change with two potential traitors in their midst. HQ had announced that police officers would get extra bonuses for any report on anti-German activities leading to an arrest. He hadn't shared that yet. It likely could turn any unreliable man into a rat. In spite of his assurance of being non-prejudiced at the start of his speech, he must do something as the commander. He stepped back into the adjoining corridor.

From the doorway of the squad room, he barked: "Peters, Dijk, into my office."

The two men looked up from their paperwork, then at each other, paused a few beats before they got up, and followed him into his office with hanging shoulders.

Jacob sat down behind his desk but let the two men stand. Not caring if the others in the squad room could hear him, he raised his voice.

"Goddamn you. What brings you to want to join the Germans? Don't you have any loyalty to your country? What do you have to say for yourselves?"

"Gosh, boss, I told you, I'm after advancement," Peters said.

Jacob couldn't control himself any longer. "You, idiot! If you'd deserved advancement, after all those years in the service you'd be Sergeant. If you'd done more than just the minimal amount of duty work, your previous boss might have picked you for a promotion. I was warned about you, an opportunist and a dishonest man. I'll propose you for a transfer. I can't see how we can work together now."

Peters recoiled and looked down at the floor, clasping his hands. He looked up at Dijk, who nodded to him. "I didn't really mean it, Opper," he said. "I just wanted to know about it, just in case. I don't want to move. Please don't transfer me." The man wiped a hand over his face. He looked pale, sweat on his face. "I am not what you said."

Jacob scoffed, didn't believe a word of it. "What about you, Dijk? You didn't mean it either?"

The man looked back at him, head raised, nose in the air. He didn't have the subservience of Peters.

"I have my own opinions and you can't tell me not to have any. It's a free country."

Jacob shot up from his seat. Leaning over his desk with both hands, he yelled at the man: "No, it's not! That's the point, you dumb-ass."

He sat down again and proceeded slowly with deliberate diction: "I assume the pressure is getting to you bastards too. But why the hell would you speed up the breakdown of our laws and our freedoms? You think the Nazis have better rules and more fairness, is that it? I could just fire you both for incompatibility with the job requirements."

Dijk's eyes flitted from him to Peters and back. A few seconds passed as his eyes alternately looked back at his boss and down at his feet. He then spoke again, his eyes trained on Jacob's.

"Jesus Christ, I didn't know you cared that much. To answer your question, I'm not political and haven't made a study of the Nazis' rules. It's just, like, I don't know. We've been defeated and now they get to say what happens. To the victor go the spoils. I said it before, I might as well get some benefits for my family..." Dijk's soft voice trailed off. He stared out the window.

Defeated, Jacob sat back in his chair, staring from one man to the other. After a few minutes, he spoke again.

"I can't understand this attitude, but you can have your opinions. Just know I'll keep my eyes on you both. One mistake and I'll fire you. Understood?"

Both men answered with quiet voices: "Yes, Chief."

"Dismissed."

After the two officers had left, Jacob started pacing, then decided to leave and check up on the horses. Oh no, they're gone. He missed them terribly, those big animals he loved so dearly, always loyal. Maybe he should get a dog for keeping the night crew safe during those lonely patrols. He left the brigade early, needing the soothing, or at least distracting presence of his boys and his wife. His bones hurt, and he had a headache, making him nauseous. These days, when he combed his hair in the morning, he noticed his comb was full of dark hairs. He was going bald in a hurry.

Chapter 43

Even in desperate times, life itself was unstoppable. When the baby announced her arrival, Margaret was home alone with the children. She felt the first contraction but didn't pay much attention to it. When her water broke, she sent Hendrik to the office to get his dad. Jacob wasn't in. The sergeant was the only one left at the squad room, and Hendrik didn't know enough to leave a message.

Margaret told herself she was getting used to Jacob's absences at crucial times. He hadn't been around for either of the boys' births. Intense fatigue overwhelmed her, nevertheless. The only other family living in the compound were the Van Houtens, and they had no children yet. Besides, Margaret had seen Nelly Van Houten leave on the driveway that morning.

She called the midwife, but the man to whom the operator connected said the midwife was away in a neighboring town, attending to a delivery. The boys played in the backyard, as Margaret slowly made her way across the front. She stopped every couple of minutes when a contraction hit her, making her nauseous, and each heartbeat pounded behind her eyes. She perspired profusely.

Holding onto the wall, she stared down at the packed dirt floor of the compound. The bits of straw mixed with dust gave off a faint smell of old piss and horse manure. She was about to vomit. The contractions were coming fast and furious. She recalled her labor with Hendrik's birth; the tearing at her cervix then had been just as painful, but it had taken her hours longer to get there. This baby was going to be born any second.

Ruth's row house next to the police compound seemed miles away. Her neighbor had been distant since Bram's deportation, but Margaret needed someone now. It felt like half an hour to get to the back door. She slammed her fist on it. As Ruth opened the door, Margaret sank to her knees with her hands pressed to her back. Every contraction pierced with the pain of a blade.

"Thank God. You're home. Please help me, my baby is coming," Margaret breathed.

Ruth told Rosanna and Peter to go watch Margaret's children in the backyard. She slowly walked Margaret back to her home and up the stairs into the bedroom, where towels and sheets already sat ready on the dresser.

The operator put her through immediately. Ruth mentioned emergency to the doctor and told him the baby was due any minute. She took the largest pot she could find in the kitchen, filled it with water, set it on the burner to boil, and then went back upstairs to help Margaret through the contractions. The doctor arrived on his motorbike in time to quickly drip some ether on a diffuser and hold it over Margaret's nose and mouth to relieve the pain. He delivered Elizabeth within five minutes of his arrival, a healthy and beautiful baby.

When Margaret came to from her brief ether-induced insentience, she turned to Ruth and grabbed her hand. Stumbling over her words, getting them out as fast as she could, she whispered: "Thank you so much, Ruth. How can I repay you? The Germans lied when they said the Jews would be respected in Holland. We both feel so bad."

"Shhh, no matter." Ruth whispered.

With a hoarse voice, Margaret went on. "Can you forgive Jacob? His boss forced him to be at the arrests. Can you forgive us?"

Ruth replied with sudden anger and raised her voice: "I cannot forgive Jacob. He should've protected us. Sure, he told you to warn me, but way too late. Nobody should've been arrested." Then she softened. "But you? I truly have nothing to forgive you for, Margaret. You need to rest now."

Grateful and at a loss for words, Margaret sank back in her pillow. Life is strange. Despite Ruth's own misery, a baby brought the promise of a better future. Margaret hoped Ruth would get that future too, that Bram would return to her.

Ruth retrieved the children from the yard and took them upstairs, where all of them crowded around the bed and admired the tiny, squirmy baby sister.

"I'll take your boys home with me until your husband comes back," Ruth whispered.

On her way, Ruth opened the door to the squad room and, from the corridor, told the duty officer to tell Jacob he had a baby girl. She quickly left the brigade, unwilling to spend any time conversing, acutely resentful of the police.

***

Jacob and Margaret were delighted with their beautiful girl Elizabeth, Elly for short. She had a head full of dark curls and big, brown eyes, and she hardly ever cried. When Jacob first held her in his arms, he said: "When I was born as the first dark-haired child after the string of blond ones, my father said I looked like his mother — the Huguenot from France. She takes after me and my grandmother," and he kissed her softly on her head.

"You never told me that before but it would explain your elegant constitution," Margaret joked.

The two boys were eager to hold Elly but needed to be taught how to handle their sister. The baby was gasping around for food with open lips, like a carp in a pond. While Hendrik was too wild with her and Margaret had to warn him to be gentle, or she would take Elly away, Jaap always tried to stuff anything edible he could lay his hands on into her tiny mouth.

The fall was a happy time at the home front. The family often went out for walks together, enjoying the still-warm weather. Their friendship restored, Margaret showed her gratitude to Ruth by sharing with her and her children the bounty from Johanna's farm.

Chapter 44

In the spring of 1943, Jacob closely followed the renovations going on at Camp Star. He observed how the former camp dedicated to the Indian philosopher Krishnamurti was converted for an utterly opposite function. Heusden kept him informed as the preparations took shape. After several misfires, SD boss Schwier received all parties' approval for a labor camp for criminals, operated German-style and managed under Security Services, but staffed with Dutch guards, a *Lager*.

SS Chief Rauter appointed Werner Schwier as its superintendent. Schwier hired an NSB member, Charles Nauwaard, as the manager. This former cop had already worked for the SD in Amsterdam as a translator since the invasion. He obviously was on a career path in the Nazi realm. When Nauwaard stopped in at the Wehrmacht headquarters, Oberfeldwebel Heusden called Jacob in for an introduction to the camp warden.

The man's boasting demeanor was the first thing Jacob noticed about him. Charles Nauwaard was a slightly-built person of average height with wispy blond hair, and nothing else stood out about him. With his iron-rimmed glasses, he looked more like an intellectual than a security agent. Nauwaard told him he'd brought his own personnel: 48 guards from the ranks of Amsterdam's unemployed and a couple of Dutch SS men, plus two former marines. All guards were to receive special Nazi training for the job and were outfitted in recycled army uniforms from the former army surplus depot.

Against his expectations, Jacob didn't immediately detest the man. Both were born and raised in the country's western region, and he spoke with the same coastal accent as Jacob, with the same jovial turns of phrase using the same vernacular, often with a dose of irony. Nauwaard said he had all personnel swear allegiance to the German military authority on Commander Schwier's orders, so, in essence, they all were German soldiers now.

No prisoners would be admitted during the training period, he said. For most of this year, Star prison camp would be open for business at a low level for staff to get a chance to practice. He assured Jacob, he would let him know when to expect the first batch.

Back at the brigade, Jacob sat in his office and reflected on the man he'd soon have plenty of dealings with. It had been a relief to understand Nauwaard perfectly. His conversations with Heusden were always in German, a language he couldn't speak even semi-adequately, although he understood most of it. The local dialect was a dense secret to him as well, with its *oo* and *uu* sounds and extra syllables tacked onto a word, or some omitted altogether, and words he had never heard before. He had trouble catching the precise meaning of a local's story, and he relied on his local men for the interpretation.

He expected his own cooperation with this warden wouldn't be controversial. They both worked for the Justice system under the same rules, after all. In any case, it would be helpful to get more information on the man. Jacob called Hansen to inquire about Nauwaard. Hansen indeed got news for him.

"You've got Charles Nauwaard there? No way. That means shit for you, bud. Our undercover crew arrested the guy in Amsterdam on suspicion of spying before the invasion. He's a member of the Dutch Nazi club — which he denied — and he lived in Germany for a while too. He said he had quit the NSB, but there's no evidence of it. You watch out for him. We found out he's a born liar. So, he hired on with Schwier. Good to know."

"I thought his name sounded familiar. Thanks for the info."

Damn! He would have to adjust his opinion of the bastard. He slowly hung up. He could have suspected that the campsite would change from a mind-improving anthroposophical retreat, but not that it was to become a god-forsaken place of inhumane punishment and cruelty.

Chapter 45

The call for assistance with the first batch of prisoners came later that summer. Charles Nauwaard requested the Marechaussee to guard his prisoners on the three kilometers from the railway station to the camp. The chatty manager added some interesting facts.

"Van Noorden, just letting you know the first batch of knackers is a gang of fifteen NSB members, convicted for assaulting the mayor of Rotterdam. The louts attacked the mayor, a Freemason, and thought it funny to dress him up. They tied a tea towel on him as a carpenter's apron and pinned a Star of David to his chest. The Nazi wannabees took photos of him, with them draped around him like a big-game hunting trophy. Then they beat him into the hospital."

"Despicable. Serves them right then to be put into your hands," Jacob joked.

Nauwaard just went on talking. "The judge convicted them to us for punishment and rehabilitation. Not sure about that last thing, rehabilitation. I don't like the NSB. I quit my membership before the war broke out. They're a bunch of nitwits and the frigging leadership discriminated against me, so to hell with them."

"I'm with you there!" Jacob didn't think it much of a gamble to say so.

It produced a scoff from Nauwaard. "Schwier doesn't like them either. Anyway, they'll be here tomorrow to try our guarding skills on."

"So, you got Dutch Nazis. You couldn't do any better?" he said.

"At least it's a damn start. I'm not complaining. My guards were slacking off, were bored stiff. Dutch Nazis are better than nothing. Those shysters expected the Germans to approve the mayor's harassment and get them acquitted. To say it nicely, the boss considers them Nazi-wannabees with little integrity or conviction, uneducated pretenders. I agree with Schwier. They are low-status opportunists, and their leader, Mussert, is a nobody. You gonna be available with a few men?"

Well, finally, a Dutchman and a Kraut agreed on something, but Jacob didn't say it out loud. "Sure thing, Nauwaard, I can be there with a few of my men. What time do you expect the train?"

"Ten-thirty. Two of my men, or maybe Heusden's men will be there with the paperwork. Talk later then."

***

Heusden had sent two Wehrmacht soldiers. They stood with their machine guns at the ready when Jacob and his men showed up at the station. When the train arrived, Jacob and his four men greeted the prisoners at the platform. Jacob instructed the soldiers: "You can finish the queue."

The walk started in silence. A few brave ones started asking about the work a kilometer in. "You'll find out soon enough," said Corporal Peters, walking closest. "The work is hard. You'll be turning over soil for the vegetables and digging peat bricks for fuel." That kept the others from asking more questions throughout the three-kilometer-long march.

Jacob signed for the prisoners' delivery at the office inside the palisade fence. Two female office clerks worked in the separate administration barracks, which bordered the inner court yard. Charles Nauwaard shook hands with Jacob and invited him for a quick tour with his men.

The center of the camp consisted of a hard-packed field, meant for soccer, exercises, and roll-calls. The prisoners' sleep barracks were located along the area and the mess hall next to these. Across at the far end of the camp were the latrines and washing facilities.

The visitors noticed a few wooden cabins outside the wooden palisades. "The guards' sleeping barracks," explained the warden. Adjacent to it, they saw a large area fenced off with 4-foot pickets, with several wood sheds inside it. "Our gardens and the pig sties. We also have a few cows, and we'll keep enough prisoners handy who know how to milk a cow. We'll produce some of our own food, and we have the fence to keep the deer out."

The various camp sections inside and outside the palisades were secured by an unbroken electrified wire fence all around, topped by razor wire. Nauwaard took them outside the wire fencing and pointed out a lovely house in the distance under the trees.

"There's my comfortable residence. The modular unit next to it is for Commander Schwier, when he chooses to stay. He's here most Fridays taking over from to give me a day off."

After the tour, Jacob sent his men back to the brigade, because Nauwaard had invited him to his residence to meet his family.

***

Nauwaard's wife was a nice-looking blonde with an easy, loud laugh who spoke only German. She was pregnant. "Due in November." They had one daughter of six with a golden halo of curly hair around her face. She looked small for her age.

"My wife just had a daughter," Jacob commented.

"Congratulations. How many children do you have?"

He answered politely, and Nauwaard translated. She reminded him about his own baby daughter and his boys, and he felt friendly towards this family — so much like his own. He was acutely aware of the divide between them: the occupier versus the occupied.

Apparently, Nauwaard was feeling strange as well, as he acted tentatively, politely, without any cursing or blasphemies in the presence of the wife. Jacob realized the effects of their differences would certainly produce difficulties for his brigade. He couldn't assume they would hold similar views, even if it looked that way. Jacob shook hands with Maria on saying goodbye.

Walking back from the residence to the exit of the terrain, Nauwaard disclosed with a big smile, "I've had the voltage jacked up on the perimeter fence to 200V. I also hired more guards. My trained men were siphoned off to other places, and some just quit, bored to pieces. I had proposed Jewish prisoners at first, but didn't get them, and also didn't get the juvenile delinquents I wanted to rehabilitate."

"Too bad, Chief."

"Just call me Chuck, since we'll be working together."

Not wanting to look too eager, Jacob didn't reciprocate the offer. Maybe later, they might get to that point, and maybe not. He left Nauwaard with a firm hand-shake.

***

An unpleasant, lingering sensation he couldn't precisely place stayed with him on his walk back to the village. He had a stomach ache. He wanted to believe the family was just another mixed Dutch-German family caught up in the war, much like his own family.

On the other hand, the image didn't jive with what Nauwaard had told him and what he had heard from others. Nauwaard must hate Jews, and he was already too eager to please his Nazi boss. It made no sense for him to be the man to reform criminal youth.

Back at home, Jacob told Margaret right away about his march with the prisoners. He described the facilities to her and his visit to the warden's family, but he didn't share his ambiguity about the man. He ended his story with his conclusion: "In any case, if the job entails guarding the sort of criminals we saw today, this occasional sideline might not be so bad."

Chapter 46

That week, the Reich's Police Chief Rauter announced the new rules for Jews on the ANP radio, on the first page of the censored newspapers, and on posters tacked on trees and walls around the nation. The rules were hard to miss.

As expected, the deputy of the DOJ ordered the police to enforce the new rules. Jacob got word from his boss in Hardenberg in a personal call. Den Toom hammered on his expectation for enforcement. By that point, Jacob knew he couldn't expect anything else from his leadership but bowing down to everything-Nazi. He decided to ignore them and their obnoxious servitude to the Germans and see where it would lead.

Van Houten posted a copy of the list up on the squad room's noticeboard and read aloud.

"It says here that all Jewish gathering places must attach signs on the exterior, stating Jewish Venue. Only Jews Allowed. Law breakers risk a fine of up to 1000 guilders, or a prison term of up to 6 months. What are we supposed to do with this, Chief?"

"With the average income of about $25 a week, who can afford the fine?" Dijk complained.

"Not only that, but it's a pretty ridiculous order. In our town, there's only the synagogue, where Jews go, mostly empty now. The rest of the places are mixed. The bastard already took the Jewish butcher, and his wife sells to everybody in town. We can't arrest her customers," Leversma observed.

"You're correct, all of you," Jacob said confidently, his tone jovial. "Enforcing that law isn't a big priority, so let's ignore it for now. All you need to know is to tell me when there's a situation, and I'll take care of any requests for the needed permits."

Sergeant Van Houten had to put his ten cents in. "The Nazis want to alienate the Jews from the non-Jews. It'll be easier for them to cart off the remaining Jews when nobody bothers to protest."

Jacob nodded.

Dijk wanted to know, "What about wearing the Star of David? It's been a rule for a while, so do we enforce that?"

Jacob used his prerogative to shut down the discussion. "Like I said, don't pay it any attention. Anything else we need to talk about? No? All dismissed."

***

Ruth was furious about the new laws, although she didn't let it bother her friendship with Margaret. Their renewed friendship blossomed. In their interpretation, these restrictions didn't apply to them, so they ignored them. Their children played together, and life continued as usual, with one difference: Ruth was desperate about Bram's imprisonment. He told her sparse news about himself in the scattering of letters she received.

"He doesn't complain," she told Margaret. "He doesn't want to worry me. He was transferred without a forwarding address, so I can't send him any food anymore." She looked devastated.

Margaret asked: "Don't you think it's time to hide, Ruth?"

"Not yet. I'm hopeful Bram will satisfy the German requirements and come home soon. Then he can resume our shop. I'm not cut out for it. I don't even know how to instruct the hired man. No, I don't want to go into hiding without him."

Margaret sensed Ruth's doubts despite what she said and gently tried to convince her.

"I understand, but are you sure? It might be time to hide. Bram could join you in hiding, when he comes back. I can let him know where you are. The Germans are not getting any more lenient. You know it. I don't want to scare you, but look at what's happened in the Ukraine, where the locals joined the Nazis in killing the Jews, and in Poland, were all Jews that had stayed were deported to camps after the German invasion. In Germany all Jews have been collected as well without any resistance of the non-Jews. Who knows where they are. It seems the life of a Jew is in danger everywhere. The Star of David is a sign too. Ruth, dear, you need to pay attention. All is ready for you at Johanna's — just say the word."

"Not yet." Ruth's face was expressionless, like a stone statue.

Margaret tried one last time. "Would you meet with my mother first and get to know her? Maybe that would make a decision easier."

Ruth looked at Margaret with an embarrassed look on her face. "Thank you, Margaret. Not yet."

Both knew Ruth and her children lived on borrowed time. Fearing Johanna's reputation had cast a shadow on her plans, Margaret wished she could convince her friend, but she didn't find the words.

Chapter 47

Word spread about Jews refusing to wear the Star of David. They were arrested and transported to a holding camp in Mauthausen, Austria. Others wearing the Star just disappeared into hiding. As a result, further resistance had died among the Jewish population. Jacob's director in Zwolle especially emphasized to Jacob he wanted the segregation orders enforced and the Star of David rule. All thinking civilians knew by then that reporting Jews to the SD would mean their deportation. Certain death was rumored to await them in the concentration camps.

Ruth wasn't shy about letting her ever-fewer customers know about her thoughts. She talked their heads off in the store and complained needing to hire a butcher to keep the shop running. She told everyone her husband had been carted off to a camp for no reason. Soon her customers stayed away for fear of being fined for visiting her store, in breach of the segregation laws. It was hard for her to make ends meet. How could she possibly keep the store open?

When Margaret told Jacob about Ruth's refusal to wear a star, Jacob decided to visit Ruth at her home after closing hours. He had only known Bram from Margaret's stories — besides the arrest's disaster — and felt sorry they had not met before as free men, a missed chance. It was time to act. He went around back and knocked. He saw Ruth sitting at the kitchen table peeling potatoes. She looked up, then came to the little window in the door and opened it a crack.

"Yes?" she asked softly.

Jacob could only see part of her face and one eye. A wayward curl of auburn hair had fallen over her forehead, obscuring part of the eye visible through the crack. He felt too large and too official. He should've change into his civvies.

"Missus Groenheim, Ruth. I'm here to talk to you, could I come in, please?" He used his gentlest of voices, aware of her low opinion of him.

"What do you want," her voice devoid of emotion.

He shuffled his feet, looked down at his polished boots, took his tall cap off, and twirled it in his right hand. "Ruth, I would just like to talk to you, nothing else. Please, would you let me come in for a minute?"

She relented, unlocked the door, opened it just wide enough to let Jacob through, then closed it behind him and locked it again. She stood there, not moving, hand still on the doorknob.

Jacob moved into the middle of the kitchen. "Thank you. I want to talk to you about the German orders. You must be aware of the star insignia and the segregation orders? The Jewish Council sent them around some time ago." He paused to give her a chance to respond at her own pace.

She wasn't going to make it easy for him. She sat back down at the table, not looking at him, and picked up a potato and kept it in her left hand as if she had forgotten the procedure of peeling. She answered slowly, still not looking at him. "Yes, I'm aware."

Jacob thought of mentioning her husband, weighed the pros and cons, and decided he'd better not ignore history. He cleared his throat and sighed.

"Ruth. I'm so sorry your husband was taken away to a labor camp. I apologize on behalf of the Marechaussee. Our management forced my crew into helping, but in the end we refused to participate in this perversion of justice. I can't tell how much I regret this action of the Germans. Let's hope your husband can rejoin your family soon." He stopped talking.

She didn't say anything.

Standing in the middle of the kitchen, feeling like an animal out of its natural environment, ready for flight, Jacob wondered how Ruth might feel. His intention was to convey the opposite and assure her of his good intentions. His compassion took over, and he spread his hands with open palms, his uniform cap tucked underneath his left arm as he explained.

"You see, as police officers we're in a difficult position, because our superiors order us to collaborate with the Germans. If we refuse, we'll risk dismissal from our job and possibly, arrest by the SD. But those are my worries, not yours. I'm here to implore you to wear the Star of David. I cannot begin to understand how difficult this must be for you, to be singled out like that."

He stopped explaining, checking whether he was getting through. The distance between them was too great.

Ruth looked up, and their eyes met for a second before she quickly looked down at the potato in her hand.

Jacob started again. "You're observed around town without Star insignia. Violating the order may mean imprisonment, possibly followed by a more severe sentence, like deportation to Germany. If the SD catches you, Ruth, counting on the Germans for clemency is unrealistic. There's nothing I can do for you, but ask you to wear the Star."

He remained standing, feet apart and hands behind his back, hoping to project a relaxed person, non-threatening, just waiting for her reply.

Ruth Groenheim still looked at the potato in her hand. After a minute, she rose from her chair and looked him in the eye. Standing with a straight back, she spoke in a soft voice, clearly enunciating each word. "I-am-not-going-to-wear-that-outrageous-star. You-can't-make-me. Try me."

Jacob savored her words. For the rest of his life, he would remember those words of defiance seared on his brain. He looked back at her, his eyebrows raised.

"I completely get that. No, I cannot make you, nor would I want to. It's your choice. Just know you'll be in danger when you go outside without the star, and in the shop, and your children will be in danger as well. How many children do you have?"

She seemed to soften and looked up at him.

"You already know from Margaret I have two, a boy of ten, Peter, and a girl of twelve, Rosanna. They miss their dad. My children cannot write letters to Bram, and we don't get a lot of letters from him. It's incredibly hard for us. We already stay indoors as much as possible. There's nobody left to visit with anyway."

Her voice turned hard again, and with fury in her eyes, she spat out the words: "That's your fault. You should've protected us. The police should protect us, Jews, and prevent the Nazis from putting us on the train for the camps. We're citizens, just as good as your family. I hate the police. You're all just collaborators doing nothing for us."

Slowly she sank back on the kitchen chair, all defiance gone.

Jacob swallowed. Ruth's accusation hit him hard. He took a step forward and touched her lightly on her shoulder. "You are right. We're all complicit in some ways.

I'm so sorry. I wish I could change what happened. Maybe you could have your groceries delivered, and please, wear the Star in the shop. Let's hope this war ends soon."

She didn't answer, just nodded her head in agreement, looking down at her hands.

"Ruth, if I may, could I suggest while there's still time you'd consider finding a place with your children where nobody can find you?"

She looked up at him, her face soft, tears about to flow.

"I've thought about it, believe me. We haven't socialized much outside of our synagogue. Who would want to shelter three Jews anyway, and if they do, can we trust them? Your wife offered me a place, but I'm not sure how safe we'd be at the property of an NSB member. No offence to Margaret's relatives, but Dutch Nazis are famous for ratting Jews out to the Germans. Besides, if Bram comes back, he'll never be able to find us. I won't leave without him. I'll stay indoors. I can assure you that much. You'd better leave now."

She sat quietly, her head still held high, a small, joyless smile on her face, looking at him — the alien object in her kitchen.

Jacob sighed and quietly unlocked the door, let himself out, leaving Ruth Groenheim behind, hands in her lap staring out the window.

He noticed the exhaustion in his bones as he dragged his feet home. He hadn't known about Margaret's plans to hide Ruth's family. Why hadn't she told him? Ruth was right that he should have protected all Jewish husbands that day and each day. He hadn't slept much since.

He had dreams about Moses coming down the mountain throwing his tablets down in anger, about the flood and about Noah, crying in exasperation about losing everything he had. In the dream, it was all his fault. Today's attempt to help Ruth bothered him. He wasn't sure what to call it. It felt like coercion, not help. He implemented the segregation laws of Jewish citizens on behalf of the Nazi enemy and wasn't protecting anybody.

Although she would've been better off not knowing wat a failure he was, he shared with Margaret how it had gone, in need of somebody who loved him despite all his faults. He didn't bring up the hiding place at Johanna's. Margaret had a right to her own secrets. He had to agree with Ruth it wouldn't be a safe place.

He kept washing his hands that week, as if he had acquired dirt that wouldn't come off, like the hands of his elder brothers, who worked in the bulb growing indus-try. Unblemished and Courageous, as the Marechaussee slogan goes. He didn't feel unblemished at all, nor courageous.

***

That same week, the noose tightened a bit more. Jews were no longer allowed bikes, nor were they allowed in the streets after 8 p.m., while other citizens had a curfew of 11 p.m.

The following month, all Dutch were ordered to bring their bikes to the Wehr-macht. An exception could be applied for but was seldom granted. Margaret now relied solely on her brother for transportation. The brigade crew was allowed to keep their bicycles as police vehicles, but Jacob had to surrender his motorcycle. It wasn't as heartbreaking as the loss of Suzie had been, but nevertheless, with his diminishing freedom in his corrupt job, his enjoyment in life disappeared.

Chapter 48

With the top brass firmly in SS Commander Rauter's pocket, the national police force fell in line without a hitch. The Marechaussee Commissioner took the trouble to travel from his head office in Zwolle to Overdam for an in-person briefing with Jacob's crew to announce the additional changes for the corps due to a prison camp operating within his region.

When all crew members were present in the squad room, Commissioner Feenstra announced the Department of Justice was organizing a celebratory Police Day for the first time in history. He expected all members of the now-unified National State Police and their families to attend. He encouraged all to donate at the fundraising events held throughout the country. The only charity that was not prohibited yet — Winterhelp — was the recipient.

"I am sure everybody will give generously," he said confidently. Under deep silence, Feenstra continued to sing its praises. He proudly listed three deputy ministers and a dozen provincial department heads and police commissioners on the board. "And the most important honorary member is the Deputy of the NSB, Rost van Tongeren," he bragged.

As the portly commissioner spoke, several of the crew members rolled their eyes or raised their eyebrows. Jacob silently concluded the top brass must have felt their reputation needed a boost. Why else do charity works? Feenstra granted the crew a ten-minute session of questions and answers. Aware of which way the wind blew with this man, nobody had anything to ask. Even Peters was subdued.

After having graced the tiny unit with his presence, in itself strange, it was time for the director of police services to leave. He wanted to wait for his driver in Jacob's office. After some polite chitchat, Jacob took a deep breath, shoved his discomfort down somewhere in an obscure corner of his brain, and addressed Feenstra.

"Major, could I share some delicate information with you about the Star Camp?"

The man shifted in the too-narrow, wooden office chair. "Go ahead Van Noorden. What's on your mind?"

"You were once concerned the Overdam brigade did not fulfill its obligations to the occupying authority. I'd like to let you know that my men regularly provide services to Star Camp. I heard the reports from my men and I've got my own observations and have to conclude that the camp staff perpetrated some serious irregularities against the inmates. A number of unusual injuries occurred, and one death so far. I wouldn't presume to know how to be a warden, but I thought you should know, since the camp falls under our department. If there's any justice left in Holland, these guards should be stopped and punished for their abuse of the prisoners..." his voice trailed off under his superior's stern gaze.

After a few seconds of silence, Major Feenstra responded, speaking slowly.

"Is that so? Well, uhm, I'll think about what needs to be done about it, if anything. I might be calling you later for details, if needed. Thanks, Van Noorden, appreciated. Oh, here's my driver now."

After the commissioner had left, Jacob went back to the common room. The men were all atwitter. He stood in front of them with his usual relaxed stance, feet spread, his hands in his pant pockets, and waited for silence.

"As you may well know, the whole idea of a Police Day is from the Nazi blueprint of SS-boss, Heinrich Himmler. There is no doubt in my mind our new leadership will be doing their darnedest to keep the country afloat and their own positions, of course, by collaborating in all matters with the occupier. You might agree with my prediction, or not. I won't insist that all of you go to the Police Day. If you don't go, I won't take any disciplinary action."

"Oh, great," someone said. Several men nodded.

"Only one condition: you'll need to apply to me in writing for an exemption and provide a reason why you can't make it to the celebration. I will accept any reason, as it's just a formality to satisfy the top, but don't advertise I said that. Some minimal staff complement will stay behind at the brigade for emergency duty. Just give your letters to Van Houten and if you want to volunteer for a shift, sign up with him. I'll be here at the brigade during police day. Understood?"

When the crew members mumbled right, and fine, he was satisfied and dismissed them. He waited around in the squad room for a few minutes longer, just to see the effects of his words. Peters and Dijk seemed enthusiastic about Police Day, the others not so much. The men needed to sort this out among themselves. He left the room.

He had pissed off Feenstra before. The humiliating tirade of some months ago was still fresh in his memory. The threat of being fired still echoed in his ears. The major hadn't seemed enthralled with his disclosure of mistreatment at the camp either. Well, that was the major's problem anymore now. Relieved, he lit a cigar — an unusual luxury he granted himself today.

Chapter 49

Warden Nauwaard recruited Jacob for another job. "I need somebody to immediately accompany a prisoner with a serious injury to the hospital. He may not survive. In that case, your people must be involved anyway to take care of the death certificate."

Jacob got off his chair and put his jacket on. "Good grief. What happened?"

"Oh, nothing much. He tried to climb over the fence and a guard shot him." Nauwaard's voice sounded casual.

Aware of the camp's security measures and the razor wire fence, Jacob found this course of events hard to believe unless the man was suicidal. He asked, "Would it be possible to send the ambulance by the brigade and pick up my man on the way to hospital? It'd be faster than you having to wait for my crew to bike to the camp. Sounds like your prisoner won't run away between there and here, if he's in such bad shape."

"Of course. I'll instruct the EMR to pick you up. The prisoner's name is Hans Willemse. Thanks, Jacob."

Jacob wanted to do the job himself to check out what was going on instead of sending one of his men. He wanted to make a record of all the camp's suspicious injuries. Fifteen minutes later, the watch commander told Jacob an ambulance was waiting up front. Having heard the siren, Jacob was already there and climbed into the back with the injured prisoner.

Hans Willemse was conscious but in bad shape and breathing raggedly. His face was ripped up, unbandaged, with parts of his cheeks hanging down, the muscles exposed, and the shot wound in his lower belly was bleeding through its bandages. He moaned with little pauses as if exhaling caused pain.

"Hang in there, Hans. We'll be at the hospital in a jiffy. Can you tell me what happened?"

With a barely audible, staggering voice, he replied, "The bastard …shot me…I didn't do anything, …but he shot me. Ahhh." The effort of speaking made him cry out in pain.

"Weren't you trying to escape over the fence?"

"Lies. That what he said?" The prisoner looked at Jacob with hate in his eyes.

"Who shot you?"

"That Kapo Bakker shot me. I was working in the garden, minding my own business and the bastard started fired at me, for nothing." He gasped and closed his eyes. "He told me to dance and laughed…." He stopped, and a few seconds went by before Willemse softly resumed in a whisper, "…when the bullet hit me. He then hit me with the rake in my face." Willemse's moaning became louder, and his eyes stayed closed. He fell silent.

Jacob bent over the man. "If I wrote this up, would you sign the report?"

It took a few moments before the chief heard a faint alright, and then Hans lost consciousness.

The ambulance reached its destination. The emergency room staff carted Hans Willemse off to surgery. Jacob's only job was to wait around to see if the man survived. He walked up to the administration desk. "I'm leaving now. I can be reached at the Marechaussee brigade. Would you please call me when there's any news?"

***

About an hour later, the doctor called, telling the duty officer to let the chief know Hans Willemse had died from his injuries. The death certificate would be ready for pick up later in the day by six. Jacob sent a man to retrieve Willemse's personal effects from the camp, to be forwarded to his family together with the death certificate.

He was too angry to face Nauwaard. He wanted to confront him with this non-accidental death, but without a signed report by the victim, he had no leg to stand on. He didn't doubt what Willemse had divulged about the guard and had already written his report. Major Feenstra would be no help on this, and Den Toom would just cow-tow to Feenstra. He got only his crew to solve this: seven man against fifty guards, impossible. The rest of the day, Jacob spent brooding in his office, trying to develop a strategy.

***

A week later, he called a special meeting to share a tentative solution with his crew.

"Next time something happens, I want you to pull your weapon, aim at the responsible guard, and tell him to get lost. Then report it to Nauwaard. I need hard evidence, so put your written reports in my basket. Triple carbon copies."

"The Krauts can be bastards," Leversma said, "but I can't understand how our countrymen can be so cruel to their own kind."

"I agree," Jacob said and continued in a serious, softer voice. He had an open look on his face that his men didn't get to see often. "We can blame the Nazis for unleashing hate and destruction on the Jews, because they think they can get away with it. But some of those guards are taking advantage of the occupation by attacking all prisoners. Godless sadists, morons without a brain, they are."

"Beg to differ, Chief," Van Houten said. "The proper term for them is criminals. They were trained by the Nazis to do this." His sergeant — always on the ball.

"I stand corrected, Sergeant. Good observation. We need to think about what other avenues are open to us. I'll forward these new facts to Den Toom and to Feenstra, but the commissioner doesn't like me much, as you know, so I'm not sure what he'll do about it, if anything. I surely will submit my record to the authorities after the occupation has ended. Don't you forget it: one day the Krauts will be sent home."

***

Soon after Henk Willemse's death, Corporal Dijk expressed his objections.

"Chief, the cruelty and lawlessness of those camp louts, I have no words for it other than crimes. They call themselves elite commandos, but have no rules, don't abide by any laws, and are terrorizing the prisoners."

Van Houten agreed. "The other day, a prisoner was badly beaten. Nauwaard should've called the ambulance right away, but he just called us. I had to call the ambulance. It became another death report. Those sons of bitches. That inmate died right in my arms."

Jacob shot up and sat down again, trying not to let on how the news affected him as the chief.

"Since we are regularly called on to escort prisoners to the hospital in cases of critical injuries or death, we'd better make a shift schedule for it. Van Houten and I shouldn't always have to go. I want to see a schedule for Star calls involving all of you. And make sure you write the report immediately. I am making a dossier of the incidents."

The increased police involvement and ever-more reports of abuse at Star Camp led to the camp becoming a standing item on the brigade's agenda. Two weeks later, Leversma made a report. "I was there at lunch time and the prisoners had only three minutes to eat their meal. The guards threatened to shoot the man who kept eating after the three minutes were up. No wonder they look like skeletons. They must be starving."

At the end of the month, Peters reported: "I saw a guard fired at a prisoner for no reason. When I asked him why he did it, he said the fleabag was trying to breach the parameter, clearly a lie. I saw it with my own eyes. The asshole was just shooting for his own gratification. Luckily, he didn't hit anybody, that time."

"And the guards always give the Jewish prisoners from the west the shit jobs," De Wit said, "like hauling those heavy barrels out from the latrines to the dump. But who knows, maybe they're lucky sitting here, instead of deportation to Camp Westerbork with the rest." Typical De Wit, always thinking ahead.

Jacob's dossier of incidents grew. Nauwaard had told him in an unguarded moment about two men, shot by a visiting SS officer, and he had them buried on the grounds behind the guards' cabins. Usually, prisoners who died in the camp were buried in the Overdam cemetery. He added it to the growing list of evidence in the case against Nauwaard on his criminal lack of care. He created a detailed record for later use, believing that this crazy occupation would end.

***

Jacob couldn't let go of Nauwaard's role in the prisoners' abuse. He compared that public conduct to the man he knew. The warden hadn't seemed devious. Obviously, his first impression had been wrong. He'd expected Nauwaard to be like a regular policeman, but the bastard wholeheartedly accepted Nazi principles, and extreme cruelty ruled in his camp under his leadership.

Jacob called in Henk to strategize and stop the guards' reign of terror. More than three years after the invasion, the British and American armies weren't close enough to be of use. Henk figured it could take at least another year before they'd see friendly faces, so impatient Henk had formed a resistance cell. He got his men to be proactive and collect inside information. They had begun to facilitate escapes of captured men and found hiding places for the fugitives.

He promised Jacob the group would capture those bastard camp commandos, and he charged Jacob with the job to give him all the info he could gather about the Star Camp leadership, and while he's at it, about the Wehrmacht activities as well.

After its amateurish failures of the first year, the Illegality had collectively become smarter, at the cost of many lives. Now the movement was growing more potent and effective every day. As the leader of his region, Henk was always well-informed and well-connected with other groups throughout all corners of the Low Lands. He kept Jacob abreast of everything going on.

"Did you know Governor Seyss-Inquart has canceled all city councils? I heard many mayors are refusing to be isolated and keep most councils working anyway. What about your mayor? What's he like?"

"He's alright," Jacob said, "a decent fellow, even if he belongs to the nobility. After all, it's not his fault the government excludes the plebs for those appointments. Maybe that'll change after the war. Hah! Looking forward to it."

His politics had always been anti-revolutionary based on Christian-democratic principles, but the war was changing him. He saw the benefits of a people's revolution under certain conditions. Henk was probably a socialist, but the occupation by a foreign power had made those distinctions irrelevant. He asked Henk, "Have you ever thought about how strange political affiliations can run within one family?"

"No, that's not my concern. For me the only ethical choice is anti-fascist. You might test your mayor for his views on the Nazis. He could be useful to us," Henk suggested.

When they spoke the next time by telephone, Henk had gathered some devastating information. "The Nazis have transported 1,137 Jewish citizens from Camp Westerbork to Auschwitz in Poland, and get this: the political branch in the cities played a significant role. These fascist cops didn't only arrest their fellow citizens, but went back to the empty homes, and hauled everything out and divided the loot amongst themselves."

Having chewed on about the traitors in the leadership of the Justice Department for some time, Jacob kept his cool. "I should apologize for the conduct of the police, but I consider those reprobates no colleagues of mine. I suspected something like that might have happened. Schwier told Nauwaard it took only a small number of SD and SS officers to organize the deportation of the Jewish *Holländer*, thanks to the political branch of the Dutch police. If conditions are anything like those in the prison camp, women and children won't live long in those camps. And my neighbor, Bram Groenheim won't survive." Jacob shivered and thought of Ruth.

"I heard rumors the Nazis are killing the Jews with gas in Auschwitz," said Henk.

They both were quiet for a minute, unable to believe this might be true, unable to comprehend how any government could let such atrocities happen and how normal men — not unlike themselves — could participate.

In the face of the cruel deaths, Jacob's impotence, his sense of incapacity overcame him. "I fear for my neighbor's life," Jacob said softly. "She won't go into hiding, and I can't make her. She's got two children."

"I'm sorry, man," Henk said quietly.

There wasn't a lot left to say. They agreed not to use the phone. The Germans had ways of listening in. Henk provided his illegal contact number with a code word to pass on messages. Then he reluctantly disconnected to return to the reality of his life.

Chapter 50

The second Jacob disconnected, Margaret burst into his office. In a panic and her cheeks wet, she shouted through her tears: "The SD is taking Ruth and the children away. Do something. Stop them, please, please." She pulled at his arm to get him mobile. Jacob got up, ran to the exit and, passing the squad room, called to the three crew members to follow him.

In front of Ruth's house, he saw a canvas-covered army truck, and an army sedan was parked behind it with some SD men. Two SD agents in civilian clothes led Ruth by the arm to the vehicle, while a third SD agent behind them pushed Peter and Rosanna along. Ruth's frozen face was as white as Margaret's linen towels. The children were sobbing softly.

Margaret ran towards them and placed herself between the group and the truck. Jacob followed closely, three marechaussees at his heels.

"Stay back, Margaret," Jacob told her, placing himself directly in front of Ruth, the children, and the SD agents, forcing them to a halt.

Margaret stopped crying and stood at his side with fiery eyes. The three Marechaussee members lined up on his other side. Rosanna grasped the arm of one agent, trying to loosen his grip on Ruth's arm. Peter just stood frozen.

Jacob formally greeted the man in charge with a hand to his cap. "Commander Van Noorden, Chief of the Overdam police." His broken German was getting better all the time, and he asked: "What authority do you have to arrest these people? Can I see your orders? As the chief, I should've been informed. What's your name and rank?"

The SD officer said, Heil Hitler, but kept holding on to Ruth's arm.

Jacob had no trouble making out what the man wanted: He wanted Jacob to stand down and let them do their SD job of arresting German-hostiles — *Anti-Deutschen*. He gave Jacob an arrogant tilt of his head, abruptly nodding once to confirm his words.

Jacob stood his ground with his men beside him, hands on their holstered weapons.

"I don't take orders from Germans. Verzeihe, but I cannot let this arrest proceed. If a crime has been committed, that's another matter, but this woman has committed no crime, unless you can show me different. I know her and demand you let go of her and her children."

Peter and Rosanna stood beside their mom on each side of her, holding her hand.

In his peripheral view, Jacob noticed two other SD uniforms approaching. When they were close, the security commander in front of him gave the nod in his direction. The SD agents pushed their way past the three marechaussees towards Jacob. He felt a firm grip around each of his upper arms.

Margaret had moved beside Ruth. She spoke in her Hanover-accented, perfect German.

"This is my friend, she's no criminal — *keine Verbrecher*. She has done nothing wrong. You, soldiers, should be ashamed to arrest innocent women and children instead of fighting at the front, like real men — *echte Männer*." Her voice was strong and beautiful. Without hesitation, she looked the SD agent in the eye: "*Ich schäme mich für Ihnen.* [I'm ashamed of you]."

The SD agent averted his eyes and focused on Jacob. "If you insist on harassing us in our work, we will arrest you, and your men too. Tell your woman to go back to the kitchen, *zurück in die Küche*."

Jacob tried to catch Margaret's eyes and shook his head no. But she didn't look at him and glared at the commander, who nodded to the agents holding Jacob. As he saw what was coming, he managed to instruct his men: "Go tell Den Toom of my arrest."

The two SD-men led him forcefully away to the waiting sedan. All the while, Jacob protested loudly, "I demand you contact the Wehrmacht Commander Heusden to confirm your jurisdiction. This is a breach of trust with the local authorities."

"Halt das Maul," growled one of the goons.

Jacob yelled louder: "Women and children are not your enemies. Your leadership promised to leave our Jewish citizens alone."

The SD-men roughly pushed him into the car and took a seat beside him. Two other SD agents were waiting inside the vehicle. The driver accelerated hard. As they left with screaming tires, Jacob heard Margaret shouting at the SD commander, but he couldn't distinguish her words.

Chapter 51

The sedan pulled into the parking lot at the back of the Wehrmacht headquarters, not half a block down from where they had arrested Jacob a minute ago. Two of the SD men got out, one of them pulling Jacob by his arm with him, so he tumbled on the gravel of the parking lot. The goons grabbed his arms, hoisted him on his feet and led him between them into the commander's office. They dumped him in the seat in front of Heusden's desk and left immediately.

Heusden looked at him with a hint of a smile. "So, Von Norden, you can't leave well enough alone, and now you're here. *Dumkopf.* You haven't learned anything. Should I lock you up?"

Jacob was surprised at Heusden's tone, then relief set in. He could handle Heusden. With a belligerent voice, he demanded: "I wonder why the German army has to resort to such dishonorable conduct. Is that how you Germans will win the war? By incarcerating and killing our Jews, their women, and children?"

Heusden frowned and shifted in his seat. "Shut up already. I'll let you go back to your brigade, if you give me your word you'll not interfere further with the job of the SD. You know they'll complete what they came here to do. You can't fight it. I'm sorry about your wife's friend and her children. We're at war and I don't design the methods."

Jacob heard the same excuse *we can't fight it* within the police — and with vehemence, he replied: "You say so, but you, Heusden, are *ein Werkzeug* [an instrument] — "

Heusen cut him off, his mood changed: "You, idiot! The SD will arrest the five remaining Jewish families from Overdam today and take them to the refugee camp in Westerbork. Other Jews will join them. All will be transported to a camp in Poland. *Es interressiert uns nicht* [We don't care what you think about it]. You're a fool for trying to stop the unstoppable. Think twice before you get your men involved with the SD. They have no mercy. If it's any consolation, let your wife send her friend care packages." Even if Heusden believed that possible, it turned out to be another lie: Jewish prisoners didn't get care packages.

Defeated, Jacob stayed mute. He'd assumed all of the other Jews in town had gone into hiding after the first raid. It would've been sensible. He hadn't expected that more people in that precarious position thought like Ruth: hoping that all would turn out for the best. And why wouldn't it? They'd done nothing wrong. The only mistake they made was to be ignorant of how bad things were, and whose fault was that? He suspected most of the Jewish men from the labor camp in Friesland were abroad in some unknown town with a large concentration camp or dead already. Ruth and her two children would die too. That much was clear.

Until his conversation with Henk, he hadn't thought much about Ruth these last months. Whenever she came to mind, he'd been reminded of Bram and had pushed away from the guilt. Margaret had not spoken about her either, although he'd known she was taking Ruth food. Bram had been taken before he'd had a chance to get to know him. Jacob realized this dynamic must be happening all over the country — Jewish families, isolated and vulnerable, no non-Jewish people fighting for them, just as Van Houten had correctly identified when the segregation rules came down.

Across from him, Heusden observed him working out the reality of the situation. Finally, the German spoke again. "Alright. It's a terrible thing. I see it'll be hard for you to face your wife. But go home, be a man and face her."

Jacob spat out: "*Mein Respect für Ihnen ist verschwunden* [I have lost all respect for you]." With that, Jacob got up and walked out of Heusden's office.

Chapter 52

When Jacob got home and faced Margaret, she broke down entirely and couldn't speak. Standing in the kitchen, he held her close and waited. She grabbed on to him and sobbed. When she recovered enough, she finally admitted to him about her plans for Ruth at Johanna's.

"Why did this happen now? How stupid I was. Why didn't you warn me? I would've made her listen."

She looked at Jacob with that expression he so hated. It made him feel despised, inadequate. Tears streamed down her face again. She impatiently wiped them away with the back of her hand.

He led her to the table in the dining room, pulled out a chair beside her, and held her hand. "Margaret, dearest. It was brave of you to say what you said to that SD agent. Don't blame yourself. You did what you could. I, too, told Ruth to find somewhere else to stay, but she wanted to wait for her husband, so they could discuss it together, and she didn't know anybody she could trust. It's not like they didn't know it was dangerous to stay. Most of the others hadn't gone into hiding either. I'm so sorry Heusden didn't give me an advance warning."

"What others? What do you mean? The SD arrested more families?" She stopped crying and got up and stared at him.

He got up as well. "Five families were going to be arrested, Heusden told me just now."

She brought her hands to her head and looked at him with eyes wide. "Oh my God, that's terrible." The realization made her cry again. Her hands dropped, searching in vain for a hankie inside her sleeve, so he gave her his.

Jacob heard the children playing in the front room, but they would be alright there for a while. He had to look after their mother first. He tried to soothe her. "You're right. Maybe I should've stepped up my pressure on them to hide right after the first raid, for sure after the second raid. I had no idea you already had a plan, until I spoke with Ruth about the Star. She didn't think it was safe enough at the home of a Dutch Nazi. I had to agree with her."

He paused, but unable to remain quiet, he asked, "For God sakes, with Johanna? What were you thinking, Margaret? How could Johanna keep this secret from Juergen?"

She stopped crying, and the hate was visible on her face. "I hate this war. I hate your job." She stopped short of saying she hated him.

Jacob kept still beside her on his chair, forcing himself to stay there and not leave.

Then the words, swirling around in his own mind all this time, came from her mouth: "Why don't you quit? You could disappear too, go into hiding."

He pulled back and looked at her, his eyes wide, eyebrows raised. "I could. I've been thinking about it, believe me. I'd love to go into hiding and get active in the resistance. You and the children could go live with your mother. You want to do that then? Say the word, and I'll disappear." He made his voice determined and full of hope, baiting her to say yes, but she wouldn't.

"I don't know," she said slowly. "I didn't mean it. I just..." her voice failed.

Then she cried again; through her tears, she said, "This is just too hard. How will our kids grow up? This is no life. They'll ask us what we did to stop the Nazis from taking our Jewish friends. What will we say?"

It reminded her of the children, who were quietly playing in the front room with blocks and the Mechano set that his uncle had given Hendrik for a birthday present. "Come boys, bedtime," she called. The boys were staring at her red face and quietly followed her upstairs. Elly was already in bed and would wake up later for another feed.

Jacob sat down on the divan in the front room and stared into space, not even in the mood to read the paper — which didn't have news anyway — or to absorb the approved radio news with its distorted facts.

He went upstairs to join Margaret, hugged the boys tightly, tucked them in, then stood beside Elly's crib and quietly watched her sleep. He bent over and kissed the sleeping baby on her soft head. She smelled of sweetness.

Downstairs, he put on his warm uniform overcoat and went out into the cold night. Hours later, he crept into bed, exhausted, and cuddled up to Margaret, who was also still wide-awake. "It'll be hard if I leave. I will miss you," he whispered." She replied, "Me too."

He must have nodded off anyway. After a couple of hours of sleep, he woke from a nightmare. He was undercover and in hiding, when SD officers were coming up the stairs to arrest Margaret and the children.

***

A week after Ruth and her children had been taken, Margaret asked Juergen for a ride to visit Johanna. It wasn't the usual social visit. She bitterly complained to both about what evil things the Germans were doing. She vehemently distanced herself from her German heritage: "I'm ashamed of the German in me."

In the following weeks, Jacob and Margaret didn't talk much. Beyond that one time, Jacob couldn't share his pervasive feelings of guilt about his failure to save their neighbors. His job was vital for the family; he couldn't quit. He just held on tight to Margaret with a lump in his throat as she wept for her friend and her children at night. She moved through her days with a somber face. Similarly unhinged, Jacob had no words to comfort Margaret.

***

The pogroms had arrived in full force in The Netherlands and shortly afterward, completed, just as they had already swept through Germany, Austria, Poland, and the Ukraine. Not even a fortnight later, Jacob heard from Heusden about the fate of the last Jewish citizens in town. The SD had raided the private school on Castle Eerde and the houses on the estate. They found two Jewish families, who had lived under the protection of Baron Van Pallandt, and nine Jewish students, who attended the international Quaker boarding school there.

Jacob decided not to tell Margaret about this and add to her distress. Margaret and he both couldn't shake off their low moods. Even the antics of their little baby girl could not chase away the blues. Jacob second-guessed himself in silence and wondered what he could have done differently. He wanted to spare Margaret from talking about what couldn't be reversed anyway and not pick at the scab, so he didn't share his feelings or ask about hers. They both stuffed their emotions down deep, from where they couldn't quickly rise up.

He felt lacking in judgment and blamed himself for the likely death of the Overdam Jews. As the Chief of Police, he was responsible for the Overdam civilians and he questioned himself about having done more to prevent their deportation. Was this the start of the end, and would it all be over soon? Or would things become worse?

Chapter 53

The ultimate order that changed everything for Jacob arrived a fortnight later. The Wehrmacht requisitioned all horses for the war effort. The announcement hit him like a blow below the belt. His gut ached all day, the day after, and especially the day he had to implement the decree. All night he lay awake, inventing all the curses he could possibly formulate. He was unable to pray. This was the work of no God. If he had believed in the devil, he would have fingered him for it. No escape was possible: anybody found with a horse without a special permit after the implementation date would face arrest.

The order was akin to asking him to sacrifice his first-born son. He couldn't think straight about it, was looking for a way out, hoping that God would send a distraction or an exemption. Feenstra's henchman, Den Toom, instructed Jacob to feed and water the horses well, so the animals would survive the day-long trip by train to the front. Jacob knew his animals would face certain death at the front.

"We must request an exemption, Adjutant," he pleaded in a state of delirium for lack of sleep. "We need our horses for crowd control at demonstrations. We've already proven we needed them on Carnation Day. And how are we to get to those awkward places in the forest after a meter of snow, or in the rainy season with mud covering the dirt roads in the spring? We can't just give our animals up for being slaughtered at the front. They're way too valuable. Please, would you reconsider that decision?"

Den Toom didn't care.

"I hear your arguments, Van Noorden, but Major Feenstra told me no exceptions. Sorry. It has to be this way. The Wehrmacht will take possession at the brigade, ride the horses to the train station and load them up. Your men don't have to do that."

He had one last argument left and couldn't stop an uncharacteristic but heartfelt curse.

"Jesus Christ, Chef! First, we lose our status, and now the horses. It's hardly worthwhile staying in this damn job." As he said it, he heard his own voice trembling but he didn't care if he was too emotional.

The department head's voice was cold, flat, without sympathy.

"In that case, you can send me your resignation letter. I've got no time to argue with you. This is an order that must be executed." The man had disconnected, leaving Jacob devastated at his desk, his head in his hands.

***

On the day before the transfer, Jacob took Susie for a long run. He couldn't stop thinking of ways to avoid the verdict, such as saying he fell off when Susie's foot got caught in a rabbit hole and she had escaped, then hide her somewhere, maybe at Johanna's farm. Or he could feed her too much green grass, so she'd get bloated and sick — an excuse to keep her at the brigade to recover. Then maybe they'd forget about her. But it was no use. Whatever he came up with, the counter arguments popped into his head just as fast. It spoiled the ride's pleasure and his last moments with her.

The following day, he arrived at the brigade at daybreak to spend as much time as he could with the gleaming, coal-black mare. He tried not to imagine the misery Susie would have to endure at the front. He softly spoke sweet words while feeding and grooming her one last time.

When the Wehrmacht soldiers arrived, Jacob led her out of the stables. The other three brigade horses and his crew were already waiting in front of the brigade. He wasn't successful in holding back his emotions. The dam broke. He handed her reigns to the soldier with great effort, and as the soldier grabbed the lead, Jacob drew back his hand and punched the soldier in his Nazi face, this time, his right hand. Susie reared back. The soldier bent over, called out, "Scheisse," grabbed his jaw with his free hand but didn't let go of the reigns.

"Look after her. She's a good horse," Jacob said calmly and turned around.

With watering eyes, he walked into the building and into his office, where he spent the day hiding, keeping as busy as he could with paperwork. The thought arose that none of the soldiers could've been a relative of Margaret. They were too young. He still hadn't asked her about her military uncles. He didn't even know whether the men were still alive. He certainly wasn't going to ask Johanna.

Chapter 54

Jacob's motivation for law enforcement seeped out of him. The night of Susie's transfer to the Wehrmacht, Margaret asked why he was so quiet as they were still at the dining table and the boys played in the other room. "Was the transfer of the horses difficult for you, dear?" She looked at him with worry on her face.

That was all he needed. With a breaking voice, he said, "I punched one of the soldiers in the jaw. Susie knew she was leaving and reared back. I can't…" Then the tears came. He hadn't cried since he was fifteen. It felt like a dam broke inside him. As he exhaled and inhaled deeply to make them stop, the tears kept flowing, and he was powerless. He couldn't control anything that was happening.

Margaret had grabbed his hand and held it as she told him, "It's alright, Jan, I understand."

They sat together quietly, until he had regained some control, and the tears had stopped streaming. Then he finished his sentence. "I can't find enough reasons for staying in this job," and sighed.

Margaret nodded. She got up and called the boys for bed.

Everybody went to bed early. For most of the night, Jacob lay sleepless as Margaret held him.

***

Jacob's version of what the job meant clearly deviated from what the leadership had in mind. He sorely missed Susie and their runs across the moors. And yet, he continued on, stamping around the brigade in a somber cloud. His crew avoided him. Most days Jacob sat in his office, brooding.

In the dark about an appropriate response to the dismantling of his world, he was nevertheless acutely aware of the slowly tightening string of Nazi orders. It was as if the air was pushed out of him, like a slowly deflating Messerschmidt sinking to the ground. Judging by the spells of intense thumping of his heart and shortness of breath, he might be developing a heart problem. This happened two times in the last week, immediately after a jolt of intense anger at the state of affairs grabbed him — a visceral experience. When he told Margaret about it, she said it was an anxiety attack. Yet, he was aware his experiences were much like those of other colleagues in the nation. He wondered how in the hell they coped.

Of course, he was happy about the new baby, although a third child increased his worries and diminished his capacity for making decisions the way he wanted. A newborn would also limit Margaret's abilities. She would need a sitter, just even to get groceries, and she hadn't taken steps to find someone. Johanna was the only option for childcare, but he doubted she'd come to the brigade since he'd told her she wasn't welcome. Margaret would need to ask her brother for a ride, and he wasn't welcome either. What a mess. They had not visited after their last dinner together. Yet, Juergen dropped off fresh supplies each week. Juergen's willingness to look after two families had surprised Jacob, but he was grateful. His family had not yet experienced a lack of food.

For a moment, Jacob arose from his own misery and realized the estrangement was brutal on Margaret. That night, he asked her how she was doing, a relatively rare occurrence these days. He admitted to her he had been a bear, selfish and detached from her and the boys.

She nodded, and searched his face for more signs he was coming out of his sadness.

He bent over and briefly hugged her as she sat in her chair. "Is all going well with the baby?"

Margaret looked pleased — he was paying attention.

"Yeah, I feel alright, just a little tired, my dear husband. I'm hoping for a girl this time. What would you like best, a girl or a boy?"

He replied with a quiet voice, "Oh Margaret, that doesn't matter, as long as the baby's healthy." He pulled a chair up and sat beside her, took her hand, and added, "But it's nice having a little girl."

She kissed him. "I was hoping you'd say this. I'm having some trouble keeping up with the boys. Hendrik can get into so much trouble with his curiosity. I didn't want to tell you. You can be hard on the boy."

Jacob raised his eyebrows. "If I spanked him, he deserved it but I try not to spank. Remember the fire at Johanna's barn? I didn't spank him, although I wanted to, and he deserved it then. I was afraid I wouldn't stop and hurt him. You're telling me spanking doesn't help?"

She nodded vigorously.

"Exactly. I expected you to spank him and was happy you didn't. It would have made things worse. We all had a good scare that day. He just gets more nervous around you with spankings. Hendrik isn't only active and impulsive, also ultra-sensitive."

"Really? He looks like a *rauwdouwer* [a rascal], tough to me, but you may be right. I never was allowed to have any other qualities at home than toughness. Come to think of it, I had lots of other emotions but if I showed any of that, my brothers beat me up." Jacob said and softly stroked Margaret's hand.

Margaret looked inquisitively at him, then said, "Luckily, Hendrik will be going to Kindergarten soon, so it'll make things easier for me. I can't look after him every minute. Things are stressful enough with the occupation going on, and you're busy and never home to help me. I really wanted us to raise our children together —"

He saw where the conversation was going and cut her off. "Yes, school will help him. If not spanking, what do you do? I'll have to teach Hendrik some discipline. You're too soft on him. For the record, I am trying to raise our children together."

Her comments had surprised him. He knew spanking didn't help, only instilled fear. Hendrik had to get tough, somehow. The Bible said 'spare the rod, spoil the child.' He'd had enough lessons to be tough to last him a lifetime. His father used to say: I will not pass on the sins of my father to my sons, but the man's harsh shaming and put-downs had been just as bad.

Margaret pulled her hand back and said with vehemence, "Not true. I do try. Yesterday, I lost my temper with Hendrik when he kept pounding on Jaap, and I gave him a spanking. And today, after he kept running into the street, I broke the wooden spoon on his behind. It's no use, he just laughs. You should get a lockable gate on the compound, or get a section of the compound fenced off for the boys."

He noticed Margaret's raised eyebrows and heard the strain in her voice.

"I know. I used the truncheon after I caught him going into Susie's stall, but only that one time because I lost it. Even a good smack on his butt didn't make an impression on him. Yeah, he just laughed then too. Susie was a gentle horse, but could've kicked him in the head if he had startled her. Well, no danger it'll happen again." He felt beaten, his shoulders ached and his sadness returned.

She shrugged and spoke in a weak voice: "Yes, it's time we had a girl. They are gentler. When Hendrik is in Kindergarten, I can give Jaap more attention; he'd like that."

He watched her wipe her hair out of her pale face. He wanted her to be healthy and live a long life next to him. Not like his parents and grandparents — dead from being worn out before they hit sixty. He wanted to see his grandchildren.

For a moment, the troubles of the world melted away in the light of their precious lives. He looked at her with concern, got up, and gave her a kiss on her head. "I'll make us some tea. I'll try to be home more often. Honestly, I'll try."

Chapter 55

After Major Feenstra's speech at the brigade, Jacob had prepared his absence from the celebratory Police Day. He resented the upper echelon and their mindless spreading of Nazi propaganda. Especially Himmler's slogan that a policeman is a citizen's best friend, got his goat. The reality of the job right now was arresting and sending citizens to their death. It put the Marechaussee slogan to shame: Fearless and Unblemished — the ultimate lie.

After he sent his summary of incidents of criminal neglect and abuse in the camp to the commissioner, he followed up with Major Feenstra by telephone. He should've known better to alert the man, as he got another verbal licking.

"Don't make a fool of yourself. I got a call from one of your men about SD agents having to remove you from the scene of an arrest. If not for your local Wehrmacht commander's intervention, your arrest and deportation for obstruction would have been a fact. Don't let it happen again."

He despised the Justice Department's hypocrisy and its officials' willingness to put on a good front for Rauter for the sake of getting funding for a central State Police. Goddamn it — in the service of the German Reich. For the moment, he ignored that the commissioner might hold on to his job just like him for personal reasons. The clear difference between them was in the scale of its effects on the victims.

Jacob knew that the excuse I followed an order wouldn't help him much on the day of reckoning, so he had to find other ways to disobey. He wouldn't expose his family to this Police Day farce. He had enough excuses as he was busy. After the deportation of the Baron of Castle Eerde, the Nazis claimed the estate as their playground and turned the stately home into the Hitler Jugend clubhouse. And not least of Jacob's problems was the NSB's regional meetings in town, with hundreds of home-grown Nazi troublemakers using the resort town to let loose. He sent Den Toom's assistant his regrets for the Police Day. He received no answer.

***

After the Police Day had passed, Jacob went to a meeting with Henk in the forest. It was a clear evening. Henk lay prone in the heather, leaning on his elbows and smoking his pipe, and Jacob sat with his back against a tree, smoking an imperfectly-made cigar of locally grown tobacco. They shared a thermos of lousy coffee and some sandwiches between them amidst the beautiful scenery. Jacob had continued to keep Henk abreast of all the Wehrmacht developments, the camp, his corps, and the community, as agreed. They often agreed with each other about the current state of national affairs, primarily related to the police force.

"Your top brass is crossing the line, taking the concept of accommodation-when-possible into factual collaboration with the enemy," Henk remarked with a mouth full of sandwich. "The police force has become a tool in the Nazification of the nation. It forgot the condition as long as the enemy follows the international rules."

Puffing on his stogie, Jacob said: "I'm sorry to say, but I couldn't agree with you more. I heard that when Deputy Tenkink quit long ago, he commented he'd seen the country change before his eyes from a state of law to an authoritarian state. I don't think his replacement is much more than a puppet of the Nazi's, an academic, completely useless for keeping any integrity in the force. Rauter is our factual boss now."

"Damn, the soil is wet." Henk got up. "Complete absorption into *Das Deutsche Reich*. The country will be irreversibly ruined." He went to his motorbike and took a tarp from the bag.

"Like the bastard Rost van Tongeren arranged with Seyss-Inquart," Jacob commented." He should've never become the Council's Chair or President of the National Bank.

Henk spread the tarp and draped himself on top.

"Rost's been successful: only Kraut-loving politicians are left, and the traitors are running the government. The Nazi institutions are synchronizing our country, the slogan of the day. Did you know that a third of the civil service are now NSB members? What a disgrace!" He blew smoke circles, which disappeared in the darkening day.

"You took the words out of my mouth," Jacob said. "Our units in the cities are taking their directions straight from the SD and the Security Police. I'm ashamed of my superiors, and especially of my city colleagues." He sat down beside Henk on the tarp. "The commanders of five cities refused to arrest Jews. They got fired. Only one

Marechaussee commander in Amsterdam refused to have his men hunt for Jews. He was arrested and sent to a concentration camp. It stopped me in my tracks. I've got nothing good to expect from Den Toom, my department head or from Commissioner Feenstra. I told you already about Heusden's rescue when the SD took me to his office?"

"Yes, you did," Henk said, smiling with a twinkle in his eye, the same sparkle Johanna sometimes could have.

"Don't smile. It wasn't funny. I guess I didn't realize at the moment how close I was to being carted off. By the way, last week I got three new trainees from Schalkhaar, Van den Berg, Van Hardenberg and Van der Gulik. Do you know them by any chance?" His brother-in-law was widely connected, and if there was anything fishy, it would surface.

"No, but I'll ask around," Henk replied. "Better keep a close eye on them. They might think it's normal to kill and torture people after that training." He took a deep swig of coffee and spat it into the heather. "Horrible coffee."

Jacob shrugged. "Not on my watch. I hear the Illegality has stepped up the number of assassinations. Is that true?"

Henk calmly said: "Indeed. That traitor Seyffardt got his punishment for recruiting our men to die in Russia."

Jacob disagreed. "That's murder. I still don't condone vigilante justice. If only these Nazi turncoats could be captured and held somewhere, until they could be dragged before a real judge."

"My friend, you've got other things to worry about. Let the Illegality worry about the traitors, and about their own safety. I heard a communist-led group took care of that scumbag Seyffardt. A student shot the general when he opened his front door in Scheveningen."

"I had no clue. They don't talk about it on the radio. You seem to know a lot." He studied Henk's face with interest.

The man didn't let on he felt observed and said: "I've got my sources. Of course, you won't hear about these assassinations on the radio. Seyss-Inquart doesn't want us all to know that some people rebel. I heard the SD couldn't catch the group who did it and picked up the usual trouble makers, of course always students, hauling them from the libraries. They're still raiding the city streets as I speak. The snakes want to send them all to Russia as punishment for Seyffardt assassination. I hope the deputy ministers at least will object, but those cowards probably won't. What a mess."

Jacob spat on the ground and pushed his cigar butt in the dirt, turning it repeatedly around until it was a flat mess fanned out in the soil.

"What about the Reydon assault? Did he die yet?"

"No surprise to me that he got what he asked for. No he still lives. That propaganda artist was putting his neck on the line for the Nazis. No wonder he was perfect in the job of the DM of Public Relations." Henk said. His defense was sarcasm, and he was free to think and say what he wanted. Jacob envied him, sickened by his own available options: death by instant verdict or letting the Nazis continue to destroy the nation.

Henk went on explaining. "The SD traced the gun back to a particular C-6 member, a communist group, and they jailed him in the government cell block. By the way, did you hear the news today?"

"No, I didn't have time."

Henk took a deep breath and, in a flat voice, continued, "The ANP announced, and I quote, the assassin of Reydon cowardly escaped standing trial for his crimes by jumping out of an upper story window, end quote. The bastards. The SD found him dead in the court yard before they could interrogate him. He saved all the men of his group. I hope I'll have the guts to do it too, if it comes to that. He's a hero in my book. The communists are really stepping up in the resistance. And Seyss-Inquart negotiated another division of Wehrmacht out of Der Führer."

The two men stayed silent for a long time until Jacob resumed talking.

"Nauwaard heard from Schwier that the SD already arrested eighteen-hundred young people. At least six-hundred were university students."

"Yeah. What a shame. Want to be more active in my group, brother? Blow up a few targets?" His voice sounded eager, upbeat, and inspiring.

"Am I not already working for you, brother?" Jacob asked peevishly.

"Sure, sure," Henk said, "but I meant, more actively."

Soon, they said their goodbyes, and each went their way, not optimistic about the near future.

Chapter 56

Jacob and Margaret had decided to try taking the kids to church for the first time as a family. Although their clothes were wearing thin, the family still looked pretty good at their Sunday's best, including the children. Margaret wore her hat and leather gloves, her grey tweed coat over a decent winter dress, wool stockings, and her sturdy, best shoes. Jacob wore his rather shiny-worn suit and overcoat, topped with his grey fedora. He had had an extra go at his face with his Philips electric shaver that morning. Margaret possessed sewing skills and could always sew a new outfit for them from an old dress or coat, take it apart and cut a child's pattern from it.

Their shoes were more of a problem, but the lack of leather goods was out of their hands. They weren't forced to wearing wooden shoes and the scarce, leather linings yet, and Margaret could always replace the worn soles — as long as rubber soles were available — with glue and a few well-placed nails using her grandfather's cobbler's last.

Jacob was always on the job, hyper-vigilant. In the habit of scanning the space and its occupants before the sermon started, he noticed Van Houten and De Wit in the pews. When the service proceeded, the Referent's message from the pulpit made Jacob want to quit his job, or quit going to church. The Minister spoke to the congregation in an urgent appeal to the nation. He said that all other religious leaders read the same message on this day in churches all over the country. He read: "It is forbidden for a Christian to collaborate with the arrest and deportation of the Jews, nor should a Christian assist with the arrest of youth for the Arbeitseinsatz and slavery."

Wow, thought Jacob, this is something. The Minister equated the German labor organization benefiting the German industry with slavery. It indeed was slavery. Jacob drank in his words.

He demanded more of his congregation. "You must be strong and firm on this directive, even when refusal to collaborate with the German authority meant making personal sacrifices." He said that the congregation members should be satisfied, knowing they would make this sacrifice willingly in their duty to God and country.

Jacob held his breath together with the rest of the congregation; it was dead quiet. Margaret looked at Jacob with regret in her eyes and grabbed his hand, which he impatiently withdrew. The boys sat unusually subdued on their bench and didn't need a whole roll of King peppermint to stay silent. Elly napped on Margaret's lap.

So that was God's will: he should put his own family at risk. Jacob wondered what his crew mates were thinking. The prayer at the end of the service seemed suddenly fresh, as if new meaning had been revealed by the Minister's few clear sentences about moral responsibility, about not abandoning their brothers and sisters.

Jacob and Margaret would usually say hello to a few fellow believers on leaving the nave. Today, they stopped to chat and shake hands with Van Houten and De Wit and their wives. Neither couple had kids and the wives readily interacted with the boys. Elly acted shy on Margaret's arm. Jacob invited the two young couples for a coffee at their place, and they accepted.

All enjoyed the aroma of Margaret's strong coffee, made of chicory roots roasted in factories, which rather successfully invented the substitute coffee. Margaret always added a tiny spoon of Buisman flavoring into the grounds before pouring the boiling water into the filter compartment of the coffee pot. "You like some hot milk in your coffee? If I'd known of the visit, I would've gotten some cream from my mother's farm, but I do have some cookies."

"It's delicious as it is, Margaret. Amazing, the cookies even taste like butter," Nelly Van Houten assured her.

"A heck-of-a sermon," Jacob said.

"With all Jews of Overdam already deported, what can we do now?" said De Wit. "I guess we'll have the youth left to defend. I would like to quit the job, but I can't."

Jacob was surprised to hear this from De Wit. He was usually so unassuming, such a quiet man at work.

Van Houten was more direct. "Don't you wish you could be more active, Chief? What are our options for doing more at the brigade, for example collaborate with a local action group?"

Jacob jumped on it. "What are you talking about, man? What kind of action? Are you talking resistance? Speak your mind. Don't worry, I am definitely not pro-Nazi, if you haven't figured that out yet." Jacob laughed heartily, reminding himself of his standard advice: the walls have ears.

The others laughed as well. Then Van Houten said something that alerted Jacob's sense of caution. "Well, Chief, we surely do know it. The reason I'm going to share something with you."

"Just one moment," Jacob interrupted. "Let's just leave the ladies to the coffee klatch and go for a smoke in the back."

The men readily traded the private residence for the squad room across the corridor, and followed Jacob, who carried his cedar box half-full of cigars.

In the squad room, Van Houten continued speaking and blew Jacob's mind.

"Chief, we've seen you in action and we know we can trust you. Whether you would like to hear this or not, I'm going to say it anyway. De Wit and I are members of a resistance group. We are involved in illegal work. We protect those who are helping men and women in hiding, making sure they're not caught. We always do our work at the highest level of careful. We ensure what we do stays secret. Without me going into detail, you might want to consider joining us. Please, think about it and maybe talk it over with your wife. We share only on a need-to-know basis, but thought you should know whom you can trust. That's all. Yup." He looked at DeWit, who confirmed with a nod.

The room was getting smoky, and the mixed fragrance of cedar and cigars enveloped the three men in this extraordinary situation inside an ordinary squad room. All three were quiet for a few, long minutes, until Jacob spoke.

"*Verdomme* [damn], I didn't see it coming. You covered this up well, you sly dogs. I have to say, today's message from the pulpit hit me hard. The first raid on the Jewish homes with the Wehrmacht left a foul taste in my mouth. I can't get that day out of my mind. I'd do anything to prevent a repeat. I might join you, Van Houten, but considering my position, I'd be limited as to what I could do. You'll probably know my brother-in-law then, Henk Zondervan. I'm in touch with him. I will think about it and let you know."

De Wit and Van Houten nodded. "We know him," mumbled the Sergeant.

With a big smile on his face, almost as happy as if someone had told him Susie was back in her stall, Jacob spoke again. "Thanks again, for staying on the right side. I needed to hear this."

They talked for a while longer. When the cigars were half-smoked, they shook hands with gusto as if solidifying a pact between thieves and left the room to join the ladies.

After their guests were gone, Margaret and Jacob had their Sunday dinner, a meager meal of mashed potatoes mixed with onions and carrots, called *hutspot*, and a fried egg for each on top with *kaantjes*. The boys were asking for more meat. "If you put your *kaantjes* on top and take a bit with each bite, it'll feel like you have a lot of meat," said Margaret, meaning the little bits left after rendering fat. The salty bits crunch between the teeth and are usually spread on a sandwich with some fat. Little Elizabeth was happily making a mess out of her bowl with mashed potatoes.

"We'll get some *draadjesvlees* soon," Margaret promised, not having any idea when they'd get a beef roast again on the coupons. Without company now, she asked what Jacob thought about the minister's message.

"It came a bit late, too late for the Jews of Overdam. The minister hit the nail on the head for me. Alas, I can't undo the disaster."

He sat with hanging shoulders and spoke with a gentle voice, his hands in his lap, looking at Margaret. Noticing Margaret's expression, he changed his position, sat up, and leaned back against the upholstered back of the indestructible, solid oak chair at the head of the table.

She was looking at him with concern. "I know you did your best. I am behind you, Jacob, whatever you do."

"I appreciate you saying that, dear wife. I love you for it," He blew her a kiss, conscious of his diminished look due to stress and exhaustion, but he had to be strong for the family. They needed him to be the anchor. He was startled by her following question.

"So, why didn't you fight Heusden? I know you aren't willing to do anything you don't believe in. What happened? Did Heusden threaten you?" She laid a hand on his, still folded in his lap.

"Well, yeah, he did, but it was my department head who threatened me. It never really was the Wehrmacht that could stop me. I should've stayed back at the brigade from the very beginning and refuse to help, which was my prerogative. In the future, I will tell Den Toom to stuff it. In hindsight, I knew Heusden wouldn't do anything against me, and Den Toom wasn't even there in person. What's the big deal if he fires me, when he finds out I defied his order?" He laughed bitterly. "Exactly what I want, right?"

Margaret's eyes teared. "You did the right thing, dear husband," she said quietly, wiped her cheeks with her free hand, and looked at him with compassion in her eyes. "I miss Ruth," she said quietly. "I wished we could've saved her and the children. What will they be going through?" She let go of his hand and folded and unfolded her own hands in her lap as if they ached and needed a massage. She looked at him with an expression of intense sadness.

"I know," he said softly. "Maybe they'll survive and we'll see them again, someday. I miss our old country." He stared into the distance, reliving the moment of having to make the decision to defy an order. He was cold and tired. He tried to shake it off, stretched his arms overhead, and then got up.

"Can we play outside, Mama?" Hendrik asked from the corridor. The boys had left the table, taking advantage of the intensity of their parents' conversation.

"No, it's too cold," Jacob answered gently, getting up and pushing the boys in the direction of the front room. "And it's dark. You boys can play in the living room for a bit."

***

Jacob tossed and turned, finally got up, and went downstairs. He didn't want to disturb Margaret with his agitation. He sat in his easy chair in the dark living room, his brain fully engaged. It was clear what the minister had meant. He had to face it; he'd been powerless and was coming up short as a member of his church, his community, and especially, in the eyes of God.

He felt pity for his historical, Jewish namesake, who was loved by his mother — like him. That Jacob was born after his twin brother, Esau — loved by his father — and whom Jacob deprived of his first-born rights by bribing him with food, which resulted in a feud between them. That Jacob fought God's angel over his destination as the father of the tribes of Israel, and it left him an invalid. Yes, he knew very well about sibling rivalry and about parents who stoked it, intentional or not, and about trying his best for his father to start liking him. His parents had named him aptly.

Chewing on all of the things he heard in church, a window opened in his mind. He got a message from his crew mates. The day's visitors might've been sent him by God, and the message was one he should heed: a call for action. Joining the group would mean more secrets between him and Margaret, but also less loneliness, and he would gain compadres against the Nazi rot. He must do something, if simply to save his soul. It was time: tomorrow, he'd tell Van Houten to sign him up, and he knew he'd also make Henk happy.

Chapter 57

Resistance spread across the country like a petrol spill in a still lake, even when — or just maybe because — immediate consequences followed. In five cities, the front-line policemen flatly refused to arrest the Jews as ordered. The police leadership ordered the arrest of these marechaussees exceedingly fast for refusing to follow Nazi orders. The same day, the rebels were subsequently put on transport to Camp Vught. Their deportations were telecommunicated via the police alarm and notification system to warn to all brigades to fall in line.

The German weapons industry demanded more laborers as Germans disappeared from the factories to the army. In the following weeks, thirty-five hundred university students were picked up and sent to work in Germany. The announcement of their disappearance was touted as an admirable voluntary contribution from the students, made to fit the occupier's propaganda machine. Margaret knew someone from church, whose son at university had gone into hiding to avoid the same fate.

The day after the minister's instruction to the congregation, Jacob tried to contact Henk through the usual third party to tell him he'd signed up with Van Houten's cell, but the man — alias Tinkerbel — said he could no longer reach Henk. To make sure, Jacob called Henk's home number. His wife told him he had left; she didn't know where he was or why he had left.

"He said to tell you he'd contact you soon, Jacob. Do you know anything about this?" She sounded worried.

Jacob knew she had her relatives close by, just like Margaret, and would be alright. "I couldn't tell you, but I wouldn't worry about him. He'll be landing on his feet." He spoke the truth in a way. Henk had gone into hiding and probably increased his resistance activities.

When he let Margaret know that evening at dinner that Henk had left, she had some news too. Juergen had a call from their elder sister, Elfriede, whose husband had disappeared after the last big raid for laborers.

This news reminded Jacob to write his sisters and ask how they were making out. Two of his sisters lived together. Adriana, a spinster school teacher, had taken in

Sientje, who was weak and had Polio as a child. His youngest sister, Josefina, was married to a baker. She would be alright, as long as there was flour to bake bread from. He hadn't seen them since long before the start of the war. He might ask Johanna for extras and send a care package to Adriana if they needed his help.

"So how is Elfriede coping without Karel?" he asked.

"She is planning to join us here and stay with Mutter for a while with her boys," Margaret said. "That'll be fun for me and our boys. I've been lonely and the kids need some distraction as well."

"Weren't you always jealous of her?" He was teasing but was surprised by her answer.

"True, I was, but I got over it. If you had not changed your mind and chose me instead of her, I know you and she weren't likely to last. She's just too vain. I am looking after you well, am I not?" She blushed.

He smiled at her. "Yes, *lieverd,* you are. And you, do you have any complaints — oh wait, don't answer that," he laughed heartily. He got up from the dinner table, kissed her, gathered the empty plates, and took them to the kitchen.

He got his coat and, about to leave the house, told her, "Got to do something, won't be back late, dear," and was gone.

***

A month later, Elfriede bicycled with her sons from the west of the country, to stay with Johanna. Margaret asked Juergen to pick her and the boys up for a visit at her mother's. The sisters tearfully but thankfully embraced. Elfriede had some tale to tell.

"I travelled at dusk and at night," she said. "I brought Koos first on the back of the bike. Ms. Wiebe, my employer, looked after Erik. The next day I went back to get him."

"Gosh. You had the guts? I admire you, Elfriede. You still had a bike?"

"I borrowed the bike from Ms. Wiebe. She paid good money for it on the black-market, but said she didn't mind me taking it out of hiding. Don't tell this to Jacob. A Wehrmacht soldier stopped us by the bridge over the IJssel. It was getting dark, so I made a run for it and he started shooting. The soldier gave up. I was too fast for his bullets."

As the women laughed about Elfriede's characteristic boldness, their mother prepared lunch, and Juergen went to the property's back for some repairs. With Juergen out of the way, Margaret could no longer contain her curiosity and asked the question. "Tell me, what's happening with Karel?"

"His shop closed for lack of materials. Without a job, he'd be a prime target for forced labor in Germany but he was damn well not going to work for the Krauts, he told me. He's in hiding. At least we'll have food while staying with Mutter," Elfriede whispered and continued in normal volume. "Food is getting pretty meager in the west."

"You can trust Mutter, she's on board," Margaret whispered back.

And so, Margaret and Elfriede reinvented their daily routines, giving each a break taking turns looking after the children once a week. At times, they combined all four boys and spent a happy time visiting together. The four rowdy boys always went wild in Johanna's yard.

On one of these afternoons, Margaret boldly addressed a beef she had carried for at least a decade, if not more. "Dear sister," she began.

The formality of her address got Elfriede's attention, and she looked with curiosity at her.

"I always have been jealous of you," she continued and stopped talking.

"Really?" Elfriede said with a hint of irony.

"Yes, especially when Jacob took you out a few times. I thought he was into me and liked me, but I got confused when he started with you."

Margaret looked at her hands, to her chagrin feeling bashful like a twelve-year-old. Jacob had asked Elfriede out in the beginning stages of Margaret's dating him before Jacob had set his sights permanently on Margaret. She recalled her intense jealousy and wanted what Elfriede had. She had a secret she was never going to divulge, she had told herself, until now.

"Oh, come on now, that's ages ago, Margaret," she scoffed. "Anyway, if he liked me he was out of luck, because I wasn't impressed with him. He's too boring, too serious, a stick in the mud. If you liked him then, that's good, because he didn't like me either. I like Karel, who's much more adventurous and attractive, and lots of fun.

You must know that," Elfriede said softly, changed seats to sit down beside her, and grabbed her hand.

"That's not what I want to confess," Margaret, impatiently wiping her bangs from her forehead. "Just wait till I'm finished. I have something of you that I want to return." She got up and took something wrapped in a men's handkerchief out of her handbag, handed it to Elfriede, and sat down again.

Elfriede unwrapped it and held a necklace of greyish beads from a natural mineral. "Oh. There it went. I always wondered where I put it. So, you pinched it, you little *ekster* [magpie]." Elfriede laughed louder. "Thanks for keeping it safe for me or I might have lost it by now. You know how much at sixes and sevens I always am."

"You're not mad?" She asked and touched her sister's hand.

"Oh, God no," Elfriede laughed. "You are my little sister. How could I stay mad at you? You're such a goody-two-shoes. For once in your life you dropped a stitch. I'm glad. Who wants a perfect sister? Let's forget it, dear." She bent over and kissed Margaret on her cheek.

Relieved, Margaret got up. "Let's ask Mutter if she keeps some liquor somewhere. I want to drink on us as friends, not only sisters."

***

After her first visit with Elfriede, Margaret told Jacob about the pleasure she and the children derived from her visit. "When are you going to visit your sisters, dear," she suddenly asked. "You haven't seen them in a long time."

"It'll be hard to go away, it's too far," Jacob said, "but I wrote them to ask how they're doing."

"Not really, you can hop on the train, stay over one night and come back the next day. You should do it, you never know when you get another chance. Sientje is not healthy and Adriana might need more help with looking after her. I think it's sweet and brave of her to devote her life to her weak sister, in addition to her teaching job. Don't you? Besides, the physical handicaps from Polio might increase over time as a patient gets older."

"Yeah, you're right. I will try to see when I could travel west and maybe I could bring some extra veggies or bacon from Johanna. I'll pay her for it," he had replied.

"Even Elfriede travelled to the west with her boys, twice, on a bicycle. That outrageous sister of mine puts everybody to shame," she laughed. Jacob had joined her, heartily laughing as he said, "You got that right."

***

At their next visit, Margaret told Elfriede of the latest problem with Hendrik.

"He takes advantage of Jacob's absences and sneaks out of the compound with Jaap when I'm busy. They roam the neighborhood together. Jaap is only four and wants nothing else than to follow his big brother around like a puppy," Margaret said.

Elfriede chuckled. "Yeah, I know what you mean, my boys are real comrades in crime too."

Margaret shook her head, her face worried. "It's almost as if with his dad a policeman he feels challenged to misbehave. One bad day, I saw Hendrik yell dirty Kraut at a soldier passing by the brigade on a bike. It brought back memories of when we first arrived in Holland. You won't believe it, but that coward stopped and took a shot at the running boys. I yelled at him to find somebody his own size to shoot at. The soldier stared at me, probably because of talking to him in German. I told him I would report him to his commander. He got back on his bike and took off as fast as his bullets, but in the other direction."

Elfriede laughed out loud.

Margaret chuckled. "Where does he get that from?"

Her sister sympathized. "Oh, yes, I know what you mean. Boys just have too much energy. But you're right. These German soldiers are cowards, firing at women and boys, underhanded snakes they are."

"Jacob is struggling with finding ways to avoid his superiors' orders. I wonder, if the Germans and their supporters feel threatened, I mean with the Illegality stepping up its actions. Will this war ever end? I want life to go back to normal." After a few minutes of silence, she brought up the question, occupying her mind for months. "We could surely do something, but I don't know what."

Elfriede jumped at the chance as if she'd been waiting for the question to materialize. She hugged her sister and said: "Sure, we can. We're smarter anyway than those young bucks of the resistance. Who would suspect us, decent and honest housewives? Marvelous idea, Gretchen."

With Elfriede's use of her childhood nickname, Margaret felt transported back to her years in Germany, and she recalled her sister's wildness, always playing with the boys, half a tomboy herself, until Elfriede brought her back to the present.

She said, "Alone, we'd be house-bound with our children, but together, we could share the job between us, just like we now do with childcare. We could take turns. I know they need couriers. We'll take a courier's job. It won't look strange, as women have taken over those jobs now men can't show themselves in the streets anymore to avoid slave labor." Elfriede was practically vibrating from excitement with the idea.

"It would put Jacob in a difficult position with his boss," Margaret said slowly. Knowing that Elfriede found her Calvinist husband too stiff, she smiled, but stopped short of offering an apology. Elfriede could know.

Margaret shook her head. "Unlike Karel, Jacob wouldn't approve his wife spreading her wings without his guidance," she slowly stated. "The less he knows, the better. But I will support you."

Elfriede agreed. "Your Jacob surely would get a bird if he knew. But how do we get in touch with someone? I know the contacts in the west, but not here."

"I know somebody. I'll put you in touch, but I will not do the deliveries. You can, though, and I will look after the children at Mutter's." She didn't tell her sister she was prone to listening at doors, not a nice habit, but ultimately, extremely useful.

Flamboyant and outgoing Elfriede started formulating plans. "If you're too chicken, I'll do it. I have the bike. And if stopped, I could say I'm a nurse doing home visits. Could you get the paperwork together? Have a look around the house, you might have something from your nursing days. We look alike, especially if I do my hair the same way and put a nurse's cap on. I may need a license for the bike too."

In no time at all, Margaret established contact with the Resistance Council, the RVV for short, which put people to work in different jobs and provided the required documentation. Not long after, Elfriede started the work on her black-market bike. It didn't take long before jobs came in regularly through a system of messages and cryptic notes. In an ecstatic mood and free as a bird, Elfriede was the one to do her bit for the country, sometimes pedaling an hour or more to the destination as Margaret did her work on child care. Luckily, the boys were of similar ages and got along great, and Hendrik did better with a boy his age to play with, and so did Jaap. All was great.

***

Margaret skirted around the sensitive issues in her conversations with Jacob. She was careful not to ask him questions. They didn't talk at all about Johanna and Juergen, about politics or Jacob's work. Once again, they were drifting apart without really noticing it, each preoccupied with their own secrets, both thriving and feeling useful. Margaret enjoyed the support of her sister and looked after the four boys and her own girl while Jacob was making his own plans for dangerous exploits.

Chapter 58

Jacob kept in touch with Warden Nauwaard, reluctantly calling him Charles in private but not in front of his staff, and the chummy name Chuck never passed his lips. Nauwaard occasionally called him Jake, which nobody ever had, although Margaret might call him Jan sometimes. Now and then they had a beer together at the warden's residence.

The warden talked about his large family back home in the west, his brothers — all blue-collar workers in the shipyards on the coast following in their father's footsteps.

"Crude people with whom I don't feel connected. I left home as soon as I had an opportunity. My father's an asshole. I don't want to end up like him, a brutal fighter who gets drunk on payday. Nobody was safe from his punches, not even my mother."

"Sorry to hear that. I can relate. My father wasn't the easiest man either, although he kept procreating, or maybe because of it. Seems to be that generation, lean and mean, hoping their brood will look after them. Too bad we're their sons," Jacob joked.

"And too bad we both got shortchanged in the physique department, right?" Nauwaard scoffed. They both laughed *als een boer met kiespijn* [like a farmer with a toothache] with difficulty. "But we're not stupid. In Germany I picked up the language really easily. I want my children to break the university barrier," Nauwaard added with a grim expression on his face.

***

When Nauwaard's child was born in November, they celebrated together. Jacob took Hendrik to the private residence to play with Nauwaard's little daughter and see their new baby, to which Margaret didn't object. To all appearances, they were friendly.

On one of Jacob's private visits, the warden disclosed a problem. "Did you know the judges have started an action against the camp?"

Jacob perked up his ears. "What? No, I didn't."

"For so-called prisoner abuse," scoffed Nauwaard.

Jacob tried to keep any excitement from his voice. "Is that right?" He waited at the edge of his seat.

Nauwaard grunted, straightened his back, and sat up from his slumped position. "A delegation of judges visited the camp and interviewed the prisoners. I lost it when they started asking me questions."

"Lost it. What did you do exactly?"

Charles threw both his hands up in the air and then folded his hands over his stomach. "I screamed a bit at them, told them to leave me the fuck alone. I might've cursed a bit."

"What happened next?"

He shrugged. "They left indeed, but not before they spoke to a bunch of people. The judges recommended for me and Deputy De Jong to be fired. I'm not worried. According to Schwier, the deputy minister doesn't want to believe their charges of abuse."

Jacob already had the same impression of his commissioner, who hadn't been excited about his disclosures either. "How did that come about, then?"

"I was told the judges started the investigation themselves, banded together and refused to convict people any longer to my camp. The funny thing is, the concerns originally didn't come from the justice ministry at all."

"Oh?" Jacob kept his fingers crossed, hoping nobody in his brigade had ratted him out.

"They came from the hospital doctors."

Jacob exhaled and casually remarked, "Yeah, I heard rumors of prisoners being interviewed at the hospital. What happened with the judges' recommendations?" Jacob kept his voice flat, curious about what exactly Nauwaard knew.

"You mean my job? I'm still here, aren't I." His tone was cranky. Reluctantly, he added, "Because Schwier protected me. He can't run this joint without me."

Jacob didn't face the man. Instead, he looked down inspecting his nails, to hide his satisfaction. "And did you change your guards' instructions?"

"No, the Justice Ministry has ended their contract with us, that's what happened. No more criminals. I'm glad. For now, we carry on as if nothing changed. Schwier told me to keep some prisoners back to look after the gardens and the livestock, to

empty the latrines and things like such. Before any new prisoners can be admitted, we
need a thorough cleaning. Those deranged louse knackers wrecked a lot, needing a lot
of repairs." Charles sounded unconcerned, as if it all was happening to somebody else.

Jacob hadn't noticed any changes on his arrival, so he pressed on. "I see people
there now. Who exactly are your inmates?"

The man grinned. "A group of students on their way to labor jobs in Germany.
Volunteers, so we treat them n-i-c-e-l-y," stretching the word empathically. "They're
leaving for Germany on Saturday."

"Volunteers, you say? For labor in Germany? Who're you trying to kid?"

Nauwaard ignored this remark and continued his story about how he found these
great tents in storage, left behind from the time the camp had been a retreat for fol-
lowers of that crazy East-Indian prophet. On Rauter's order, he was to treat the students like they were indeed on vacation. "Come July, we'll have new prisoners.
Enough already with the damn holidays. We got a new contract with the State Employment Services for the Work Effort Initiative — for short, the *Arbeitseinsatz*.

"Oh, that's a change. What are you supposed to do with them?"

Deputy Minister Verwey's is going to pay us for babysitting work-shy vagrants,
for fuck's sake. The bloody prisoners will come from labor raids, mostly younger men,
I suspect. Get this: they call those contract breakers," he snorted.

Jacob wanted to keep Nauwaard talking. "Well done, a different kettle of fish altogether. No more criminals, so you can go easy on them."

Nauwaard blew a raspberry. "Bfffft, that's what you think? You gotta be joking.
We're supposed to rehabilitate frigging vagrants, the generally useless anti-socials, who
didn't pull their weight in society, fugitives. No way. We'll make'em pay for their
keep, until they're showing signs of improved behavior. A kick in the pants and a
blow to the bleeding side of the head is what they need." Slumped back in his chair,
the man had lost his earlier levity.

Taking his cue from Charles's deflated demeanor, Jacob sat up. In a serious tone,
he started his rehearsed speech.

"Good luck with the new job then, Charles. Just a warning: you need to know I've
instructed my men to stop your guards when they see them abuse prisoners, especially
justified if they're not even going to be real criminals. If it means pulling their guns,

so be it. After each incident, my men will report verbally to you right away, and a written report to me will follow to justify their actions. It's up to you how you will stop your guards' despicable conduct. We'll talk later, I'm sure." He got up and walked to the exit.

Nauwaard shot up as well. On the way to the front door, Nauwaard replied with a sneer: "Hope not, if you're that much of a sissy." The door slammed shut behind Jacob.

Chapter 59

The start of the new employment oversight service — commonly called labor police — was widely publicized. On the order of police boss SS Commander Rauter, prison specialist Werner Schwier formed a number of inspection crews, whose job was to enforce the new labor laws. He named them after his special, man-hunting Overdam crew, Kontrol Kommandos — KK for short. Schwier delegated the training of the national labor police force to Warden Charles Nauwaard.

In tandem with the new employment plan, Governor Seyss-Inquart ordered all city administrations to open their citizens' registration records to the Employment Services advisors. They could then scour the files to find anybody unemployed and pass on their names to their local area KK crew for their arrest. The captives would be re-allocated to "where the labor is needed", which all knew was a euphemism for the weapons industry in Germany and Holland.

From the informal conversations Jacob overheard in the squad room, it became clear Jacob's crew was initially divided on this new labor police.

"At least we don't have to arrest them. We can leave that up to the KK," Leversma said.

"But they shouldn't even be arrested." Van Houten went straight to the heart of the matter when he said, "It's perverse. They did nothing wrong. Labor doesn't fall under criminal law."

"If you're young and without a job, better go into hiding," Dikkers said with some envy.

"For damn sure. Just being out in the effing street is now dangerous." Dijk put into words what everybody thought, and several men nodded.

Van der Gulik sighed and exclaimed: "They've already sent hundreds of thousands of slaves to Germany. When will it end?"

"When we stop it. If we get to know about a pending arrest, we should try to delay the KK, warn those on the list," Van Houten suggested. "We should have spies at the employment office."

At the next crew briefing, Jacob reopened a formal discussion with the crew, so they would know officially what's going on, and he could give directions for them to respond to the concerns. "I can't give you explicit direction to undermine the KK. Having said this, I also cannot accept the view that someone trying to escape labor in the German war industry is committing a criminal offence. For God's sakes, they'll be working to produce weapons to keep our country occupied. And not just us. This is completely against all international laws."

"What are we allowed to do then, Opper?" Peters asked.

"What I can legitimately say, is this: check your own conscience on what to do, just don't get caught. Be aware the KK crews get bonuses for each arrest, including escaped prisoners — alive or dead — and Nauwaard will pay out. He hates his new prisoners already. Don't let it be you who'll the KK kill next."

He hoped his new directions wouldn't backfire and get back to Den Toom and Feenstra. He resolved to keep Peters and Dijk away from anything to do with the Star Camp. He still hadn't told the crew about the exact payout for any information leading to an arrest. Just about anybody could end up arrested for any reason and be thrown into a prison camp. What a goddamn mess.

***

When Henk and Jacob met next, the new labor laws and the KK were the sole subjects of their conversation. Henk furiously drew on his pipe, puffing clouds in the air. "The Council has gone completely crazy in approving this bullshit. No man can show his face in the streets anymore. You're not safe at home either. If you're flagged as unemployed, you can just expect those brutes of the KK on your doorstep."

Jacob eyed the pipe and wished he had something to smoke. "Yeah, I know. They do spot-check in the streets. You'd be a prime candidate for the labor police, together with all others in hiding. Rauter doesn't trust the police to do the job, which is great. My men are happy enough to never make another arrest, but my department head doesn't trust me, actually, with reason. I'll try to undermine that traitor at every turn. You must've heard the euphemism for those intended slaves? Contract breakers. I'd call them conscientious resisters. The SD will be extremely busy with keeping us under control."

Henk didn't look worried at all. His hat sat jauntily on the back of his head. "Yeah, damn right." With a broad grin, he shared an observation. "Cute little women are replacing the boys. You know, the couriers on bicycles? Great, don't you think?"

Not something he had noticed, Jacob replied. "Sure, as long it's not my wife. What exactly is their job?" Henk knew everything and was the man to ask.

Indeed, he had an answer. "The Council for Resistance RVV has arranged funding for the various regional branches in the Illegality. They direct the money flow, raised by the Resistance and a few bankers, and a bunch of administration people are involved. Couriers are pedaling the loot to certain distribution spots — illegal gold, checks, and ID paperwork and coupons for those in hiding to pay their hosts for extra food."

Jacob whistled through his teeth in admiration. "I see. Brave men and women. Good on them. You take care now. Keep me in the loop."

"Yes, you too."

With Henk gone, Jacob reflected on women getting involved in the resistance. If they'd get caught, the lives of the mothers and their children were threatened. Nobody would be safe anymore. He was grateful that at least his wife was at home, out of danger.

He should soon make that trip to Sientje and Adriana, and possibly Josefina, to see if they needed his help. He knew from the letters Adriana had sent him that his brothers had not been reliable. If they had any decency, they should look after their younger siblings. But Sientje and Adriana just had to wait a while longer. That night, Jacob took up pen and paper and wrote his sisters on the west coast with a date for a visit. He inquired if they were getting help from their brothers and if everybody was still well. Satisfied to have that job completed, he joined Margaret in bed.

Chapter 60

The next day, the Wehrmacht took the motorcars, buggies, and trucks. That put the kybosh on Jacob's planned trip to the west by borrowed motorcycle; he'll have to take the train. Every kind of private vehicle was now up for grabs. Only the Mayor was allowed to keep his sedan. The villagers lived under government-sanctioned robbery. It was like the Wild West, but without guns for the good burgers, so the citizens became sly and skilled at hiding vehicles underneath haystacks, in dug-outs, in dense brush, or in deserted farm buildings. Johanna was one of the few with an exception certificate from the Wehrmacht and was allowed to keep her horse and buggy.

The Occupational Authority for the *Arbeitseinsatz* — the Work Effort Initiative announced a new order one day later: all young adults under 24, including students, must work first for the *Arbeitseinsatz* before accepting any job.

Jacob had established regular meetings with the Mayor at the town hall when Van Voorst still had two town constables to supervise. Although those men were absorbed into the general force with the police force's centralization, Jacob continued meeting with the Mayor. Going into hiding was no longer a controversial subject in the public discourse. Jacob suggested that remedy for the former constable's son, a second-year student, called up for service in a German factory. "It's pure slavery and against all international laws. How could our DM of Economy approve it? It's morally wrong too. He should tell his son to go into hiding."

The Mayor smiled benevolently and replied: "Yes, I'm aware, Van Noorden. I can't imagine what Hirschfeldt told himself to make this fly."

"What do you know about Charles Nauwaard?" Jacob asked.

The Mayor smiled, seemed eager to talk. "Well, he showed up here to introduce himself on the day of his arrival in town, pointed at the portrait of the Queen on the wall, and told me to take it down. I asked him under what authority he thought he could order me. You know what he said? He could tell Commander Schwier about it, who could have me arrested for defiance of the law. I told him he would have to take it down himself, before I would. Then the guy stepped on a chair, took the portrait down and smashed it on the floor. What a nasty man. I don't envy you, having to work with the Neanderthal."

"Yes, I know." Jacob still considered himself a military man, even without status. Not entirely sure of the mayor's loyalties, he didn't let on he had read about the oath in the illegal newspaper, *Trouw* [Loyal]. "Did you hear about the requirements for our decommissioned career soldiers to sign a new oath, Mr. Mayor?" He wanted to test the man, see whose side he'd be on, as he'd agreed with Henk. His mind had been going around and around, trying to find a reason for the nonsensical order. Maybe the mayor had some ideas.

"Yes," Mayor Van Voorst said. "I read it somewhere too. They're supposed to sign an oath of loyalty to Hitler, on punishment of deportation if they don't sign. All seventy thousand career soldiers, living free for years now. How odd. I suspect those veterans were an ongoing concern for the German strategists. Things must be getting tough for them. They must realize the danger if these military men joined sabotage groups." He smiled again at Jacob.

He smiled back, as the mayor had indeed read Trouw, judging from his answer. "Sure, would explain it. Do you think the Germans are justified in their worries?"

The sly fox didn't reveal himself. "Well, who knows, Opper. I think our men might not sign an oath to Hitler, but keep me informed, Van Noorden. I do appreciate our meetings."

***

Jacob brought up the new oath requirements the next day at the brigade. "Seyss-Inquart has revealed the plan including a time frame with a deadline for all decommissioned soldiers to sign an oath to Hitler." The discussion that followed was a lively one.

Dijk thought the demand for adherence to an oath was just Nazi naïveté, but Van Houten saw the Nazis' calculated humiliation of the military. Jacob suspected Seyss-Inquart had another, more devious, plan in the works, as of yet unknown. It was Peters who put the finger on the sore spot. "What would happen to those refusing to sign?" wondered Peters.

"Probably prison. They wouldn't dare execution," thought Leversma.

Jacob wanted to move on. "Oh well, it doesn't concern us anymore, men. We're not military. But I do hope our military won't be sacrificed for Hitler. I'll let you know if there's more news. Tell me if you hear anything about this."

The crew went on to the usual briefing subjects. That the military professionals would sign their loyalty away to Hitler never occurred to anybody. Indeed, in discussion throughout the country, most soldiers felt such a thing went against everything they stood for. The former military hotly debated the issue among themselves. Jacob couldn't help but fear that the outcome of the debate wouldn't be as expected.

Chapter 61

Henk couldn't divulge his source, but he told Jacob how it all went down. The deputy ministers could not reach a consensus about Seyss-Inquart's demand for the military's oath-signing to Hitler. Nobody wanted to go down in history as the tiebreaker, so they consulted with the Supreme Court instead.

When the Court found no legal precedent for refusal to sign the demand from the Nazis — identified as an occupying authority — the Council of DMs approved Seyss-Inquart's proposal and sent it to the man in charge of the decommissioning program. This official didn't want his hands dirty and sent it on exclusively through strictly internal channels, hoping the process would remain a secret. The recommendations were for all military to sign the non-disclosure agreement and agree to the oath of loyalty to Hitler.

Jacob couldn't believe his ears. He shouted into the phone. "The bastards, that's betrayal by our own leadership. And how far has the so-called independent Court strayed. Of course, we have no legal precedent. It's been three hundred years since we were last occupied. We have no laws about it."

"No use shouting at me, brother, I couldn't believe it myself," Henk said on the other end of the crackling line from god-knows-where. "If the council had publicly backed the men to refuse signing the oath to fucking Hitler, you can be damn sure these career soldiers would follow that example. Promising loyalty to our fucking enemy, what craziness. I would've refused. You?"

Jacob didn't hesitate for a second. "Damn sure."

Henk asked him: "I wonder what devious scheme the bloody Nazi authorities are cooking up for those men. You've got any ideas?"

"Being ex-military myself, I've been breaking my brain on it for a while. They might send them to Russia too, where the Krauts are in real trouble."

"Hope not. I'm glad I'm in hiding." Henk's line got fainter and cracklier.

Jacob spoke louder to compensate. "Yeah, lucky duck. I'm glad I'm not under military jurisdiction, never sure if you're dragged off to a prison camp. Keep in touch. Gotta go now."

The meaning of it sank in as soon as his reply left his mouth. Much like nose-diving off his horse that time, when Susie stepped into a rabbit hole and lost her footing, and he got a mouth full of dirt and a big lump on his forehead. He dropped the mouthpiece hard on its cradle. His police corps had been demilitarized after the capitulation, and he had been put to work as an ordinary cop. He didn't like it. Had he stayed in the military, he definitively would have refused to sign an oath to Hitler. God have mercy: his reassignment had saved him from a much worse fate. He was staying where he was.

The certainty didn't make him feel any better. He wondered what job Rauter would find the military to do, besides working for the Rebuilding Services. The abandonment and the devious manipulations by his own command took his breath away. He had to be smarter than them, he must increase his own level of thinking, find better schemes. He must avoid the damage of the next chapter in his life. He willed himself to think outside the rulebook, be more innovative, more creative, and anticipate what disaster would come next. It became another sleepless night.

Chapter 62

Jacob had set a date for his visit to the Westland. On that date, he left for 's Gravezande with his military backpack full of green pears and apples. These covered the cabbages, onions, carrots and some beets. On the bottom of the bag, he hid half a ham and a slab of *spek* [bacon] he had been able to secure from Johanna. It hadn't been much of a problem to get permission from the Wehrmacht for travel by train to a sick relative. Heusden only asked him if it was for real, and he didn't even have to lie.

He rode the train to Amersfoort, where he switched to the line direction The Hague. Riding along the countryside, he saw the country's changes, floating by from the window seat: the devastation and the rubble of the many bombs in city centers the train went through. He saw trucks with soldiers on the streets and the occasional sedan with officers of what he assumed were the SD or the SS. It looked like little agriculture was practiced. He had expected to see the green fields of the sprouted winter sowings and the yellow stalks of ripe crops of oats and wheat. Nothing of the sort went by his train window.

At the Amersfoort switch, two SD officers coming off the train he needed to take looked at him, glancing up and down, and their eyes stopped at his backpack. Afraid they might go after him, he quickly got on the train and walked through the corridor to the very last wagon. Riding through the Westland, he saw that the bulb fields were destroyed and not cultivated, endless pits of dirt with the bulbs gone, harvested for food. There would not be a new crop come spring.

In The Hague, the scenery was even worse. The quays were filled with Wehrmacht, and the station's restaurant absolutely full of them with a mix of lower-ranked soldiers and officers and many SS in their distinct, ultra-neat grey uniforms. He quickly got onto the side-line to Hoek van Holland, already waiting at the end of the quay. The train didn't leave right away after he got on. The ticket checker came by and went through the seats, followed by two SD agents, who requested to see Jacob's ID. One of them said, "*Was haben Sie im Rucksack* [What do you have in the back-pack?]"

As the train moved and gradually sped up, Jacob identified himself and told him the purpose of his visit, about his ill sister and their lack of food, and the gifts from his German mother-in-law for the women. The SD agents nodded, gave him his ID back, and didn't bother looking into his backpack. He saluted them with a tip to his cap. Clearly, it was a good thing he decided to dress in his police uniform that morning, or he'd have lost his meat for sure.

He arrived in the town of 's Gravezande. After half an hour's walk, he arrived at the modest duplex of his sisters. Adriana had expected him and opened the door before he rang the doorbell. With a big smile on her face, she opened her arms, and when Jacob stepped over the threshold, she hugged him tightly, then let him go and kissed him on both his cheeks.

Adriana looked slight, her dress baggy on her thin frame, and her face didn't show any of the previous plumpness in her cheeks or neck. Jacob saw a sad expression in her eyes and in her smile. She looked at least forty pounds lighter than he had last seen her at their mother's funeral. Times must be worse than she'd let on in her letter.

"Jacob, my dear brother, you look good, older, but how we can expect anything else in these hard times. How are you? I'm so glad you made it." She grabbed him by a hand and pulled him down the corridor into the living room.

"I am fine, dear." He took off his backpack and set it on the linoleumed floor. After the initial assurances of being fine and inquiries about the family, Jacob looked around the living room, and, peeking into the kitchen through the open door, he asked, "Where is Sientje? Is she alright? Is she resting?"

Adriana's face lost her smile. "I wanted to tell you but decided against telling you in a letter." She stopped talking, and looked at the floor.

Jacob's held his breath, exhaled and, expecting the worst, asked with a halting voice as he grabbed Adriana's hand, "Adri, you, you scare me, what, did, did something happen?"

Adriana burst into tears as if he had pulled the chain of the tank in the water closet that kept flowing freely as she muttered through her tears: "Oh, I should've told you, I should've."

Jacob put his arm around her shoulders and couldn't help noticing only bones underneath his fingers. "Shhh, it's alright, Adri, it's alright," as he waited for his sister to calm down, understanding something had happened to Sientje. It was too late. It dawned on him he'd been naïve in assuming an already weakened and often ill person could survive the last three years of deprivation under the Nazis.

Adriana hung on to him, her hands dug into the material of his jacket at his back, which he hadn't had a chance to take off yet. He held her tightly and stroked her head with his other hand. "Shhh, it's alright. I know, it's very hard. It's alright, Adri. Is Sientje gone?"

After about five minutes, Adriana had calmed down enough to speak, and she whispered through her tears, "Yes, Sientje's gone."

His first impulse had been tenderness for his sister, but always thinking practical, Jacob had to get her moving to hear more, so he said, "Would you make us a cup of tea, or whatever you have to drink, Adri? Then we can talk as you make that tea. Tell me everything. Was Sientje in the hospital, or has she passed away here?"

Adriana stepped into the kitchen as she talked. Jacob followed her and watched her brew an herbal concoction of undetermined surrogate tea as she described the last few days.

"It happened three days ago. I could've called you, but I didn't know what to say. You would've have been too late anyway. Sientje said not to bother you, so I didn't. She was so weak, but always knew what she wanted." Saying this brought another flood of tears.

Holding the tray with the tea and cups Jacob went to the dining table. Adriana followed him as she got hold of herself and sat down beside him with her handkerchief in her hands. She looked up at the ceiling, slowly exhaled and inhaled, and said, "The doctor said it was severe post-polio syndrome."

"Och, I didn't know it could return and make people sick again," Jacob said quietly.

Adriana nodded. "We didn't either. Of course, like everybody else, we didn't have a lot of food and she had been weak already, so it wasn't a surprise to us she felt weak and fatigued, and she had more muscle pains. She got a bad headache, and within a day she fell into coma from which she didn't recover. There wasn't even time to take her to the hospital. She is now in the funeral home. The funeral is tomorrow." She stayed quiet and leaned back in her chair, defeated, no more tears available to her.

Jacob noticed his sister's leg brace in the corner where it leaned against the wall. So strange to see the brace without Sientje. He felt numb, didn't know what to say. He stared at Adriana and said nothing.

"What are you thinking, Jacob," she asked quietly.

"I don't know what to say. I'm very sad not having been here for you, and for Sientje, of course. I'm devastated, no, disgusted, with myself. I seem to be a useless dick all around. Did Sientje suffer, Adri?"

"No, I don't think so, at least not very much. She had just the increased muscle pain and then the headache, and only for a very short time. There wouldn't have been anything you could've done."

"Sientje's life wasn't great. And she was smart and so sweet, even with all her problems. Life isn't fair. What about Josefina and our brothers, did they help you?" He referred to his brothers and their married sister. "I know that Koos has disappeared, so I assume he's in hiding. But the others could help you out, are they? Are Maarten and Piet still working at the same place? And the other three bastards. What are they doing?"

"Jacob, they're your brothers, don't say that." Adriana looked at him with a frown.

"Well, I say it because they weren't nice to any of us at home. They were mean bastards, took after father. Don't tell me you can't remember," he quietly said.

"I do remember, dear Jacob," she replied with an even voice. "But that's all water under the bridge. Their lives weren't easy either, and father died a lonely and miserable man. In his last years after mother's death he turned to religion, was a reclusive. I tried to visit him regularly, but we just sat in silence, until he asked when I was leaving. He wouldn't visit with mother's relatives either."

"Yeah, I can see that happening," Jacob said and scoffed.

Adriana ignored his comment and continued speaking with a trembling voice.

"Our three youngest brothers have become better men, they grew up, have families. If you had stayed after mother's funeral, you would've met them. One minute you were there in the back pew and the next, you were gone. They're just normal people, flawed, but human, like all of us. Don't hold a grudge, Jacob. Holding on to anger will hurt you." She looked at him with compassion.

Again, he didn't know what to say. Finally, he said, "Much had happened in the last six years. I wasn't ready to meet them but I'm a different man today. What are they doing now? Jaap was the strongest one, did he use his strength in any way?"

"No, he moved on, became one of the managers on the auction floor in Poeldijk. Dirk joined the merchant fleet, and Willem went to work for Philips in a bulb factory. They're all married and have children — your nieces and nephews. The men won't come to the funeral, it's too dangerous."

Jacob relaxed, knowing life went on and had its course. "Oh, that's okay then. Sounds like they made something of themselves. They shouldn't have been so envious of me, back then. I hated it at home because of them, and because I couldn't stand father, who was always angry at me for something I'd done wrong. My life isn't easy now either."

"I know, it was horrible how they targeted you. Thank you for helping us. I love you and will never forget what you did for us. It would've been much worse, had you not gotten mother to make them stop. Sientje often said so. They were awful, their rough wrestling games hurt us and their putdowns were mean, especially to Sientje, calling her peg-leg." Sitting beside him, Adriana grabbed his hand.

Reminded of the poisonous family dynamics, Jacob's eyes filled with tears without advance warning. He was powerless to stop them from falling down on his hand. Impatiently he wiped his cheek, but it was no use. His elder sister pushed her hand-kerchief in his hand and laid her arm around his shoulders, now shaking with silent sobs. Slowly, Jacob got hold of his breathing and made his sobbing stop.

They sat for a long time together, hand in hand, each lost in their own thoughts. Later that evening, Jacob and Adriana unpacked Jacob's gifts with sadness; these precious foods, no longer beneficial to their sister.

***

The next day, Sientje's funeral was a simple affair with few guests in addition to Adriana, Josefina, and Jacob as the only man. The *Arbeitseinsatz* was looking for any chance to kidnap laborers hoping to catch them without proof of employment, and sometimes the labor police ignored those anyway.

Jacob requested to see Sientje's body before the closing of the casket. She looked peaceful, no signs of a wrinkle or blemish on her face. Jacob touched her face and softly spoke his last words to her. "Goodbye, dear sister. I will see you in heaven."

The casket was made out of rough pine planks and rolled out into the front of the small church's nave. The minister kept the service brief, as the church was cold without heating. Adriana had paid the minister in advance with the piece of bacon for his service. As food and money were scarce, no official reception took place. After the internment was completed in the rain, the wives of Sientje's brothers and their children walked back with Jacob, Josefina, and Adriana to her rental home.

Instead of slinking off, like at his mother's funeral, he stayed at the social gathering.

This time, Jacob spoke with his brothers' wives, and all the children were introduced to their uncle Jacob. As he got to know the people who loved his brothers, his heart softened. They painted a picture for him of Jaap, Dirk, and Willem as unremarkable, normal husbands and fathers. Koos' wife whispered in his ear that Koos had left early on to join the British army. She sounded proud.

"Good for him," he whispered back. "Can you manage without him?" She nodded. He wondered if any of his other brothers had joined the Illegality but was afraid to ask. He got everybody's address, just in case he wanted to get in touch.

Jacob left for home in the late afternoon. The train ride was uneventful, and it allowed him to reflect on his youth and his present life. Sientje's death had changed him. Mourning her and their youth together with Adriana had relieved him from his sense of responsibility for them. The anger against his brothers was becoming a distant memory, although his heart felt bruised by the emotions he had experienced these last days. Adriana was right, hanging on to old grievances — all water under the bridge.

Chapter 63

After each new prohibition from the Reich's Office, Jacob called a meeting with his crew. These orders always took away more civil rights. This time, it was the decommissioned military. On Wednesday, April 28, 1943, Wehrmacht General Christiansen announced their arrest and imminent deportation. The only exemptions would be made for those soldiers who accepted employment in the weapons industry.

Jacob burst out in front of his men, no longer able to contain himself, losing all caution, and unabashedly showed his emotion. "There you have it," he spat, pacing the floor in front of his men in the squad room. "The Kraut showed his hand — Seyss-Inquart wants to enslave another 300,000 men. This time our former colleagues."

Van Houten stood with balled fists in front of him.

"What idiot would sign up to be taken prisoner? They'll all go into hiding. The Gestapo and the SD-bastards will be all over the country looking for them. God help us."

As his Deputy joined him in his emotional mood, Jacob remembered his position. He suppressed his anger and told his men in an icy voice: "That's correct. Let's use our heads and stay calm. I warn you all to be more careful than ever before. If any German tries to have you arrest someone, do not participate, and immediately contact me."

He left for his office but listened with one ear to what went on in the squad room.

Some of the crew were on the telephone, trying to contact others for more news. By coffee break all brigade members were gathered in the squad room. Word of mouth to start to general strike had been effective. The message about a wildcat strike spread nationwide as fast as a flash flood at a spring tide. The nation was angry. Hardly any men were left to work the fields, man the factories, sail the ships, and keep the country generally functioning. The Netherlands was going to the dogs rather than submit to the Nazis.

"Those textile workers in Twente started it," Van Houten said. "Forty companies are on strike already, their workers walking the streets, yelling and singing. Marvelous. I wished I was there."

Leversma, son of a farmer, said: "Even the farmers refuse to deliver milk to the plants. Who would've thought those stoic flatlanders would take the hit from lost milk sales? I'm proud of my dad!"

Van Hardenberg danced around the room and shouted his news. "Stork Metal Works has stopped production completely. The workers just sat down on the factory floor in front of the German guards, and refused to work. What could the Nazis do, kill them all?"

Van der Gulik announced an update: "Twenty-one thousand in our province. Hello, rebellion."

By the end of the morning, the brigade was buzzing with nervous activity. Nobody was doing any work. By 2 p.m., many industries were on strike throughout the country. Government services stopped work and engaged in sit-downs, and many workers left their worksites to demonstrate in the streets.

Van Houten went to Jacob's office and demanded: "Why can't we join them?"

Jacob leaped up from his desk and grabbed his Deputy by the arm. "Come," he said and they joined the crew in the squad room.

"I'll tell you why we can't strike: we are essential services. Striking under any law, Dutch or German, would be a breach of our contract with the risk of being fired. But we can slow down, work to rule. We're not going to arrest strikers. If anybody, it will be the SD to do that job. You heard the Krauts are already out there, including the Wehrmacht and the SS firing at strikers, but you don't hear about marechaussee helping those bastards."

He stopped talking, and his thoughts raced to find methods to convince his rebellious men, saving them from themselves.

"Alright, we'll stay inside, but I'd rather join the strike," grumbled Van Houten. As a second thought, he added in a thoughtful tone: "Not our problem if farmers pour their milk in the streets, but I do wonder what Seyss-Inquart will do for revenge this time."

Peters, always the obedient German defender, said, "You really think we shouldn't at least try to get those farmers to deliver the milk?"

Everybody ignored him.

"I heard they're singing We're Not Working For The Krauts No More," De Wit said with a dreamy look on his face. "I wished I could join them in Zwolle. It must be a gas to openly defy the Nazis."

***

They heard that day, Thursday, April 30, that the state-owned and the private coal mines in the southern region stopped producing, supported in this Roman Catholic area by the clergy. By the end of the day, Phillips had ceased production in many of its factories throughout the country. The German weapons industry in the Dutch territory was halted.

The crowds walked the streets singing and chanting and welcoming others. As in the olden days, they savored their freedom of expression, if only for a little while. Curiously, Radio Orange didn't broadcast a word of the strike all day, although the brigade crew took turns sneaking away to listen to the illegal radio elsewhere. In any case, the wildcat strike was a complete success, and everybody in the nation knew about it.

***

On Friday, Jacob got a call from his department head, Den Toom. "I want you and your crew to listen to the 10 a.m. news. The governor is going to speak."

The brigade crew gathered around the radio. The voice of Governor Seyss-Inquart declared in his perfect German, with an interpreter talking over him.

"The circumstances of the emergency demanded I instated martial law, with the death penalty for strikers. I have designated high ranking SS officers as my representatives and delegated them to sentence to death any striker who violates the command to go back to work. They will be executed the day of their arrest, or the next. Oberst Rauter has ordered his men to shoot to kill."

Van Houten had anticipated problems, but not this, and he burst out: "My God. I told you they'd take revenge, but this is the devil's handiwork."

Beaten down, the crew stayed quiet. With Seyss-Inquart's order to shoot to kill, they all knew Hitler's Adjutant no longer believed the Dutch would fall in line. The Nazis never sanctioned insolence before — after all, they were still at war — but this was going to be a slaughter.

"This battle is turning into an all-out war with the whole country," Jacob sighed before he retreated into his office for the moment.

***

All that day, the bad news trickled in. Jacob kept a close eye out to prevent individual members from doing anything rash. Dikkers got a call in the afternoon. When he got off the line, he told his crewmates about it.

"My uncle got shot in Groningen. He refused to bring his milk to the factory. Some SD in uniform saw him tipping the milk into the ditch and told him to get on with delivering it. When he still refused, the SD shot him point blank and left his body lying there. My aunt found him in front of the farm bleeding out. The bastards. My aunt and cousins are devastated, but my dad doesn't dare to travel to them now."

Dikkers was a young man at the start of his career, and the look on his face told of the shock, eyes wide, his face pale. He was about to cry.

Jacob crossed the room and shook his hand.

"My condolences, Dikkers. Your uncle died a hero, standing up to the SD. You can be proud of him. In a day or two this will be over. You can leave then and accompany your father to Groningen, but I would advise for all it's worth to travel in uniform."

Jacob required the marechaussees to finish their backlog of reports. He wanted one report for each incidence of police involvement, regardless of its significance. Writing an incident report was a tedious job, and thought of as useless, to be avoided at all cost, but today the crew was remarkably uncomplaining. It was rule-to-work and saved their butts.

***

On Saturday, Commissioner Feenstra himself called and induced in Jacob another bout of resistance: "I want your crew to arrest the local strikers, including the farmers, who refuse to deliver milk."

"With all due respect, Major, it's Labor Day and the crew is at home, with only two officers scheduled for duty shifts," Jacob argued in a reasonable tone of voice — respectful but as an equal. "You may not be aware, Sir, but enough SD and Wehrmacht lately arrived in town for any arrests. They don't need us. Den Toom agrees with me." That was a plain lie, but he didn't think his regional boss talked a lot to his subordinates.

The commissioner's voice rose in pitch and volume as if trying to shout across the actual distance.

"I don't care. Go out there. This is an order, *verdomme*. Do as you are told."

In a patient voice much like the one he used to explain a rule to Hendrik, Jacob replied to his boss.

"Major, I instructed my men to stay inside and catch up on paperwork. That's what most brigades are doing. Den Toom was fine with it. Even if I tried, I wouldn't get our men to arrest their relatives and friends for something senseless, like helping out their farming uncle. You can't expect them to do that. Striking used to be their right. And what will happen, Major, if I did give the order and they defied it? I'd have to fire them all for insubordination — and then I'll be the only policeman left standing."

In a high-pitched voice squeaking like a woman, the commissioner made a last-ditch effort. "Goddamn you, Van Noorden, this will go on your record. Get out there, man, even if it's only you." He disconnected without another word.

Feenstra couldn't scare him anymore: in Jacob's eyes, his authority to order him about had melted like snow before the son with his dereliction of the law and complete lack of morality. Jacob quietly lowered the phone to the cradle, rubbed his head, sat back, and thought about tackling this problem. Duty officer Van den Berg had told him a nephew of his and some other entrepreneurial citizens had arranged a co-operative sales point where they sold their milk privately. The least he could do was go and see.

He put on his jacket and left the office. He observed stalls with all sorts of used items at the market square, including homemade products on offer. According to the old custom, on a civic holiday, citizens had organized a free market; no licenses were needed. Some of the entrepreneurs offered unpasteurized milk and cream. Such a market didn't require police intervention, as everything was within the legal parameters. He nodded in approval and left the market. He had covered his ass and acted within the Dutch law.

As Jacob pedaled back to the brigade, he wondered how Henk had got on with his plan to alert the government-in-exile, hoping the strikers would get help from the Allied Forces before the Nazis' terrorism would've killed all their enthusiasm.

Chapter 64

The following day after dinner, Jacob finally got around to talk about the funeral and the shock on his arrival that Sientje had passed away. He added news about his brothers in some detail, and ended with, "They're tough fellows, they'll survive it."

"I always wondered why you never talked about your brothers. What is the deal with you and them, dear," she asked. "Why didn't they come to our wedding?" She sat across from him, with only Elly still in her highchair at the table and the boys in the front room noisily playing with tin soldiers.

Jacob exhaled and shifted in his chair. "You really want to hear the sorry tale, *lieverd?*" he asked with raised eyebrows.

"Of course, better late than never. We shouldn't have any secrets anymore for each other, right?" She smiled and took her lab coat off.

"Yes, that is true. I told you that my mom taught me bookkeeping and I used to do the books for the store. When I was fifteen, my dad kept harping on a mistake he said I'd made but I couldn't tell him that my brothers made me steal cash from the till for them — I hadn't got around to justifying that somehow in the books. So I left. My brothers were a lot stronger than me. I hated them. They didn't like me either."

"Och, Jan, *wat jammer* [that is a shame]. And what about your mom, couldn't she do anything?" She reached across the table and laid a hand on his.

Jacob told her how he recruited her to protect his sisters and himself from his brothers' cruelty. "It's a shame you didn't meet her, you would've liked her. She was kind, like you."

He sighed with the memory, and added in a brighter voice: "It was all for the best, because it made me leave home. Anything was better than that strict and unbendable man lording it over me, and I told him I quit, was done with penny-pinching, stealing, and church-going. I'd rather leave than beat the shit out of my father. The Bible says a son can't raise his hand to his elders."

"Jacob, what a sad story. I wished I'd known this before. I wouldn't have bugged you so much to invite them to our wedding, and it explains a lot about why you think you have to be so austere. Are all of your brothers like that?"

She looked with sympathy at him, soaking up each word that left his lips. He looked defeated and vulnerable, his face sad as if he might start weeping. She got up and walked around the table, sat down beside him, and took his hand in both of hers.

Jacob wiped his other hand across his face, squeezing the hand Margaret was holding.

"You might as well know the whole damn story. I never told anyone this, dear, so keep it to yourself. You see, all my five brothers worked in lousy jobs in the fields, getting their hands dirty, while I was paying for my room and board by working at home. In my eyes they had the better life, away from Father too, and maybe they thought I got the best deal. Envy can do strange things."

Margaret empathically nodded her head. "Yes, it can," she said quietly, thinking back of her own bout of envy. "What kind of work did you do?"

"Delivering groceries, doing father's books, and the books for the church. The minister paid him. I didn't get a cent. I quit that job too, packed my bags and slinked out of the house. Mother might've talked me out of leaving, so I didn't say goodbye to her. I felt terrible and have regretted that part."

"I couldn't imagine doing that to Mutter," Margaret looked shocked. "You must've felt really bad, you loved your mom. So, did you ever tell her why, or make up with your relatives?"

Jacob pulled his hand back from hers, and a deep frown appeared on his brow.

"I called her after finishing my training and apologized to her. I wasn't willing to go home, as that meant facing Father too, and later it was too late. She suddenly died when she got pneumonia. That's now at least fifteen years ago. I regret most of all not seeing her alive. I did go to the funeral, but slunk away without meeting my relatives." He stood, ready to leave the subject alone.

She stared at him in consternation, looking for words.

Quickly, he asked, "Any other things we need to talk about, love? I want to go outside and get some fresh air."

Margaret raised herself up from her chair, standing close to him, and touched his face. "Very sad, I'm sorry for you. You must have been scared, so young."

He grabbed her hand, kept it to his cheek for a few seconds, and quietly said, "Yes, I was fifteen, and scared, but I lied to the recruitment officer. I slept on a park bench, afraid in a city I'd only been once before with Father. The officer must've accepted me out of pity — I was a puny kid, sad, and I looked terrible, I probably had dirt on my face. I'd been crying for a while, I can admit that now. You wouldn't have recognized me then."

Margaret wrapped her arms around him and hugged him tightly. "Family is so important," she whispered, "I know."

He accepted her embrace and held her, tears prickling behind the eyelids that he kept shut. When he let her go, he felt lighter with his isolation broken and more sadness released from his soul together with the truth, and a bit of the pain as well.

***

In the morning, Jacob received a call from Henk at the office. Henk's voice had changed; it had a hard edge.

"I'll have to disappoint you. The British government and MI-6 knew already about our situation. Others had wired telegrams requesting military backup. Prince Bernhard, Queen Wilhelmina, and Gerbrandy met with frigging Winston Churchill to evaluate the situation. They've decided a British strike in Holland now wouldn't be feasible. Goddamn it." He exhaled sharply.

Jacob threw the telephone down on the desk, cursed softly, and picked it up a second later. "Bad connection, sorry. Christ. That's too bad. Why aren't they helping us? What a waste of good people."

"There's a little light in the darkness," Henk said a few seconds later in a conciliatory tone. "We've got a line of communication going, the purpose of sending the Marconist. We've got a system now with hiding places for the sender and a trained man who knows Morse. He has laid the connections with MI6. At least we can get the supply route going. Did you know that Wilhelmina replaced that coward De Geer with Gerbrandy as the PM? Our Queen is some powerful woman, gotta admire her."

Jacob grunted. "Yes, I knew. But not enough to convince the British."

"Gerbrandy will speak tomorrow on Radio Orange," Henk added.

"Some comfort. Talk later," Jacob replied and plunked the telephone on its cradle. It bounced off and fell on the desk. He left it as it was, not wanting to talk to anybody else, and got up. He kicked the office door closed with a bang and started pacing.

Without much hope, to begin with, he had secretly hoped nevertheless that the tiny spark of rebellion would light the fire of mass resistance, and they would chase the Germans out of the country. He must set his targets lower, maybe wait till the weapons start coming in. All hopes dashed for a quick rebellion, he went home early.

***

Margaret was busy with the laundry and hung her corset on the line next to his boxers in the backyard when he got home. He put his arms around her waist, soft to his touch now without corset, pulled her close and held her for a few seconds, and tickled her.

She giggled and pulled herself free, as she said, "Stop it Jan, later, I promise."

He was going to wait for her and stretched out of the divan, while the boys were outside playing, and Elly was happily cooing away in the wooden playpen in the living room. His eyes closed.

Chapter 65

On the third strike day, Jacob listened to the contradictory speech of Gerbrandy at his radio hiding place. The cabinet leader strongly recommended that all Dutch should resist and refrain from collaboration with the German measures against the former military. The clincher was his last sentence: his appeal mustn't be mistaken for a call to armed resistance. PM Gerbrandy ended with wishing all citizens much strength and God's protection, blah, blah, blah.

Jacob returned to the squad room. He worried about the Mayor and feared the man might challenge the soldiers next door in his frustration and get himself into deep trouble. He had no doubt Mayor Van Voorst kept himself informed. For a long time already, the old man hadn't seemed firmly attached to life. Jacob charged Peters to stand guard at the Mayor's office.

"We should protect him, just in case the Wehrmacht gets an inappropriate order," he explained.

"What sort of order," the dumb corporal asked.

"To arrest him, of course," he barked. "Call me immediately. I'll be at home for lunch."

***

Before the end of the day, Jacob rode by the mayor's office for a chat but didn't see Peters. The *Burgervader* [Burgermeister] seemed alright and promised to do nothing risky. "I'm an old man," he said, "why would I speed up my demise? It'll come soon enough without my help."

In a casual tone, Jacob asked, "Have you seen my corporal, Mayor?"

"I don't need a childminder. I'm not dement yet, Van Noorden, but thanks anyway," Mayor Van Voorst grumbled. "He was here for an hour or so, but I told him to leave. You go home too, Chief, and have a good evening."

"Alright, Mayor, goodnight then," Jacob said and went home, brooding about Peters.

***

By Sunday, the Security Police with the Wehrmacht had arrested a thousand strikers and executed nineteen workers on the spot, right on the factory floor. In the northern province of Groningen, the SD filled a whole soccer stadium with arrested strikers.

That Sunday morning, Jacob got a call at home from Oberfeldwebel Heusden of the Wehrmacht.

"Last night, one of my men arrested a farmer, two of his sons, and six others. You should know what happened. My soldier locked them inside an empty barracks, somewhere in the fields. These partisans had erected a barricade and he needed help, so he called the SD for back-up."

Heusden's explanation sounded like an apology. Irritated, he asked, "Why would he call the SD? A barricade? Seems farfetched to me. Maybe a fallen tree from the storm we had a few days ago. Where's that barn? You could've called me earlier to help sort out the problem, but with the SD on their way, I can guess what's going to happen: they're going to be deported."

"Well, it's too late. It's sorted out," Heusden said briskly. "The SD arrived an hour ago with a transport truck. The prisoners tried to escape. All are dead."

Jacob gasped. "My God, Heusden, that's… I have no words for it. Ruthless doesn't cover it. You know farmers are no terrorists. How stupid. What crime did they commit? You tell me, Heusden. Dead men can't bring the milk to the factory." He waited for an answer, but it stayed silent on the line until it dawned on him, and he demanded: "Why did you call me then?"

Heusden didn't reply.

Anger and disappointment made Jacob drop his vigilance. In an aggressive tone, he continued. "Did you instruct your man to call the SD? You told me you didn't like Rauter's men. I can't believe you anymore." Jacob realized he was walking a fine line, but he wanted to test Heusden. "Next time, get me in on it earlier. We could've saved some lives."

Heusden sighed, and a couple of seconds passed before he replied.

"This isn't my kind of war either, but you, Dutchmen, can't be trusted, and you proved that with the raid on the school. Rauter wants the SD on all political arrests. You are not needed anymore. It's why I didn't call you until now. I can't save you from your own recklessness, *mein Freund*, but I wanted you to hear it from me, is why I called. I'm not a coward."

Jacob scoffed and disconnected.

Later that day after church service, he heard that the SD had shot a 13-year-old kid in the back, who was at the farmers' arrest.

***

On Monday, Jacob received Den Toom's order by courier to submit attendance lists for each day of the past week. He didn't lose any time and reported all crew members present on the job according to schedule, and returned the attendance forms with the courier. That job completed, he called in Peters.

He frowned. "Sit down. Where were you Friday night? Didn't I tell you to stand guard at the Mayor's office?"

Peters seemed to have cold hands and had them tucked in his pockets, glanced at him briefly, then looked out the window and said: "Oh, that. Yes, I did. I left when the Mayor told me I could leave. Had a beer at the hotel bar."

With an impatient jerk of his head, Jacob demanded to know: "What's to see outside? Look at me, man. Oh, so the mayor is your boss now? You didn't return to the brigade either. When I tell you to stand watch you do that and nothing else, until I dismiss you. Understood? I'm deducting a half-day of pay as your consequence of dereliction of duty. Dismissed." With disgust on his face, he ignored Peters and went back to his paperwork. Peters got up, slithered out of the room, and softly closed the door behind him.

***

The previous night, Jacob had heard from the Radio Orange broadcast that most employers had used the phrase *absent with good reason* for strikers, so he had used it for his crew today. A decent number of other employers simply refused to submit anything. News of their gutsy response ran through the country's offices with the speed of a snake's strike.

"Good for them to take a principled stand. I respect them," Jacob said when Leversma brought him the news.

Van Houten, always well informed, was the first to bring up what followed next. "Did you hear the latest about the Limburg mine directors? That viper Rauter had the SD arrest them."

An hour later, after his call with Hansen in The Hague, Jacob had more news to share with the crew. "Rauter sentenced ten mining CEOs to the death penalty. I hope Rauter finds a way to commute the verdict, or else the Illegality just might...." Before he could finish his sentence, a brick crashed through one of the windows of the squad room. It landed at his feet, leaving a shattering of broken glass on the floor.

Leversma ran outside. When he returned to the squad room, he reported no sign of the perpetrator. With a big smile on his face, he said: "Chief, I think our villagers want us to do something about the raids. Any ideas how we could boil that German swine and stick a fork in it?"

"Shut your mouth and clean up the mess," Jacob replied in a sober tone.

Van Houten smiled, shook his head, and winked at Leversma. Jacob saw it. He didn't comment and disappeared into his private office but couldn't help hearing Van Houten's comment. "The boss doesn't appreciate our input."

Jacob heard both men laugh as if they knew better. He appreciated the affection, but it was also dangerous in an office with potential traitors.

***

That Monday, four days into the strike, Jacob gathered his crew. The members were chatting quietly in small groups of two or three to discuss the increasingly disastrous news as the day went by. They updated each other informally, then went back to work.

Around four in the afternoon, Van Houten came to see Jacob in his office, plunked himself into the chair looking disheveled, as if he hadn't slept and bathed in a while. His jaunty mood of that first morning had disappeared, and he seemed to have trouble finding the words.

"Fifteen strikers in Haaksbergen were arrested today. On their way to jail in Enschede, the SD bastards shot seven men in the back, after letting them out of the van telling them to make a run for it, like a hunting game. The sons of bitches. Three of them escaped, and one of them went home, the stupid jerk. Of course, the SD found him there and executed him on the spot in front of his family. Isn't there anything we can do? I'm ready to go to their office, go on a rampage and kill them all."

Jacob got up, left his chair and stood beside his deputy. Looking down on his sergeant he replied in a stern voice.

"Sergeant, I know what you mean, but it would be the end of you. We just have to sit tight. I hear this sort of thing is happening all over the country. Let's just wait for our chance. It will come, one day soon, I'm sure of it, when we will have decent weapons to fight back with, and I want you alive for that day. Go home, rest up. Take a bath." He briefly laid a hand on Van Houten's shoulder, then opened the door, grabbed him by the upper arm, and walked the desolate man out of the office.

Before leaving for home, he instructed his men to keep their eyes open, to stay vigilant on and off the job, and be careful on their way through town. That night, on his knees in front of the bed, he prayed for the strike to end. It became another sleepless night.

***

The next day, a Tuesday, Jacob let the crew know last night's news, standing before them in the squad room. "Radio Orange reported more than 400 strikers were severely injured." Most knew about it already.

When he saw the Reich's Office's delivery man with the mail, he knew Governor Seyss-Inquart's retaliation had begun. Like all other brigade chiefs, Jacob received a list with a notice of the execution of 80 strikers. Their names were printed on posters the SD had distributed throughout the nation. The crew looked with grim faces at the list as they circulated it among them, passing it from hand to hand without comment.

***

By Wednesday, the strike was over. Jacob heard from the mayor that many other mayors had lost their jobs. Henk told him that the enemy-aligned managers in the civil service had sacked more than a hundred public servants for refusing to collaborate with the strike-busting. This level of brutality had never been seen before in a strike. That day, Jacob didn't insist on completing paperwork and frequently joined his men in the squad room, sharing their concerns or just listening.

Van Houten clarified: "Seyss-Inquart commuted thirty-six death sentences to a lower sentence. The viper called it a gesture of goodwill to the Dutch. Guess what? Those were the CEOs who at first refused to submit attendance lists. The manipulative bastard didn't mention that the SD had already shot ninety-five more strikers in the streets that day."

Jacob added: "My contact in The Hague said that many dozens are still in jail, all sentenced to death. I wonder what'll happen to them. They must be praying for a commuted sentence. We should pray for them too."

De Wit replied: "We will. But why did Hirschfeldt allow it? You'd think the head of Labor, Trades and Economy would be more understanding. As a Jew himself he'd undoubtedly be aware of the misery of his fellow Jews. It's unbelievable."

The sergeant summarized it succinctly: "Business as usual, the way a capitalist society works, even an occupied one," and he spat on the plank floor of the squad room.

Jacob let it pass. "After the war, he'll be called on to answer for his conduct," was all he could come up with.

For now, defeated, the men tried to go back to work, but with growing anger in their hearts, waiting for an opportunity to release it. Meanwhile, Jacob was brooding on making his plans.

Chapter 66

The second strike and its disastrous aftermath revived the spirit of resistance. The nation's citizens were animated with a wave of anger, determined it was time to end this German madness. The Illegality grew by the day. Many burghers were leading alternative lives, and the covert planning activities to provide for the members of the Resistance influenced every-day-life. It was called the *ondergrondse* [the underground], hoovering like an invisible, magical mantel over the nation. As Nazi terrorism reigned the country, citizens disappeared in large numbers to join the invisible anti-terrorism force.

One evening, Jacob sat resting next to Margaret on the divan after the censored ANP newscast had finished. He took her hand and spoke in a gentle tone of voice: "What would you say, if I went into the underground?"

She looked up and stared at him. "You mean in hiding? Attacking Germans, blowing them up? We've been through this. Why would you do this now?"

Jacob looked down at her hand, covered by his. "You know my job is getting harder. I've talked enough about it. Dikkers' uncle got shot. I defied Feenstra's order. He let it go this time. I'll continue to do whatever I can to get people off from arrests by the SD, but then we also have the KK here. There's only so much I can do on the job. The risks for me are getting higher." He didn't tell her about the risk of getting caught passing on information to the Illegality or having to potentially drop his cover to save somebody.

He looked up and saw a frown on Margaret's forehead.

"What's wrong? Don't you want me to pass on the news from Radio Orange? How else are you — sitting at home — going to know what's going on in the world? Did you know a National Organization for Hiders exists to provide for those in hiding? The North-East Polder is now known as Hiders' Heaven."

She still faced him but bent her upper body backward as far as she could manage without falling off the divan.

"Sure, I do. Don't mind me. I'm just a housewife." She got up from the divan and grabbed a pile of laundry from a chair, and dumped it on the table. Some pieces fell on the floor, and she ignored those.

Jacob didn't recognize the signs of Margaret getting angry. "I've got nothing good to expect from the job, relegated as we are to functioning as instruments of the Nazis. I was thinking I'd be more useful if I disappeared, like Henk."

He stopped talking and studied her face while smoking his awful-smelling, locally-made cigar. He wasn't used to having to explain himself to her. He stayed silent on how disappearing would make things easier on his conscience. His religion would tell him that his life goals should be doing God's will, practicing humility and selfless love. Happiness was not included. How to put that in practice was a mystery to him, but staying on the job certainly wouldn't get him there. What would be God's will anyway?

Margaret thought for a few seconds, then replied: "Henk is a show-off and was always reckless. You're not him. Getting back to what you said. What kind of things does the Resistance do? And what will you wear?" Her face showed a certain measure of doubt, and an ironic smile curled at her lips with her last question. She looked at Jacob with her head slanted sideways.

He sensed irony in her voice. He dismissed it. Margaret always said she liked him in uniform, and the idea of him dressed in some worn civil garb obviously didn't appeal to her. He ignored her skepticism and her last facetious comment. Oblivious, he prattled on.

"Well, for instance, I could work for the Organization for Assistance to Hiders, or the Council For Resistance, the RVV. I could steal food coupons and ID papers and rob the offices of the distribution system. People in hiding need to eat, and they need an illegal ID. And money is needed, lots of it, gotten legally or illegally."

"My God, you don't mean it. You, of all people, you'd rob a bank, would you?" She stood looking at him from a distance, holding a piece of laundry.

"*Ja*, I mean it. How else do you think the Allied pilots are kept alive and travel back to England? National Fight Groups, called KPs do that sort of thing. I'd do good joining them, and let's be honest, I'm in good shape with my boxing skills. I'm well suited."

This was one of the few times he'd been honest with Margaret instead of protecting her by keeping the facts to himself. He had no idea what really went on in her head. She usually tried to please him, but not this time. She just stared at him. Finally, she spoke.

"You must've completely gone crazy. It's more than dangerous, it's suicidal. If the SS or SD catches you or somebody else betrays you, you'll be killed. And what about our family? What'd I do without you? Stay here by myself with our children?" Her movements got choppier, throwing things after she folded them into the basket so that they fell apart again. It was becoming a mess.

"Well, what I told you already: go to your mother. You have your precious family." He stated it as a very matter-of-fact.

"You, jerk," Margaret burst out, "Yes, they are my beloved relatives, but you are my family too. Did you forget Elfriede and her two boys are staying with my mother? I can't go live there with three kids. Mutter only got a bedroom downstairs, and one in the attic, as you well know. Where would we all sleep? The attic is not even insulated." Turning her back to him, she resumed the laundry job.

Jacob scoffed. He didn't quite know why he was such a jerk, only knew he wanted to push. "Oh, come on now! There's lots of room on the farm."

Margaret didn't answer. He wasn't sure whether she was going to cry or run away. In a more conciliatory tone he pleaded with her. "You said yourself you had it ready for Ruth and her kids. We could put some bunk beds there for all the kids and put a fold-a-bed in the living room, or in the stables, or insulate the attic. You could just say we're separated and I left you for somebody else."

Done folding laundry, she got up and walked through the open door into the kitchen while talking. "The German security services might harass me, trying to find out where you are. The first place they'd go is to my mother."

He called out his answer, and a second after he said it, he regretted saying it. "Oh, so now you're concerned about the Germans?"

She stood by the door, eyes flickering, hands balled into fists. "Of course, I am. You think I'm blind? I hear things. I know what happened to Ruth's husband." Then she nodded as if she'd decided something and continued talking as she stepped back into the living room. "Since we're honest with each other: Charles Nauwaard is not the man you think he is. I don't like you being so chummy with him, or with the

Wehrmacht lieutenant, for that matter. They act nice in my face now, but what if you go into hiding? They won't be nice then."

Her hair had fallen over her forehead, and she brushed it away impatiently. She sat down on the far end of the divan across from Jacob. She spoke, coolly and distanced. "If you feel you have to, go into hiding and join the KP then."

Jacob didn't believe her feigned indifference. He stayed seated, put on his most earnest face, and grabbed her hand again, holding it more forcefully.

Margaret flinched and softly whispered, "Ouch." He loosened his grip.

"You must know I don't want to arrest innocent people knowing I'll be sending them to their death in the camps. I wasn't adequately prepared with the first raid to stop it, but now I am. What if I get fired when Feenstra finds out I disobeyed his orders? Or arrested? In that case, you'll lose me too, just as if I were in hiding, no difference."

Margaret didn't answer and looked at him, disbelief on her face.

Jacob continued. "But one difference is, when I'm in hiding, I can help you through my connections. The Illegality will help you. I'll make sure of it."

"But why now? You've worked above-ground all this time. Can't you do it a bit longer? The boys will miss you terribly."

Jacob kept his cigar alive by taking a succession of drags as if his life depended on it, drawing clouds of smoke, more so than with a good cigar, and Margaret disappeared behind the clouds. "The time is ripe now. Things are getting much worse. Deputy Schrieke died of a heart attack. His second in command, Hooijkaas, isn't a stand-up guy. Now we have Boellard as inspector, a traitor. My commissioner and my department head turned out to be a Nazi-lovers. I can't tell you exactly what, but things are bad."

Margaret got ready to stand up and leave, but Jacob had to vent and wasn't to be stopped now. He grabbed her by her arm and pulled her down on the divan.

"Wait. Remember Adjutant Kaasjager, division commander? You met him at the formal photograph sitting. You liked his wife, Madeleine. When he refused to make arrests, he was promptly fired. From now on, I'll refuse too. Being fired might be the least of it. Being shot is a real option, depending whom I'm faced with. Don't think I am just saying this, I mean it."

Margaret got up, and he had to let go of her arm. She went into the kitchen, leaving the folded laundry pile behind.

Jacob called after her: "Don't worry, dear, I won't abandon you."

She returned a few minutes later and sat beside him.

Jacob put an arm around her, and she turned closer. He was making headway with her. She was softening up. "You don't have to be afraid for Heusden and Nauwaard. They're basically harmless to us. They told me they just want to survive the war. Even Nauwaard, as I read him. He's already sorry he started working for the SD and now he's afraid to quit. Did you know his wife left him?"

Margaret continued to just stare at him.

He felt her fingers relaxing. He swung his legs onto the divan and cuddled up beside her. "How are the kids? I don't get to see them a lot lately."

Immediately, her face became more animated; a half-smile played around her mouth while she spoke. "The kids are fine. We have a good time with Elfriede's boys when we get together, although I know they miss you, especially Hendrik. He can be hard for me to handle. The other day he'd gotten hold of your cigar box and was lighting a cigar." Margaret's smile grew larger.

He smiled too. "Darned kid. He didn't learn from the fire at the farm. I'll have to hide my cigars, especially the matches. From now on I'll lock them in my roll-top desk." He took his pocket knife out and started cleaning his nails that were already perfectly trimmed.

"I wish you'd come home before six, then you could take him for a trip on your bike. He loves it. Since Elly's birth he feels sidelined in your attention. How about you calling in sick once in a while?" She took her lab coat off and folded it, holding it on her lap, and pushed her hair with her hands to give it shape.

"I hate to bring this to you. The clever Rauter also stopped that, since many of my colleagues, or their wives, had the same idea as you. Sick days were up significantly in the force, especially long-term illness. If we're reported sick for more than twenty-four hours now, we'll have to hand in our service weapon and uniform, so it means a suspension without pay. Calling in sick won't work."

Jacob didn't tell Margaret about his membership in Simon's group. He didn't mention that police boss Rauter had ordered the arrest of all direct relatives of officers who failed to turn up for work. Their wives and children had been taken to Camp Vught to be held hostage until their husbands showed up on the job.

They kept talking for a while, sharing their worlds — or at least partially — confident and happy about their renewed intimacy until it was time for bed. Jacob carefully hung his new uniform of the State Police on a hanger, upstairs in the closet. He hummed a psalm and washed his hands and face.

Chapter 67

Margaret was always busy with jobs, the laundry taking the most time of all out of her week. Three days, it took: one for soaking, prewashing, and washing by hand on a washboard. Another day for drying, and hopefully, the weather would be good; otherwise, on frosty days, the laundry had to be hauled up to the unheated attic, and it would hang there frozen stiff. That was followed by a third day for ironing. Not much time was left for playing with the children or planning meals, let alone visiting, but she always found time for her turn at the courier job. Good thing Jacob wasn't all that demanding about the quality of his dinner that he didn't have to cook. He was okay with any food that she put in front of him unless the potatoes were burnt.

A few other blessings in her life had materialized. The minor irritation of his harassment about her closeness with Johanna and Juergen had stopped. They were good to her, and this benefited the whole family. The Wehrmacht's door-to-door collection of all radios had not ended her listening time, thanks to Johanna's permit, and she enjoyed her time with Elfriede. Occasionally, Johanna joined them in the backhouse, where all three of them laid down to rest in the hay while Juergen looked after the boys.

She suspected that Van Houten, who had got her the contacts, might let on to Jacob eventually about Elfriede's courier job since the men had grown close. After one successful day of deliveries, Elfriede told her: "I'm so happy we can manage this job, aren't you? I feel more satisfied with life. Doing this is a chance of a lifetime. Even if the rest of our lives is awful, I love doing this with you."

Margaret confessed, as her sister saw through her anyway: "I agree, dear sis. We're being useful, and honestly, leading Jacob down the garden path feels good. All for the good cause, of course. But I am not lying, just not telling everything." She winked at her sister.

Elfriede chuckled. "Oh, Gretchen, you Goody-Two-Shoes. You're funny. That's a complicated way of putting one over on your man."

They had a good laugh, forgetting the disastrous circumstances in their lives for a while.

***

At night, while Margaret was still putting laundry away, Jacob went to bed. He anticipated her giving in to him, as she usually did. Not much would change for her with his going underground. To keep her safe from the SD, he couldn't just disappear but would have to quit his job first to get Rauter and the SD off his back, and she'd move in with Johanna.

At her mother's place, Margaret would process the vegetables from Johanna's farm in canning jars, like always. Rows of glassed-in beans from last fall's harvest still lined the shelves in the cellar. The potato bin was full of potatoes. The farm had an in-ground cold room in the backyard full of carrots, beets and cabbages.

They hadn't faced hunger yet, and most likely wouldn't in the next year either. Jacob's absence wouldn't change it. He was glad he hadn't pushed Margaret to choose between her mother and him. Family, in some ways, had caused the most conflict between them, but he also relied on them. So be it: resisting the Nazis was worth a family fight.

He was no longer prepared to walk the tightrope of his present life with no benefits but so much risk. If he put his life on the line with resisting the Nazi regime, the benefits should be substantial and make a difference in their lives. Satisfied with how his talk with Margaret had gone and in the delusion he would soon follow Henk's example, he faded off into sleep, while Margaret still rummaged around somewhere in the house at some household job.

Chapter 68

Jacob exploited his freedom of mobility courtesy of his job, and he obtained much detailed intelligence on Wehrmacht positions and strategies. Heusden didn't care one iota about the local police, so long as Jacob could satisfy him of the reason for his presence at military sites. Knowing Jacob's German wife and his pro-German in-laws, the Nazi captain seldom asked him difficult questions. He must've forgiven Jacob's resistance, as he was now as friendly as ever. Heusden surely must assume he'd tamed the chief of police.

Counting on the goodwill between them, Jacob tested Heusden about the KK crew. Having a beer together in the hotel bar, he told Heusden in confidence that his skin would crawl when he accidentally ran into Schwier's man-hunters. Heusden just nodded, then said he couldn't get stuck between the police and the camp's delegates; that was Rauter's business. Heusden sucked his beer back and left immediately as if Jacob had made him an indecent proposition. So much for help in controlling the KK from that side.

***

Jacob met with Henk in the forest that evening. Jacob rode his bicycle, and enviously saw that Henk rode out on his motorbike. Only riding at night, Henk hadn't been caught yet. On this mild summer night, they were both dressed in dark-colored civvies.

"Thanks for those details on the Wehrmacht positions, Jacob, so helpful to us. Our priorities are changing rapidly, with the Allied initiative intensifying. I like what I see. You?" Henk offered Jacob a cigar, while he filled a pipe with tobacco for himself.

"Thanks. It's been a while since I had a real cigar. You need to ask? Yup. I can't wait to have the Allied troops closer."

Henk poured French brandy into two Bakelite cups from a flask he fished from his motorbike's saddlebag. "Let's drink to the Allies." Somehow, he always happened to stumble on some good liquor and smokes during his Illegality adventures.

Buoyed by this good news and the brandy, they lay on their backs in the heather, smoking their tobacco rewards of the week, excitedly discussing the ins and out of the recent Allied battles.

On an impulse, Jacob asked Henk whether he had given his wife any say in his decision to go into hiding.

"No. It's my responsibility only. I can't offload this onto my wife. Of course, your position is different from mine, and you happen to be in the thick of law and order. You've got no way around having to deal directly with whatever law the Nazis want to see enforced. I don't know how you cope with it."

Jacob liked the answer about decision-making. He tried to read Henk's face in the shimmery light of the moon to see what he meant about dealing with the Nazi decrees. Henk was always much less fearful and more adventurous than him, maybe even light-hearted. He envied him. "Thanks, but what about Juergen, and your mother? Do you ever consider what they might think, or, more importantly say about you, especially to certain others?"

Henk grunted. "Ach, what could they do? They don't know where I am, or what I'm thinking, and they wouldn't dare rat on their own brother and son anyway. Anyway, Mutter is now looking after Elfriede and her boys. Don't worry about them, Jacob. What about your relatives. Where are they? Who are they; any of them in the Resistance? Mind you, you've got bigger problems with those KK monsters, and that bastard Schwier with his sadistic henchman, Kapo Bakker, and not to forget sissy Nauwaard, who can't control his men."

In a thoughtful voice, Jacob said: "You got that right. They terrify me, but so far, I haven't been threatened, and am keeping my fingers crossed. About my relatives. I have some brothers who are involved. My uncle and aunt on my father's side live in Westland. They are with the black stockings church. After my mom's death, my father joined also, until his death. I'm not fundamentalist enough for them, we didn't visit," Jacob grinned.

Henk laughed and said: "Hard to imagine. You're too Christian to me, good man." Then took a swill of his cup. "Too bad we had to get rid of all those guns. We'd already have a defense team together. I did tell you about the guns, didn't I?"

Jacob sat up and turned to Henk. "No, I don't know that story."

Henk was a natural storyteller. Jacob could tell he loved the attention of an audience.

"After the capitulation, the mayor and his two town constables collected all long-barreled guns, mainly hunting rifles and also some pistols and they stored those in the townhall. As the fire brigade commander, I've got a key. One night, a firefighter and I took those guns out of storage and dumped them all in the river. Better rusting in the Vecht than ending up in Nazi hands."

"No, you didn't."

Henk laughed heartily. "Sure did."

It was quiet for the moment. Both laid back, enjoying the silence and the drinks, a rare moment to relax, each with lives to reflect on.

Henk sounded much more self-confident than Jacob ever had felt — even before the war — and he started comparing what might be the cause. He had worked in his father's grocery store after primary school because too many children at home prevented any kids from pursuing advanced education. Self-study had been his education, reading whatever books he could lay his hands on, and that included the new library in his parents' town, supplemented by what he could borrow from the minister of his mother's Dutch Reformed church.

Jacob remembered his first impression of Margaret's brother at his initial visit to Margaret's family. He saw an entitled, self-satisfied twerp with his higher education that Johanna bragged about. Re-evaluating his old life, he had to admit that maybe he was envious of the guy. Things certainly had changed between them. Henk was the most trusted man in his life now, an older man, and this bond with Henk was a different experience than he had with his own brothers.

Margaret's siblings had more education. It made him the country bumpkin from the Westland, if not for his military training. In Johanna's eyes, he still didn't measure up compared to her own, successful children. What did he care? Johanna — a Hitler lover — wasn't known for her excellent judgement. Her superficial sentimentality about her home country had turned her into a blind fool. She should be grateful for finding refuge in Holland with a Dutch husband and even owning land. Maybe she wasn't feeling as secure as he'd always thought and was more like him.

His own family had been slaving away for generations, building dykes, backbreaking work on the bulb fields, and growing vegetables on land they didn't own. They had made rich bastards even wealthier in the town of 's Gravenzande — literally: the Dukes' sands. Lucky for him his father had married one of the rich girls of the wealthy grower Bakkenes.

Geziena Bakkenes' very modest inheritance as the daughter and not a son got his dad only a starting fund for a store through his marriage. Too bad for him, the store hadn't earned more. The depression and the economic downturn interfered with earnings. Maybe not so strange that his father hadn't wanted to socialize with his wife's wealthy relatives.

Jacob suddenly realized the similarity between his father and him — envious of his in-laws. Father had tried to preserve his dignity by discouraging his children to avoid the rich and self-satisfied in-laws, as he called them, to prevent comparison. After leaving his parents' home, Jacob could've started to visit his mom's relatives but hadn't. It dawned on him he'd just followed his father's example — easier to accept his authority than fighting it, a habit coming home to roost now. Goddamn, that's why he has so much mixed feelings about defying Feenstra's authority — only now, he can't run away from it.

His train of thought got interrupted when Henk got up and put his cup away.

"What are you thinking, brother? Jacob, I got exciting news about those promised British weapon drops: they've already started in the west. It'll be our turn soon. Marconist is our emergency radio contact, but the regular drops will be announced in code via Radio Orange. I'll take care of it." Almost as an afterthought, he added: "They made me regional commander."

Jacob got up, grabbed his brother-in-law's hand, and shook it vigorously. "Congratulations, Commander, you deserve it. You're a born leader."

Henk interrupted him and pulled his hand back. "Alright brother. No big deal. We all do what we can."

They both sat down again on the ground and stretched their legs out in front of them.

"Yes, we do need weapons," Jacob agreed. "I fear it's only a matter of time before Rauter takes our police arsenal from us everywhere. My biggest worry is being shot before the Allies arrive. I was thinking about your family and mine just a minute ago. You got lucky you got an education."

Henk nodded. "Uhm-hum, that's because my parents worked hard in Germany and had saved enough to buy that farm and a house. The children didn't have to go to work right-away, and got a few years of secondary education — if we wanted it," and he remembered something else. With delight in his voice, he went on: "Say, did you know all Illegality branches are now combined? We are the new army with the moniker *Nederlandse Binnenlandse Strijdkracht*, the NBS — Dutch Interior Force. The commanders of all cells got notice."

"No, I didn't know. Thanks. That's a sign of progress. Good to be part of the army again," Jacob said dreamily.

Henk then asked him the crucial question that had played so much on Jacob's conscience.

"Well, what do you say, my man, it's now or never. You have so far been all above-ground, and you've told me of your agreement with Margaret about not going into hiding."

Jacob couldn't completely hide his eagerness when he interrupted. "Never mind Margaret. Actually, Henk, I joined my sergeant's group. There's one more man on my crew who's a member. Our Commander Simon says it's better I'd stay clean and in the public eye, so I can protect them."

"Now, that is news. Simon hasn't let on about it to me. Good man." Henk punched him on the arm.

Since Henk was now his official High Command, he elaborated on his activities on the new role. "Simon says he needs me to divert attention from the group and bail them out, if needed. I suspected some actions were happening, but Van Houten, my sergeant, doesn't tell me, and I don't need to know. I haven't been in any sabotage actions yet, but try to cover for the others."

"Excellent. That needs another toast." Henk got up to grab the flask. "You keep doing what you always do. I'll leave it up to Simon. That Nauwaard and Heusden trust you, works for us. It'll be essential to know the plans of Schwier's bastards, as they're the real danger to the Illegality around here." He poured Jacob another drink. "Cheers." He drank from the flask.

Jacob swallowed and enjoyed the burning liquid traveling down his throat and into his esophagus. "Piece of cake," he said. "I'm just not sure how much they trust me. My sergeant and I keep track on a daily basis. We're on top of any developments."

Henk was all about business. "Don't worry about the air drops, my group will take care of it, but you with some reliable men might have to distract the KK and the Wehrmacht patrols. As long as the coast is clear, we can disperse quickly. My men will make sure the loot gets to where it should go. It's time to take back the nation from the Nazis, brother." He chuckled.

Jacob laughed with him but softly. They rose from the heather and, slightly drunk, slapped each other on the back, hard, until it hurt. They had trouble keeping their voices down, buoyant with the idea of the end of war arriving before the winter.

Henk grabbed his upper arm. He could see Henk's eyes shining in the dark and felt the pressure on his arm, which didn't let up. Jacob turned and put his other arm on Henk's shoulder, facing him. In a solemn voice, he replied: "I'll do as you ask. I can't stand by while you and others put yourselves at risk."

Henk let go of his arm and gave him another slap on his back.

Jacob's voice was not as firm as he would've liked. "About Nauwaard, I think — I hope — he trusts me, and about Heusden, the Wehrmacht guy, he's also not interested in pursuing any nastiness."

"Good to hear. Time to go now."

Jacob wasn't finished talking. "The KK is another matter, even without weapons. The Ordnungspolizei took those from them when they raided the camp and arrested Nauwaard. They only held him for a week. I fear Schwier will give those weapons back. He needs the KK for his own hunting trips finding Illegals. Dismantling the KK might be too much to hope for. The difference is they work no longer for Justice, so no judges are holding them accountable anymore. We'll need bigger guns trying to stop those demons."

"Alright, we're aware of it. We'll find a way to eliminate them. Got to go now."

The men embraced again briefly, right shoulder to the right shoulder, a sentimental gesture completely against their natures, but both needed to seal their commitment. As always thorough in his methods, Jacob was not finished yet.

"Just one more thing, making sure we both know the consequence. I'll help when possible, but can't prevent the SD from killing anybody. If the SD finds those British weapons on someone, it means a death sentence for all involved. You need to tell this to your men. Agreed, Henk?"

"Agreed."

"Another thing, if a Kraut stops anybody with contraband with me present, I wouldn't be able to do anything. It would be the end of my cover. You realize that, right?"

"God, you're a pain. Alright, understood already. We all have our decisions to make. So be it. I accept those limits."

Jacob took his fedora off, stroked his head slowly, then replaced the hat, and exhaled deeply.

The shrill whistle of a night predator in the vicinity pierced the night. They both fell still and listened intently, not moving at all. The whistle sounded again, three times in quick succession. Henk had a come with a buddy.

"Alright, here's the sign, talking about the devil," whispered Henk, and he disappeared into the shadows, pushing his motorbike along. A few minutes later, a two-tact motor's rumble started up and faded away in the distance.

Ten minutes later, Jacob — virtually invisible in dark brown — got up, picked up his bicycle, and rode home at his leisure in good spirits.

Chapter 69

On a foggy Saturday, a tragedy played out in the sky over Overdam in the early morning hours. A steady stream of Allied bombers buzzed their way through the air traveling east towards coastal Germany, accompanied by many fighters. The sound abruptly changed from its droning equilibrium to a fast-approaching, high whine right over the burghers' heads. The brisk rat-ta-ta of big-gun fire burst from all directions, stressing the spectators on the ground. They anxiously looked at the sky, trying to see something through the misty layers of varying density.

Working in his office, Jacob heard through the open windows the engines of several planes diving and climbing. The changes in the engines' sounds as the planes jockeyed in midair alerted him to an unusual event taking place. The crew members ran outside and scanned the foggy sky. Not a minute later, all watchers heard and felt a big explosion and ran for cover while plane parts flew through the air, slowly landing over an unusually vast area.

Jacob and his crew sped on their bicycles in the direction of the explosion. With other searchers' help, they found one debris site in the hamlet of Arrien near Overdam and another outside the Overdam boundaries near Dalfsen.

Corporal Peters and new recruit Van der Gulik accompanied Jacob to the Arrien site. The chief sent his other men to the second site. Commensurate with the orders from the Reich's Office for just such an occasion, Jacob did his job: "Close it off to the public, locate the dead, arrest any survivors, and protect the area from looters. Collect all parts and sensitive documentation. When we're ready for it, I'll inform the Wehrmacht." Resistance to the order wasn't worth the punishment of deportation to Germany, although somehow never anything worthwhile remained to hand over from a crash site.

Within minutes of the crew's arrival, the mayor and Air Defense chief Piet Koster joined them with two other Air Defense members. They set out on the rescue mission and dispersed across the field. It was dead-quiet, now that all droning sounds had disappeared.

After a few minutes, Peters yelled out. "Chief, I found somebody."

Jacob ran towards him. A black, mangled thing not resembling a person had sunk in the grass, a few feet from the plane. The incinerated body was unrecognizable.

"Looks like the poor bastard died instantly in the explosion. He must've been dead before he hit the ground," Peters concluded. He looked a little pale. "Poor chap, but in a way lucky. He didn't suffer."

"Thanks, Peters," Jacob cut him off.

What more was there to say? The smell of burnt meat permeated the air all around them. Jacob looked at the recruit, whose face was as white as the skiff of wet snow in the rows of the plowed field. A second later, Van der Gulik ran away to vomit.

When he returned, he looked at Jacob and said sheepishly, "Sorry boss."

"No problem. Van der Gulik, go look for the rest of the plane wreck, see if anything is still salvageable. It'll keep you busy. Papers are important."

The three marechaussees looked for IDs, dog tags, papers, and anything else that might indicate who was killed. They collected what artifacts they found, and put them in a cardboard box from the mayor's vehicle. Mayor Van Voorst got blankets and carefully draped one over the corpse. Under Jacob's instruction, the Air Defense boss and his crew helped cordon off the large debris field.

"Koster, I'll inform the Wehrmacht later. Could your men stay here until they arrive? Alright with you, Mayor?"

"Yes Chief, that's fine."

The smell of metal mixed with smoke, freshly plowed dirt, and mowed grass hung in the air, which didn't cover the sickeningly sweet fragrance of the burnt flyer.

"Go look in the fields. There must've been more crew members. Buckle up Van der Gulik and keep breathing. You'll get used to it. The war's not over yet, son."

While the mayor stayed with the Air Defense crew, Jacob went on the search with his men. He didn't feel good himself.

They found two more bodies. One flyer had been thrown with force into the soil, his body forced an inch-deep into the soft grass, his limbs in positions not humanly possible. The remains looked like a prop in a lousy movie but less burnt than the first man.

The third corpse was hidden under a piece of the wreckage and had to be extracted from it. A fourth man had to help the three policemen forcing up the wing, still attached to the fuselage part and half buried in the soil before the body could be recovered. If other crew members had survived the crash, they weren't near the wreckage.

Jacob collected several weapons. The whole area was searched for anything that the Germans could use. The men then carried the bodies on blankets nearer the road for the undertaker. The valuables disappeared into the mayor's trunk to never arrive at the Wehrmacht station. With muddy boots and dirty hands, both crews stood silently around the crash victims, covered with more blankets from the mayor. These had been young men, defeated by the ultimate enemy: death.

Van der Gulik's face was streaked with smudges. Peters was scouring the skies, although no sound could be heard. Koster's lips moved in silent prayer, hands folded in front of his chest with closed eyes. Jacob was reluctant to break the silence but staying in the face of the carnage was also excruciating.

"Let's leave the honor guard to Koster's crew. We're finished and can leave now. Attention!" All saluted in the military custom.

The mayor wanted to say a prayer. Jacob's softly spoke his command: "At ease."

"Dear God, we commend these brave men into your care. Amen." Then Mayor Van Voorst left with the box of collected items and various valuables in his trunk.

Without another word, the three policemen left the crash site on their bicycles, their part of the recovery mission completed.

The wreck was an American plane, a Boeing/B-17, nicknamed the Flying Fortress for its firing power. It had exploded midair; its usual escort of American Liberator fighters unable to save it in the fog. The policemen pedaled home in silence. Jacob thought about the terrible grief of the young soldiers' loved ones when they would be notified.

**

The Dalfsen crew under Van Houten's leadership had found four more American bodies at the other crash site. The crew members sat around the squad room, listlessly shuffling a piece of paper here and there, but otherwise quiet. Van Houten said prosaically, himself not much older, "It really doesn't matter whose side you fight for. Death is the great equalizer that came too soon for these young lads."

An hour later, Jacob informed the Wehrmacht: nothing much left at the site to hand over. Van Heusden released the bodies to the funeral home for burial shortly after.

Chapter 70

Later in the afternoon, another call came in. Jacob listened, nodded, sighed loudly, then disconnected. He called young Van den Berg into his office: "There's an American flyer at a farm, he's injured. Go tell the mayor, but make sure nobody else at the townhall hears your message." Within ten minutes, Van Voorst arrived at the brigade in his vehicle, and off they went to see the soldier.

At the specified farm, they found a young man dressed in brown flyer coveralls. He sat with his leg resting on a pouf in the living room, the portion of his pants cut open and flaps of material hanging down. The farmer's wife said she had fed him, applied a bandage on the cut, and had tried to share what she and her family knew about other allied pilots escaping to England. Then she left to give the visitors privacy.

Introducing himself with his full name, Mayor Van Voorst Tot Voorst took the lead, as his English was good. Van Voorst stood with his arms folded over his chest in front of the young American. Jacob stood next to him with his hands stuffed in his pants pockets, observing, leaving it all up to the mayor.

The pilot said he was Francis, the gunner of a B15 crew. He flew with six other men but had no idea where they were. Able to jump from the plane in time, he had unfortunately poorly landed on one foot, and the other had been caught on the barbwire.

The mayor informed him that a police officer would take Francis to a city hospital for proper treatment. "Would you be up to returning to England?" When he got no answer, he tried again: "What do you propose?"

Jacob noticed a small stack with civilian clothes beside the injured man on the floor. The guy seemed out of it, unfocused, whether from the shock of the crash or something else was not clear.

The mayor asked him again. "Is your injury severe, would you need a hospital? No problem, we'll take you there, but you will be officially reported, and become a POW then. You understand?"

Finally, the poor guy seemed to shake it off and answered the questions.

"I honestly don't know. Doesn't seem to be broken, probably just bruised. Where are my men? Were any of the crew found? Could you tell me, please? I went down somewhere in the fields, and didn't see any sign of my plane through that goddamn fog. An explosion just after I jumped pushed me off farther." He sank back and stared out the window.

Jacob and Van Voorst quietly discussed what to do with the man, as his injury was clearly not a break and just needed some time to heal. They concluded it'd be best to take him to Zwolle and for him to stay in the hospital as long as possible. "He might then escape from the hospital with some help, but ask him what he thinks," Jacob said.

The mayor told the young man with a soft voice, "Son, your crew, I'm sorry to say, most were found dead. We found the bodies of some of your crew members at two crash sites. My condolences. I'm so sorry." He put his hand on Francis' shoulder, squeezing it for a moment, then let go. He pulled up a chair beside Sergeant Francis and sat down.

Hearing the news, the young soldier bowed, his hands covering his face, his elbows leaning on his knees.

Jacob grabbed another chair and sat down in front of Francis. Unsure how to proceed, he looked at Van Voorst, and asked the mayor to translate. He spoke directly to Francis.

"What would you want to do? Will you try to make your way back to Allied territory, or would you prefer to become a POW and join the others?"

Francis raised his head and sat up. He looked exhausted, pale, with sweat on his brow and shaky hands. He wiped his face and eyes with both hands. When the mayor had finished translating, Francis didn't take long to answer.

"I'm fine with dropping out of the war. Just let me be a POW. I'm sure it won't be long before we beat the Huns. They're losing all over."

"Okay," Jacob said. "*Kom wit mi.*"

Francis stood up. Leaning on Van Voorst for support, he said he wanted to thank his host.

Jacob opened the best room's door leading to the threshing floor alongside which the cows were stabled. He noticed the heat of the cows, and their smells hit his nose. He called out: "Mevrouw Meulman, *waar bent u*, are you there?"

The widow Meulman came from behind the back, where she was feeding the cows. It was getting close to milking time, and it would be easier to milk them as they ate. She ran the farm together with her mother and her teenage children. Jacob knew the family as hard-working and upstanding members of his church. Mrs. Meulman didn't speak English, so the goodbye was brief but no less heartfelt with a big hug for the soldier. She had picked up the small pile of her dead husband's clothes and pushed it into Francis' hands.

The mayor dropped them both off at the brigade. He had agreed that he or the chief of Air Defense would transport the American soldier to the hospital in Zwolle the following day with a policeman as an escort. The proper central authority of the Wehrmacht there would register Francis as a prisoner of war. The mayor assured Francis he'd be safe. "At least you can take a break and sit out the rest of the war together with your POW comrades."

Francis looked at him with a blank stare without replying.

Jacob shook his head. "You're not yourself yet, son. You need a rest."

Chapter 71

Jacob took Francis first to the office to fill out a form for the essential identification details, and informed the watch commander of that night of the pilot. He received the man's weapon, and stored it in the vault. Then he showed Francis to his cell, leaving the cage door open, and he left the exterior door unlocked as well. "*Frisse lucht* [Fresh air]," he said, opening and closing the door once. Francis' face was still ashen.

He gave the flyer two horse blankets and a pillow, a bar of soap, and a military towel. He signed with his hand to his mouth for mealtime and added, "*Mai wife wil kook.*" Then he left the man to rest up.

Jacob went home across the connecting corridor and stepped into the kitchen, where Margaret had a meal going since it was getting close to six o'clock: the mandatory start of dinner at his home. He quickly explained he had a prisoner in the cell, one of the good soldiers, an American in his twenties and that he had left the cell door open.

"Margaret, the man needs a meal. Do we have extra today? He just survived a plane crash, and all his buddies were killed. The poor guy's exhausted and injured."

She slowly shook her head. "Oh, terrible," she said, "I'm sorry for him."

"A pot of tea would be nice too, and a jug of water. If we still have an aspirin, you can bring him that too, and maybe a toothbrush, if we have one. You can translate for me, if he has any questions. Take the boys too. I bet Hendrik would like to meet a real flyboy, wouldn't you Hendrik?"

The boy sat at the table, wide-eyed, watching his dad.

"Yes, I would," he exclaimed and got off his chair.

"Me too, me too!" Jaap said, not wanting to be any less important than his brother.

"Finish your dinner first and then both of you can go visit with Francis, is his name."

The boys quickly shoveled their food into their mouths, hurriedly said their two-second prayer, and stood already beside the table. "Ready!"

Margaret confirmed she had enough food, but there'd be no leftovers for tomorrow. She and the boys had a brief conversation about what to call the soldier, Sir or Francis. Margaret told them Sir is good form. As Margaret, Hendrik, and Jaap took the meal, the tea, and the water jug to the man in the cellblock, Jacob ate his dinner in peace and quiet.

On her return, Margaret reported that the soldier had been sleeping when they arrived. He woke up on hearing their voices and was visibly surprised to see children. The boys were impressed by his coveralls with the many zippers and pockets, and they both wanted to wear the flyer's cap. Francis found some chewing gum in his pockets and had given the boys the treat. They were in heaven and wanted to stay. Margaret had to drag them home.

***

Jacob heard the exterior door clanking open in the middle of the night, got up himself to go to the bathroom, looked out the bedroom window, and saw Francis stand in the courtyard, staring at the sky. It was a cold and misty, starless, and moonless night, although no sleet or snow was left on the ground. Jacob went back to bed. It took ten minutes before he heard the door closing. He imagined the Gunner having a fitful sleep, probably full of experiences of falling from the sky, being hunted by a Messerschmidtt, and burning alive.

The following day, Jacob brought the captive a breakfast of tea and cheese sandwiches. When he gathered the dirty dishes, Francis said he changed his mind. From what Jacob could make out, Francis wanted to go into hiding and try making it back to his base in Britain.

"I must fight on for my crew mates, in their honor. They'd would want me to."

Jacob nodded. "Stay here," he said, then went to the squad room and returned to the cell with Van Houten.

He introduced the two to each other. "Van Houten, my deputy, a good man," said Jacob, passing the young flyer's care over to his sergeant.

Van Houten placed a couple of calls to get Francis on his way. When it was time to leave, Jacob shook hands with Francis. "Good luck, man." He took a good look at the guy. Francis wore rubber boots, was dressed in woolen farmer's pants, a hip-length, padded jacket of black wool, and a butter-yellow woolen cap topped by a pom-pom, covering his crew-cut. Francis was unrecognizable.

Jacob watched him leave with another farmer, who'd take Francis to his hiding spot, then returned to the office to write the crash report with a smile on his face.

***

A few days later, the report was completed.

The investigation results described the most likely scenario: German fighters pursued the Allied fleet on its way home from bombing several coastal cities in Germany. From witness accounts and the debris spread over an a-typically broad area, it became apparent that a midair collision or at least a battle among several planes had taken place with a direct hit at close distance. The B17 American plane had ten crew members with only six bodies found.

Chapter 72

The following day, Jacob got a call from Nauwaard. "Hey Jake, how are things? Haven't spoken to you in a while. Thought I'd give you a call to catch up." Charles' voice had a strange tension, his tone a new, soft quality with a careful formulation of the words.

Jacob instantly sat up and paid attention. "Good morning. I'm alright — considering the circumstances of an occupation by a foreign army. Have you been keeping on the straight and narrow? And how's your KK crew?" No time but the present to ask the most awkward questions. When people could any second disappear with a gunshot, you might not get a second chance to get the information you need.

"Here's the thing, Jake. I'm calling to warn you about an exotic bird in the woods. Schwier's KK will try to catch him tonight. There's nothing I can do to prevent it, so consider this a last-minute warning. Hope you catch my drift. We should have a beer soon. Call me when you have a chance."

Before Jacob even had a chance to thank him, Nauwaard disconnected. Dang it, all he needed was those beasts on the prowl. Jacob got his drift alright. He closed the office door, picked up the phone, and dialed the operator. After three tries, the operator was still unable to connect him to his contact. What to do now? He could send a note, but who could deliver it? Maybe Van Houten? He got up, opened the door, and called his deputy into his office.

"There's trouble. Do you have a contact number for Francis?"

"No, sorry, Opper. I don't have a number. I don't think there's a phone out there, but I could run out."

"No, I'd put you at risk, and it might lead to other problems. Never mind, I'll find a way. What's the address of the location you took him to?"

Van Houten gave it to him with a shrug and left his office.

Jacob's cover could be blown. He expected no mercy from Schwier and Rauter if any policemen were implicated. He hoped Nauwaard was sincere, and it wasn't a trap. The man couldn't be trusted. Jacob asked the operator to try the number again. Still no answer. He was getting twitchier by the minute and took his jacket off, despite of the cool temperature in his office. He tried to reach Henk via another contact.

A man who identified himself as Tinkerbel answered. Jacob gave the coded greeting: "Peter Pan here." The safety measure was completed, and he asked Tinkerbel if he could send an urgent message to the address of last night's bird, and he provided the location.

"Yes, I could. What's the message?"

"The bird was spotted in the woods and Chuck's bird catchers are out to catch him tonight, if he doesn't fly away before sundown."

Tinkerbel replied: "Yes, I'll give the rookery instructions to let the bird go as soon as possible. Thanks. Bye."

He sat back and relaxed but not completely. He hoped that Bakker wouldn't change his plans and go hunting earlier or that the message wouldn't be misunderstood or delayed for some reason. He prayed that nobody had a flat tire or was held up by controllers. A thousand things could go wrong.

He went home early as Margaret looked sad and worn like she needed some support. These were hard times, and the effects of aging showed on her. Probably on him too. With an unusual sense of premonition, he kept listening for the ring of the phone. He didn't believe in superstition. It was against his religion, but this sensation came close to what he understood the word to mean.

The boys were unruly. Baby Elly was whiny and needed him to rock her in his arms and sing to her. Jacob was good at walking the floor, softly singing a lullaby while gently rocking her to sleep. He scooped her up. "Sleep baby, sleep, in the pasture runs the sheep with white feet and drinks his milk so sweet, sleep baby, sleep." It always worked, even with his deep, never hushed voice. After carefully laying baby Elly in her crib upstairs, he joined the boys in the living room.

Hendrik and Jaap wanted to play cards. Although Jacob's father had frowned on card games as the devil's game, Jacob thought it harmless, and it improved the boys' numbers and memory. He'd teach the boys chess, but they didn't have the attention span for it yet. That night, he received no call.

Chapter 73

The following morning, the telephone rang as soon as Jacob sat down at his desk in his office. The operator connected him to Nauwaard, who tore into him without preliminary niceties.

"What the hell happened yesterday? I told you the crew was on the war path. Bastard Bakker is like a bloodhound. You know he is. Why didn't you take care of it? The intel was solid. They went to the area by the railroad and the goddamn flyboy was still there. They found the effing sod somewhere alone in a vacation cabin. He's here now, not much I can do about it. Damn it, I put myself on the line for you and you botched it. Some mickey mouse operation you run."

"Oh, no." Jacob tried to find the proper tone of voice to calm the warden down. "I got on your message right away. What time did the KK leave camp last night?"

"Must've been around five. Before dinner time. Why?"

"Oh, I see." Jacob's voice sounded flat. "What can I say. We tried. Thanks anyway for the call, Charles. Good of you." He planned to disconnect but Nauwaard was chatty and interrupted.

"Schwier's hunters have trouble finding targets lately. They were happy catching this one." Nauwaard's laugh was more like a growl than the sound of mirth. "What's the news from the front? Any updates?"

Jacob was sure Charles' question was meant to bait him. So be it. As a strategy, it would be alright to give Charles something already out in the public domain. Trying to project innocence, he kept it light as he confronted the accusation.

"I'm not sure what you mean. Except my brigade, I'm not the organizer of anything. Don't know what's going on at the front either, but I guess we can say with some certainty the Allies are still stuck in the south."

"Tell me something new," Nauwaard growled.

"Sure. You might be interested to know that the Allies arrested the NSB members right away, with help of community partisans. I don't know what became of them. Right now, the armies on both sides are looking at each other over large stretches of no-man's-land between the rivers and the Biesbosch watershed. But the fighting continues. The front will soon reach Overdam, Charles. Then what are you going to do?"

"Yeah, heard about it. I'm sure the Germans won't sit still either," the warden scoffed.

"No, they aren't," Jacob said in a somber tone. "I heard they inundated some of the floodplains of the big rivers, and the Allied tanks got stuck. I guess we're waiting for the next offensive to get to the precious Rhineland. At least the V1s and V2s have stopped hitting Britain. Did you know? I wonder if the Germans or the Allies will start the next battle. Doesn't Schwier tell you anything?"

Charles saw through the attempt and made light of it. "You know I'm not his fucking favorite to talk to."

"Oh, come on now. You're the warden, you should know some things." Jacob chuckled.

"Sure, I hear things when the commandos talk among themselves. I don't know where they get their info, but they said Romania and Bulgaria surrendered last month and troops joined the other side. Maybe I'll do that too."

"You don't even have to go eastwards. Just sit and wait a while, and the Allies will get you first," Jacob joked.

Nauwaard ignored him. With an air of importance, he continued talking.

"The Soviets came only as far as Hungary, but they've cleared the Balkans in the north. When comrade Stalin ordered his army relocated to Poland, that surely would've been the start of the Führer's sleepless nights. Not sure if the Polish will be happy with Stalin," he scoffed and followed up with: "I guess our young prisoner might try to escape."

The non-sequitur startled Jacob. He always tried to guess what Nauwaard knew, and especially what his motives were for sharing this precise information. He ignored the comment about the American. He wanted the turncoat to continue divulging what he knew. He had to give something in return. Keeping his tone light and casual, he replied.

"I heard the Germans have evacuated from Greece, and the Soviets captured Belgrade with the aid of Yugoslav Partisans. How 'bout that Schwier, isn't he making plans to leave the camp yet?"

"So, when are you coming to get that beer?"

"Soon, I guess. How 'bout tonight?"

"Tonight, it is."

When Jacob had disconnected, he imagined all the information spilling out of young Francis: locations and names, including those of Van Houten, the mayor, the Meulmans, and his own. He paced his small office. Nauwaard's suggestion was unrealistic. Francis wouldn't have a chance to escape, not from the KK, not from the camp, unless he was put to work outside the palisades. Not likely with an injured ankle. He couldn't ask Nauwaard to surrender the American to him. What did he mean by mentioning escaping? The bastard must be setting him up. He tried to remember what else he'd confessed to Nauwaard. Was it enough to hang him? Good thing he hadn't involved his sergeant in taking a message. He could've run right into the KK men's hands.

He shook his head, thinking about all those pilots and the Illegals, all barely in their mid-twenties, young lads risking their lives. How could anyone know what was right and wrong and what was illegal? The criminals were making the laws. Those on the right side were turning into lawbreakers. If they survived the war, would they be seen by the public as criminals or as heroes?

How the KK got wind of the flyboy was another problem. Was the presence of a mole in the group a possibility, or was Nauwaard just setting out bait? He would have to work on Nauwaard. Bakker or De Jong would surely torture Francis to get information about his helpers if they hadn't already. The likelihood of Francis still being alive seemed fainter with each passing hour. He stopped pacing and left his office.

He told Peters — the watch commander — he was going on a routine visit to the Star Camp. Peters nodded approvingly.

Chapter 74

Jacob arrived at the camp shortly after noon and requested the guard at the gate to let Nauwaard know of his arrival. The guard let him in, and Jacob marched to the office barracks.

Nauwaard was surprised to see him. "What's the deal, Chief van Noorden? I didn't expect you this early."

"Hello, Commander. I realized I've got something going on tonight, so thought I'd come by now. Alright with you? "

"Fine, I'm going home for lunch. Join me. I couldn't get anything down my throat here anyway. These filthy varmint breeders really stink."

It was late fall, and the weather clear with a smell of frost in the air. Jacob noticed that the prisoners were dressed in layers of clothes to keep warm. No wonder they didn't want to undress for a shower with ice-cold water in unheated barracks. The two commanders left the camp to cross the 500 meters to the commander's residence.

Walking along the path towards the large home, Jacob began his plea at a safe distance from the gate.

"Say Charles, I thought I'd discuss something important to both of us. You need to protect the prisoner from Bakker and De Jong. Who knows what they'll squeeze out of him. If he starts to talk, others will get picked up, and somebody will let it out you sent me a message. Under the circumstances of late, you can't afford it, right?" He left it at that. Better to stay quiet and let Nauwaard work out the domino crash for himself.

Everything that used to be green around them was a solid brown color now. The branches were naked, just like human bones after putrefaction when the flesh had disappeared. The two men kept walking. Nauwaard, deep in thought, stared into space. He opened the front door, went into the kitchen, and pulled a beer out of the icebox in the cellar. Then he looked at Jacob. "Want one?"

"Why not? They say a beer is worth a sandwich in calories." Jacob was hungry; it was his lunch time too.

They sat down in the living room and sipped their beer from the bottle.

Nauwaard, a small curve of displeasure stuck around his mouth, frowned.

"You, jerk, you do realize this whole thing could take a nasty turn? I'm fucking sorry I even called you about the bird. I can't do much now. We'd both be in shit."

Jacob felt he was crossing a line once again. He had to say it, for both their sakes and for the sake of Francis. Despite the coolness in the unheated room, he was hot, and his forehead was forming drops of sweat, a fire burning inside him.

"Yes, I know. It's why I decided to come to see you right away. We need to protect the fugitive, if only to stay in the clear ourselves. Turn him over to us and I'd put him on transport right away, if there were a train. What do you say about arranging a camp car? I'll have one of my men take him to our main office in Zwolle. Who knows, the Allies might get here soon."

Nauwaard still frowned, and his mouth's corners had turned down even more. With fury in his eyes, he glared at Jacob and growled: "Why the hell would I do such a thing? Schwier won't like it. The POW should go to the SD office."

Jacob kept up a light tone of voice, feeling incredibly disingenuous. "Well, the man is a prisoner of war after all, and you have the responsibility to treat him decently. He doesn't belong here anyway. He's a military man. Don't hand him over to us then. He can go to Vught to join the other POWs. Isn't this where the SD would send them? As long as he is kept out of the Butcher's hands..." He didn't finish his sentence and stared at his opponent, tempting him into insubordination.

Nauwaard's eyes were dark pinpricks. "A demanding son of a bitch you are, if I may say so."

"Jeez, man. It's not just for me. Having a POW in your care murdered won't look good on you. On the other hand, saving his life will bring you favor in a trial for war crimes, when your actions at some point in the future will be scrutinized. Wouldn't you agree?" Saying this brought him to the edge of the warden's collegiality and it might push Nauwaard over into plain hostility. Jacob got his handkerchief out and blew his nose, which allowed him a wipe over his forehead. It took more talk on Jacob's part, but after some back and forth, the unhappy warden agreed to the proposal.

Nauwaard promised him he'd make the afternoon arrangement to have the POW transported to Camp Vught in the camp jeep. "I don't need you, better stay out of it. You're contaminated as a cop; your crew's sons of a bitches can't be trusted. The prisoner is ours now."

On leaving the camp, Jacob shook Nauwaard's hand and thanked him, assuring him he'd made the right decision, perhaps saving three lives. Nauwaard didn't look happy, but Jacob pedaled home full of energy.

Chapter 75

One dark November night, Jacob was late at a management meeting in Hardenberg with Department Head Den Toom, when the phone rang. His supervisor passed the phone to Jacob as the call came from the Overdam office. Dijk reported two employees of the distribution office had been robbed at gunpoint in the center of Overdam, just after office closing time. Dijk had met with the two victims at the brigade, took their information, and had let them go home. The robbers took a box containing two hundred blank *Ausweiss* ID cards and a box with the region's labor inventory. It had all eleven hundred employment registration cards. Dijk proudly said he had already reported the incident to the proper authorities. Jacob grumbled a thank-you and hung up.

An hour before midnight, Jacob finally arrived at the Overdam brigade from his meeting in Hardenberg. When he read the watch commander's note, he cried out: "Goddamn, can't those beginners get anything right?" One of the crew member was still doing paperwork next door and must have heard him curse, but Jacob didn't care.

Just then, the phone rang. When Jacob picked up, the operator put him through without telling him who called, and a second later, a German voice barked at him. *Polizei Offizier* Steiner from the Betragter's office was one of the four authorities alerted by the watch commander as per protocol. As far as Jacob understood Representative Steiner's tirade, he told him to arrest the victims of the robbery and pronto. Steiner of the region's designated SD didn't wait for his answer and disconnected.

Jacob sat back in his chair. He needed to think about how to handle this. Guns were involved in the hold-up, so it was undoubtedly a Resistance action, and likely with the employees' cooperation. The Germans expected specific SD protocols to kick in. He didn't want to be accused of co-conspiracy with terrorists and end up in a concentration camp together with his crew, but he had to do something to save the fools of the Illegality with too much brawn and not enough brains. If only Dijk hadn't been so diligent. Or such a coward — afraid for his boss finding fault with him for not doing his job. Damn. Damn. He wished he had been clearer in his instructions not to act but first talk with him.

Jacob went to the residence next door and woke up his deputy. He stood by the man's bed and shook his shoulder. "Wake up, Van Houten. You men on duty screwed up the robbery report. Dijk should've only informed Den Toom's office. Did you have to sing it out to all the world? Call Lambregts, the distribution manager, and get him to the brigade. And have the two robbed employees brought in as well. We're going to lock them up — orders of the *Betragter*. Dikkers is still at the office here and can help you. The SD will process the robbery in the morning. It's going to be a long night." Without waiting for an answer, he turned around and left Van Houten's residence.

When the manager arrived an hour later, Jacob had a quiet talk with Lambregts. He suggested that his employees had taken off as fast as the wind, the second they'd been threatened, and that no guns were involved.

The man looked at him with eyebrows raised and briskly replied immediately: "Nonsense. Wouters was in the army and knows a weapon when he sees it. What are you getting at?"

With fake friendliness, Jacob suggested a different story. "I don't know, of course, but your men are no saboteurs, right?"

He got no answer. The man just stared back.

"I'll interview your men when they get here and will suggest to them also that they saw no guns and have exaggerated their story. Guns raises suspicions of the Illegality. No guns — no Illegality. I can't say it any more direct."

The phone rang and it was Steiner again, screaming in his ear.

Jacob put his hand on the mouthpiece and asked the manager: "Do you speak German?" The man nodded and Jacob handed him the phone. "You explain it to Officer Steiner."

After what looked like Steiner's intense response, judging from Lambregts' face, he hung up. "He said they'll come in the morning to interview my employees."

"Well, you can be present for it, if you wish, Mr. Lambregts. You can go home now."

Chapter 76

An hour later, Dikkers woke him from a brief snooze and told him one of the robbed employees had arrived. "Watch Officer, you take notes. Bring the man into my office."

Dikkers sat him down across from Jacob, got another chair from the squad room, and sat next to the desk facing the distribution employee.

Without the preliminary chitchat, Jacob opened a note block in front of him and started his questioning. "Officer Dikkers here will also take notes. I'd just like to confirm what you told the watch commander. Your name?"

"Wouters, I'm Pieter Wouters."

"You are the department supervisor?"

"Yes."

"You have been robbed, you say, and lost documents?"

"Yes." The man looked at his feet with pain on his face, as if his feet were hurting him. His voice was low. He was dressed like a public servant, but nicely, especially considering the country's lack of goods, obviously a neat and conscientious man.

"What happened exactly?" Jacob leaned back. The snooze had made him more tired. He was aware the man across from him was nervous, and with the sagging skin and dark half-circles under his eyes, he looked exhausted.

Dikkers took up his pencil and looked down, ready to write.

"Well," Wouters began, "it was after closing time. We were riding our bicycles from the outreach office to head office when three men stopped us on Main. They took the banker's boxes from our bikes' carriers. As I already told your man, at the end of each day we take the papers back to our vault at the main office."

"Alright. What did those men look like?"

"I didn't see their faces. Two of them lifted their jackets to show guns stuck in their belts underneath their jerseys, and all of them wore balaclavas." He rattled off the sentence as if he had rehearsed.

Jacob wrote down this observation on his writing pad.

"So, how tall where they?"

"Gosh, I don't know, hard to say. It was dark and we were in a hurry. It was darn cold and it rained. We wanted to get home. I didn't really look hard."

"Sure. Why weren't you looking too closely? Did you know them already?" Trick question. Jacob still didn't look at the man, giving him space.

"I didn't say that. No, I didn't know them."

In his peripheral vision, Jacob saw the man's right leg vibrating as if keeping time with a song's fast rhythm.

Wouters went on explaining. "Besides, I couldn't see their faces, like I said, I was scared. I was trying to avoid looking at them, so they wouldn't get angry with me. I'll admit it, I'm not good at facing bandits with guns."

Good save. Jacob finally looked up. He saw a pencil pusher, a fish out of water wriggling to get off the hook. He looked gently at Wouters, his tone friendly. "What would you say, if I said you knew at least one of the robbers?"

Wouters didn't respond and stared back at him, wide-eyed, and shuffled his feet.

Satisfied with the effect of his suggestion, Jacob leaned back and, in a conciliatory tone of voice, continued. "I'll tell you what we'll do. You're a smart man, I'm sure, or you wouldn't be a supervisor. You don't have to say yes, or no, but I'm going to tell you what I think happened. Afterwards you can always confess to conspiracy. I would recommend you say this: you're the victim of a robbery. I bet you took off as soon as you felt threatened. I bet there wasn't a gun at all. I put it to you that the alleged gun, bulging underneath the man's sweater, you thought you saw, could in reality have been only a tobacco pipe, or a wrench, of whatever. You didn't actually see a gun. If you insist on guns having been involved, I want you to know these circumstances you painted are difficult for you."

Jacob took a breath and paused a few beats before he went on, giving Wouters time to think. The man stared back with his eyes full of hate. The fool didn't get it, so Jacob had to spell it out.

"We don't want the SD to run this public office, but they get overly excited when guns show up. I can't let you go without doing a proper investigation, or I'd be putting this whole brigade under suspicion of fraud, or co-conspiracy with partisans. It happens. My hope is, if we do the job right, the SD will let you go."

Jacob leaned back in his chair, clasped his hands together behind his head, and looked directly at Wouters. The man looked a bit less nervous and stared back at him with curiosity, the hate gone for the moment. His feet had stilled, and his hands were balled together in his lap.

Dikkers stayed bent over his notes.

Jacob tried again on another track. "You know these blank ID cards and the employment cards of over a thousand registered people would be useful to people in hiding. The KP surely loved taking those from you. We could call it theft, sabotage, or fraud. It might save a good number of fellow Dutch, at least for a while longer. I'm not saying it's good or bad, but I cannot do nothing about it, even if I wanted to, when guns are involved. You need to know the robbery was already reported to the SD, and Officer Steiner already called to make sure you'll be around for an interview. We'll keep you here for the night. Your manager has vouched for your co-operation."

He stopped talking, got up from his chair, and walked around the desk to stand beside Wouters, who leaned back as much as he could, away from the chief. "Did you tell your colleague of the plan? No matter. You're the supervisor, so it's on you, anyway."

This would be hard for a boss who wants to be right, as he knew from experience, and indeed, Wouters pursed his lips tightly shut. He hoped Wouters read between the lines, take his advice, and deny that weapons had shown up.

"You have placed yourself and your colleague in a compromising situation. I'm going to consult with my superior in Hardenberg. I'm not paid enough to take the risk. Tomorrow he'll decide together with the SD what to do with you and your buddy. You understand?" He laid a hand on Wouters' shoulder.

The man looked at him now with his mouth half-open. Dikkers was also staring at him.

"Good," Jacob added. "One more thing: may I remind you of the fact that the walls have ears nowadays?" He took his hands off the man's shoulder and gave him a light tap on the back. "You can go now. Dikkers, escort him to a cell and let me know when his colleague arrives."

Wouters shot up from his chair and ran to the door.

"Leave the door open," Jacob said. Dikkers opened it, and the men disappeared.

Jacob saw the other chap through the open door seated in the squad room under Van Houten's guard.

"Bring him in, Sergeant," he called out.

Van Houten brought him in, and sat him down.

"You can go home now," Jacob told the sergeant.

Van Houten left, closing the door behind him.

Dikkers knocked at the chief's door, came back in, and sat down next to Wouter's colleague.

This one was much younger, really a kid, not much older than Sergeant Francis, who had occupied the same cell not long ago. The image of a burned body flashed before Jacob's eyes. He quickly focused his thoughts. "Name?"

"Yes, sir. I'm Friesema," the young man said brightly, as if he was in a job interview.

"How old are you?"

"I'm twenty-one, sir. And you?"

Jacob felt Dikkers grin more than he saw it, as his eyes were on Friesema. "Alright. No need to get cocky now, son. You're too young to spar with me. I'm just going to hear from you what happened earlier today. In your own words. Go ahead."

Jacob sat back and didn't bother writing anything down, as Dikkers was on it. The strawberry blond youth eagerly told the story Jacob knew already. The man was pretty confident and didn't give signs of nervousness the way Wouters had. Jacob quickly concluded Friesema wasn't in on the KP deal. Too bad he'd just have to sit in jail for a while. On the other hand, he'd be safer in jail than out in the community. Good thing he had work already. A strapping young lad was always a desirable target for the *Arbeitseinsatz* labor recruiters.

"Alright, I've heard your story, Friesema, thanks. I'll tell you the same thing as I told your boss."

He went on with the interview for a while and suggested the same thing: that no weapons were involved, and he told him he was staying in cells for the night because the SD wanted to make sure he's around for the SD interview.

Dikkers was catching up on his notes.

"I'll take him, Dikkers."

Jacob walked Friesema to the cells and wished him good luck. He locked him in next to Wouters. "*Welterusten, heren* [Goodnight, gentlemen]."

Van Houten had gone home. Jacob told Dikkers to go home and finally went home himself. He ate some bread. Exhausted, he fell into his bed, thinking how screwed up his job was, before he drifted off to sleep beside the sleeping Margaret.

Chapter 77

The following morning, Jacob initiated a warrant for the three robbers' arrest with the vague descriptions the victims had provided. Before the Betragter would arrive, he called Department Head Den Toom and discussed the situation again, withholding his assessment of suspected KP involvement. He assumed asking Den Toom was the men's best bet to avoid continued involvement with the SD, which would surely lead to imprisonment.

He'd guessed wrong. Den Toom told him the commissioner, Major Feenstra, wanted to have the two men transferred to "the proper authorities": the German SD. He should talk to Feenstra.

Without any trust in Den Toom considering his previous decisions, Jacob called Feenstra himself. "Major, sir, I've already thoroughly interviewed the two, and the watch commander interviewed them too. The *Betragter* will be here this morning and interview them again. He'll find no evidence of fraud or sabotage. These employees are certainly the victims here, no perpetrators. I'll send you the transcripts. They really don't need to be sent to the SD. If you could call the *Betragter* and tell them this, we'd be saving them a trip in vain. Our hope is to catch the perpetrators."

Catching the perps wasn't a goal he'd be crazy about either, but it sounded good. He strongly suspected involvement of Van Houten's Illegals with the robbery, or maybe the KP, but didn't ask; he didn't need to know. His pleading fell into the commissioner's abyss of cover-your-ass strategies.

"Sorry, Van Noorden, you might be right, but I don't see a good enough reason for my intervention with the SD."

The same morning, Herr Steiner, the *Betragter* — the liaison with the Security Services — briefly interviewed both men in the presence of their regional manager, Lambregts, and Jacob. Lambregts scowled all through Jacob's suggestions he peppered throughout the responses from the suspects. However, Officer Steiner seemed to like those. For instance, the two yellow-belly public servants' lack of courage during the robbery. Or that in their fear, the men thought they'd seen guns, but in reality, no firearms were involved — making a mountain out of a molehill to justify their behavior. Steiner then quickly announced his decision: the two employees would be further detained in Arnhem "to teach those saboteurs a lesson". He winked at the chief, upsetting Jacob's peace of mind greatly.

***

After the men had gone, Jacob cursed a blue streak in his office. His trusted men were furious as well. On his return to the brigade from Arnhem later that day, Van Houten straight-up accused him.

"You should've never have had me bring those men in, Chief. Why did you? Now they're in the SD hands in a Nazi jail. If they're tortured, you're the one to blame."

"Yeah, I'm aware of it," Jacob grudgingly admitted. But he couldn't offer his sergeant any consolation, or even a defense for his failed attempts to set them free. It was below his dignity to cowardly blame his diligent Watch Commander Dijk, or his Department Head Den Toom but Commissioner Feenstra should know better — the turncoat.

Van Houten and De Wit reported they had taken Wouters and Friesema on the train with a special permit to Arnhem, where they delivered the employees to the SD office as instructed. Van Houten told Jacob he had offered the two men with De Wit's agreement a chance to escape on the train. To avoid repercussions, they would themselves go into hiding as well. Wouters and Friesema had declined the offer, because they'd promised Lambregts not to disappear.

To the community, Jacob had only proven his reputation as an overzealous chief. In the KP's eyes — the likely robbery's organizers — his reputation became even more sinister: a dangerous traitor who delivered the brave co-conspirators to the SD.

***

A week later, Jacob got an anonymous letter at the office. The sender told him to stop his devious collaboration with the Nazis, or he'd end up belly-up. He showed the letter to his deputy. "What do you think this is about?"

Van Houten's reaction was vague. "Oh that. I guess somebody got pissed off about the results of the robbery investigation. Don't worry about it." He wouldn't look his boss in the eye.

"I hope those two won't be tortured in SD custody," Jacob commented wistfully and rubbed his chin.

"I hope so too," replied the sergeant, studying Jacob's face before leaving the chief's office, slamming the door shut behind him.

When Jacob followed up with Commissioner Feenstra, the man told him the SD held the two employees for refusal to cooperate with an investigation and for suspicion of co-conspiracy and fraud. He made a last-ditch effort.

"Major, couldn't you please inquire with the SD what their evidence is? We need to protect the robbery's victims. They're innocent. They are our citizens and entitled to fair treatment, not as criminals, but as the victims." He held his breath, expecting a scolding.

"Sorry, it's out of my hands, Chief."

"Thanks for nothing much, then," Jacob said and threw the phone down. He didn't tell Feenstra about his own punishment. The SD made his office work twenty-four hours straight on replicating the stolen labor inventory, together with Lambregts' other staff.

***

About a fortnight later, Mayor Van Voorst Tot Voorst told Jacob in a call about other matters of a chance meeting with Schwier, who had happened to be in the Zwolle hospital at the same time he was there. The mayor had pleaded for the two employees of the Distribution Services.

"I questioned the SD's decision to keep Wouters and Friesema incarcerated, two innocent employees, without any evidence of their guilt. I told him if an investigation by several police officials in Overdam hadn't found any evidence of a crime, and the SD investigators didn't find anything either, there wasn't any to be found. I argued the men should be set free. You might be interested to know the SD released them two days ago, just in time for Christmas. Didn't anybody tell you?"

Jacob gasped. "No, I didn't know. Great. Thank you so much for your intervention, Mayor. I hope the men got treated well?" It was the most crucial detail.

"They could've been tortured, but no, they weren't, no thanks to you! You should've left well enough alone. Why would you get involved? It rang alarm bells!"

"Not my intention, mister Mayor. I had no choice. Tell them sorry for me. I was sure Steiner would let them off after we had talked to them. I tried to convince the Betragter of their innocence, but I wasn't going to set them free against Steiner's order to pick them up for safekeeping. They shoot people for less."

The mayor sighed audibly before he replied. "We all do what we can, Van Noorden. I'm not judging." He hung up abruptly, leaving Jacob with the impression he had been judged.

So, his reputation was on the fritz. Nothing new there. What a debacle. Yes, life was sure complicated. He tried to sort out his mixed feelings. He had dealt with the fall-out for his stupid watch commander, covered his bases with the SD, had navigated the interviews, and made plenty of enemies among which Feenstra, his boss. He'd been too damn subtle with his suggestions to Wouters and Friesema.

On the other hand, the men had time to think about it jail and then set free in good condition. The Illegality was provided with plenty of blank Ausweiss ID papers, and no labor inventory, so they could falsify to their hearts' content. His brigade was not implicated in a cover-up. In the end, not a bad outcome.

Nothing was what it seemed. He promised himself to speak with Friesema and Wouters after this would be all over, and the Kraut had left the country. That cold January night, Jacob slept well, knowing Wouters and Friesema slept unharmed in their own beds.

Chapter 78

Whenever a call from the Star Camp came in at the brigade, the crew expected a disaster to follow. Charles Nauwaard informed Jacob of the new developments in his latest call.

"Just so you know what's happening here. Superintendent Schwier has started up a special force under his leadership and De Jong as his deputy with a selected few of my KK guards. Their assignment is to hunt day and night for law breakers. I'm not happy about it."

Jacob's patience with the Nazis ran short lately. "So, what's new about that? Your KK have been doing exactly the same thing for some time."

"No need to be nasty. I'd thought I'd let you know. It's official now."

After the call, Jacob started to see more prisoners with black eyes and head wounds, who looked as if they had fallen down a long set of stairs. His crew reported frequent incidents in the community, and not just within the camp boundaries, with the guards as criminals. The Kontrol Kommandos terrorized the towns around the camp, assaulting citizens without good reasons. Van Houten reported on a case of arson by the KK.

"Yesterday, Schwier's KKs burned the property of a farmer they caught hiding someone. The bastards first took the valuables from the house and divided everything among them. They're animals. I'm ready to kill them myself."

"What happened to the man?" De Wit asked.

"Arrested and off to the camp."

"And his family?" Jacob asked.

Van Houten's reply came softly: "His elderly wife is homeless. Luckily, their children had already left home."

The image of Ruth and her children flashed before him. "How fortunate," he quietly said. "She can move in with her children. Be sure to write it up in triplicate." He shook his head. This surely won't be the last disaster with the KK.

***

A week later, Camp Superintendent Kommandant SS Schwier himself called the police brigade. He ordered Jacob to report to one of the camp's satellite work sites in the nearby hamlet of Junne with an extra man and guard a few saboteurs, suspected of hiding enemy pilots. Schwier and his men were now interrogating them.

When Jacob asked for volunteers, he saw Van Houten's expression waver between alarm and anger, and he asked him to get his bicycle and join him. "No, thanks," Van Houten said. "I got things to do, calls to make." The sergeant turned around and walked away with purpose.

Before he could question Van Houten's conduct, Leversma stepped forward.

"I'll do it."

***

When Leversma and Jacob arrived at the barracks — a converted barn — about fifty uniformed SD men and camp guards were already at the site, some of them still beating the bushes at the edge of the clearing. One SD agent was holding a Rottweiler on a long line. The dog was sniffing around, nose to the ground, the handler giving it the entire length of the line.

Others were standing around smoking cigarettes and chatting. Apparently, the hunt was still in progress.

Jacob and Leversma entered the barracks in the center of the clearing. Three young men were tied to chairs and had been beaten, with deep cuts on their faces and bleeding from their heads, probably from gun butts. Schwier was the only officer inside the barracks. He told Jacob to guard the men closely, and then left.

The two policemen stood staring at the captured men. Jacob frantically thought what he could do to save the men. Seconds went by. He looked at Leversma, who looked back with panic in his eyes. The seconds crawled by. His heart slowed, and he lifted his hand for the handkerchief in his pocket. He accidentally hit his gun in its holster. No use now.

"Please untie us," one of them pleaded with a cracked voice, looking at Jacob. The other two captured were only half-conscious and stared at the floor without any reactions.

"Sorry, man. We can't do that," Jacob said empathically. He had his hankie in his hands and stretched his arm to wipe the blood, then froze. "You can't run, even if we let you go, we're surrounded, it'll be too obvious. With dozens of security men out there and a dog, you'll be shot, even if we help you. You want us all to be shot?" He went down on one knee and pushed his cloth against the worst injury on the man's face. When he got up with the soaked cloth, he folded it and put it in his pocket as he looked at Leversma on his haunches at the other side.

The man moaned. "Goddammit, those bastards will beat us to death anyway. Give us a chance."

"The chief is right, Wim," Leversma said, close to the man, whispering into his ear. "We can't do anything. Should we warn your people, maybe your wife? Who're they looking for? Are any still out there?"

The fellow he called Wim was bleeding from a large gash over his eye.

Leversma pulled out another hankie, pressed it on the injury, and kept his hand against Wim's head.

Wim replied in a whisper but loud enough for Jacob to hear.

"Leversma, go to my house and warn everybody to hide right away, but don't lead the bastards there. Schwier set us up, to pick up some pilots. There were no pilots, just them. They're hunting for more Illegals but we're the only ones here. Tell my wife I'll be alright and give her my love."

"I will. Shush. Here comes the Bruin." Leversma stepped away from Wim, the bloody cloth in his hand.

SS officer Schwier stepped into the barracks with two SD men at his side, pistols in hand, one of them a Dutchman. He grabbed Leversma roughly by his arm and pressed his weapon against Leversma's temple. His German was sharp, precise, and loud. "Are you in cahoots with these partisans? What did he say to you? Did you give them the guns? They had Dutch police guns. Show me yours, if you still have it."

With all three Germans aiming their guns at them, Leversma and Jacob slowly took their own weapons from their holsters and showed them to Schwier. Jacob wasn't worried, but maybe he should've been. At that moment, he realized he didn't know everything that was going on in his brigade.

The SS boss removed his pistol from Leversma's head and put it back in its holster, but his sidekicks still had their guns aimed at Jacob and Leversma. Schwier inspected the Belgian-made marechaussee guns, and after a short hesitation, handed them back to the cops. He then told the Dutch SD member to translate for him.

Jacob stepped forward, moved closer to the SS boss, and started talking in a soft tone of voice.

"Kommandant, these men are *jung und töricht* [young and foolish]," he said. "I ask you to spare their lives, *bitte, sie sind Abenteurer* [adventurers at the most], but *keine Terroristen* [no terrorists]. I can…."

Quickly for such a pudgy man, Schwier drew his gun and pushed it against Jacob's head.

Jacob stopped talking midsentence and inhaled. He held his breath for a few seconds, and time slowed down. It seemed like minutes before he started pleading for his own life. "Oberst Schwier, *bei allem Respect* [with all due respect], I must object. *Steck ihre Waffe weg* [put your gun away]. *Keine möglichkeit zu reden* [we can't talk like this], from one officer to another."

Schwier seemed to get it and put his gun back in its holster, spitting out the words with a sneer: "*Fange an zu sprechen* [start talking]."

Jacob exhaled sharply. Murmuring, he summoned up all his imagination. The Dutch SS man, sensing his importance, translated immediately after each half-sentence.

"I don't know how police weapons would end up in these locals' hands, but these are not ours. I'd know if any were missing from my brigade — none are missing. My men haven't heard anything about terrorists, and certainly wouldn't help them if they knew of any. You have to believe me. These men you got here tied up, they're villagers. My constable knows them. They probably carry guns to defend themselves against those work-shy louts, escaped from the Star Camp and roaming the forests, and robbing innocent people just going about their business. It's a crime."

"*Beschwindeln mich nicht, Käsekopf* [Don't try to bamboozle me]. I don't trust any cheese-head. What do you suggest we do with them?" The portly officer stood with folded arms over his chest and glared at him.

The SD agent had to translate some of the words, as Jacob's accent was awful, and Schwier didn't get everything.

Jacob cleared his throat. With enormous difficulty, he formulated his sentences, hoping it would give them the escape they needed. "*Bitte.* Let my constable go back to town and search their homes. If there's any evidence of sabotage there, Leversma will find it. If, not, then you can let your prisoners go." By now, he was recovered from the shock of a gun against his temple and took a deep breath. A bit of his mojo came back when he saw he'd convinced Schwier.

"Alright then," barked the man. "Send him to search the location but you'll come with me. I assume your man knows where they live?" The Nazi looked with an intimidating scowl at Leversma, who nodded yes. "Good. Ten of my men will go with him."

This hadn't been his intent, dammit, and Jacob looked at Leversma with eyebrows raised. As the SD men marched him outside, Leversma avoided looking at him on purpose, like a pouting child. Damn it.

Once outside, Jacob pointed at their bicycles, "*Fahrräder* [Our bicycles], please," and the Dutch SD man threw them in the back of the truck with Leversma, and they left. Jacob couldn't think of a plausible reason to offer Schwier for not riding in the sedan with the German officer. The three prisoners followed in another truck guarded with the SD.

Jacob sent up a silent prayer for the most critical house, Wim's, to be devoid of illegals and pilots on their arrival. He wished the trip would last longer, they'd get a flat tire, or Schwier would drop dead from a heart attack, or even himself — not altogether an impossibility judging by his heart beating at a weird rhythm inside his chest.

Chapter 79

They headed for a small vacation house in the woods. The Wehrmacht truck with Leversma and the ten SD agents was already waiting on the sandy path to the cabin. Schwier, sitting shotgun, turned to Jacob in the backseat.

"Get out. You lead the search, Von Norden. Two of my men will stay with you and your constable, and the others will search the area. Don't let me get wind of another sabotage. Your neck is on the line." As soon as Jacob got out, the sedan pulled away, throwing up a cloud of fine gravel, followed by the truck with the prisoners.

Leversma stood already waiting on the path with the two SD men, one of which was the Dutchman — a traitor. The rest of the SD crew spread out through the surrounding forest and started searching; they had the dog too.

Jacob's heart sunk into the bottom of his shoes as he slowly walked the path to the cabin. Leversma followed behind him, and the Dutch traitor and the German SD agent followed Leversma. After two steps, Jacob turned around, stopped, and called out as loudly as he could: "Leversma. Is this the house, are you sure?" Not expecting an answer, he nevertheless waited on the spot as long as he could, until the traitor brushed past Leversma and punched Jacob in the back.

"Get on with it." The Dutch SD agent followed him with his gun drawn as he forced Jacob to continue walking towards the cabin.

The front door was locked. Leaving his weapon holstered, Jacob entered the house through an open window, making a racket by tripping and breaking the window with his elbow as if he tried to break his fall.

The Dutch Nazi hissed: "Do you have to make so goddamn much noise?"

Jacob waited in the front corridor of the home, uncertain whether his fortissimo had warned off the occupants. The two SD men brushed past and dashed into the home's interior. In case there were any residents, Jacob continued to loudly chitchat with Leversma like an idiot about his alleged plans to go on vacation. Leversma stared at him but didn't participate in the conversation as the two Nazis searched both floors of the place.

It was clean. The chief could breathe again.

With the search inside completed, the exterior needed to be checked next. As Jacob walked around the house to the back, the two SD officers stayed close behind him as if they sought protection, using him as shield. Jacob halted, close to the house with Leversma beside him in the backyard, their backs pressed to the wall. A field with a ripe crop of wheat stretched out in front of them towards the edge of the forest, where the other SD agents could be heard trashing through the bushes some distance away. Jacob listened for sounds nearby other than the birds; he saw no movements in the tall crop.

The SD traitor walked a few meters into the wheat field with his gun ready, halted, and called out, "There's someone," as he fired a round into the air. After this, something indeed moved then in the field. The traitor pointed with his free hand in the direction where he had seen the crops move and yelled. "Halt, *handen omhoog* [hands up]!"

A young man in civilian clothes slowly rose with his hands up in the air. A few seconds later, another man stood up a few yards deeper into the crop. Jacob cursed softly. Leversma looked at him with sadness in his eyes.

The SD agents arrested the young foreigners and took them to the truck, and waited inside it, for their other mates to return from the hunt.

Jacob turned to his man and quietly said, "Let's go, Leversma."

They got their bikes out of the army truck and left without speaking to the SD agents. On the ride back to the brigade, Leversma gave it to him.

"What the hell, boss, why did you have me go there? The bastards could've arrested Wim's whole crew, if they hadn't escaped. Those three men in the barracks are my friends. You, dick. You saw what the SD does to prisoners. They're going to be killed."

"You don't know that for sure. I didn't know what else to do to save us from being shot," Jacob said with a rare admission of his plain ineptitude. "We wouldn't be the first men Schwier shot on the spot. I couldn't know they'd send those bloodhounds with us. Those poor lads. I feel bad for them."

"I sure hope so. I don't know how to tell their families. Or will you do that?"

"If you want me to I will, but they know you. Anyway, how did the SD know about them?"

"I don't know how that bastard knew the KP was running an escape route. Somebody must've ratted them out. Now the whole network is in danger. You heard Wim. The men were set up by Schwier."

Leversma ferociously powered down on the pedals of his bike as if his life depended on it sending its chain rattling. "We could've tried to let them escape. We should've pulled our weapon on Schwier and taken them hostage. Those SD bastards wouldn't dare risk their boss' life."

Jacob's breathing became ragged. He burst out in a guffaw, and yelled, "Come on now. We're not Bonnie and Clyde. Man, grow up," causing an icy stare from Leversma, who accelerated and moved ahead. With difficulty, he caught up with Leversma again and continued talking in a serious tone. "Be reasonable, man. What chance did we have against dozens of sharpshooters? Even if we had our guns on Schwier, the others would have picked us off in a second, once we left the barracks. It would've been suicidal."

Leversma didn't answer.

Jacob ran out of patience and barked: "You've got lots to learn before you'll ever be a good copper." He was out of breath and stopped talking.

Leversma stared at his front tire. "Thanks, boss, and you're a lousy chief."

Jacob nodded as he powered down on the pedals and breathing hard. "Sure, I know," he managed to say between breaths and fell quiet.

After another stretch, Leversma had slowed down some, giving Jacob a chance to recover enough to be able to speak again. "They should've instructed the pilots to hide better, though," he mused. "But Leversma, how were you able to warn the group?" Jacob's tone was conciliatory. He hoped the absence of KP members at the safe house hadn't been just dumb luck.

"Van Houten made the call when we left the brigade," growled Leversma.

"Thank God for the sergeant," Jacob said softly. "That traitor Wietsema, he just tried something when he called out. He didn't see anybody, I was watching too. Those pilots shouldn't have shown themselves. Why the heck did they get up? Wietsema wouldn't have gone deeper into the wheat; he's too much of a coward."

They pedaled the rest of the trip in silence and arrived at the brigade in record time. Each stomped into the building, slamming doors, and each hid in his own space.

Jacob sat down, elbows on the desk, and covered his face with his hands, praying silently for the life of Schwier's captives, and for forgiveness for himself.

Chapter 80

On a snowy Sunday in February, a fire broke out on a farm. A fire wasn't always just a fire. The occupier relied on citizens betraying their fellow countrymen, who used the SD to gain an advantage or take revenge against a particular person. Schwier's KK would eagerly torch a house or a farm if they suspected the owner had hidden a fugitive and the bird had flown the coop. No evidence was needed. *Kontrol Kommandos* would shoot anybody running away — maybe a fate more desirable than capture.

In this particular instance, on this cold February morning, the fire's cause wasn't clear at first glance, and nobody was talking. A large crowd of farmers, all dressed in black, refused to clear the farm's driveway and prevented the police officers from accessing the farm. Jacob addressed the problem by pushing the farmers in front of him out of his way while calling out in his strong commander's voice.

"Police! Step aside, step aside, let us through. Police. Step aside. Out of the way, people, step aside."

In response, the farmers turned their backs and closed ranks even tighter. As he shoved the unbending backs, those stocky, black bodies, Jacob shouted louder. His crew of three followed his example, trying to make a sweep across the width of the driveway, all of them calling out, pushing, and shoving the unmovable men, but the crowd wouldn't budge.

The firetruck's arrival didn't change the situation one bit.

Jacob was just about to pull his truncheon when thirty-odd farmers grabbed him and his officers. He wanted to scream at the crowd that he was on the right side and not worry, just needing to secure the farm and make sure everybody was safe, but he knew by then nobody trusted the police. At the end of his patience, he wrestled one of his arms free, managed to pull his revolver, shot three rounds in the air, and loudly shouted his directions. "All of you, get back, or people will get hurt. Anyone resisting gets arrested."

Finally, the crowd yielded, letting the police officers and the firetruck pass to pump up the water from the interconnected sloughs dividing the pastures. By that time, the farm was fully engulfed in flames and burnt like hell's fire, melting the snow around it in a three-meter radius. Nothing could be done for the building, but somebody had freed the cattle in time to run out into the fields, where Van Houten spotted them.

"Take their names and addresses, we need witnesses," Jacob said. His crew members started taking down names, but most of the men had disappeared within seconds.

The crew returned to the brigade, except one man, left behind to assist the firemen. A couple of hours later, the fire crew gave up, reportedly only able to dowse the farm's glowing remnants when the heat had subsided enough for them to come closer.

Sergeant Van Houten took the lead in the investigation. He reported to Jacob the following day: "Some of the farmers said they'd tried to put out the fire. Not likely, as nobody had any mud and soot on their wooden shoes or was soaked from hauling water pails, confirmed by police witnesses. We all saw that."

"Do you think that obstinate bunch was buying time?" Jacob asked casually but observing his sergeant closely. "Maybe they had weapons or people hidden on the farm. What's your sense, sergeant?"

Van Houten replied in a neutral voice, "It's possible. Lots of options. You could hide someone in the orchard or take them across the fields in the back of the property." It's all he said.

Jacob simply had to trust that his deputy would let him know if he needed to know. He balled his fists in his pockets, then let go. The case was closed.

Chapter 81

That month, Jacob got a call from Nauwaard. He didn't know why the warden chose him for the news other than that the man had to unload to somebody. He didn't have many friends.

"This morning I instructed the canteen crew to make up bagged lunches for a bunch of prisoners and to allow for more than the usual food ration. I sent them off to freedom. If the SD wants to catch them again, let them." He chuckled.

To Jacob, it sounded like genuine glee, and he inhaled sharply. "What the heck's going on? Did you discharge them because you know something I don't, Charles?" After this, he couldn't get a word in, while Nauwaard just rattled on, high on his own courage.

"Well, let's see. The city of Nijmegen lost more than eight-hundred citizens in a bombardment, because the stupid RAF had made an error in navigation. But, no, that's not it. The SD brought me a lot of beggars, refuseniks, and street bums. That's the reason. We got four-hundred knackers here and more on the way, but goddamn it, we already have over two-thousands inmates, way over capacity. We've had to expand the camp, just for these goddamn losers. I'm no frigging Salvation Army! What are these fools at HQ thinking? These slobs are no good for labor either: half of them are already sick and look like bags of bones. They're surely going to die in my camp." The idea made the warden catch his breath.

Jacob could finally get a word in. "How nice of you to let them go, but stupid."

"I don't give a damn," Nauwaard shouted, and continued in a belligerent voice. "I've had it. This is no prison. It's an effing make-work-project. I'm not wasting my bloody time on them. So, I let them go, since you told me to get a pair. Fuck it, I'm standing up for what I believe, come what may. Jake, talk to you later. If I survive this, come by my house and we'll drink a few cold ones." He disconnected.

Jacob was stunned and also excited by Nauwaard's change in attitude and the fact he had shown some common sense and decency. He wasn't sure how to interpret it, hoping Charles wouldn't have to pay for it with his life, although the man deserved jail. Jacob would just have to trust God to protect the bad fellow for doing a good deed. To seal the deal, he sent a short prayer up to remind Him.

But Nauwaard was right to expect repercussions. That same afternoon Jacob got the news that the SD had arrested Nauwaard on charges of sabotage. The Ordnungspolizei would run the camp for the next weeks and transfer the prisoners elsewhere, while awaiting the assignment of a new commander. The interim job of Warden of Star went to De Jong.

***

Ten days went by in which Jacob and his brigade crew enjoyed a brief vacation from camp mores until Jacob got another call from Nauwaard.

"Hey, bud, I'm back from my vacation in Arnhem. You're talking to the hard-boiled Warden of Star. I guess the SD couldn't find another stupid ass to run this goddamn joint. The Germans have left camp, except Schwier, of course."

"Congrats. Too bad our nice quiet time had to end," Jacob said wistfully.

Nauwaard ignored the jab. "The boss got me my job back. Schwier didn't want to disarm his *Kontrol Kommandos*, but the SD made them submit their weapons. They don't like guns in any other hands but their own. That's how it will stay, if I've got any say. I'm talking to Schwier about the crew just carrying Billy clubs. Bastard De Jong made a real mess of running the camp. Why don't you come over to celebrate this win with a few beers?"

"Sure, maybe later today. Does eight suit you?"

***

Seated in Nauwaard's living room with a bottle of beer in his hand, Jacob, curious as ever, tried to take advantage of Nauwaard's upbeat mood. He asked his question with a big smile on his face: "Congrats, man, you did it! Good for you to put a stop to Bakker and his cronies with that sly move. I have to say, setting yourself up for arrest and having the Security Police disarm those KK men of yours was ingenious. Tell me, did you anticipate it would exactly roll this way and you'd be back?"

Nauwaard sat back in his chair, broadly smiling like the Cheshire cat. "Ah, Jake, for you to guess and for me to know! I'm not going to offer myself up for high treason, or give the SD an excuse to do away with me. No Sirree! It's fine how it turned out, and let's leave it at that. I know Schwier likes what I'm doing. We go way back. I saved his ass and he saved mine. Hey, I heard a few more jokes, wanna hear?"

"Sure, let's hear it." Jacob sat back to enjoy the jokes; Nauwaard's happiness must be rubbing off on him.

With much aplomb, Nauwaard began. "Question: what's the difference between De Gruyter's Groceries and Hitler? Answer: De Gruyter offers us ten percent rebate and better products, and Hitler offers us Six-and-a-quarter (Seyss-Inquart) and Rommel [junk]."

"Good one," Jacob laughed. It was common knowledge Hitler had just charged General Rommel with the job of finishing the Atlantic Wall to stop a British invasion. The work on this miles-long fortification of bunkers, landmines, and beach obstacles on the west coast sucked up many slave laborers. "I got one too," he said. He only knew the good-natured jokes he heard from Van Houten.

"A joke from you? I gotta hear this," Nauwaard said with a smirk.

"Heard the one about the German soldier coming home and riding the tram? That soldier got on the tram in Frankfurt and the conductor asked him for 20 pfennigs for the fare. He replied he'd just come back from Holland and never had to pay for rides. The conductor went: In Holland you'd be treated like air — and in Frankfurt you're normal and 70 kilos."

"Ha-ha. Talk about Germans leaving. I can't wait for that day," Nauwaard said. "I have another one about your Six-and-a-quart." He was already grinning.

Most jokes were too crude for Jacob's Calvinist's sensibilities, but these were virtually family-approved. "I'll be generous and say as Dutchmen we're in this together. He's your Seyss-Inquart, more so yours than mine, you working for the SD and all. But go ahead!"

"Back off and listen. Question: which of the two streets in The Hague are named after Seyss-Inquart? Answer: Lange Poten (Long Legs) and Korte Poten (Short Legs)."

Seyss-Inquart had a solid limp, and a war disability was not something to joke about, but Jacob smiled anyway.

Nauwaard seemed delighted, his posture alert, sitting upright full of energy, his eyes were clear and focused on Jacob's reactions. He immediately went on talking.

"And here's another one. Question: what's the motto of Mussert? Answer: to build the pure German race you must first marry your auntie. Good one, hey? The hypocrisy of that man, keeping his love life all in the family! Talk about wives. Did I tell you I got divorced?"

"No, you didn't. What about your kids?" Jacob wasn't just pretending he had compassion. Leaving a wife was unimaginably sad, especially for the children. Relationships with loved ones were difficult to maintain under the best of circumstances, but even more so under the isolating demands of an impossible job — something they had in common.

Nauwaard seemed unperturbed, even boastful.

Despite his congeniality with Charles, Jacob's underlying distrust was overwhelming him now, and he wondered how long he could keep up the charade. The stories floating around town about the KK and Nauwaard were always in the back of his mind, stories of torturing the prisoners, baiting them and beating them to death, how he blasphemed and mocked the religious piety of his captured as they prayed for divine intervention. The KK's cruelty on their raids in town was worse than what the SD did. With this man, he couldn't ever know the truth. The thought that Nauwaard might be playing him was always present. That Nauwaard would've acted out of compassion when he let those wrecks go was hard to believe or that he even possessed the attribute. He didn't seem the least bit upset about his marriage troubles.

"Like your wife, Maria's German."

"Yeah, I'm aware of it, but my wife is Dutch, like your first wife." Jacob frowned, his lips pressed together.

Nauwaard shrugged. "We fought a lot. Sometimes it became physical. Maria left me as she thinks I'm a monster. She blames me for what happens at Star Camp. She saw the damned dead being taken away and the poor bastards arriving, the louse knackers put on transport to labor camps in Germany. She heard the shots fired and the screams of people being beaten up, you know the sort of thing." He still looked rather content, had accepted his work environment as part of the deal for survival.

Jacob had an inkling of Charles' domestic problems but had never asked. The talk about it was *verboten*. And yet, here they were talking. He shifted uncomfortably in his seat and didn't respond.

"I admit, Jacob, what we do is no life for a woman. When this is all over, Maria and I might get back together. I will definitely change my ways. I'll tell you something I've never told anyone. I suspect my sister's first child is mine. We fooled around when I was fourteen and she was thirteen. My father used to drink himself stupid every Saturday. As my mother was hiding in the bedroom with the door locked and he was passed out in the living room, we were in the shed doing it. She got pregnant and married some fool. Never mind, shit happens. Rejoice, a new world is about to arrive when the Germans will be gone. I only hope I'll survive it. Will you put in a good word for me, if it comes down to it? I'm not a monster, goddammit, just a man caught up in this fucking war."

His bravura was gone; he started biting his nails and stared down at the floor.

Jacob had a lot to say but thought it wiser to keep his mouth shut. He wasn't done with Nauwaard and reminded himself not to let down his guard until after the Allies would have arrested the man. He cleared his throat. "You didn't look perturbed about Maria leaving you or the Allies arriving. Somehow, you even seem happy a minute ago. Charles, what's going on?"

"I'll tell you a secret. I've got a new woman, a local girl," the man replied with a broad grin on his face.

Jacob gasped.

"I visit her in town at her place, so she doesn't have to hear what's going on here. She's single, no kids, about ten years younger than me, and she doesn't care about politics. She's a happy-go-lucky gal, built like a brick house with great gams, just the girl for me." He made some movements with his hands, indicating how shapely his new lover was, unsettling Jacob to his core. "So, tell me, Jake. How's your wife?"

Jacob silently stared at him, needing a few seconds to clear the words he really wanted to say about Nauwaard's corrupt conduct before replying. He felt pity for the fatherless children in the world.

"My wife's fine. I'm fairly honest with her. She understands I'm keeping work secrets and she accepts it. She knows I won't make any life-changing decisions without her. She trusts and respects me. But the war's not over yet. What I wanted to talk to you about. You know what the Germans have been doing on their retreat from Russia, Poland, and other places, right?"

Jacob never used the word Kraut with Nauwaard. The man was too closely aligned with his benefactor, Nazi boss Schwier.

"You mean the scorched earth thing? Killing prisoners? Yeah, I know. What about it?" Nauwaard was less happy now and looked at him with a frown on his face.

Jacob stubbornly continued. "The Germans killed hundreds of thousands of prisoners in camps on their retreat. You can't kill all of them. I mean, killing prisoners is not a solution. One or two will always escape and be potential witnesses in trials. You could just leave the prisoners behind alive instead for the Allies to find them." He waited to see Nauwaard's reaction.

Nauwaard kept sipping from his beer bottle — nearly empty — tipping it while bending his body backward. Without any visible emotion, he then replied: "Yeah, it's a bitch if you happen to be a prisoner."

Charles' frostiness didn't throw off Jacob. "I'm going to ask something, Charles. Could you give me your word you won't let that happen at Star Camp, even if your superiors give you the order? Luckily, we don't have the death penalty, but I would hate to see you convicted to something like 25 years in jail."

Nauwaard jumped up as if bitten by a viper. "Man, Jacob, Goddamn it, you sure can bring a fellow down." He took off to get himself another beer from the cellar.

Lost in thought, Jacob sat motionless in his chair. Had he gone too far? When Nauwaard came back into the living room, he looked at him with some curiosity.

"There must be some reason why you're such a pain in the ass," Nauwaard commented. "What're you trying to say? I want to hear it."

Jacob took a deep breath in. Now was the moment.

"Nothing else. I put it before you, so you can think about it and prepare for what you need to do. The war is ending, you know that. The Allies might target Zwolle next. How many more will have to die? Don't you ever wonder?"

Nauwaard took a gulp of his new beer, leaned back in his chair, and glared back at him. Calmly, he answered Jacob's questions.

"Yes, I know, and I'm looking forward to the end. I'm sick and tired of this bloody craziness. Come what may, this shit can't be finished soon enough for me. I never believed Hitler's crap about the scourge of the Jews in Europe. Yes, I know I am with the SD, but you know what? It's a group you can't just resign from, exactly like the

Mafia. They're a rather trigger-happy bunch of bastards, especially Schwier who lets De Jong do his dirty work when he isn't out hunting himself. They'd shoot me in a heartbeat."

Without his usual bravura, he had spoken quietly, and looked at Jacob, who noticed the fear in his eyes.

Jacob returned Nauwaard's gaze, leaned forward in his chair and answered with the same intensity. "I know what you feel. I've felt similar all the time since the capitulation: when will I get the bullet? It's the randomness of it all."

Nauwaard observed him with curiosity and kept quiet.

"The Nazis are not rational," Jacob went on. "Their theories are based on some dream of Aryan greatness and a future with Aryans only. The secret rules of the club are changing all the time, and we're kept in the dark. You and me both, we're all just trying to survive doing the best we can. It's how I feel." He exhaled slowly, not sure what he would get in return for taking such risks. He was so hot his shirt was soaked through, but he was at peace.

"You took the words out of my mouth, Jake! Want another beer?" Nauwaard's voice was not facetious, as far as Jacob could tell.

"No thanks, I'd better be going, got things to do, but thanks anyway. By the way, I heard the Allies might be invading France soon at Pas-de-Calais. They've already installed some equipment there."

"Well, you know more than me. I haven't heard."

That probably was a lie. No doubt Nauwaard also listened to Radio Orange's news. From being too hot, Jacob was cold now despite the brightly burning fire in the fireplace. He got up, ready to leave, and Nauwaard also got up. They shook hands, wordless, aware any meeting might be their last one.

***

That night, Jacob couldn't sleep. He wondered whether he had been too forthright with Nauwaard. After all, he was the camp's warden and an SD employee, and in thought and affiliation a Nazi, if not a current party member. He was implicated in many cases of cruelty, was responsible for many camp deaths. Nauwaard had demonstrated unacceptable conduct during drunken rampages in the village, and there were rumors of assaults. Jacob wondered if the man had no conscience at all or just hiding it well.

Jacob got up and left the bedroom, leaving Margaret to sleep. He thought back to the first night of the invasion, with Margaret peacefully asleep and the bombers buzzing overhead. He couldn't believe it had only been four years. He felt a hundred years older. The burden of constant insecurity had aged him faster than the years would justify, and his body ached. This life was like the years of civil service in the colonies: each year counted double towards their pensions.

He went down the stairs in stocking feet, put on his rubber boots, and went out in the cold February night. The empty stables smelled of dust and mouse droppings. He missed the more pungent horse smells and his spirited horse, which needed a confident handler. An old blanket hung over Susie's stable's half-door. He brought the rough cloth to his nose and took a deep sniff. It brought back the animal's image for an instant. She would be dead by now. Everything had been taken from him, all stolen, and it wouldn't stop there. The requisition of their weapons couldn't be far off. He wondered whether that day would come before or after his death.

Chapter 82

Two months later, the Van Noordens went for a visit to a farm in the area. Desperately needing a change of scenery, Jacob left work early. They made the trip by bicycle, Margaret on a borrowed brigade bike, a boy seated behind each parent, and the baby in Jacob's front basket. Contrary to a woman's bicycle with a low, downward slanting bar attaching the steering column to the central column, the man's bike has a horizontal metal bar from the saddle straight out to the steering column. This bar presented a problem for Margaret and her skirt. She wasn't able to swing her right leg over the seat, like a man. She needed Jacob's help getting on and off, which produced some hilarious moments for the boys, who watched the undertaking.

The days were getting longer, and the weather was lovely. They knew farmer Dirk Lantink and his wife Els from church, and Margaret occasionally bought eggs from the farm when Johanna's hens were not productive. They often chatted after church service. Dirk and Els had once come back to the brigade to see the horses and had stayed for coffee. Els Lantink thought it'd be fun for the kids to come to visit the baby pigs and the other animals, ducks, calves, and a foal they could keep until it had matured.

Riding along, the Van Noordens noticed in the distance on the highway many people walking or on bikes, and some people were pushing horse carts.

"What are those people doing, Papa?" Hendrik asked, always active and curious.

"They're looking for food, son. There's next to no food left in the cities, so they go to farms to buy food, or trade their stuff for something to eat."

"What kind of stuff?"

"Well, it could be anything, from a gold ring to extra clothes they don't need, or maybe money, if they've got any."

"Why don't they have food, Papa?"

Jacob took a minute to formulate how to explain this strange situation. "There are no shops anymore that have everything. You can only buy food with coupons our government sends us, because there's not enough food to go around, so we have to share what little there is with everybody."

He explained that not everybody has an Oma or Uncle Juergen to give them food. That many people in the city live in houses without gardens and can't keep chickens in four-story-high apartment buildings on a balcony. Unlike him, lots of fathers don't work, as many factories have closed now because of the war, or they make only a few guilders, not enough to buy extra food illegally on the black market, like rich people can. He hoped Hendrik wouldn't ask what a black market was.

"Oh. Look there, Papa, that bike doesn't have any tires, that lady's just riding on the rims. Did she ride on with a flat, and then the tire shredded? Is that what happened to her?" He sounded pretty proud of getting to the conclusion on his own.

"It's exactly what would happen. Well spotted, Hendrik. The shops don't have any spare tires anymore either."

"But how come, Papa? When will the shops have things again? Is it the fault of the Krauts?"

"Where did you hear this word?" He glanced over his shoulder at Hendrik behind him. The sharpness in his voice had an effect.

The boy knew he had done something wrong and let his head drop. Finally, he answered with a timid voice. "Everybody at school says it. I didn't make it up. It means the German soldiers, right?"

"That's right and you'd better not use this word, because the soldiers don't like it. They might arrest you if you're disrespectful to them." Jacob sighed and continued in a milder tone. "I think it'll be a while before things gets back to normal again, Hendrik, even after the war is over. We'll just have to make the best of it. Do you know what you want to be when you grow up, son?"

"Yes, Papa, I want to be a soldier."

Not expecting the particular answer, he quickly looked over his shoulder again and saw that Hendrik sat upright with hope on his face. It reminded him of what he had wanted to be when he was the same age. He made his voice gentle again. "Is that so? Soldiers could get killed. You know this, don't you, Hendrik?"

"But they keep strangers like the German soldiers out, and soldiers from other countries, like Sir Francis fights to save us. I know, because our teacher said there's fighting going on all over the world."

"Your teacher's right. But, Hendrik, listen carefully. It might be dangerous to talk about it with others. These are tattle-tales and the soldiers may not like it. You can tell me and Mama, but don't go talking at other people's places about it."

He was surprised how mature Hendrik had become while he hadn't been watching — eight years old already. He promised himself to spend more time with his sons.

"Well, we're here. I'm getting off first and then will help Mama. You watch Elly."

Jacob stopped his bike by the side of the driveway. His feet solidly planted on the ground on each side of the bike, he took little Elly out of her basket and sat her down in the grass. Hendrik climbed off the back seat and joined her. Jacob then swung his right leg over the central bar and dropped his bike flat in the grass, after which he quickly ran towards Margaret to help her off her bike, holding on to her bike's saddle. With his other arm, he plucked Jaap off the back seat and set him down. "Alright dear, you can get off, I got your bike. Careful now."

Margaret's full skirt allowed her to worm her leg over the central bar while still staying decent. Jacob had never known her to wear slacks, although it would make riding a bike a lot easier. She simply wasn't the kind of woman for it and left trouser-wearing to the modern city types. "Thanks, Jan." She used his diminutive nickname.

At the end of the long driveway, Els Lantink stood in front of the farm, waiting to greet the visitors. She walked Margaret and the kids to a separate building, a few yards to the side of the big house. Familiar with the place, Jacob walked around to the back entrance. He opened the small door within the huge, double doors — large enough for a horse and wagon — and peered into the threshing floor with the stables alongside it. In winter, the cows would be lined up on either side of the concrete floor on their straw bedding, their waste neatly dropping behind them in the concrete troughs, easy for the farmhands to clean. But now, in springtime, the cows were out grazing in the pasture, and the cement floor was gleaming.

As he lifted his feet to clear the small door's extra-high threshold, he startled Dirk and two other men, who looked over their shoulders at him, then at each other with concern on their faces. They were operating a stenciling machine and obviously producing copies of the banned newspaper *Trouw*. He recognized the paper immediately, as he would read it whenever he could get hold of a copy. It was right up his political alley. The three men stopped abruptly and stared at the police officer in uniform. It flashed through his mind he should've put on his civvies.

It was a rather primitive setup and highly illegal. The smell of ink was strong. Jacob looked behind him, and when he didn't see anybody outside, he made up his mind, then spoke.

"I apologize for barging in like this. I thought you were expecting us, Dirk. Anyway, I've seen what you fellows are doing. After I've left, move this machine elsewhere and pick somewhere harder to find you this time, or set out a watchman, if you appreciate living a little longer." He stood by the door with his hands in his pockets.

"Van Noorden, I didn't expect you in here." Dirk's voice sounded higher than usual and he had a deep frown on his face. "My wife was going to show you all to the barns." He wiped his hands continually on his pants, although they weren't wet.

"Well, too late. I know it looks like we're heading for the last months of the occupation, but you know the Nazis are still a virulent pest. Instead of me, it could've been the KK dropping in on you and then, off to camp with you. You'll never talk about this to anybody. I was never here. Good day, gentlemen." He didn't wait for their answer and practically ran out, hoping to God the men would follow his advice. He took his jacket off and walked towards the animal out-buildings.

Chapter 83

After admiring the chicks, Margaret and the kids were on to the pig barn when Jacob caught up with them. Els showed them the tiny piglets, only a week old, not more than one foot small, pink and adorable, making squeaky grunting noises. Hendrik was in his glory when allowed to handle a wiggly piglet, holding on tightly to the squirmy screaming thing, which only wanted to get back to its mother in the straw bedding. The sow was confined under a heavy iron cage as the piglets were free to roam around her. Hendrik counted twelve of them. So many marzipan-pink babies for one sow, it was a miracle. The children were enthralled.

"Luckily this time the sow has a working nipple for each of her babies," Els said. "Sometimes we have to feed one with a bottle. That's no fun for the baby, and a lot of work for us."

Jaap also wanted to hold one, but he needed his dad's help to restrain the uncooperative piglet at just five years old. They knelt down together in the straw bedding with the piglet and let the baby return to its mother after a few minutes. She rolled over, miraculously not crushing any of her babies. Each piglet in the pink gang scrambled over the others to find its assigned nipple and started to feed with much sucking and grunting noise. Little Elly let go of her mother's hand and closed in on her wobbly legs, then tried to grab the rolled-up corkscrew at the closest piglet's behind.

Margaret grabbed her hand and pulled her back. "Can't get it, honey, it's a tail. It belongs to piggy."

They went to see the foal in her paddock. She was beautiful, toffee-colored and playful, darting away and throwing up her hind legs and then her forelegs, shaking her head and whinnying. She ran back and forth between her mother and the fence, where the audience watched, fascinated by the ebullient horse child.

"Els, thanks so much for having us visit you, for giving the children a chance to see all these lovely baby animals, so sweet. Thanks again." Margaret shook hands with Els, and Jacob followed her example. At that precise moment, Dirk came out of the main farmhouse and joined them.

"Hello Margaret, how are you? Hello, young 'uns, I have something you might enjoy. It's a gift from the pig." He had a gunny bag in his hand and gave it to Margaret. He whispered in her ear. "It's half a ham."

"Well, it's time to ride back now." Jacob shook hands with Dirk and admonished the kids: "What do you say now to Missus and Mister Lantink?"

The children's cheery *dankuwel* [thank you], spoken in unison. Jacob and Margaret gathered their bikes from the front and rode back the same way, enjoying the mild early-May weather, the scents of flowering fruit trees and freshly mowed hay. The boys couldn't stop talking about the piglets, the chicks, and the foal. It had been a splendid day.

Chapter 84

After that day in spring, Jacob left home late at night most days to listen to Radio BBC at Dirk Lantink's hayloft, where he heard of D-Day. On June 6, 1944, nine divisions of Allied troops burst onto the west coast of France. At the staff briefing the following day, the mood was buoyant, as everybody knew about it.

"Great news, men. With the Allies landed on the French coast to take the five beaches of Normandy, we'll be looking at the end of the occupation soon. Forget the failure of Dunkirk. This time the fight went swimmingly, not least because the Allies surprised the Krauts. They were led to believe the offensive would be at Calais in the Channel, where they had concentrated their troops."

"I'd love to be there right now," Van Houten said.

De Wit nodded vigorously. "They said four thousand Allied soldiers got killed on the beaches, but so many landed that enough soldiers broke through to dismantle the Nazi strongholds in the dunes." The corporal added more quietly: "It would've meant hand-to-hand combat. They'll have to sort the dead Krauts from the Allies. I wouldn't like that job." His face now showed feelings of sorrow after his initial delight.

"I imagine they won't have time to look for the wounded or missing. They sacrificed themselves for us," Jacob said. "I sure hope the Allies will push through…" His voice trailed off, stopping short of the possibility the Allies could fail.

***

The cheerful mood among the crew lasted for weeks, and Jacob felt unusually close to his men. The squad room was filled with speculations and wishful thinking about the liberation, so near they could smell it. De Wit became the officer with the best army intel, and all turned to him for information.

That summer, the Canadians pushed through to Belgium, ending up in Dieppe by September and continuing towards the big rivers in the south of The Netherlands. At that point, the Americans and the British armies were pursuing their assignments elsewhere, towards Germany.

The Overdam Illegality anxiously followed the Canadians' progress and prepared themselves for the Allies' arrival. After Schwier's capture of Wim Smit's KP crew and the close escape of other group members, Van Houten clued Jacob in on some his group's actions. By then, Jacob completely trusted Jan Van Houten, the man with the most accurate and up-to-date information about illegal business and a direct line to Commander Simon. He felt just as protective to Van Houten as he had to his sisters in his childhood.

"Simon asked me to pass on the decision of the government-in-exile to appoint Prince Bernard as Commander of the NBS," Van Houten told Jacob in their briefing meeting.

"A good opportunity for the Prince to prove himself. I hope the Allies aren't bogged down forever before that bridge near Arnhem. The Nazi's arsenal and factories in the Ruhr — that's where they need to end up, and soon."

"Yeah, another winter would be too hard on all of us, Chief." Van Houten looked defeated, sitting with slumped shoulders on his large body across from Jacob in the office chair. "The British fancy-ass Montgomery has completely miscalculated that operation. He picked the wrong strategy."

His Deputy reflected his own worries. Jacob had heard from Nauwaard that the Allied Market Garden initiative had failed already, although he didn't say it out loud. "Let's hope not."

Remembering something else, Van Houten perked up.

"What about the speech from PM Gerbrandy calling on the railway workers to start a general strike? Do you think it'll work? The rails are the most essential services the Krauts need now. All those supplies, weapons, and prisoners, and not to forget the laborer, all need the trains. Everything would damn well stop with a strike."

"Yeah, you've got that right. They should've joined last year with that labor strike. We could've taken back the country then. What about the code on Radio Orange, wasn't that funny: the children of Versteeg have to turn in."

They had a good laugh, which alleviated the depressed mood for a few seconds. Reminded of their old boss, Versteegh, who had resigned rather than corrupt himself, they took courage.

The next day, Jacob listened to the conversations around him in the brigade about the National Railway. He wished they could participate in a strike, but that horse had left the barn. All of the crew sounded excited about the strike's success, except Peters and Dijk, whose faces showed something akin to fear. They stayed quiet, daren't participate in the conversations. The other crew members generally ignored the two dissenters, and especially now, strong and secure in the face of the pending liberation.

"Hot damn! Already 30,000 men on strike. Hurray for the NS! I didn't think they had it in them. The whole railroad out. It's a miracle," Leversma said.

"Well done! Since the government called for the strike, it should damn well pay the strikers, now we don't have unions anymore to pay them out. How odd for a cabinet in London to call for a strike, but it worked. I wonder if Gerbrandy instructed Hirschfeldt and the NS (National Railway) to pay out? There must've been some contact. I wonder how they'll justify that in the books," Van Houten snorted.

"I wished I worked for the NS," Peters said quietly.

"Keep dreaming, buddy," Van Houten replied. "We'll be on duty till the last day, and then we'll just carry on after the Krauts have been kicked out."

"We should strike too," Leversma said.

"Good luck convincing the chief," Van den Berg said.

"I bet the National Support Fund for Hiders will take a hit." Van Houten suggested. "Many more will go into hiding now."

"How would you know?" De Wit replied.

"I took a course in bookkeeping before I joined the Marechaussee," he chuckled.

"Smart-ass."

As the Illegality's National Support Fund found out soon after, the resistance movement didn't have to fund the strikers, as the personnel branch of the State Railway — NS — paid out whoever was on the government-sanctioned "leave of absence" list, approved by Hirschfeldt, the Deputy Minister. How that went to pass was a miracle. Just as a precaution, many strikers went into hiding anyway, so the Employment Police wouldn't haul them off under the *Arbeitseinsatz* [Labor Effort].

Chapter 85

Elfriede regularly borrowed Johanna's horse and buggy. She preferred it over the bicycle. Under the guise of delivering of wood or straw to the Wehrmacht HQ for Johanna, she would make a drop for the Illegality. The soldiers didn't harass her, as Johanna's pro-Nazi reputation had been well established, and the burghers and soldiers soon recognized Elfriede and the horse cart. Hiding papers, money, or even weapons under a load of hay was easy.

Not Margaret, who had decided not to work with the animals anymore, ever since the young marechaussee officer had made her blush by commenting loudly he would like to be the cow she was pulling along on her way from the pasture to the stable. "You wish," she had told him despite her embarrassment. That he had liked her enough to court and then marry her was beside the point.

She barely found enough excuses to explain her absences and late homecomings, but luckily Jacob wasn't asking. The boys didn't complain either. Every two weeks, Juergen picked Margaret and the children up from the brigade in the morning. They got to play in Johanna's yard with Elfriede's boys all day, as Margaret visited with Johanna and made their lunches.

Elfriede would meet with a member of the RVV at the back door of the Distribution Services to pick up the "goods," and then deliver them to the various addresses. The job would take most of the day. The women had the courier service running like hot molasses over fresh pancakes. Elfriede was a born courier and she delighted in her work.

"It's a great feeling, fooling those soldiers and those upstanding citizens. I can't wait to see Jacob's face when he hears about what we did. Can you imagine? I told Karel about it when he called me the other day. He's delighted we do our bit for the country just like him."

"But you are taking the risk; I am just helping but I won't tell Jacob. He's so overprotective of women, he thinks we're made of porcelain. Only his sergeant knows."

"Better keep it quiet then. I just love doing the runs with the horse and buggy. I'm good with the horse. He listens to me. I've got it down pat now: I click my tongue, and he walks, and at how he stops right away. At the stops I give him a carrot, and halfway we take a break at the watering trough by the post office. We don't need men to get things done, right?"

"Sure, sis," Margaret said, smiling about Elfriede's happiness for having excitement in her life. Luckily, Jacob was too busy to notice things around the house. She said out loud: "I'm not up to snuff with my house work. His shirts aren't always washed and he often has to wear the one from yesterday."

"Boohoo, big deal. He should try to do his own laundry." They both laughed heartily.

"See you next time. Look after yourself, Elfriede, dear. Don't get too cocky." They hugged. Margaret and the children arrived at the drive, where Juergen waited in the buggy to take them home.

Hendrik climbed up front with his uncle on the seat, while Margaret and Jaap climbed in the back on a mattress of hay covered by a warm blanket. Johanna lifted Elly up to Margaret.

"Mama, Uncle Juergen lets me hold the reigns," Hendrik proudly shouted.

"Yes, Hendrik, it's great. You'll be a real farm boy yet."

"Me too," Jaap piped up.

Chapter 86

Even more exciting than the strike was the news from the south front: the Allies liberated Breda in the south of the country. On the following day, September 5, 1944, close to 60,000 Dutch Nazi Party members headed north and eastwards on a trek to safety in Germany.

A few days later, standing in front of the brigade, Jacob and his men watched well-dressed citizens pushing carts, wagons, and anything with wheels down the streets. Their frightened eyes didn't rest for even a second on the policemen as they trundled by. To his surprise, Jacob felt sympathy. He thought of Juergen and wondered if he had taken off yet, or if he would weather the storm at home.

In a quick meeting, Jacob and Van Houten shared their ecstatic moods. Making sure the office door was closed, they discussed implications for their resistance group. Despite his happiness, Jacob was concerned. He stroked his head several times before he changed the mood. "We better be prepared. The Kraut won't sit still and wait to be captured. What about those British weapons? Will we get them any time soon?"

"Any day now. I wonder what the Kraut will do with the V rockets. I heard our government is moving to Breda from London."

"Yeah, terrific. Finally, again on the same soil as the rest of us. It's just a matter of time before we'll all be free. I guess it made it easier to tell Hirschfeldt to pay for things."

Van Houten couldn't sit still, and he danced around the office.

"Did you see the panic in the eyes of those NSB Nazi snakes today? I laughed and laughed, and my wife too, tears were streaming down her cheeks. I had to kiss her. Those traitors saw the writing on the wall. Good riddance."

"One of those might be my wife's twin brother," he said in reflective voice. "Don't celebrate too soon. It's not over yet, Jan. Be careful."

That night, Jacob couldn't get to sleep. He wasn't so sure all would go as planned. Nothing was easy with the Nazis. This couldn't be the end yet.

Chapter 87

The following day, many Wehrmacht soldiers arrived in Overdam looking for a place to stay. The odd one rode a horse, others pulled carts, or rode bicycles with wooden wheels, hauling their meager possessions on their retreat from the southern front, in a hurry to reach the *Heimat* [home].

Van Houten came into Jacob's office, still excited from the previous glorious day. "Chief, what are we supposed to do with those people hanging their flags out? Dutch Nazis leaving doesn't mean the end of the war, or does it?"

"We'll let them. I've got no orders to do anything about it. It wouldn't surprise me if Den Toom and Feenstra joined those NSB rats." He and his sergeant were having a good laugh when Peters opened the office door with a question for the chief.

"Why are those people celebrating, Opper? The whole of Main Street is in flags and banners. They're breaking the law, and besides, the Allies are only in Breda. It may be months before any troops show up here, if they take the north at all." He waited for an answer by the open door.

Leversma yelled from the squad room: "You're just hoping, Peters!"

The careful attitude among his crew was disappearing fast and needed him to curtail the further deterioration. "Hold your horses. Let's see how it goes," Jacob said. "It might not last long. I'll give it till tomorrow, unless, of course, I get an irate Heusden screaming at me, but somehow, I doubt that'll happen. Close the door, Peters."

***

It became apparent in the days following *Dolle Dinsdag* [Crazy Tuesday] that the Allied forces had failed to push back the German army and were stuck in the area of the big rivers. As a result, the Germans consolidated their strategic positions with extra Wehrmacht units, and all Orange banners and Dutch flags were hastily stored away. The crew's disappointment was overwhelming and a general mood of depression was apparent.

The mayor arrived at the brigade to complain about it to Jacob in his private office. Jacob had Margaret bring him a cup of coffee.

"What am I supposed to do with all these extra Wehrmacht soldiers? I'm told these *Organization Todt* engineers and their laborers will stay for a while. They'll be digging up every damn street and little bush. The whole town is going to be a mess."

"Yes, you might be right, I can see it happening. I hope those Russian prisoners understand German by now, or else they'll blow up the town by accident," Jacob said, smiling.

The mayor didn't smile. "Good point. The Wehrmacht boss ordered me to take care of their accommodation. I'm supposed to clear out the schools, or any other building, the hotels, what have you. I'm afraid some of the Russian POWs will have to be interned with civilians, probably on farms. They can sleep in the barns. Heusden says they can use the empty Employment Services' youth camp, since there are no young men left to train anyway."

Mayor Van Voorst was the age of a senior citizen and looked even older, worn-out. The war years had ground him down. Jacob felt sympathy for the man and wondered if he would make it to the end of the war.

"For some that'll be alright, Mayor. I'm sure my son Hendrik will be happy to surrender his school. He's not a boy for sitting still in a desk."

The mayor smiled. "One heck of a time to raise kids. I feel for you."

"Yeah, it's alright. Margaret's family is helping us. I do feel sorry for those Russians, forced to dig in the mud for the Krauts far away from home. They darn well treat them like beasts of burden. I wondered if we somehow couldn't get them involved, make them lay dud landmines, or let us steal the ammunition the OT makes them haul around. It may save lives when the Allies come through."

Jacob had already talked this over with Van Houten but was interested in what the mayor could contribute, and he observed him closely for his reactions.

The mayor sat back and enjoyed his coffee. "I'll think about it. I believe they're now mostly digging holes in the ditches for soldiers on the move to jump into. If the OT activity is any indication, we can assume the overhead traffic will increase drastically."

Jacob leaned back. "Sure. What's your sense, mister Mayor? Will we be free soon?"

The elderly mayor exhaled deeply, then rubbed his face with both hands before he replied. "I sure hope so, Van Noorden. This is no life. I've had enough. What did those damned troops have to get stuck?"

Jacob nodded. "Same here. We'll have to hang in, Mayor. The last mile is the longest, but it'll happen soon, any day now. Something else. I worry about the camp staff, especially Schwier. If I needed it, would you cover for me? Would you help free somebody arrested by the KK?" He pulled out his cedar box from his desk drawer and handed it to the mayor. "You can take those home."

The elderly man opened the box a crack, smiled at the ten cigars, then closed it again. "I could be helpful, but give me a heads-up. I can't read minds."

"Thanks, Mayor. Times are unpredictable, so are my superiors. To tell you the truth, I still dream about those young fellows the KK caught in that SD raid in Junne and hauled off to Germany. I keep seeing their bloody faces. I couldn't do anything for them." He sat back and shook his head, remembering the particular, stressful situation. His voice wavered when he went on. "Their leader's name was Wim Smit. Did you know any of them? Their KP group was dismantled after Smit's arrest."

The mayor looked at him with curiosity, then spoke in a soothing tone of voice: "No, I didn't know them. Don't worry about it. We all do what we can, Van Noorden."

Spoken to as a child with the inference of forgiveness, the mayor's remark sounded to Jacob nevertheless as if his efforts had fallen short. If only he could forgive himself.

Chapter 88

Again, the liberation seemed far off. The Allies' progress had stalled, dashing all hopes for freedom before the winter. As the risk for detection increased with time, the Illegals' family members felt acutely more vulnerable. On Sergeant Jan Van Houten's insistence, his wife had returned to her hometown to live with her parents for safety reasons.

Jacob started listening to Radio Orange at Jan's house to keep his deputy company. In the small residence's attic, they listened together to the small receiver next door to the brigade offices. At that point, it seemed irrelevant and unlikely that an SD team would bust them. After absorbing the latest news, Jacob would go home and rest in his easy chair, smoke his daily pipe, and let his thoughts run free. He contemplated which words and phrases to use for talking to Margaret, who was still busy with something in the kitchen. Caution had become second nature.

Margaret entered the living room in a critical mood. "You're always coming home late these days. The kids haven't seen much of you."

"You have been away lots yourself. But let's not quarrel. Dear, sit down. I want to tell you something about the Illegality."

"Oh? What about it?" She sat down on the divan.

"Radio Orange has just reported the ambush of a German army sedan with two officers and two soldiers, near the bridge between Putten and Nijkerk. In the attack, one of the Resistance fighters died."

"I know that. I'm aware of what goes on." Her face was determined, lips tight, and eyes averted.

Jacob didn't know her like that, prickly, edgy, or maybe the war had changed her too, and he hadn't noticed. "Really? How would you know?" He looked at her with a smile on his face but with a sense of uneasiness in his gut. She scared him. He crossed his arms over his chest.

Margaret dried her hands on her lab coat, then pushed her hair in shape with spread fingers. "If you really want to know, Elfriede and I are listening in the stable in Mutter's back yard." With a satisfied look, she faced Jacob, who couldn't have been

more surprised. She raffled off her subsequent sentences. "I know the partisans abandoned the injured German, who was later found alive, and another SS officer escaped
to a nearby farmhouse and raised the alarm, then died of his injuries."

He knew his face showed his surprise. "What do you know, my wife has turned
illegal," he said in a mild voice. "Oh no, correction, it's not illegal for Johanna to
listen to the radio. I don't know what to say, Margaret." Then his face changed, and
his eyes turned fierce. He uncrossed his arms and balled his fists in his pockets.

"I have a mind to be so angry with you, placing our kids in danger with whatever
you're doing. Why are you doing that at the house of an NSB member with the end
of the war near?"

She waved her hand in a gesture of dismissal. "Don't patronize me, Jacob. You're
doing the same. What's good for the goose is good for the gander. And it's my
mother's house." Margaret, steadfast, returned his stare.

Pushing back his anger, he reacted. "You sound like you've joined Aletta Jacobs'
feminists."

Confused, she asked: "Who's that? I joined nothing." Then, with more determination than Jacob ever heard from her, she continued. "Don't change the conversation. I also know the German retaliation for that attack was ruthless, and the Wehrmacht surrounded Putten, where the Wehrmacht soldiers captured all citizens." Her
voice caught, then she went on. "I know how they separated the burghers by gender,
and then torched more than a hundred houses. In the end, six men and a woman were
shot dead during the raid. Isn't it ghastly? Those poor families." Her voice had turned
quiet and her face was sad. "Yes, dear husband, I'm aware of the harsh punishment
for illegal work."

Margaret, now full of grief, her shoulders slack, all her defiance seeped out of her,
continued in a soft voice. "Do you know about the seven hundred men from Putten,
dragged off to a camp in Germany?"

He relaxed his fists and carefully replied. "I am very careful, dear wife. I have an
inkling you're doing more than listening to Radio Orange. I was worried to tell you
about it, but now that you are aware of what Illegality membership means for families,
I am determined you should know. Any town can expect this kind of consequences if
an Illegal kills a German. We also have a group in Overdam. You know some of the
members."

He went over to her, sat down beside her on the divan, and took her hand. "The ANP news omitted the German retaliation and many don't know about that part, but you do. I wished I could spare you all of that misery."

She looked at him with kindness in her eyes and laid her head on his shoulder. In a quiet voice, she said, "Don't worry about me, dear. I'm tougher than you think. I'm aware you have a dangerous job and that anything could happen. Just don't tell me about your secrets and I won't tell you about mine."

So, Margaret had secrets. He wanted to ask what those were. He had kept his deals with Henk and with Simon from her, including his meetings in the woods. The less said, the better, so she would not divulge anything about him if ever questioned by the SD. He realized the same danger existed for him about her secrets. Jesus Christ. This goddamn war is ruining everything. He decided he didn't want to know her secrets.

"Good," Jacob said finally, defeated. "I'm satisfied you're aware. Maybe one day soon we can openly share again. You're right. It's better we don't share those secrets. You're beyond surprise, I see it now, which worries me even more." He got up, pulled her to standing kissed her passionately. She kisses him back and clung to him, her arms tight around his waist. He let her go. "Can I do something for you, take those jars to the basement or something?"

Margaret took off the white, but now-stained lab coat. She sat down again.

"Sure. Would be nice, thank you, Jan. After they cooled off."

He returned to his easy chair. "It's really generous of Johanna to keep us stocked. I'm glad you know about Putten, so you're prepared for what could happen here. If I don't show up one evening for supper, you don't need to worry about me. I'll be in hiding. If I'm not back the next day by evening, you must go to Johanna with the children, to be on the safe side. Can you promise me that?"

He bent forward in his chair, elbows resting on his knees, looking at her with an intensity he used to scold the kids after disobedience. She seemed to shrink on the divan, hugging herself tightly, as if cold. The earthy smell of boiled beets penetrated into the living room, even with the kitchen door closed. He didn't really care for beets.

"I understand," Margaret said in a whisper.

They sat together in silence, holding hands.

After five minutes or so, she had recovered her voice. "Let's hope it won't come to that. I would rather not go to Mutter, it's full there now as it is. How long do you think before the Allies will arrive?"

Jacob straighten his back. "Hard to tell, dear. I hope sooner, rather than later for all of our sakes but especially the hungry. If a Messerschmitt started firing at all those people looking for food on the roads now, they'd be falling over like bowling pins. I can't see the Germans becoming more lenient about Red Cross food deliveries to the starving cities. The Allies are standing on the other side of the Rhine. From Breda it's a hop and a skip to us and into Germany. It can't be long now." His demeanor belied his words, and he exhaled sharply, then got up and walked away with slack shoulders. As he left the room, he turned around and said, "By the way, I got word from Adriana. She did get our package and she said, thanks."

Chapter 89

In the absence of Henk and Karel, Elfriede's husband, the family visits at Johanna's continued. On those occasions, a whole other awareness level lived underneath chatting about farm work as the children played. Anything and everything in some way connected to the Nazi occupation wasn't talked about. The news was not the real news, and the actual facts were hidden. An honest discussion could never happen. Stating real opinions would lead to conflicts, which could cause serious damage to relationships and maybe endanger lives.

Jacob behaved exemplarily. He was unusually polite, even friendly, and always shared his appreciation for the food supplies out of gratitude, and also avoiding raising suspicion. More flies are caught with honey than with vinegar. Johanna and Juergen had become less vocal about Hitler's divinity, and Jacob didn't bother trying to convert anybody to the war's political realities.

"You need to know I'm truly grateful for all your help, Mother, and to you too, Juergen. Look at the boys. It's so nice they can play with their cousins."

Margaret smiled at him.

"No problem. What else is family for? Times are hard enough as it is." Juergen said this, his gentle brother-in-law, the Nazi. How could this man believe in the Hitler dogmas?

Jacob patted him on his back in acknowledgment, then turned to Johanna. "Have you seen Henk lately, Mother?"

"He stopped by briefly the other day. He won't tell me where he stays, but it's alright. He's safe." Johanna was friendly as always, polite.

"It's all I wanted to know," Jacob said. "I like him and miss him at our family get-togethers." He wondered if Johanna still believed in Hitler but didn't want to ask. He reminded himself to ask Margaret tonight about it.

"Me too," Johanna agreed. "I wish he would stop what he's doing. It's not a nice time right now."

Jacob couldn't help himself and had to ask. "Don't you wish the war was over, Mother?"

"Sure, I do. Who wouldn't? But it's nice to have Elfriede here with the children, and Margaret is here often too, just like the old days. It's wonderful to have my children close."

If it weren't for the duplicity of it all, these visits would have been enjoyable again.

***

Jacob went outside to smoke a pipe. He admired the sleeping quarters Margaret had long ago arranged for Ruth in the back of the orchard, unused now. He let his thoughts roam freely without anybody to observe him. He must stay vigilant. This news about the Putten retaliation showed the nation that the Nazi monster hadn't lost its talons. Standing out in the yard, he prayed for the end of the occupation. He realized he couldn't last in his deception much longer.

It seemed that half the population had gone underground or undermined the Nazis in other ways. It was satisfying to know his co-conspirators in the Illegality were all part of one government-sanctioned Interior Forces — BS for short — and soon they would join the Allies under the Prince's command. But when?

Commander Simon led his Overdam group under the banner of the Council for the Resistance RVV, one of the three leading organizations, each with a different function, now unified under one umbrella. The commander had come to his calling after the SD had caught him for operating a communist magazine in the north. Once the SD had released him, he had left his province and was hiding in Overdam under a pseudonym. Jacob had never met him in person, nor had anybody else he knew and might have unknowingly bumped into Simon in town. He had to give it to the man: it was a smart move to keep his identity hidden religiously.

A massive national shadow system administered the care for the many hundred-thousands living undercover, the so-called *onderduikers* [hiders]. The Illegality accumulated blank official documents in any way possible including fraud, robbery, and forgery, and it distributed many books of coupons for food, clothing, and other products. It maintained illegal telephone lines and short-wave senders. What didn't it do? The nation thrived on illegality.

Jacob had suspended his sense of the law as he had known it. What was up was down, and down was up. It made him dizzy thinking about it. Living by his conscience and his wits, he had discovered that knowing right from wrong was much more complicated than the law. When the usual rules didn't apply, making decisions became a crapshoot. His crew members and his bosses and others in his network might have their own versions of the truth and the law. He fretted on the outcome of this way of life and wondered how his decisions could bite him in the butt. He hoped he could restore his sense of the law after this crazy occupation ended.

Chapter 90

Air traffic overhead wasn't letting up but too high in the sky for visual identification. The nationality of these countless planes traversing the heavens in waves might be assumed from their direction and the time of day. Once in a while, a plane flew over so low that the villagers knew there would be a crash. They then waited for the explosion. Most of the impacts had been elsewhere.

Some nights a plane flew over low, but no crash followed, and those in the know identified it as a British plane on its first covert flyover, to check the ground crew's readiness. The ground men would scramble to make their presence known with swinging light beacons before the plane would dump its load between the beacons on its second flyover. It was a crude system that worked pretty well — most of the time.

It was late October in Jacob's fourth year with the Nazis. The season of dark nights with windy, wet weather had arrived. Fog hung low between the trees on this particular night. For the first time that month, a plane had dropped out of the sky. The call came in after office hours and was put through to Jacob. Taking young recruit Van Hardenberg along, he decided to investigate, quickly leaving the brigade to prevent Peters or Dijk from getting involved.

The moor was enveloped in darkness. At the suspected crash site, the two policemen spotted a pilot hanging from a tree in a shaft of light from their lanterns, his parachute caught in a high branch. The plane was nowhere to be seen. Two civilians, known to Jacob, were halfway up the tree, cutting the harness ropes. The British pilot appeared unharmed.

One of the men in the tree, startled by the light exposing their activities so blatantly, complained. "Turn the damn light off, you amateur!"

"Hello there. I'm Van Noorden." Jacob spoke loud enough, but not so loud for anybody to hear passing on the adjacent road. "Making sure you fellows are alright. Don't mind us, just carry on and get that fellow the heck out of here. Good night." To Van Hardenberg, he said: "I've seen enough. They seem to have it under control. Let's leave them to it. We'll look for the plane."

They rode their bikes along the forest road. It wasn't raining, although gusts of wind shook the trees overhead, so showers of drips fell on them, occasionally drenching their caps and faces making them wish they'd put on rain gear. The smell of rotting leaves and mushrooms was overwhelming. The drizzle soaked the men's uniforms, dripping down their necks.

Jacob's unofficial job was to guard the British supply dump — planned for the other side of the moor — against surprises from the KK, although he kept this bit of information from his companion. He suspected an accident during the fly-over had interfered with the mission. Most likely, the fog had caused the crash. After searching for several hours, Jacob and Van Hardenberg still hadn't found the wreck. They had circled the suspected crash site and patrolled the area, covering the vicinity twice.

"Hey, Boss, what's that?" Van Hardenberg pointed at two side-by-side light beams ahead of them in the distance. They heard voices. Jacob grabbed his constable by the arm, forcing both their bikes to stop. "In the bushes, quick."

They dragged their bikes off to the side and fell into the wet heather, sheltered from the dirt road by some shrubs. They watched two heavily armed KK men approach, their carbide lights exposing part of their faces. They held their carbines pointed forward in their hands, and their pistols were visible in holsters at their belts.

Jacob whispered in his companion's ear: "Prepare your weapon underneath your jacket, make no noise and do as I do, quietly, and stay on my left. You take the left man. Take your cap off and nod, if you understand me." Van Hardenberg nodded. Both took off their uniform caps and put them down beside them in the ditch.

As the two KK men walked by, chatting and kicking up fallen leaves on the path, Jacob stood up, his weapon aimed shoulder-height at the black uniform ahead. Van Hardenberg closely followed. When Jacob was one meter away, he jumped forward and pressed the gun against the head of the man on the right. "Stop. Don't look behind you. One move and my gun goes off."

"What the fuck," the guard cried out and immediately froze on the spot.

Just one beat behind Jacob, the young recruit had followed his example and held a gun against the KK guard on the left. Jacob nodded at him and instructed his targets. "No sense in hollering. Nobody around here but us. Slowly drop your carbines with your left hand on the ground behind you."

The guards followed his advice.

"Now we're taking your pistols." Jacob changed his own pistol to his left hand while still holding his gun against the man's head, and took the KK's pistol out of its holster with his right. He tucked the German pistol in his belt, switched hands on his gun again, still pressing it against the back of the KK's head. He nodded to Van Hardenberg, indicating his turn. Once both KKs were disarmed, he ordered: "Take your belts off and lie down on your stomachs, noses on the ground."

After this, it was just a matter of immobilizing the captives' hands behind their backs with the belts and tying the KK's woolen scarfs over their eyes. The policemen gathered the German carbines and slung them over their shoulders.

In a threatening tone, Jacob promised: "Stay down and we'll let you live. If not, you get shot."

While Jacob and Van Hardenberg recovered their bikes and caps from the ditch, one of the commandos managed to get up on his feet and started slinking away to the bush at the other side of the road. Jacob spotted the movement before the guard reached the shrubs and aimed. A shot cracked, and the man toppled over, screaming in pain as he clutched his right femur. Jacob pushed Van Hardenberg forward by the shoulder. "He'll live. Let's go."

They jumped on their bikes and sped off. Jacob glanced at his mate after a few minutes. Van Hardenberg wore a big grin. Less than five minutes of hard pedaling away from where they had left the guards, they saw a car parked by the side of the road: the camp's sedan.

"Those buggers would've been wiser staying in their vehicle," Jacob commented.

Van Hardenberg stayed quiet all the way back to the station. The marechaussees arrived at the brigade close to midnight without further sightings of unusual activities. Jacob turned to his constable in the bike shed. "We'll resume the search for the wrecked plane in the morning. Be ready."

Once inside the office, Van Hardenberg started asking questions. "*Opper* [Chief], were we doing anything we shouldn't be doing?"

Jacob raised his eyebrows and stood still, observing the young man. "What do you mean, Van Hardenberg? Speak up, man, don't hold back."

Van Hardenberg shuffled his feet and righted his back.

"Well, for example, Chief, why did we disarm those commandos? And aren't we supposed to report any pilot sighting to the Wehrmacht? It was an alien plane and if we don't report it right away as per Rauter's instructions, we might be in trouble."

Jacob couldn't withhold a smile, recovered quickly, and in a stern voice replied.

"Van Hardenberg. I'm going to say this only once in the hope you'll keep this in mind for the next time. We are Dutchmen, not Krauts. We work for our government to protect our citizens. We do not work for the Nazis. Whatever you do, keep what happened tonight between us. We went on a search for a crashed plane and that's all. Let me rephrase what you said: this is not about an alien plane, but an Allied plane, and anyway, we didn't find any plane, right?"

Jacob's stern gaze on the young man made him shuffle his feet some more.

His eyebrows raised and his eyes fixed on Jacob's face, Van Hardenberg said: "No, Sir. We didn't see a plane, but we did see a pilot and some KK men. It seems clear to me there has to be a crashed plane, somewhere."

"That's right. Constable. I'll spell it out for you. Our country will soon be liberated. All we did was delay those KK traitors, so the Illegals could finish their job saving the pilot. If we were to report this suspected crash immediately and the SD, or the KK found anybody at the indicated location, the pilot and the men helping him would be arrested. Our fellow Dutchmen would be sent to a camp from which they likely wouldn't return. Do you want their arrest on your conscience?"

"No, sir, of course not." Van Hardenberg looked surprised. The look of slow understanding changed the expression on his face. He smiled.

Jacob noted it and nodded. "Good. In any case, we disarmed those KK men before they could hurt us, or others. We didn't kill them, right? No doubt they would've killed us, given a chance. And if the SD was so keen, why weren't they out there already? There's no lack of them in the village. As you saw with your own eyes, they weren't there. If they're too scared of being knocked off in the dark by so-called terrorists, let that be their problem. So, after we search for the wreck ourselves in daylight, I'll make a report and give it to Heusden. Does this answer your questions, Van Hardenberg?"

"Yes, Opper. Sorry I had to ask." Van Hardenberg glanced at Jacob and then looked down.

Jacob smiled. He laid his hand on the man's his shoulder for a second, a kind gesture. "No problem. These are confusing times and you haven't been with us for long. You'll learn. At least you ask the right questions. I'm going to ask you something. If you see anything you don't understand, you should talk with me, not with your colleagues. Do I have your word?"

The recruit nodded frantically as he responded. "Yes, Chief. No problem. You can trust me."

"Good. Go home now. Good night."

They both went to their homes with hope in their hearts and a renewed appreciation for each other. Jacob valued his youngest recruit for having a working brain and an ability to "see" what wasn't observable and say so. The recruit now had seen an aspect of his gruff boss he hadn't expected.

Chapter 91

The deputy chief was off duty the next day. To his surprise, Van Houten called Jacob at six in the morning to let him know the KK had arrested one of the men from the weapons drop on his return to town last night. "Gert Klooster couldn't justify his presence on the forest lane after curfew, and the KK took him to Star Camp."

Jacob sighed. "That's a shame. Alright, I'll see what I can do. Let's hope the KK haven't started the interrogation yet. We met two of them on the way home and I shot one in the leg. They weren't happy," he chuckled.

After a quick wash and getting dressed in his uniform, he jumped on his bicycle, hoping Schwier wouldn't be in town. He arrived at the camp before the inmates had finished breakfast. He requested the reluctant guard to let him in to see the warden. It took a while and a changing of the guard. The new watchman told him the boss was still at his private residence, called Nauwaard, and told him the Marechaussee Corps' chief was at the gate to see him.

As Jacob walked to the residence in the forest, he mumbled words, trying to find the proper phrasing. The front door opened before he had arrived on the doorstep. Charles Nauwaard glared at him, a frown on his face.

"Goddamn, Jake. What are you doing here at this God-awful hour?"

Jacob forgot his prepared sentences. "Sorry about that." He tried to find the right tone but didn't want to beg either. Already sweating this early in the morning, he just barged in with: "I need your help, Charles. I've got a small problem and thought I'd better catch you before the day starts taking over. Could I come in, please?"

Without an explanation, he handed Charles a brown bag with a bottle of Dutch gin, a gift he'd saved for just such an occasion. "I thought you might like this. I don't drink gin myself." That was a lie, but the goal justified the means.

Charles opened the door wider and let him in.

Jacob continued talking. "Anyway, there's this young man I know from my church, Gert Klooster. He's caring for his elderly parents. The KK caught him without an ID last night. I heard he is here. Could we get him released? He was just in the wrong place at the wrong time."

Charles looked at him with eyebrows raised and a sneer around his mouth. "I was told the man is a partisan and involved with an enemy plane crash."

"Sure. I can see why they'd think so, but it's wishful thinking," Jacob said in a lighthearted tone of voice, and he shrugged. "Looks deceive."

Charles said nothing and just stared at him.

Jacob's voice became grave when he spoke again. "If you want to know the truth: Gert was out poaching for food. He was out late checking his traps, but lost track of time. He understandably didn't want to incriminate himself and wouldn't tell the KK what he was doing. He didn't bring his ID but I can vouch for him."

"Stupid of him then. Why do you care?" The warden still stared at him.

Hoping to project a shared sense of charity among compatriots, he said in a confidential tone, "He's from my church. I know his parents well, good Christian people, and elderly. His father is in a wheelchair and his mother is debilitated by arthritis and can hardly get around. They completely depend on him. The fellow is doing no harm."

Charles heard him out, then growled: "You've got some nerve bothering me this early for a goddamn Calvinist. It must be your lucky day: Schwier is away in the city. Do you know by any chance who shot one of Schwier's commandos in the leg?"

Jacob had expected this question and made sure his face didn't change. "No idea. What happened?"

"Some assault by partisans, but your fellow Klooster was indeed unarmed," the man said. "Thanks for the gin anyway. Let's go."

They walked to the camp in silence. At Nauwaard's direction, the guards located the prisoner. The young man looked surprised but kept his mouth shut. Charles released Gert Klooster into Jacob's control without a blemish on him.

Jacob took him back to town on the back of his bike, but not before admonishing: "In future, you'd better hurry up after a drop, otherwise there might not be a next time, son."

***

By nine in the morning, he was free to continue the crash investigation with Van Hardenberg. They found the wreck and a few hours later, stripped of everything, and he submitted a copy of the crash report to Heusden with a small cedar box containing six cigars. They had a little chat. Heusden felt the end of the war was near. Heusden hoped the transition of power would be smooth. Jacob agreed. The day had started well.

Chapter 92

A few days later, Charles Nauwaard called Jacob to tell him SS boss Rauter had suddenly terminated the national labor inspection with its Dutch employees. Rauter thought the German *Ordnungpolizei* [Order Police] were more trustworthy, and should do the job of recruiting laborers for the *Arbeitseinsatz*. The economy must go on, and the production of army supplies could not stop whatever else happened.

"The Dutch are out of a job," the warden said.

"Is this the end of the KK then?" Jacob did his best to keep any sentiment out of his voice but didn't wholly succeed.

"I'll have to disappoint you, my friend. Schwier has privileges with Rauter: he could keep his KK men, forty man strong. I suspect he's got a leg up after handing over those millions from the sale of assets of Rudolph Steiner's club and that Krishnamurti holy man. Rauter trusts good soldier Schwier," he chortled. "We're still under the Ordnungpolizei. I can still charge all expenditures back to the Labor Department. Governing a country cost big-bucks and the Germans weren't going to pay for it." The sarcasm dripped from his voice.

With the goal in mind to keep the conversation positive and to keep him talking, Jacob played along. "Nicely put, but governing is not what I'd call it. By the way, I see you've changed colors, from black to green. The townies call you, fellows, the Greens nowadays."

"That's the only change: to the green unis of the German police," Charles said.

"But like the leopard and his spots, your KKs won't stop their tricks." Jacob laughed at his own joke.

The prison boss made the sound of laughing, but there was no joy in it. "Your jokes are terrible. Stop trying."

"Thanks anyway for the update. We'll see how it plays out." Jacob disconnected and went back to his paperwork. With the KK becoming ever more vicious and no longer supervised by the Labor Office, he was relieved he had intervened on young Gert's behalf. This time, it all had ended well.

***

Besides delinquent, the KK also seemed better informed. Henk called Jacob a fort-night later in a panic about them.

"Jacob, would you please send some men to the Calvinist church in Lemelerveld? We've got a big weapon's stash there. The KK caught three of my best men and I'm afraid they'll not keep quiet for long under torture. We got to get rid of the weapons before the Kraut gets his dirty claws on them. Bring a vehicle or two if you can. There's a lot of stuff."

"I'll do my best. We first have to find a truck. Is a sedan big enough?"

"Maybe two or three sedans, a farm cart maybe?

"Have you talked to Simon yet?"

"No, but I will, right after our call. So please, get to it. I hope to God my captured men won't give us all up. Let me know what you come up with."

Jacob called his contact, AKA Tinkerbel, who promised to pass on a message to Commander Simon. Next, he called the mayor to ask to borrow his sedan. To get info on the three arrested, he called Charles Nauwaard with some excuse about one of the wives requesting to deliver extra food. He learned they were still there, awaiting interrogation.

Then he called a befriended farmer to ask if he might borrow a cart, but the man said he had none. At last, he called Johanna, asking to borrow her horse and cart. She was surprisingly accommodating, and without asking questions, told him to come and pick up the cart.

After half a day of organizing, he finally had a farm cart, a sedan, and a plan. Farmer Dirk Lantink would pick up Johanna's cart filled with hay, and marechaussee De Wit would drive the mayor's sedan; they would drop off the materials at Dirk's farm. The vehicles would travel separately and stop a block from the Calvinist church at 7 p.m., an hour before curfew. Jacob would first check out the situation at the church and prepare the janitor. If all was safe, he would meet Dirk and De Wit a block from the church and give the go-ahead. In case of a last-minute problem, Jacob would place the church's garbage container at the curb. In that case, all would just drive by and go home. Simon approved the plan.

Luckily, it wasn't a garbage day. Around six that evening, Jacob cycled over and found the janitor in the sanctuary room at the church's back. He was about to explain his mission when they heard the sudden sounds of a many boots resounding on the nave's plank floor.

"Go see what's going on," Jacob urged the janitor, who rushed through the door leading into the nave.

Jacob quickly slipped out the back door. Several dented galvanized-zinc garbage cans sat in the backyard. He hauled one of those along the side of the building, staying in the wall's protective shade. When he peeked around the corner, he saw two army trucks parked in front and no guard. He dashed to the curb, positioned the garbage can, picked up his bicycle from the picket fence, and sped off.

Later that night, he heard the men had returned the sedan and the cart to their owners. He hoped their failed rescue mission wouldn't cost any lives. He couldn't reach Henk but left a message with Tinkerbel. Distraught, he prayed on his knees before his bed for Henk's men, until the pain in his kneecaps made him stop.

***

A couple of days later, they had a chance to meet briefly. Standing at the dark side of a hotel in Hardenberg just before curfew, Henk told Jacob what had happened.

"Henk Houtman, one of our most active members, and a new fellow, named Dovelaar, transported jerry cans with stolen petrol on the back of their bikes, on their way to a secure address. Three KKs stopped them in front of Muller's butcher store in Lemelerveld."

Jacob, always on the lookout for moles, interrupted him. "Did you know that Dovelaar?"

"Yeah, I know he joined the German army, but deserted in the spring and went into hiding. He had just joined our group. So?"

Jacob pursed his lips, then asked: "You trust a guy who volunteered for the Nazi army?"

Henk shrugged. "Well, he seemed alright. People can change. Doesn't matter now. Shut up, let me tell what happened."

"Alright," Jacob said, throwing up his hands.

"Houtman tried to escape with Bakker on his heels, and got cornered in the stables. Houtman's girlfriend told me this all happened at her parents' farm. She witnessed Bakker empty two clips of bullets from his 08-caliber gun at her fiancé's head. The bastards left his body lying there, but took Muller, that butcher, and Dovelaar to the camp for interrogation."

Jacob swallowed hard. "The degenerates," he panted. "I should've killed those two bastards when I had the chance."

With a wavering voice, Henk continued. "We can guess what happened. Bakker must have "convinced" Dovelaar to give up names and addresses. We didn't have time to warn anybody. I fear they're all dead." With bowed head Henk just stood there, kneading his hands.

"I'm so sorry, Henk." He put his hand on Henk's arm. His own fear had morphed into Henk's reality. "It's what I fear every day myself," he admitted.

"Yeah." It was quiet for a few long minutes until Henk continued with anger in his voice. "We've been sending messages to England asking them to bomb the camp and kill those brutes. Those man-hunters have trapped many of our good men. They get their information by torture, you know that. They're always well informed. Why the hell are you still talking to that snake Nauwaard?"

Sensing Henk's pain, he didn't know what to say. He disagreed. After a brief delay, he slowly replied to Henk's searing, implied accusation.

"I'm truly sorry about your men. You know Simon's assignment for me is to talk to the prison director, become friendly. I don't like it myself. I don't want to save the KK, but if the British bomb the camp, they'll also take out the prisoners, all innocent men hunted down for the *Arbeitseinsatz* and the like. Maybe capturing the camp leadership might be an option. We could smuggle in weapons to arm the prisoners and cause a revolt."

Henk's anger had dissipated. In a quiet voice, he said, "Wouldn't know how. My group doesn't exist anymore, so it'll have to be your group to do anything. I'll talk to Simon and let you know," spoken in a dull monotone. Henk turned around without saying goodbye and left on his motorbike.

It was evident in Henk's eyes Jacob had failed in whatever little he had been asked to do. He tucked his scarf into his jacket and mounted his bicycle. He resented that

Henk accused him. At a snail's pace, he rode home, unable to turn his thoughts away from the question: what if it had been his crew and not Henk's.

***

He met Henk once more on a moonless, cold December night. Henk looked like a hunter, all in dark green, dressed in plus-fours and boots, with a hunter's oil slick jacket and an ascot cap. Jacob was dressed in a seldom-worn pair of grey slacks and a dark brown woolen jacket, and a fedora. They stood close to each other and shook hands, keeping the shake going a little longer than usual.

Henk spoke first. "Does your family have enough food?"

"Good to see you alive, brother. Yes, we're fine. Johanna and Juergen are good for it. Is your family safe? What's up with you? You're looking smart today."

Henk got to the point. "Yeah, my boys and wife are fine, my wife went home to her parents. My in-laws are looking after them. About the KK: it's impossible to get any action off the ground. Simon won't risk his men for an action on the camp, and the front is moving too slow for my taste. I'm going to travel south and join the Allies, probably the Canadians, or the Polish, or the English if I get my hands on a boat. I'll see where they'll send me. All was ruined by that monster Bakker and the SS bastard Schwier. Nauwaard and De Jong also played their parts. Most of our men eventually sang. I don't blame them for it. Does any man really know his breaking point?"

Jacob groaned. "You got that right. It's my worst fear. Tremendously motivating. Gets you in gear to prevent it from happening again. What happened to the Lemelerveld janitor?"

"About twenty SD men arrested him after they found the British weapons in the attic. I guess they didn't believe his claims he didn't know about it."

"Yeah, I could barely slip away, hadn't even told him why I was there, just not enough time to arrange it all. Sorry about that."

"I'm sorry too. Don't worry about it. There's a good chance the SD will let him go. He really didn't know about it." Henk took off his cap and ran his hand through his full head of hair.

Jacob watched with envy, then remembered something. "I hear they've arrested the marechaussee from your town, Pieter Lievers."

Henk put his cap back and stuffed his hands in his pocket, his gloves tucked under his arm. "Yeah, I don't give him much of a chance for survival, he's an old man. You should try to get him out of there."

"Sure. I'll try. I hope we'll make it till the end, Henk. Got any of that good brandy left?" It was cold. He could do with a bit of heat.

"No, I'm all out of everything including brandy. So far, we're lucky to be alive. What's keeping those Allies? Damn, it's taking them long to get here." He started stomping his feet for some heat.

Jacob nodded. He was still warm from pedaling to make it to their meet. "I'm not sure how long Nauwaard is willing to back me. I don't like my chances in a confrontation with Schwier, or Bakker. God willing, we'll both survive a little longer." He exhaled deeply and slowly.

Henk had some advice. "Don't put your trust in God only. Can you even still believe in any religion? I don't anymore. We make religion up to make us feel better. What God lets this all happen, I ask you? No, don't answer me. You watch those bastards."

Jacob sensed his anguish, which reverberated in his own soul, but he couldn't let that desperation overtake him. "Yes, I believe in God," he said quietly. "I bet your men will be praying right now. Just like all those in the Scheveningen prison, and the captured in the SD head-offices in Amsterdam and The Hague are praying for their lives. Faith can make one stronger. Don't knock it; you still have your freedom." He sounded like an evangelist and didn't like it. He wasn't usually publicizing his belief: too many hypocrites in that crowd.

Henk looked up with a guilty face. "If you say so. Sorry, didn't mean to insult you."

Jacob nodded and said, "Thanks. But I will heed your warning. I will. Believe me, I know the danger. Working with the camp boss is like a game of high stakes poker: you win big or you lose big." He told Henk about the English flyboy pilot in hiding and his capture, the suspicion that Nauwaard tried to set him up. "There're plenty of traitors around here."

"It's possible, no — probable. But watch Schwier. In the last four months alone, ten people died at the hands of the KK."

"Yes, correct. Schwier is at the camp now each damn day. Don't discount De Jong neither, his right-hand man." He touched Henk on his arm. "I'm sorry to see you leave. I wish I could go with you. Good camouflage, by the way: the beard, I mean," Jacob commented.

Henk smiled and caressed his full beard.

It was a freezing cold night, and they didn't linger. Shortly after they exchanged the V1 and V2 launching sites' exact coordinates, they said their goodbyes. Each looked at the other a tad longer than usual — barely able to see each other's faces in the dark — while shaking hands, solid and hard.

"God be with you," said Jacob. Henk groaned in response.

Jacob didn't want Henk to go, his closest and most trusted relative now, even more so than Margaret. The man had become the substitute for his own brothers. So strange that Juergen and Henk were so different, but brothers. He wondered what would make one weak and the other courageous. As far as relatives are concerned, Henk made it alright in the world. Adriana and Josefina came to mind. With his monthly food packages, they'll survive. He thought of his brothers. Was there still time to make things right? He sighed and made a promise to meet them in freedom after the war.

On his trip home in the frigid air, he thought about the risks of the coming months or however long this war was going to last.

He worried about Margaret, his children. He didn't want to alienate her from her relatives, even as he held contradictory opinions about them. He wondered how she reconciled those complicated family ties. He should ask her.

Margaret somehow bridged the gap and lived with the contradictions in her family. Contrary to her, he had just discarded his difficult relatives, taking the easy exit. His mom had died of influenza within days of getting ill. He hadn't visited her, just because he didn't want to face his father, hurting her in the process — the parent he loved. He regretted she hadn't met Margaret and her grandchildren. After his parents' deaths, he had scarcely visited the coastal relatives and only saw his sisters once.

He had loved his mother dearly and appreciated her protection against his brothers using him as a target for their pent-up aggression. He hated his father because of his harsh punishments and his constant put-downs, even for even minor offenses — demeaning humiliations that wrecked his life. On the day he left home, the bastard had so criticized his work on the shop ledger that he would have liked to murder him.

Instead he left home and signed on with the military. He had always assumed that his father had died of misery, but he heard later from Sientje he had died of a heart attack. He hadn't felt guilty about not attending the son of a bitch's funeral — still didn't. You can't choose your relatives, but you can choose whom to love.

He recalled his years at home with sadness and bitterness. He would never forgive his brothers for making him steal money from the till. Was it still healthy to hold a grudge that long? In the face of death, it was a foolish thing. Time to let it all go.

His thought returned to Margaret. He loved her. He should tell her that more often, but somehow that was difficult for him. The burden of caring for Margaret and the kids — his chosen loves — was growing over his head. At least he was able to share his worries with Henk. He envied Henk his enthusiasm for joining the Allies. Not everybody was arrested — Henk was still safe. A good thing he was leaving. Today he was different — it smelled like desperation. Henk got the freedom to go, because he had lost all his men.

With the Allied forces stuck in the south, this year's winter had become desperate for everybody. The ultimate blackness of the night engulfed Jacob, and his loneliness overwhelmed him. He felt heavy. His limbs had trouble moving the bike forward. He was exposed. Even in the dark he could be a target, a silhouette against the sky for a sharpshooter on the ground. He was anticipating the final shot, not knowing when it would explode his brain.

Chapter 93

On January 14, 1945, at two o'clock on a quiet Sunday afternoon, a couple of Allied bombers attacked the railway lines to the Overdam's station and the railway bridge across the river Vecht. The bombers had also hit Star Camp. Charles Nauwaard called Jacob with fear in his voice.

"It's a bloodbath here. Extensive damage. We need help. Don't know how many are dead, but we've got many injured. We need help to get them to the hospitals. Recruit all the vehicles you can locate."

"Alright, we'll be there as soon as possible. Did you call the ambulance yet?"

"No. The fucking Wehrmacht claimed the two town ambulances for the front. Hurry up."

Jacob quickly instructed his men, not giving it a second thought to assist the camp.

"Take as much first aid stuff as you can find and tell your wives to join us there. I'm going to call the mayor. Peters, you stay here on duty. Could you ask your wife to come and get my kids, or stay with them here? Whatever works for her is fine. Margaret's a nurse, we need her at the camp."

When he called the mayor, Van Voorst agreed to pick them up and added he'd call the Air Defense crew to help out. About fifteen minutes later, the mayor arrived in his sedan and took Jacob, Margaret, Van Houten, and two other crew members to the camp.

"Did somebody call the doctors?" Margaret asked Jacob in the car. She had her lab coat on and had tied a scarf to cover her hair. She looked like a cross between a doctor and a house cleaner.

Jacob reached out from the front seat, grabbed her hand and pressed it. "I'm sure Charles would've. I'm glad you could come with us. Thank you."

When Jacob with his companions passed through the wide-open camp gate, he saw a horrific scene: bodies all over the camp, blood everywhere. Injured men lay sprawled on the frosty ground in their tattered prison garb. The mayor parked the car by the nearest injured.

"Oh, my God. It's worse than I thought," Margaret called out. She got out of the vehicle and ran to the first thin bodies.

Jacob slowly got out of the sedan while scanning the area. He could hardly recognize the prisoners, already in bad shape, as humans. The injured looked like small heaps of discarded, bloody remains, roughly wrapped in striped canvas pieces laid out on the ground. Three bodies lay in the compound covered head to toe by pieces of canvas.

He looked for Margaret and saw she had joined the two local doctors. The three of them were busy with the triage of patients. He heard Margaret instruct a group of guards to take the most-severely injured to the office.

He walked up to Charles, who was aimlessly running from one side of the yard to the other. "Charles. Could you stop for a minute? Sorry about the attack. How can we help?"

"Oh, yeah. Some of my guards are injured, but my men will look after them. Goddamn it, what a mess." The warden stood wringing his hands, unlike a man in command.

"Maybe tell your men to pick up those injured prisoners and bring them inside as Margaret and the doctors will tell them to. We need vehicles." Jacob felt sympathy for him. His confidence had been so easily dislodged. "Did you ask the Wehrmacht to help you? They've got plenty of vehicles."

"Yeah, I did but those bastards haven't arrived."

Jacob had the feeling they wouldn't join the party.

Charles did as Jacob suggested, and charged his staff to follow Margaret's directions and those of the doctors for the care of the twenty-nine injured. While the secretary was calling around for vehicles, all others at the camp did what they could. The brigade's materials came in handy, but more supplies were needed, and calls were made. Within a half-hour, volunteers arrived from town, carrying sheets and towels.

Under the guidance of the doctors, Margaret instructed the police wives and other volunteers from the community to put blankets underneath and on top of the injured, who could not be moved yet. Some volunteers tore up thin, worn sheets into strips. If a man could walk, the guards and prisoners led him inside the barracks that were still standing and laid him down on sacks filled with straw — the camp stand-in for mattresses.

Charles handed Jacob three bottles of brandy from the well-stocked camp stash, and he, in turn, distributed it to his crew members and to Margaret. The plentiful brandy kept some life in the injured who were able to swallow, and it generated some heat and dulled the pain.

Jacob was wrong: the Wehrmacht arrived with six men and two trucks. The men carried the injured as directed into the vehicles and laid them down on a bed of straw, after which the trucks took off for the closest hospital.

Out of nowhere, cars and commercial vehicles appeared with villagers behind the wheel, and these volunteers also ferried the injured to hospitals nearby. After the living, the dead got their turn. The camp guards carried the three deceased to the guard barracks outside the palisade fence for the undertaker.

The camp kitchen staff prepared a meal for all at the end of the afternoon. The volunteers were shocked at this wealth of food in a prison where the inmates were bone-thin, but the guards looked well-fed and healthy. Van Houten wondered out loud: "Is all this quantity of food today an everyday event? Or a showing-off for our benefit." He asked a prisoner, who answered him between big bites.

"Who cares, I'm hungry," said the man wolfing down thick slices of buttered, real bread with ham or cheese intermittently swallowing sips of the whole milk served with the meal. After the man finished eating and leaned back in his seat, looking ill, he added: "I ate too much. We never get this much inside us within three minutes."

It slowly dawned on the sergeant he had heard this before. "Is that all the time you get for your meals?"

The man nodded, got up in haste while making retching sounds as he pressed his hands before his mouth, and ran out the barracks.

"Good God," Van Houten said to Peters, seated beside him.

***

Just for one day, the helpers on either side of the Nazi divide acted in unison as compatriots. Even the Wehrmacht soldiers pitched in. With the Allies so near, all sensed the end of the war was near. The pain and suffering were coming to an end. It took all day and most of the evening to establish some order in the chaos, and it was late when Nauwaard locked the gate. The civilian ghost vehicles mysteriously disappeared again before any authority could lay a hand on those.

Jacob invited Charles to come in when the warden dropped off the paperwork for the dead a few days after the bombing. When Margaret reluctantly put a cup of chicory coffee before him, the man looked up at her with the expression of a beaten dog. She averted her eyes, and when he spoke to her, she focused on his chin.

"Margaret, you were great. I appreciated your help," he said, sounding sincere. Then he looked at Jacob. "Thank you both for all you did. I couldn't have managed without. I won't forget it."

Charles Nauwaard had a chat with the boys. He was remarkably subdued and friendly, and not a single curse came over his lips. After he had left, Margaret commented: "This is the first time I've thought of him as a person."

***

In the months of rebuilding the camp, Jacob and Nauwaard met regularly. In this time of scarcity, shipments and stored materials had to be guarded to prevent the locals from stealing the goods during transport or after delivery. Cooperation now came naturally to the two chiefs. Jacob believed he was operating within a neutral space between collaboration with the enemy and resistance to the occupier. He was wrong. Eyes watched and tongues wagged.

Chapter 94

During February, British and American planes frequently flew over Overdam, feeding the expectation that the Germans' demise wasn't far off. Since the railroad strike, the Nazi leadership had restored the essential train routes, now run by German railroad personnel but only for strictly German purposes. Private citizens were forbidden to travel by train unless they obtained a special permit. The Reich's Office gave the order to restore the Overdam railroad line lickity-split for a new launching site of the V1 and V2 rockets.

The Wehrmacht OT commander in charge of the engineering division ordered Jacob via Overfeldwebel Fritz Heusden to close off a vast forested area surrounding the side-line, south of the mainline. This section included his secret meeting place with Henk, but that was no problem since they wouldn't meet anymore. He had passed on the coordinates to Henk in their last meeting, so the Allies knew them too. The rockets targeted the Allied positions at the front, still up to two hundred kilometers away.

The OT installation became another potential deadly concern for Jacob. The day the rockets became active, he put the item as number one on the agenda. "Have you heard the racket at daybreak?"

"Yep, I heard the impressive launch," Van Houten said.

"That's the pits for our town, because it invites more Allied spot attacks with undoubtedly also civilian victims. We don't need those monsters here, Van Houten. I wonder if there's anything we could do."

"I wonder why it takes so long between launches. Do you know?" De Wit asked.

Jacob had an answer this time. "Heusden told me it takes hard physical labor to get those monsters loaded off the train, then onto flatbeds to the launch site, and more time to load the heavy suckers into the launchers, without dropping them and setting them off."

Van Houten related his own experience. "I did do a drive-by this morning. I'll tell you, it's a sight to see. That V rocket rises straight up into the air, then slowly tilts 90 degrees and after a split second of hesitation, it continues its horizontal trajectory. You'd think it would crash, but it doesn't."

Jacob resented the admiration in his sergeant's voice. "The Krauts didn't perfect that weapon yet. Heusden said sometimes 90 degrees becomes 180 degrees. It will often crash and dig into the earth, causing an enormous explosion. You can guess what happens to the crew then."

That detail hit Leversma, and not so much Van Houten as Jacob intended. "We don't want to see that happen. It's too damn close to town," Leversma said in a grave voice.

Van Houten disagreed. "Oh well, it's far enough from the town and our people. We don't care about the Krauts at the launching sites."

That comment triggered Jacob's thoughts about his boys. He had already forbidden them to venture far from home, but kids are forgetful. Merely thinking aloud, he murmured: "From the camp road you can see those damn things being launched. Maybe I should take my boys to watch from a safe distance, before they venture out on their own."

"I'm sure any boy would like that," Van Hardenberg enthused, himself apparently not outgrown that stage.

At the end of the meeting, the crew went back to work with renewed energy, the front noticeably coming closer.

***

In spite of Henk's pull in the Illegality and the subsequent Allied attempts to bomb the V 2 site, it remained untouched, camouflaged too well, and the Kraut OT crew moved its location frequently.

Jacob knew from Nauwaard that the Wehrmacht used the secondary railroad track to bring in alcohol or some other industrial liquid for fueling the rockets. He told Van Houten: "They move the launch site too often. Keep your eyes on that line and be sure to give Simon frequent updates."

Chapter 95

Nine-year-old Hendrik and six-year-old Jaap played rockets in the driveway with their contraption made of planks on a set of discarded perambulator wheels. Hendrik used his body as the rocket, showing Jaap how a rocket demolishes a tank: the impact instantly separated the wheels from the body.

Suddenly, they heard the sound of a real plane nearing rapidly, and a few seconds later, an Allied fighter dove down. They could see the white star on the fuselage. A spray of bullets hit a Wehrmacht truck they hadn't noticed until then. The engine pulled a large flatbed through the street with a monstrous thing hidden under tarps. The clatter of the bullets hitting metal and the street pavers sounded like a giant, throwing rocks at them. The boys froze and stared as the driver and by-rider jumped out and dove into the ditch.

The plane disappeared; it was tranquil in the street as if nothing had happened. Hendrik and Jaap ran out of the yard to the trailer and peeked under the tarp. To their excitement, they saw an enormous rocket stretched out on the flatbed right in front of their noses.

Just then, Margaret came running around the corner from the building and started yelling. "You, boys. Come here. Right this minute."

They didn't move. Two seconds later, grabbed by the arm, the boys were forced away from danger. Margaret dragged them along with her across the street and into the relative safety of the compound. Once inside the front door, she gave each boy a good smack on their behind. Then she hugged them.

The sermon followed in the kitchen. She looked angry and was almost crying.

"What you both did was foolish and dangerous," she panted. "You played with your lives, you could've been hit by the bullets. If you once more leave the compound without my permission, you'll be grounded for a month. You'll go to bed without dinner. I'll tell Papa what you did, too." She shook her head in disgust as the boys stared at her, not taking it in. Then she added: "If the plane had hit the rocket, you both would be dead, and all of us in the brigade would be dead too, because the truck was right close to us."

Hendrik looked insulted and defended himself. "We knew to be careful, Mama. We saw the drivers in the ditch. We didn't come close until the plane was gone."

Frowning, Margaret grabbed his arm and jerked hard, then bent over, her face close to his. "Don't you talk back. You were not safe, even if the rocket didn't explode yet. The plane could make a turn and come back for a second time, or the rocket could explode a bit later."

She backed off and let his arm go, as she continued explaining in a softer tone of voice. "In Luttenberg a rocket crashed to the ground, and at first it didn't explode. But while the nosy people were standing close, just like you two, the rocket exploded, killing all the people watching, nineteen people dead. Do you understand now that I don't want you close to any of those rockets? I love you and would be very, very sad if you got killed."

Hendrik nodded. "*Goed, mama, ik zal't nooit meer doen* [Alright, mom, I won't do it ever again]."

The boys played for the rest of the day in the backyard, while Margaret checked on them every fifteen minutes.

Later that evening, after Margaret had told Jacob the story, he gave the boys another good hit on their behinds for their infraction, in spite of his intent not to spank anymore, maybe just as relief for his own anxiety. And his own guilt: he hadn't taken the boys to watch the launch from a safe distance to satisfy their curiosity, as he intended. He sent them both straight to bed.

He couldn't believe his own boys had come within a hair's width of their death, right in front of the brigade. After a brief reflection, he went upstairs to tuck them into bed and explain a few things.

"I'm sorry I spanked you, boys, but I did that, so you won't forget how serious this is. War isn't a game. Many people get killed. You boys have to listen to your mother. I love you, we both do, and we'd be devastated if something happened to either of you." He exhaled deeply, then kissed each boy goodnight.

Chapter 96

It was a time of intense insecurity. Jacob turned into an edgy fellow. When he thought about it, he didn't recognize himself from the man he was before the war. One possibility was getting caught in an illegal act. Just last night, Radio Orange announced a group of Illegals had attacked a German sedan near a recreational establishment called The Desolate Homestead. He made some calls to find out more before meeting his sergeant for briefing.

Jacob sat Van Houten down, and in an austere tone of voice, he said, "Pay attention. This is important, Jan. I don't know which group did this, but please, tell your group members to double-check whomever they target. I heard Schwier's boss was in the vehicle and the K.P. men didn't know it. The men weren't paying attention, dragged the supposedly-dead Nazis out into the road but didn't check their pulses, and then took off in the sedan, but Rauter wasn't dead."

"Damn bad luck. The men should've killed the SS bastard," Van Houten said airily.

Jacob slammed his flat hand on the desk, startling his deputy. "No, it's just stupid and careless, and it'll cost more lives."

"Of course, Opper, you're right. Don't get upset, it's not worth it. Rauter fell into his own trap, after telling his upper echelon to only travel in unmarked cars. If that isn't poetic justice! Nobody knew Rauter was in that car." The younger man laughed.

Jacob shook his head, and he quietly said: "Don't be facetious, Jan. It's never justice when lives are wasted without a thought, just for a car, even enemy lives. The SS boss will retaliate. This will not go unpunished."

"That's true, Boss." The young man still smiled.

"Anyway, he survived," Jacob said but couldn't fault his sergeant — so much energy, so much youthful brawn. In a calm voice, he added: "Rauter must've made a pact with the devil. Now we're going to get it. Be extraordinarily careful when you're out there, Sergeant. I rely on you." His heart ached when he said that.

"Sure thing, Opper. I'll survive." Van Houten's demeanor changed, and his smile was gone.

"Alright. I worry about you, Jan."

***

A few days later, Jacob heard from his colleague in the capital that Schoengarth, Rauter's deputy, had instructed his security police to collect and execute three-hundred men from prisons in the area. The involved prison wardens didn't cooperate and argued their prisoners had only been arrested for minor offenses, and it wasn't fair to shoot them.

From Charles, Jacob heard the rest of the disaster. "Schwier told me they could only gather up two-hundred and sixty-three prisoners in the end, but none were from our camp." The warden scoffed, "We're not considered a prison anymore, but just a labor camp, hah."

Jacob had lost some of his fear for Nauwaard and freely spoke his thoughts. "That many of ours for four German officers is out of any kind of proportion," Jacob fumed. "Is eighty-six Dutchmen for each Nazi the right punishment? I remember Rauter's announcement he'd take three of ours for every Nazi murdered. Now it involved his own skin, he broke his prior promise. Did you ever meet that devil?" He hoped the answer would reveal more about Charles' relationship with the deadly SD boss.

"Yeah, I did meet him," Charles said reluctantly. "In the first year after opening he was here with his entourage. I don't like him. He's an arrogant son of a bitch. I hate those frigging pretenders too, like Schwier, kowtowing, bending this way and that just to make Rauter happy."

Jacob concluded that Nauwaard's commitment to Schwier was obviously personal but not absolute. Good to know. He launched his bait. "Did you know your employer came close to his death?" He was sorry he couldn't see Nauwaard's reactions. It was quiet on the line for a few beats.

Charles cleared his throat, then said: "I doubt it. It's just the Illegals bragging. Sure, he was injured, but he'll recover."

In his most innocent voice, Jacob asked his next question. "How come your KK clan is so quiet these days?"

"Are they? I wouldn't know."

"You handimen must be getting worried about your reputations," Jacob chuckled.

"Don't you worry about us," he barked. "Better worry about the SD and what they'll do to the Illegals. Those saboteurs better watch their step. It's complete extermination now. I heard the SD shot over a thousand hostages from the prisons last September. Gotta go now." He disconnected.

The callous remark proved it: Charles Nauwaard lacked a soul. Jacob wondered if a person could become numb to atrocious acts simply by frequent exposure. Jacob understood fear. The fear for his own unveiling and his extreme caution in everything he undertook had protected him and his family until now, but it might not be enough. Looking for new ways to protect himself from those degenerates of the KK crew, the question of killing the animals in cold blood needed an answer. Those monsters who didn't hesitate to kill others. He doubted he had it in him to kill Charles Nauwaard, which made the man even more dangerous and he prayed for an escape.

***

Although injured, Rauter was still functional. He ordered the arrest of all unemployed men over sixteen who had no legitimate reason for their presence in the province. He also extended the curfew to start at 5 p.m. instead of 8 p.m. exclusively for Overijssel — a dangerous province for Germans.

Chapter 97

Margaret and Elfriede had become the transportation organizers for the area's Illegality. Elfriede transported the goods while Margaret made sure the paperwork, dates, and places were confirmed, and she looked after the children. Elfriede didn't care she was on her own with the deliveries, as she enjoyed the adventure, while Margaret possessed less ambition and preferred the more traditional role of childcare, which came easy to her anyway.

Except for that one time, when Elfriede was ill with a high fever and couldn't drag herself out of bed, but the goods had to be delivered. Their reputation and the lives of others depended on it, especially on the forged ID documents. Elfriede begged her with a delirious head to take over — just this once. As the panic paralyzed her, thinking about the dangers she might face, Margaret, with her soft heart, agreed, so she pushed those thoughts away.

She received her load of cash and the documentation from Wouters — the local distribution office's manager. With her carrier bags full of heavy, canvas bags — she suspected contained the money — and a number of sealed envelopes, she traveled back and forth between Overdam and nearby distribution locations. She didn't know precisely how Wouters distributed the money to its intended recipients, or what the documentation envelopes contained. She didn't realize that Wouters continued his work in the Illegality despite his experiences in the SD's jail last year — or possibly because of it.

It took her all longer than she expected. It was already a few minutes after five — curfew time. Margaret pedaled as fast as she could when two SD officers stepped into her path. One of them grabbed her bike's handlebars with a frown, distorting his potentially handsome face, making her almost lose her balance. She could see an army vehicle parked some meters down the road, partially hidden by shrubbery.

"*Absteigen, Fraulein* [Get off your bike, lady]," he said with a gruff voice. "*Whohin gehts* [Where're you going]? Don't you know it is past the curfew? *Gib mir eine Antwort* [answer me]!"

She got off the bike, and the soldier let go of the frame. In perfect German, she replied in a cheerful voice: "Good evening, gentlemen. Of course, I know that, but I was at work. I'm a nurse, and people don't always wait for the right time to be sick. I'm just coming back from a house call and am on my way home, yes, I admit a little late." She smiled.

When she began speaking, both SD-men looked more closely at the same time. They stared. One of them asked if she was German.

"German-born but I'm Dutch now," she replied, straightening her back, looking the soldier who asked her in the eye.

The agents inspected her closely for a minute. On their second inspection, they naturally became curious about an older and obviously married woman, working so late in the day when other women were cooking supper. She barely suppressed her impulse to hyperventilate and grabbed the handlebars so tightly it hurt her hands. She repeated the words stay calm and polite in her head.

"Show your ID and your nursing license," barked the one who had taken the lead.

Margaret took her papers — usually carried by Elfriede — out of her handbag dangling from the handlebar and gave them to the officer in charge. Her hand was shaking. She was glad she was the actual person in the ID pass and the license, and not Elfriede.

"It's cold tonight, isn't it? I shouldn't forget my gloves. We might even get snow," she commented lightly.

The SD agent looked at both papers, then pushed the license under her nose, his finger with its nail bit to the quick pressed under the date. "This was granted a long time ago, it's no good anymore, expired."

"Oh, I'm really sorry, *Kapitän*. I didn't think it could expire. My employer didn't ask. I work only casually, I'm married and have children." She wiped her bangs off her forehead, tucked her hair underneath her scarf, and adjusted it. Her heart was beating like crazy, sweat formed between her breast, and her corset prevented her from breathing deeply. She imagined the soldiers might see her chest work hard if they looked at her, but they only had an interest in her paperwork.

The man with her papers looked up, stared at her, then passed the documents to the other agent for inspection. "How do we know you really are a nurse? Lots of strange things are happening in this province. Who can vouch for you?"

"Of course, I can have someone verify my identity. How about my husband, the *Polizei Kommandant* [Chief of Police]? We live close by, practically around the corner." How could Elfriede do this job? Luckily, her voice stayed firm. She hadn't known before she could lie so well under pressure but she'd surely die if arrested. Then what would Jacob do? The next problem arose with her suggestion to have Jacob identify her. Oh my God, she was working herself even deeper into the hole. How to explain this to him? She hadn't wanted to do this job and here, the first time out, she gets stopped. She got very hot and wanted to take her coat off.

The agent looked at her sternly and barked, "Then we'll come with you to the police brigade. Which direction?"

Providence, if not dumb luck, saved her. She spotted two marechaussees on bicycles at the end of the street, apparently on their way to the brigade. "Wait a moment, bitte," she said, fumbling with her handbag and with the bike to make it appear as if she was trying to get the pedal in the proper position to mount the bike, giving the policemen time to catch up.

As the policemen came closer, Margaret saw the recognition light up their faces. The men stopped and got off their bikes right beside the SD officers, who glared at the newcomers, Peters and Jan van Houten, with hostility.

"Good evening. Missus Van Noorden," said Van Houten, and with a nod to the Germans, "*Meine Herren* [Gentlemen], can we help you? What's the problem, Margaret?"

Margaret looked at Van Houten, trying to tell him with her eyes and her raised eyebrows that something was up and he'd better guess what.

Before she could say anything, the German replied: "This woman is out past curfew. She says her husband is the police chief and she's on her way home from work." He looked with suspicion at Margaret beside him, holding on to her handlebar again.

Van Houten took a step closer to the man and bent over to whisper in the German's ear, raising the man's hope he was going to share a secret. As Van Houten closely observed the changing expressions on the German's face, he murmured, "That would be the truth." Grinning broadly, he straightened his back and continued in a normal voice: "May I introduce to you, Margaret Van Noorden, the chief's wife. She lives with her family in the Marechaussee brigade. Could we escort her back to her home for you, officers?"

The two SD officers stepped back. They conferred with each other in hushed tones, then one nodded. The one, who had taken the lead before, turned to Margaret.

The soldier clicked his heels and bowed slightly. "I am so sorry about that, Frau Von Norden. We're just doing our job. You be careful now not to work past curfew in future. Your husband wouldn't want that either."

The Nazi looked at the marechaussees, not satisfied but apparently not prepared to upset the applecart. "Yes, officers, take her home. *Dankeschön. Heil Hitler.*" He joined the other Nazi officer, standing to the side. Both got in their vehicle and drove off.

Peters had watched it all from the sidelines with apparent interest. He held his bike between his legs with his feet on the pavement on either side of it. Van Houten whispered, so Peters wouldn't hear him, "Margaret, what are you doing? He said you came from work?"

With a sigh of relief, she whispered back. "Oh, Jan, I just made something up. Elfriede usually makes the deliveries, but she's sick. Don't worry, it's alright now, but I need to first drop something off at the Distribution Services. Wouters is waiting for me at the back door. Would you ride with me, please, so I won't get into trouble again?"

It wasn't yet six, the time Jacob would start missing her. He would have to wait a bit longer if she didn't make it by then.

Van Houten told Peters to get on his way and tell Jacob he helped Margaret finish her errand. Peters didn't seem to think this was weird and left.

Margaret, fussing with her coat and her scarf, was beet-red. She asked Van Houten: "Don't tell Jacob. He doesn't know. I'm never doing this again but it was an emergency. I'm not cut out for this. I'm so relieved it was you. It could've turned out really badly. I'm sorry to get you involved."

"Don't worry about it. Glad I could help," Van Houten gallantly assured her.

***

About an hour later, Margaret arrived home. She hung her coat in the corridor and put on her apron. Jacob was reading a paper in the living room. The first thing he said was, "Where are the children?" His face looked grim. "Whose bike was that?" He obviously had watched her arrival through the window.

"Hello to you too, dear. So happy to see you," she said in a soft voice and kissed him. "They wanted to have a sleepover with Elfriede's boys and I agreed."

He got up out of the easy chair, kissed her back on her cheek, and followed her to the kitchen. "Peters told me about that SD stop. What's that all about? And the bike?"

His tone told her he demanded answers, and she had to think of something believable as he followed her around the house. She felt dizzy, and she needed a rest but grabbed the potatoes from the bin.

"Oh, nothing much," she shrugged. "I left Mutter's house a little late. The SD stopped me for ignoring the curfew just a few minutes over five. I was on my way to the shop for some meat with the coupons Mutter gave me. I wanted to make you a nice meal as a treat, just for the two of us. I asked the sergeant to come with me to avoid further trouble. I'm tired now."

His face softened. "Are you sure that's all it was, dear? And whose bike?" He obviously was burning with curiosity, especially about the bike, and was not keeping his promise when he asked her questions.

"I borrowed Elfriede's bike, the one from her employer."

"I don't know if I should believe you, but it's alright. You keep your secrets, and I keep mine." He looked disappointed as he walked over to the divan in the living room for his nap.

Margaret was relieved he recalled his promise and apparently changed his mind about interrogating her. She stayed in the kitchen to make a meal, just for the two of them, and worked in some leftover meat from earlier in the week into the stamppot, hoping he wouldn't notice it was the same meat. As it was all heating up in the Dutch oven on the stovetop, she started humming.

Chapter 98

Jacob's initial resolve to only accept orders from his Dutch superiors had hardened after the sermon in his church, and he didn't even obey them anymore. Rather than comply with his superiors' instructions, his conscience became his sole guidance. He would stick to what he thought was right, even if it would kill him. His lesson learned from the first time he had found the courage to defy Den Toom, he became skilled in pretending to go out to follow an order, then return to the brigade with empty hands. The bird had flown the coop, or some other mishap had taken place.

He saw his men struggle with the same dilemmas. Feeling impotent and flawed, he tried nevertheless to give them some guidance. Everybody on the crew was well aware of the police force's tarnished reputation, except Peters, possibly. The rough brush of public opinion now painted all police officers as collaborators.

In comparison, the public considered those cops in hiding, primarily single men, as heroes for risking discovery and deportation, their good reputations ensured for the future. The still-working police officers, with families depending on them, judged those cops in hiding weak. As Leversma formulated it: "I wouldn't mind disappearing, letting others look after me and escape the pressures we're under. We never know when we'll be caught doing something the Kraut doesn't like. Just about every night I have nightmares."

"I know," said De Wit. "Each day we put our safety on the line trying to do the right thing being cops, yes, but also helping citizens escape capture, and so much more." He looked at Peters and didn't further elaborate.

When he heard the discussion, Jacob had to step in and reasoned in a conciliatory tone: "Fellows, I just want to add this. Any police officer, whether on, or off the job, out in the community, or in hiding, everyone faces deportation, and possibly the death penalty. Those that go into hiding will face their family's arrest. Let's stay united and not let the Nazis divide us. And never envy the faulty cops who chose to join the enemy. They could face executions by the Illegality, and if they survive that, they'll be tried after the war. Their lives will be ruined."

"I don't think we'll have to worry, Opper," Van Hardenberg commented. "We don't have faulty cops. I think you got that pretty much under control."

Although he disagreed with that statement, Jacob stayed silent. In his private briefing meeting with the sergeant that day, he brought up the subject.

"I'm not aware of Peters or Dijk inflicting damage to civilians," Van Houten replied.

Jacob nodded. He hadn't heard anything insidious about them either, but still, he wasn't convinced. "Alright, what about their SS membership? How would you explain it?"

"They talk a good game, just to impress people. As an SS member, they get together with other traitors and parade around, but in reality, no, I haven't heard anything about extortion, ratting people out, or making deals with black market traders. They know we wouldn't tolerate it. They'd lose their jobs and their income."

Jacob exhaled deeply, then bent forward and leaned his elbows on the desk folding his hands in front of him as if praying. "You might be right. I sure hope so. Some police officers were killed when they least expected it, just going for a swim, or at a picnic in the park with their family. I don't condone the Illegals taking the law in their own hands. I would much prefer seeing those traitors brought to justice in a court of law and then lock 'em up for a good long stretch, I say."

Jacob's hands wiped his face, then caressed his bald head. He needed to stop the conversation and bring the latest news to his deputy, but Van Houten continued chatting.

"I'm glad we keep that political stuff under control here." Van Houten looked content, leaning back comfortably in his chair across from Jacob, oblivious to the chief's signs of discomfort.

It was time to share with Van Houten how he really felt.

"All this going into hiding has caused a severe shortage of police officers in the cities. We have to do more with less. I have to tell you, sometimes I don't know why I stay on, other than to be a good husband to Margaret and a father to our children. But nobody can predict what'll happen. Whatever we'll decide, it'll be dangerous and risky. I should've not even gone out on those raids and refused our support from the very start."

Van Houten interrupted. "Yeah. I know what you mean, I've never been more unsure about my job than during those raids."

Jacob wasn't finished. "The only difference now is the German police are making the arrests and we're off the hook. Rauter figured that out well. Last November, Rotterdam alone lost 50,000 men to those labor hunters, and in The Hague 13,000 picked up." He shook his head, then inhaled deeply and slowly.

Van Houten wanted to say something, but Jacob raised his hand and went on.

"Let's talk about our own problems. I heard the SD has started picking up our uniformed men right off the street in the cities. Worse: our department head informed me yesterday we have to hand in our weapons. All police officers have to be disarmed."

Van Houten reared up from his slumped position. "No way! What will our job be without our weapons? We'd be sitting ducks, for God's sakes. Don't have us give up our guns, Opper." He got up from his seat, and started gesticulating wildly. He was a decade younger than Jacob, a tall and muscular man, impressive, even intimidating, if you didn't know his character.

Now he'd finally announced the final blow, Jacob leaned back in his chair, depleted, and he threw up his hands. "Well, what can I say? We're redundant, so the Nazis are disarming us. When the battle with the Allies gets here, we'll be harmless, except what the Brits send us. It's not unexpected."

Van Houten paced in agony around the small office.

"Sit down, Sergeant," Jacob said quietly. "I'll delay disarmament as long as I can, but don't want to be accused and shot for insubordination by our own. I'll start by writing some letters requesting an exemption and use our connections. We have important jobs: Camp Star, the Wehrmacht station, and the OT soldiers. Many NSB members are still here who need protection. We have German evacuees. Lots of potentially tense situations in which we need a weapon to enforce order, and above all, I don't want to be shot by the KK."

Van Houten had returned to his seat. "We need our guns," he said, his voice hoarse with suppressed anger, his balled fists on his hips.

Now it was Jacob's turn to shift back and forth in his seat. His body wanted to pace, but he stayed put, mindful of his position as leader, which required a calm and sensible response.

"You can let the crew know, that, as long as head office doesn't order it, I won't have anyone handing in his weapons. The orders from DM Schrieke just aren't adequate anymore, not to speak about our department head, or from Commissioner Feenstra. To carry any weight at all, an order needs to come from the Minister of Justice himself in Breda. The deputy ministers are redundant now. I'll talk to Heusden as well, so he won't make an issue out of it."

Van Houten relaxed his hands and stretched his long legs.

Jacob thought of their stash — courtesy of the British — for which the Overdam Illegality had found plenty of hiding places. He leaned back in his desk chair, crossed his legs, and observed his deputy. "Just one more thing before we end the meeting today. I take it you're aware of the Military Authority under General Koot? He operates strictly for the military."

Van Houten's eyes lit up.

"Yeah," he said with gusto. "And Major Krulls as our leader in the field. I expect that day will happen soon. They better sort out in advance who does what within the *Nederlandse Binnenlandse Strijdkrachten* [Dutch Interior Forces], when the time comes, or it'll become chaos, instead of a liberation." His grin was back.

Jacob mused, "The abbreviation NBS with the same initials as the NSB (National Socialists Bond) is unfortunate. I was told the shorter BS is also a poor choice."

Van Houten burst out laughing, and Jacob joined him.

"The English and Yankees will have a ball," said the sergeant. "We can't win that one!"

"Alright, Sergeant," Jacob said, bringing the conversation back to reality. "You and I know some of the locals that will join the BS, but keep the news under your hat, until later. Understood?"

"Yes, Opper. Any idea when the BS will start operating in Overdam?" Van Houten seemed suddenly all business, ready to start the battle right this minute.

Jacob shook his head. "Just one more thing I'd like done. The KK picked up a marechaussee chap from Lemelerveld, Pieter Lievers. That group's chief — AKA Henk — asked if there's any chance we can get this man out. Lievers' son is a known key person for the Illegality in hiding. I don't think the father knows the whereabouts of his son, but the KK won't know that and torture him for it. He's 61, in poor health, and isn't going to survive their usual treatment."

"We'll have to devise a trick to get him out on the road."

"They have him working outside the camp in the bog fields, so you could get him from there, or else when we're asked to take him to the hospital. Can I leave this with you, Jan? Let me know if he gets sick."

***

It didn't take long for the weakened Lievers to become seriously ill. Nauwaard requested someone for guard duty on the trip to the hospital in the camp's make-shift ambulance — an Opel panel truck. Van Houten took his turn for guard duty and met with Nauwaard before to the trip but the warden was grim and wouldn't say anything about Lievers and his illness.

As Van Houten reported back later, the whole assault went off without a hitch. Van Houten informed the ill man in the back, so the guard driving the vehicle wouldn't hear anything. He had barely finished talking, when the driver jumped on the breaks, and a group of four masked men stood in front of the sedan, aiming their Stenguns at the driver. Without speaking a word, the men took the elderly prisoner out of the car and half-carried and half-walked him into the bush. Jan had pretended he didn't know a thing about it, said he thought the guy looked like a washed-up old guy. When he gave the driver the bottle of gin the man shut up complaining.

Jacob smiled. His bribery strategy had found a follower. "What did Nauwaard say?"

"He wasn't happy about the loss of a prisoner, even a fatally ill one. He gave me a sharp poke in the ribs and told me he wasn't fooled. But I told him he should be happy that this old prisoner wasn't gonna die on his watch and be buried at his cost."

Chapter 99

A few days later, Jacob got a call from Nauwaard's deputy, De Jong, which instantly raised his suspicion, as he always dealt directly with Nauwaard on camp matters. De Jong reported a black-market trader, a woman named Riek. It confirmed his sense of danger in this matter justified, as reporting local crimes to the police wasn't the usual procedure anymore. Inmates ended up in the camp through the KK-crew's arrests for *Arbeitseinsatz* violators, and those from the German *Ordnungspolizei* ended up in the hands of the SD.

He looked at the issue from various angles, could not detect de Jong's interest, and decided to do the investigation himself. That afternoon, Jacob went out to inspect the trader's business premises, a regular shop in the village. A handsome Dutch blonde of tall stature was running the store. She was taller than him, a fact he always noticed. Her height was intimidating. With a stern voice he asked her: "Are you the owner?"

"Yes." She said her name, smiled, pushing her substantial chest forward, and then offered her hand.

Her red lips seemed too shiny. Jacob ignored her hand. "I'm here to follow up on a complaint," he said curtly, took his cap off, and tucked it underneath his arm. He walked through the shop. At first glance, all seemed in order. The shelves contained products that were available on coupons, or were unrestricted. While he knocked on walls and stamped his boots on the floor in search of hidden spaces, the owner, Riek, followed his every move. When he stood still in the center of the store and observed the walls from that distance, she stood so close to him that her chest was just about touching him while she asked him all sorts of questions in a suggestively low, soft voice. He could smell her rose perfume and imagined feeling her body heat through his uniform jacket. He wanted to wipe his brow but didn't.

One wall was obscured by boxes. Jacob eyed it first from a distance, then took a few steps to look at it more closely, but Riek stepped in his way, touching him with her chest.

"Why don't you take a break," said Riek. "Can I get you a cup of real coffee, Chief?"

Startled, he backed up. "No, thanks, but would you step back, please?"

He focused his attention on the wall and put up his hand to indicate she should move. The stack of boxed goods in front of the wall covered its full height. The solicitous woman wouldn't step aside and kept bothering him.

"Chief, I imagine you must have a lot of stress. Would you be interested in letting loose? I could give you the time of your life."

He shoved Riek aside and started to remove the boxes one by one. "What's behind this wall? Help me remove the boxes."

Riek said nothing, stood watching him with arms folded. She wasn't making any friends, and he noted her lack of cooperation for inclusion in his report. Finally, the boxes were removed, and a wall of thin boards on hinges with a recessed handle was revealed.

"Open that. Now," Jacob barked.

He had no doubt that Riek aimed poisonous thoughts at him this minute. Unmoved by her glaring, he again demanded: "Open it."

She reluctantly pulled at the hinged panel, opened it a crack, and stepped back.

He stepped forward and pulled the door open wide. Behind it, he saw a fair-sized room with shelves fully stocked with products, probably stolen or otherwise illegally obtained, or it wouldn't be stored in this space. A small window shed some light. Jacob activated the overhead bulb with a pull on the string and had a good look around. Hundreds of shoeboxes were stacked up on one side, taking up half the room.

"How did you get all this?"

She didn't answer.

"So, don't tell me. All contraband will be returned to the distribution office. You'll be fined, or possibly face incarceration if head office thinks that is an appropriate sentence. You're lucky the DOJ doesn't use Star Camp anymore." He left the hidden room.

When he looked at her again, he saw a completely changed woman, self-assured and hostile, standing in the main store. In a loud voice, she disclosed what he had wanted to know — why De Jong was interested.

"You're making a big mistake. Commander Schwier knows about it and he doesn't feel it is a problem. He buys articles from me."

Without missing a beat, he informed her: "Doesn't make any difference to me."

"We'll see if it does, when he hears about this," she sneered.

With a calm and professional voice, Jacob told her: "You will be investigated." When he saw her scowl, he asked her without expecting an answer: "Let me ask you: beyond hiding goods from your countrymen and selling them to the rich at indecent prices for your own gain, aren't you at least ashamed to collaborate with our country's enemy?"

Riek turned away and sat down in a chair behind the till pouting.

Never mind Schwier's benefit. Who knows what the willing lady provided to De Jong. Ignoring the woman, Jacob called the brigade for assistance. Next, he called the local distribution office. "Could you ask the supervisor to send me some kind of vehicle, a cart or what else you have handy, for a room full of hoarded products, please?"

When the supervisor of the distribution office stopped by, the men recognized each other, but both chose not to acknowledge their prior acquaintance. Wouters scratched his head. "I'd love to add this to my shelves, but I can't. This is simply too much product. We're instructed to call head office in a case like this."

"Alright, could you take care of that?" Jacob had Riek close the shop and give him the key. He arrested her but had his watch commander take Riek to the brigade. Jacob called the office and assigned Van Houten to the case, instructing him to start interrogating Riek immediately about her merchandise sources.

It took two men of Jacob's crew the rest of the day and part of the evening to get all the products registered adequately as evidence. At the same time, Wouters and another employee copied the inventory and boxed everything up. They loaded the loot into the Distribution Services' truck for transport to the head office in Zwolle, first thing in the morning.

That was a good day of proper police work, all by the book — the way Jacob liked it. He dug up a cigar as a treat that night and puffed away as he told Margaret of his find.

***

A few days later, Deputy Warden De Jong walked right into Jacob's office, bypassing the watch commander to check up on his report. With his slim figure in his green uniform and the way he moved his body in front of Jacob's desk, his eyes slits in his narrow head, he reminded Jacob of a panther. "You can give me that priority pass now, Van Noorden. I need a few things."

Jacob shook his head, his senses sharpened, and his hand felt for his gun case. "Sorry, Sir, but the goods are gone. You can find them at the headquarters of Distribution in Zwolle."

True to his predatory nature, De Jong pounced and closed his hands around Jacob's neck. He had expected something like this and already had his gun in his hand the minute de animal moved towards him and pushed his weapon against De Jong's ribcage at the height of his heart. "Get away from me," he managed to croak.

De Jong let go and stepped one pace away, his face red and hate in his fiery eyes. "You, bastard. You're lying. Give me the fucking priority pass, you, slimy slug. I reported it, so I deserve some goods," the KK-man spat out, a drop of spit reaching Jacob on his chin.

Jacob didn't want to lower his pistol and wiped the man's spit off with his left hand. If he gave De Jong a chance to recover — who undoubtedly carried a weapon under his jacket — he'd be shot himself on the spot. Without much hope, he yelled: "Leave, or I'll arrest you for assaulting an officer." He kept his gun aimed at the man's heart.

To his surprise, De Jong indeed slowly backed out of his office and slammed the door shut behind him.

Jacob jumped up and opened the door. Standing in the doorway, he watched De Jong leave through the front door, spouting insults all the way out of the brigade.

The noise had attracted the other crew members from the squad room and a few of them stuck their heads around the doorframe. Van Houten stepped into the corridor and called out: "What was that about?"

"Nothing to see. Go back to work," Jacob grumbled. No, he wouldn't trust any member of Schwier's KK-clan. He sank back into his chair and wiped his face. Good God, all that for some lousy, stolen goods.

*****

A week later, he ran afoul with Riek again. She had made plenty of money with her illegal business, and it hadn't taken long before a fancy lawyer had found her and battled with Jacob to get Riek set free. Jacob walked to the common room and asked Van Houten for his statement of the interrogation. He read it standing beside Van Houten's desk, and found out it didn't mention shoes or any of the sources of the merchandise. He threw it back onto Van Houten's desk with a deep frown. "This is not finished. Where's the rest of the report?"

The sergeant leaned back into his chair and looked up at his boss with a blank face.

"It's not a priority, Opper. I'll have to finish the statement yet. I had a late night that day. Who cares about shoes?" The sergeant shrugged, got up, and walked away.

"Don't you walk away when I'm talking to you." Jacob's stern voice stopped Van Houten, who turned around and stared at him. "I care! Dammit. Black market traders get rich by exploiting their fellow countrymen. It's also illegal. Verdomme, Sergeant. When I order a thorough investigation, you will do as I tell you! Get on it." He added as an afterthought: "Her fancy lawyer's after us."

Van Houten glared at him, stuck his hands in his pockets, and declared with his head up high: "Since you care so much, I'll do it right now, but it's a waste of our time. Nobody cares about the black market, Opper. We have other worries."

Jacob looked around him. The other crew members pretended they were busy with their own work, but Jacob was well aware the crew followed every word. He ignored that remark from the sergeant, turned around, and stomped to his office, where he threw the papers from his desk into a drawer, followed by the stapler that fell down with a loud plunk. Although disappointed with Van Houten, he had no choice but to accept this delay.

For the first time since his arrival in Overdam, he realized his deputy had become greatly familiar with his boss, so much so that he dared to dissent with him and use subterfuge on his assignment. Van Houten had turned from an obnoxious employee into an equal — the other side of the occupation.

Authority didn't mean much anymore. It needed to be undermined, and that message was passed on through the ranks. With a commissioner like Feenstra, it was natural to examine every order before implementing it. He had advised his staff to follow their conscience; he should be happy Van Houten had exercised exactly that option, following his own example. It did bother him, nevertheless.

***

The slowly proceeding investigation eventually led to a black-market distributor. Two weeks later, Van Houten approached Jacob in his office with a face that showed an expression akin to meekness he hadn't seen before on the man's face.

"You'll be happy to know that your hunch was correct, Opper. We located an illegal distributor of shoes. Our colleagues in Oss confiscated hundred-thousand pairs of Bata work shoes together with a load of textiles. They told me these came from occupied Czechoslovakia and had been syphoned off from German supply lines. Those shoes were made by Jewish slave laborers in a factory run by the Nazis."

"Well, well, how great is that. All the reward of your diligent work, Sergeant. Well done." He stood up, smiling, and shook hands with Van Houten, who grinned but wouldn't look him in the eye. "Are we still friends?" Jacob said.

Van Houten looked straight at him and nodded.

"Look at it this way, Jan. We all have to do less popular work sometimes, but thanks to you, your work is going to benefit our citizens."

"Sure, Opper. Whatever you say. Going back to work now." Van Houten tipped his fingers to his head in salute, turned around, and left the office.

Jacob had to face his men's indifference to the pursuit of black-market offenders. He hoped that Van Houten's success would change their minds about stopping the flow of illegal goods — a small victory of sorts, and he badly needed one. He didn't know he had made an enemy for life in Riek and her fancy lawyer.

Chapter 100

The SD had begun to intern the Dutch police officers from the northern provinces and of Amsterdam. When Jacob heard about the new prisoners, he called Nauwaard.

"I'm really concerned about revenge from other inmates against these men. As a former member yourself, you can imagine how things might get out of hand."

Charles seemed to have forgotten their last tense meeting, and his voice was jovial.

"No worries. We'll look after them. They're no low-life work-haters, so they'll be getting special privileges. It'll be a change of pace for us after Schwier's usual scummy targets. Most are cops from Friesland and Groningen. We might play cards or have a few beers together. I might even put them to work guarding the other prisoners."

The disarming of policemen confirmed Jacob's suspicion: Rauter anticipated the Nazis' imminent defeat and the measures were intended to safeguard the retreating Wehrmacht soldiers, when the tide turned. Nothing would stop some police officers from killing the hated Nazis.

Fortunately, his crew still had their weapons. He surely wouldn't want to bump unarmed into Bakker, that crazy psychopath, or the high-strung De Jong, and even Nauwaard — if drunk enough, a nightmare from what he'd heard.

"How will the new prisoners get there?" Jacob asked. "Do you know how many?"

"A hundred men in total. Some arrived today with only one blasted German soldier as their guard. Why the hell didn't they try to escape with only one soldier to guard them? It would've saved us the trouble of looking after them. They act as if they're on a fucking field trip. The others will arrive tomorrow in about a dozen horse-drawn carts. When they're all here maybe you can speak to them. They'd accept their fate better if you as a fellow policeman told them to behave. You've managed to stay on your post through the last five years, so that should command some respect. And who knows how long I'll be around?" He laughed — a bitter sound.

"Maybe it's the anticipation of three, square meals a day, but grant them more than three minutes for eating their meals, please." Jacob said, no longer afraid of Charles Nauwaard.

"Hah-hah, good one! Stay for lunch afterwards? As long as we got any, we might as well share. It's not much, though better than most, I suspect. There're still some advantages of being boss…" His voice trailed off in a deep sigh.

***

The next day, the job of settling in the police officers finished, Jacob had lunch with Nauwaard. Both remained silent until they were seated in Charles' kitchen, where the warden continued yesterday's conversation. "You know what Rauter said about the Dutch police?"

"No idea. Honestly, I couldn't care less about Rauter and his thoughts," Jacob said with a mouthful of sandwich.

"Be nice. You gotta hear this: Rauter said all anti-German policemen had been arrested or had gone underground, and the rest wouldn't object to any new orders from him. He said that to Himmler already in 1943. Do you think it's true?"

Nauwaard studied Jacob's face, who tried to make his voice sound airy and un-concerned. "I couldn't tell you. I only know my crew. And then again: what do you really know about a person?"

The camp boss ignored the remark and mirrored Jacob's relaxed tone of voice.

"I'm not sure what's going to happen, but I don't care. It's a zoo anyway. Rauter is still in bad shape after the terrorist attack."

"That's too bad," Jacob said, meaning it: he would like him to survive until his trial.

"It seems each sector is doing whatever. There's no goddamn discipline left. It's now each for himself. Bastard Schwier is losing his control of the camp, preoccupied with other things: getting out of here. Even suck-up De Jong feels abandoned. The swine Bakker and his crew are bringing in few victims and every morning fewer guards report for duty. They're taking off as fast as the Allies are advancing. I can't blame them, but it doesn't reflect well on me."

"Is that right? Too bad, but don't ask me to feel sorry for you. You knew this was coming." Jacob kept up the careless voice.

A snarl formed around Charles' mouth. "Thanks for your sympathy. It's not my fault many of those damned louse busters died. I didn't personally kill them. Well, I don't have to tell you that. I might damn well take myself off too."

Nauwaard took off his glasses and wiped his brow as if it was hot in the room. With his narrow jaw and overbite, his face looked more than ever like a large rodent's. His skin was greyer than usual and the bags under his eyes prominent without his glasses.

With more interest, Jacob replied: "Yes? But, the guards were under your command, Charles. What's holding you back from leaving, anyway?"

Seated at the kitchen table, they ate sandwiches of solid, brown, home-baked bread with a few slices of good cheese, fat and salty, and a pickle. The bread smelled yeasty like bread is supposed to. This was not regular cardboard war bread. They enjoyed the rest of their meal in silence.

Finally, Jacob wiped his mouth with the back of his right hand and leaned back, looking at his opponent. Himself, not a large man, he knew a man's strength doesn't come from a robust body — as Hitler would have everybody believe — but from a strong mind. He suspected that Nauwaard felt close to giving up if the man's slumped shoulders were any indication.

Suddenly lifting his chin, Nauwaard looked at him with his ice-blue eyes. "Don't you have any good advice for me, Jake?"

Jacob decided to speak his mind and strive to keep to the ideal: Courageous and Unblemished. "Nothing I could say you don't already know. Don't you remember, when a couple of years ago you lost the contract with the Justice system? They found too many injured and deaths under your leadership. It's still true."

"So, what?" Charles tapped his right foot and fixed his eyes on Jacob.

Wanting to divert his eyes, Jacob kept eye contact nevertheless.

"I bet there are more unexplained deaths with plenty of witnessed left. You could say you were forced, but I'm sure that explanation won't go over well in a court of law. You hired on with the SD and actively collaborated with the enemy. I'm not sure how you could get away with it, Charles. You're going to face a trial."

"Goddamn honesty always with you. Yeah, I figured as much." Charles stopped tapping his foot and leaned back in his chair. The spunk had seeped out of his blue-grey eyes.

In a conciliatory tone, Jacob continued speaking his mind.

"Lucky for you it will be a Dutch trial under reasonable laws and with educated judges, not louts with machineguns, and the arrested will have rights. Until then, you might want to watch your back. Above all, watch Schwier."

"I'm not worried about him." The defeated man stayed quiet for a long time.

Jacob contemplated getting up and leaving but stayed. He considered Nauwaard not altogether a friend, but an acquaintance, more like a person in trouble who needed support, who had shown him some consideration, these past years. Fair is fair. Although Nauwaard was on the wrong side, the warden was still a person. He just sat and waited, observing the apparent emotion on Charles' face.

After several minutes, the man spoke again.

"I should've switched sides when it was still possible. Goddamn it, but I didn't. I should've listened to you." He slumped back with dull eyes, breathing hard as if he had given up on his future, his life.

Who knew what Charles Nauwaard might do? The bastard was unpredictable and sly, and these signs of desperation probably were a play for sympathy. Jacob knew not to trust him, but despite everything, he felt terrible for him.

Chapter 101

The radio updates on the famine were grim. The people in the densely populated cities on the west coast were eating anything they could catch and still were dying of starvation. Radio Orange reported on the exiled ministers' urgent request to liberate the west of The Netherlands before any other advances, as hundreds of thousands of lives were at stake.

On the other hand, should the German army blow up the dikes and demolish the extensive water control installations in the southwest, one-third of the nation would be inundated. The saline Atlantic Ocean would violently reclaim the low-lying areas, which would mean long-term devastation of the agricultural lands. Add to it the damage to the civilian buildings from flooding, and it became clear that inundation would set the nation back a hundred years, never mind the enormous loss of life. More would die of drowning than from starvation.

Mercifully, the cabinet-in-exile didn't get to decide. It was up to the Allied Supreme Headquarters (SHEAF) to determine the best battle strategy. If SHEAF had made any decisions, Radio Orange didn't inform its listeners of those choices.

By early March, Radio BBC reported the Allies had pushed into Germany from the south, reaching the west bank of the Rhine River — roughly on the same latitude with the south of The Netherlands. To the east of the Netherlands, the Aliied troops entered the first concentration camps. The shocked soldiers described their horrific finds on the radio and on reels in movie theatres. After that, the Allied Forces moved eastwards with ever more persistence: direction Berlin — Nazi headquarters, to meet the Soviet-Russian troops, advancing from the east.

***

March was an excellent month for rescuing the starving children of the west, and although it was still cold, the weather stayed dry. Volunteers of Overdam and its outlying areas in the province planned to move a hundred-thousand starving children from the cities in the west to farmers in the eastern provinces. In spite of diminishing yields, the farmers continued to grow wheat and rye for baking bread, maintained livestock for milk, made butter and cheese, and still had a few chickens running around for eggs. Although butchering for private consumption was restricted and only allowed with a permit from the German State Office, with part of the animal always destined for the Germans, many farmers rebelled against the German rule and illegally slaughtered a pig or a cow anyway.

When children could eat enough to stop their hunger pangs, they would think they had landed in heaven, and their lives saved were in the meantime. The volunteers argued that the goal would justify their temporary displacement; the love from their hosts would make up for the separation anxiety. They gathered many coats and blankets to keep the children warm during the trip. The city of Zwolle became the reception and distribution center. From there, the children were allocated to farm families for the remainder of the war.

Johanna lent her horse and cart to Elfriede for the charitable cause. With concern on her face, she asked, "What about the air raids, my dear daughter. Aren't you scared?"

With typical light-heartedness, Elfriede replied: "Ach, Mutter, we can jump out and hide in the ditches those engineers dug for the Wehrmacht soldiers. We got to move five-hundred kids per day, so we can't be too picky about when. It's gotta be done."

"Be careful, dear," Johanna sighed.

***

It came down to thirty children to a wagon — with high sides to keep the kids from falling off and filled with a layer of straw against the cold. Each carriage was supervised by a volunteer plus a driver, leaving in trains of six to seven carts at the time. The massive undertaking would last the whole month of March.

The adults went through the safety drill with their young cargo before each cart's take-off. Elfriede's caravan had traveled for a couple of hours, when an Allied plane dove down and started shooting at the vehicles. The drivers stopped abruptly, got off the buckboards and grabbed their horses to keep them steady.

Elfriede, like the adults in the other carts, stood, grabbed the white flag, and as she waved it overhead, shouted, "Get out, children, get out, quickly. The older ones must help the little ones, hurry, hurry."

It took many minutes for all of the adults in the six wagons to frantically wave their white flags, get the children off the wagons, and hide in the ditches. At the second fly-over, the Nazi-hunting fighter realized these little people in carts were not soldiers and disappeared.

Arrived home at the end of that day, Elfriede told the story to eager listeners at Johanna's place. She and the children had crawled out of the ditch in a daze, and she checked all the children. To her amazement, nobody had a scratch on them, although most of the youngest children were shaking and crying or frozen from fear. They'd been already fearful, traveling far away from home under the wide-open sky.

"Most kids were nervous to start with for being out in the open air on a cart. They don't get to experience that when growing up four floors high in apartment buildings. Imagine being shot at from the air. Poor babies, so much to endure. I told the older children to hug the little ones. When the worst shakes had subsided, we got back onto the carts and continued our travel."

Margaret, the worrier, was delighted to have Elfriede back in one piece. She turned to Johanna. "Mutter, thank you so much for lending the horse and wagon to Elfriede. If Jacob had been stationed in the west country, our children would've been starving too. Thank God all the children are safe."

A slight curl vibrated in the corner of Johanna's mouth when she replied. "Hmm. Yes. And thank the Lord for rain and soil — and for your brother who works so hard, no? You're welcome, dear."

Elfriede gave her mother another hug. "Yes, Mutter. You're right."

She hoped that Elfriede's and Johanna's generosity and the saved children's story would soften Jacob's heart. He'd been reticent about her relatives these days.

Margaret was aware that Johanna had always been less impressed by religion than Jacob because she used irony when God showed up in a conversation. She had an inkling her mother might even be an agnostic, but one didn't talk about these private convictions. Although Johanna's father had been a socialist on his arrival as a young man in central Germany, his children were raised Lutheran to be accepted in the new community. After immigration to *Nederland* [The Netherlands], Johanna had switched to the relaxed Dutch Reformed church of her husband. Despite joining Jacob in his austere Calvinist denomination after marriage, Margaret had maintained the same free-style thinking of her grandfather and her mother, practically by osmosis. Religion was like a stylish mantel you threw on to shield you from the cold and blend in among others, but she would never let on what she really believed.

Chapter 102

On March 22, 1945, Jacob got a call from Nauwaard letting him know Superintendent Schwier had ordered him to lock up the guards in their staff cabins after nine at night with all the prisoners locked into their barracks.

Jacob couldn't help himself and laugh out loud. "That's funny to me, sorry. It's hard to get good help nowadays, isn't it? Bakker still there or has he taken off?"

Nauwaard didn't laugh. "How'd you guess? Yes, the bastard's taken off. Good riddance. You know when the snow fell a couple of days ago? I heard some of my men joking it was preparing them for the weather in Siberia and soon they'd be looking at the sod from the other side. Hah! Talk to you later."

Jacob shook his head. One had to admire the man's morbid sense of humor. He wondered what kept Charles going and why he didn't simply flee too.

***

British and American Allied bombers advanced eastward in a steady stream as the German planes has lost any semblance of a presence. The day following Charles Nauwaard's call, Jacob noticed the constant odyssey of planes moving toward Germany. An hour later, he learned the Allies had crossed the German border at Elten — only a good hour south of Overdam in a fast car. The sounds of artillery fire and the heavier explosions of bombs became unmistakable, like premature, thunderous summer weather in the distance. His heart began beating faster of delight and anticipation or freedom.

When he told Margaret about British and Canadian troops entering the east-Netherlands, she cried from happiness. Together they stepped outside to watch the busy overhead traffic, the sign of approaching freedom. Later, Jacob heard some towns had been hit with loss of lives — collateral damage. He didn't tell Margaret about it but hoped it wouldn't become their fate too.

The Wehrmacht was still alert and tried to hit back at the Allied armada. An occasional large plume would rise high in the sky, giving away a plane crash near Overdam. Margaret confessed the smoke and bombing made her tremble, taking her back to the earlier bombing of the camp, which had affected her more at the time than she admitted.

The frequent Air Defense sirens made daily life impossible. A low-pitched sound would start up and slowly increased to its full expression — a high, ear-drum-splitting whine rising up and falling in tone, like a devil's dance tune. The sound continued for fifteen minutes at full intensity, prompting Margaret to grab her children and scurry towards the bomb shelter. An eerie silence fell over the town until the bombing started with its own tunes and light shows after dark. It ended eventually with the Air Defense danger-free short blast. As its sound slowly faded away, it left an intensely enjoyable hush behind, and people emerged from the cellars, seeping back into the streets to continue their day.

De Wit was excited. "Don't you see? The Germans on the west coast have no choice but to capitulate, ahead of a general capitulation of the whole army. Just let the rest of the Nazis fight on, but we'll be free!"

"But what would stop the Krauts from blowing up the dikes anyway?" Van Der Gulik asked.

"Because the Allied command will demand they won't, you cheese-head. They could obliterate those Krauts, stuck there between the Atlantic Ocean and the western front or they could save their lives. Do you think the Allies will just let them walk free to join the rest of their army in Germany? They can make those Nazi bastards dance to any tune."

Jacob nodded approvingly. "I agree with you, De Wit. Men, listen up. I've got a plan for the next days. Does any of you know a carpenter who can strengthen our cellar walls?" Based on what he knew, he decided it would be wise to prepare for a fierce bombing. They'd better be ready for anything.

***

While the reinforcement of the building's basement walls was in progress, Heusden sent Jacob some young boys, *wer war mutig geworden* [who had become courageous], he said, but offered no further explanation.

"I see," Jacob said. "Send them to me. *Danke schön.*"

When a soldier brought the four boys in, obviously reluctant to enter Jacob's office, the Watch Commander had to push them forward. To Jacob's dismay, Jaap and

Hendrik were among them. He made the quartet stand at attention in the squad room, supervised by the duty man. He knew his silence was more frightening than had he scolded them.

He beckoned the German soldier into his office with a wave of his hand.

The soldier explained: "These children were bothering the wife of a high-ranking Wehrmacht officer and her young daughter, who came here to escape the violence in the city."

Standing with his hands on his hips, Jacob said: "So, *was sol ich machen mit dem jungs? Was kriminelles haben sie getan?* [What am I supposed to do with them? What law did they violate?]"

The German shuffled his feet, took his cap off, stroked his head, and then put it back. "*Nah, nicht kriminelles* [Well, a law, no]. They sang some Dutch song over and over while they were following the pair. One boy scratched the girl's arms with a stick."

"I see. You can go now, *danke schön.*"

After the German soldier had left, Jacob returned to the four in the squad room. They stood with heads bowed before him. With a stern voice, he demanded to know. "What did you boys sing?"

Jaap and Hendrik stared at the floor and didn't respond. The biggest kid spoke up, while the other one just looked at Jacob with fear in his eyes. "*Oranje boven.*"

"I see. You really think it's a smart thing to make Germans angry at you? I'll leave you to think about that for a while in the cells. Hendrik, at nine years old you should know better. I'm really annoyed with you for dragging Jaap into this. I'm ashamed of both of you. My sons should show a better example to other boys."

Hendrik and Jaap still stared at the floor, but the other two boys stared at him, wide-eyed, probably feeling already better, knowing their mates would face more punishment at home. He had the Watch Commander lock the kids into the cells and call their parents, while he personally called Margaret.

"I've got the boys here for some mischief in the street. Can you come and get them in an hour? I'm letting them study the inside of a cell for a while to smarten them up."

He was not that angry at the boys for their bad behavior and also understood, and he wished he could say so to them. He and Margaret didn't talk about the war at home, who was on the wrong side, or what the Nazis did, but other parents might not insulate their children from that abnormality. Kids didn't need to know about that, but he couldn't protect them from other parents' conversations.

After an hour, closer towards supper time, he had the boys brought into his office.

This time, all four boys stared at the floor.

"I hope you thought about the consequences of your actions. Did you?" The boys nodded. After a few uncomfortable moments of silence, when and their shuffling feet finally stilled, he continued: "You must respect other people. That German lady and her daughter have nothing to do with the war, just like your own mothers, or your sisters. You could've been shot by an angry Wehrmacht soldier. Never, ever do something dumb like that again. Go the other way if you see Germans coming, especially soldiers. Agreed?"

A subdued bunch, they all simultaneously nodded vigorously.

He had Peters take home the other boys to tell their parents what had happened. He figured Peters would be best at imagining the woe a German lady might have felt in a hostile environment and be better at explaining it to the boys' parents. He then let Henk and Jaap go home with Margaret, suggesting she'd send them to bed without dinner.

After they all had disappeared, Jacob sat back, smiling. If only these were his only worries. If he were a boy, he would have wanted to know what's going on, play a part, see everything, and if there was an enemy, fight him. He wondered what his boys would retain from this time as they grew up.

The naughty boys reminded him of Heusden and Nauwaard, who looked more nervous each time he spoke to them in person. He never saw Schwier or De Jong in the village again. Bakker was long gone. Brilliant. Without the distraction of the KK, the BS men — the Dutch Interior Army — could focus on getting organized.

Chapter 103

The Canadians advanced at lighting speed northwards, and the men of Simon's Resistance group were more than ready to join them. As per Prince Bernhard's protocol, the first step for mobilizing was contacting the Allies and identifying themselves as a legitimate Resistance unit.

Commander Simon tasked a couple of members with this mission, which meant a trip across the frontline needing extreme caution to avoid the many Wehrmacht soldiers, SD-men, and OT soldiers patrolling the area — an arduous undertaking. Sergeant Van Houten and a mate returned in a funk for having failed their mission. Their youthful appearance would be a vulnerability and an extra obstacle if they'd ever be stopped.

The sergeant asked Jacob whether he'd like to try. Jacob jumped at the chance. With Simon's approval, the chief changed into his civvies and set out after sundown with some water and a sandwich. He rode his bicycle all night, often waiting for hours hiding in a ditch or behind some shrubs.

***

Around two in the morning, he saw three Wehrmacht soldiers on the road pedaling along in his direction. He looked for a hiding spot and saw some shrubs and a watering trough in the pasture adjacent to the road. As he lay flat in the damp field, head down, his bike next to him in the grass, he listened to the voices arguing about whether to take a break, when the Germans stopped. They got off their bikes and threw the rickety vehicles down on the road's shoulder.

Jacob moved a meter to the right until the cows' galvanized water basin gave him more coverage and lifted his head a couple of centimeters until he could see them. The rain had made the wet pavement shine. The biggest guy, an elderly man, put down his backpack, sat on it, laid his machinegun beside him on the pavement, and reached inside his jacket. He took out something. The other two soldiers conceded their protests and sat down beside him on the side of the road.

Only five meters away from them in the pasture, Jacob could hear their conversation. He put his head down. The cover was marginal. If the moon had been out, he would be clearly visible. His heart knocked about wildly in his chest and seemed too loud. Luckily, the grass had grown substantially under the rain of the last days. It hid his bike.

One of the young soldiers urged the others to keep going, as the border was not that far away, and the enemy was close. The heavy-set, older man cursed and said he didn't care anymore, that anything was better than this. The silent guy spoke now.

"*Ach Munzke, das kann man begreifen* [I can understand that], *für dich war das Leben sowieso endet* [your life was over anyway]."

Hearing the familiar name, Jacob's brains fired up, and with his neck hairs raised, he closed his eyes to focus on his hearing. Was he listening to Johanna's brother, who was supposed to have retired from the military?

The same bastard continued taunting the fat guy. "You said you've got relatives in these parts. Why don't you go there and ask them to hide you until all of this blows over? *Oder hast du das erfunden* [or were you just making that up]?"

"Halt das Maul," was Munzke's muffled answer between bites.

Jacob ran through his options. It would be impossible for him to take the whole lot of them, three of them against one unarmed man. If he had a gun, he should be putting the three out of commission. He hadn't brought a gun on purpose, so he'd seem innocent if he got caught — a civilian doesn't need a gun. Should he even try to save Margaret's uncle? Keeping Munzke away from the Allies was no option, so why linger on it? He couldn't even save himself. As an enemy soldier, the man had it coming what lay ahead of him, uncle or not. He had a mission to fulfill. Nothing left but to get soaked through and pray the soldiers will move on soon.

One of them went to a bike, rummaged in its side-bag, brought out a bottle, and held it out to his mates. "Want some liquid courage?" No answer. They drank in silence.

Jacob lifted his head a few centimeters and saw them each reach for the bottle. He waited patiently, his brain working faster than ever before. Johanna should have known her brother was deployed to Holland. He should've asked her about her Wehrmacht connection. Why feel indebted to her, anyway? If Johanna hadn't been his mother-in-law, he would think about this conundrum differently. It should be clear: German means enemy.

Being indebted to your in-laws is just the pits. Just like his father. Good God, he had never thought in those terms about this before, but yes, his father had married the rich girl and used her money to purchase the store — indebted for life to her family. No wonder he'd been such a frustrated son of a bitch, holding on to that grudge for the rest of his life. Father forbade visits to his in-laws, because of their godless way of life. Jacob's seen a thing or two himself, and knows it was an excuse, a cover-up. The bastard should've borrowed money instead for his children's education. What a waste of a life. He'd better not copy that bitter fool.

He heard the sound of something being thrown through the air, and something fell down with a dull smack, missing his head by a hair — the empty bottle. Somebody called out, "Alright, Munzke, find your sister. *Ich bedarfe ein Schläfchen* [I need a nap now]."

The soldiers climbed on their bikes with renewed enthusiasm. One of them even started humming, probably not the good soldier Munzke. Jacob stayed down, his cheek against the damp pasture that smelled of old cow dung, until he couldn't hear their voices anymore. His body was cold, his bladder bursting.

The rain had not returned, although Jacob was plenty wet. His clothes were soaked through from the damp pasture. He slowly got up and urinated, stretched his stiff limbs, and lifted his bike out of the field. He shook his head and wiped his face dry, mounted his bike, and took off in the opposite direction from the soldiers' escape route to the border. Gratitude seeped into his conscience for not having anything to do with the fate that would befall Munzke.

***

A Canadian scout on a motorcycle was the first soldier to notice him and led him to the section officer in charge. In the grey morning light, Jacob spotted the Allied tanks first, looming large in the mist, and then spotted the infantry at rest, a few hundred meters down the road.

A healthy-looking young Canadian stretched out a hand, smiling. "Hello, there. Welcome to the front. Who are you?"

Jacob grabbed on tightly, squeezing the savior's hand. "Hello. Van Noorden is my name, *Overdamse politie, Binnenlandse Strijdkrachten* [BS, Interior Forces]."

The officer waved at someone, and an interpreter immediately joined them. "Oh, police, Overdam, yes." Once he was identified, they shook hands again vigorously. Then Jacob showed the young lieutenant his papers and provided the name of his Illegal group commander's name, and its location. Jacob couldn't keep the joy out of his face while he enlightened the Canadian lieutenant about the Nazi positions and about what else to expect in the greater Overdam area. The lieutenant gave him a good cigar.

Jacob immediately lit up. Puffing out great clouds of fragrant smoke, he shouted, "Oh, yes, a real cigar. Thanks so much."

The young lieutenant nodded with a grin on his face. The formal part over, he told him: "Check out our equipment. Maybe you like one of our guns. Go mingle before you head home, or are you staying?"

Jacob shook his head. "Would love to, but must head home. They'll miss me, things to do."

The lieutenant happily explained to Jacob with the interpreter how the Canadians could advance so fast. They practiced a relay tactic: one section of infantry followed by a few tanks would advance and attack any Germans in their path. After substantial advancement, the section then stopped to rest until the rear had caught up, which then, in turn, became the advancing section.

"There are no German troops left to flank us now, so the speed of advancing is the only factor we need to consider. Thanks to the Illegals on the ground, we escape nests and other traps and can advance so quickly."

The men told Jacob that the Nazis — they called them Huns — were on the run and overwhelmingly were unmotivated old men and young kids, even under majority age. The lieutenant said he expected to take the northeast within a couple of days, which would only leave the lowlands of the south-west to take back.

Jacob recalled De Wit's theory about the Allied strategy to prevent the inundation of the lowlands, and about SHEAF's tactic to isolate the western Wehrmacht army. That smart man had been right.

After a good rest, some food, and a bit of Canadian whiskey, the soldiers loaded him up with cigarettes and chocolate, and he undertook the trip home. With tears in his eyes he said goodbye to the section commander. His heart was about to burst with exhilaration when he got back on his bicycle and raced the first five kilometers of his way home. The years of craziness were over.

Chapter 104

On April 5, 1945, Jacob got a call at four in the morning. When he picked up the phone, hoping for good news, the operator connected him to Nauwaard instead. "Come to the camp as soon as you can with as many men as you can spare. We're evacuating to Camp Westerbork." He sounded stressed.

"That's fifty kilometers north. Why even bother? We can practically touch the Allies," Jacob replied into dead space. Nauwaard had disconnected. Extremely annoyed and unable to keep that sentiment out of his voice, he mustered six of his crew members by phone, all of them bristling about the early hour. "It's an emergency. After today, we'll be rid of them for good."

Within thirty minutes, the peloton of cops on bicycles arrived at the camp and found it in chaos. The central field was lit by a few spotlights, and people were running around for some private purpose, while others tacked up the horses from the last batch of interned police. He spotted Nauwaard striding toward him. Maybe he could talk the man out of it.

"I'm staying behind with a few of my men," Nauwaard told him as the warden shifted his eyes from him to the field and guards running from one side of the camp to the other and back to him. "Schwier wants me to wrap up the fucking camp today," Charles said in a breathless voice without meeting Jacob's eyes. "All the others must leave, I don't care how. Help me get them out of here."

Searching for the right tone, Jacob inquired: "Where's your boss?"

As Charles walked away, he snarled: "Left at dusk with his buddies in the vehicles."

Jacob hurried along, keeping pace with Nauwaard.

"Charles, it's impossible to move four hundred prisoners safely. The Allies are practically on our doorstep. They're attacking all over the east. Now's the time to show clemency. Be reasonable."

"Fuck off, I don't need your sermon." Nauwaard's hands were shaking. With what little dignity he had left, he stomped away in the opposite direction.

Jacob didn't follow him, knowing the railway strike was still in effect. There was no line north. Only one hundred prisoners — tops — could travel by horse-drawn wagons. A few of the inmates would have the available bicycles, with the rest of them sent off on foot together with the remaining guards.

It was a ridiculously redundant undertaking. Aware of the camp's great stash of ammunition and explosives, hidden in a forest building, he hoped "wrapping up" Camp Star didn't mean its destruction.

He instructed his men to assist the guards with loading up the wagons, and organizing the prisoners into walking and biking groups. He went from group to group and spoke quietly to the prisoners, encouraging them to maintain decorum but to take advantage of any chance for an escape, and hope for the best. Most inmates were upset and already exhausted and only nodded.

Jacob reminded individual camp guards known for their cruelty to keep human decency in mind and the upcoming day of reckoning. With some solid curses for him, most guards told him to get lost.

Standing by the gate, he watched the departure of the sad ragtag collection of inmates in various garb, including old army and police uniforms and striped prison pajamas, unprepared for the soggy April weather. Some carried a small load on their backs, some had no possessions at all, and all were without food. It was clear Schwier had exerted his power over the warden once more. Before Jacob left the camp with his men, he looked for Nauwaard, but the warden had disappeared.

The camp was deserted. He didn't know whether to lock up the gate, but he didn't have any keys. Nauwaard was still around somewhere. Van Houten already picked up his bike and shouted, "Let's get out a here, Opper."

***

Jacob felt he should apologize to somebody for having been unable to dissuade Nauwaard. Back at the brigade, he discussed the strange morning with Van Houten.

"I tried to convince him to lay off, sit tight, and wait for the Allies. I'm sorry to say I was completely ineffective. I don't think Nauwaard thought he'd get a fair shake as a prisoner, that he and his guards would be treated fairly. What I don't understand is why he bothered asking us to be witness to the disaster. We were not needed. What point was he trying to make?"

"Beats me." Van Houten shrugged.

Van Houten pushed his chair back. "I'm letting Commander Simon know of the camp's evacuation."

"Sure, you do that. Sergeant, tell me this, could Nauwaard still cause us harm?" Jacob's question went unanswered as Van Houten was already out the door.

***

Both were unaware of Hitler's instructions to Himmler to have all camp operators kill the prisoners and blow up all materials before withdrawing from the camps. But Nauwaard would've known.

A farmer with his operation next door to the camp hadn't liked the possibility of being blown up in his own backyard, so he had cut the underground ignition wire to the camp's ammunition shed weeks earlier. When somebody lit the fuse on that day, nothing happened.

***

On the evening of the camp's evacuation, Van Houten — Herman in the Illegality world — proposed to Commander Simon to start dealing with the camp as part of their first action as the newly appointed Interior Forces — BS. He wanted to arrest the remaining guards before Nauwaard could do more damage and Commander Simon approved the action. After it was all over, Van Houten shared his story with Jacob. Van Houten's crew had kept the ten guards plus Nauwaard hidden in the woods for six days after the successful raid on the camp, before they were finally saved by the Allies.

"We captured Schwier's secretary too, the lovely young Rita, which complicated things somewhat, when Rita needed a bathroom break." Van Houten smiled, remembering the particulars of that situation. "Keeping those traitors under control and hiding at different places in the damp woods, wasn't easy, especially with my injured leg. But I'd do it all again."

"Better take it easy for a while and let that gun wound heal properly, Sergeant," Jacob said. A good thing he hadn't known about it at the time of the action, and was spared the stress of worrying about the men, Jacob realized.

Through the grapevine, Jacob learned of the Camp Star prisoners' fate who had been sent north. Of 450 men who'd left the camp guarded by thirty of the warden's men, only 187 arrived at Camp Westerbork, wholly exhausted at the end of their two-day trip. Air attacks had offered splendid opportunities for an escape.

Chapter 105

The Allies moved exceedingly fast, sometimes 130 kilometers a day, in a zigzagging pattern to avoid the Wehrmacht nests, thus confusing the supporting Allied planes' navigators of all stripes, navigators up in the air, who couldn't figure out the already liberated positions. Friendly fire became the danger for the boots on the ground.

One day after the evacuation of Star Camp, the Canadians took Johanna's village. Another day later, April 10, they took the town of Dedemsvaart, but with nasty aftermath. Undetected by the Allies on their way through town, a few trapped Wehrmacht soldiers led by a German SS officer captured 15 civilians as hostages and shot nine of them.

Jacob expected similar revenge actions in each town the Nazis left, so he made sure his men were well prepared and executed every task with diligence. He stressed the importance of letting him know of each sighting of enemy soldiers.

Heusden called him once more. The Oberfeldwebel had no time to meet but wanted him to know of his efforts to save the town, just in case. "An overly zealous SS officer told a dozen citizens to leave their homes in the most obvious war zones by the river and wanted to use them as hostages. He brought those villagers to my HQ. I told that zealot I damn well wasn't going to participate with this cruel and useless measure. When that bastard was gone, I told my men to let the civilians leave through the backdoor. When that arrogant SS jerk found out, he returned to my HQ and pointed his pistol at me. Treason, he called it."

"Good for you," Jacob said, and he meant it.

"Then some other ass wanted the OT engineers to load the bridges with explosives. I'm not going to. We have to cross those bridges too, and besides, it would lead to more civilian casualties. So, now you know what's happening. Got to go. Just wanted to say goodbye. Any day now. *Auf Wiedersehen*, Von Norden."

"Good of you, Heusden. I appreciate it. I always found you a straight military man with decent principles. Good luck, look after yourself."

He got off the line with mixed feelings. A bullet from this man's weapon might kill him in the next few days, even hours. Jacob would find out that Hitler's policy of leaving scorched earth had prevailed: the bridges were indeed loaded with dynamite.

**

All over the region, Resistance groups prepared to join the Interior Forces — BS, and needed their weapons, still hidden at various farms just out of town. Two members of Simon's group retrieved the horse and wagon hidden inside a ring of dense brambles on a supposedly deserted farm, waiting for that great day. The Wehrmacht, preoccupied with their own defense-and-retreat strategies, had no interest in those stoic farmers going back and forth with wagon-loads of rubble and sour-smelling silage cattle feed. The men safely delivered the weapons and ammo to the leading group, holed up at another farm under another BS Commander from Jacob's crew, Corporal De Wit, AKA Bas. They spent the night in hiding. On April 10, they dug up and cleaned their foul-smelling Stenguns, preparing the crew for action.

Just then, a group of German soldiers on bicycles turned off the highway into the farm's driveway, likely to demand some food. The man on guard spotted them in time, and Bas quickly ordered all to hide in an empty potato dugout and prepare for battle. They were now legitimate soldiers in the newly assigned Interior Forces — BS and they waited, hearts pounding, adrenaline pumping through their bodies. The Germans came closer and were finally within shooting distance when Commander Bas gave the command.

"Start shooting the bastards."

The six BS soldiers opened fire. The racket raised the attention of a number of German paratroopers patrolling the area, and they joined the fight. The unusually high firepower level caught the attention of an Allied division of Polish and Canadian troops nearby, which also joined in. The battle lasted four long hours, sustained by plenty of British ammunition from Bas' dugout. The combined efforts of Interior Forces — BS and Allies finally convinced the Nazi soldiers to surrender. When the surviving Germans stopped shooting and came out of their hiding places with their hands in the air, Bas/De Wit stood up and yelled, "Hurray. Arrest the suckers!"

The Allied troops took the POWs away, leaving Bas and his crew free to join the main BS forces with their British weapons. "That was a good practice session," grinned Bas/ De Wit, as he walked away from the dugout, a bit taller and freer.

When De Wit told Jacob later about that adventure, the chief felt sweat collecting on his brow during the account. "It could have ended badly," Jacob said softly. He added quickly, "I'm grateful it didn't. Good work, De Wit. Proud of you."

Chapter 106

At the start of it all, Jacob told Margaret to take the children and sit out the battle for Overdam in the newly enforced basement. He went next door to the squad room and invited all needing shelter to join his family in the cellar. "The last hours of the occupation have arrived, men. We'll soon be free. Good luck all."

The crew members left to find their place, whether in a shelter or in combat.

***

During his patrols, Jacob had observed Heusden's Wehrmacht digging a fortification at the back of the mayor's home. The nest was hidden behind a two-meter-high dirt hill, and the soldiers were armed with several machine guns and an antitank grenade launcher. Jacob suspected the mayor must be furious since his home was in the line of fire, and the Allies would surely target the Kraut's grenade launcher. But Van Voorst hadn't complained about it yet to him.

As most soldiers still carried a number of antitank panzer fists, it would be dangerous to underestimate the Nazis' retreat. Wehrmacht sharpshooters were hidden in several hotels, as he'd already reported to the Canadians. He had no doubt which hotels in town would receive extra attention from the Allies.

The town of Overdam shook with heavy explosions that reverberated through tremors underground, unsettling the population. The battle had begun. Henk — Regional Commander Zondervan of the BS — had mobilized all of the region's Resistance groups, and his men had been busy retrieving their hidden weapons from the surrounding areas. They had weapons and ammunition to join the battle.

***

In the middle of the bombardment, Jacob sat in his office, unable to sleep and not wanting to join the crew in the cellar. The battle lasted already forty-eight hours. He felt bold enough to get the radio out of hiding and sat listening to Radio Orange in the dark, close to the telephone, hoping the Canadians would take the town in the night.

Lit by the squeeze-cat's pinprick, a hand-operated mechanical flashlight, he took the Canadian chocolate bars and cigarettes out of his locked desk drawer and piled them up next to the radio. He unwrapped a chocolate bar, bit into it with gusto and concluded this was easily the best experience of eating chocolate ever, although it was a chewy thing, tasting more like raisins than pre-war chocolate. He lit up a cigar, a gift from the Canadian lieutenant, and leaned back in his office chair, enjoying every minute of the anticipation of freedom. This was the best-ever moment of his life.

At midnight, it grew unexpectedly quiet, and he strained to listen for any noise, turned the radio down, and noticed the silence outside when he opened a window. Suddenly, strange rolling and scuffling sounds penetrated the hush, like an enormous animal woke up and crawled out of hiding. He stepped outside, crossed the driveway, and carefully looked into the street. The cool night air caressed his bald head. He smelled diesel.

Beyond the sturdy oaks lining the street, he saw something happening. Heusden and his Wehrmacht juggernaut move out of The White Swan, kit and caboodle on loaded carts, on trailers, and in military vehicles with all they could carry, the whole darned caravan, including the Russian POWs, who were pushing carts for lack of horses.

He understood its significance and retreated into his station and called his Illegality trustee, Tinkerbel. "Letting you know the Wehrmacht unit is moving out of Overdam this minute." He said a brief prayer for Fritz Heusden, the only half-decent Nazi he had met.

An hour later, Tinkerbel called back and told him to tell his crew to sit tight while the Canadians would launch a final sweep through town at daybreak to take Overdam.

***

A lull in the fighting arrived, and Margaret took advance of it for a bathroom break. She got the children organized for another long stretch in the cellar. The tedious hours of confinement were getting to everyone. Jaap had a tendency for teasing Hendrik relentlessly, and a fight ensued. Hendrik's heart was quickly crushed, and his response to Jaap — aggression — could hurt his smaller brother, so she sent Jaap to his bedroom for his own protection.

Jaap was still upstairs in his bedroom when an eardrum-busting explosion shook the building, shattering the windows. A second later, the six-year-old boy came bouldering down the stairs shouting at the top of his voice, an octave higher than usual: "Mama, Mama, that big tank was hit in front of the hotel and he's on fire."

Margaret grabbed her slight son, holding him tightly in a bear hug, blankets draped over her free arm and a basket of food in her hand. "Never mind, quick, to the cellar. We don't want a bomb on our heads." Nine-year-old Hendrik carried little Elly, all of them hurrying together to the cellar in the beam of the diminutive dynamo light.

"Where's Papa?" Hendrik asked.

"Never mind, keep going. He'll be here soon."

The Van Noordens sat crammed together with the others in the musty brigade cellar, meant for canned goods, coal, and seasonal gear, most of which had disappeared. The first explosion was followed by many more explosions and a few hours of intense artillery fire. The group sat silently together, half-asleep or wide awake, enduring the hours in the dark because they knew these would be the last hours of the Nazi occupation.

Chapter 107

The racket lasted for hours, then it stopped abruptly. Jacob knew that infantry troops followed the tanks to take prisoner any German soldiers scattering away or surrendering on sight. He went outside and stood in front of the brigade in the grey morning mist to witness the bulk of the Canadian troops roll right through Overdam, onwards to the still-occupied north in tanks, on foot, and in trucks.

An Allied soldier on a camouflaged motorcycle pulled over in front of the marechaussee brigade. Jacob identified the regional BS leader in the sidecar by his armband, a man he knew well: Henk Zondervan, his brother-in-law. Henk got out and surveyed the damage to the building.

Just then, an Allied jeep pulled up behind Henk's bike with a Canadian lieutenant behind the wheel. Two other members of the BS-Combat Troops division got a ride with the Canadian. They were dressed in their improvised uniforms of dark blue coveralls with armbands. Commander Simon rode shotgun, the man whom Jacob finally had met after the evacuation of Star Camp. His real name was Romme Postema. The second man was Jef Last, alias Writer, Simon's deputy, the crew boss responsible for the British weapons' airdrops.

Jacob stepped forward and shook their hands without anybody speaking. Just as well, as he might not have found the right words that particular minute; something was blocking his throat. He turned away to give his watering eyes a quick wipe with the back of his hand. The three men in the jeep didn't get out and moved on to the former Wehrmacht HQ.

The regional commander, Henk Zondervan, addressed Jacob. "We got word no Krauts are left here and the Allies are moving on. We need to talk about arranging the take-over, Chief Van Noorden. Meet me at the White Swan Hotel with as many men as you can spare."

Henk got back on the bike and directed the lieutenant to ride to the former Wehrmacht HQ, now utterly devoid of German soldiers.

Jacob hurried back into the brigade building, beyond eager to inform the people in the cellar it was all over. He opened the door with a broad smile on his face and called out. "You can come out now!"

***

Blinking from spending days in the semi-dark, the Overdam residents finally climbed out of their shelters and cellars into a grey dawn. Misty clouds hung between buildings and trees, which could have been the smoke from burnt buildings. They stood around in small groups and listened to the fading rumblings. The ground still vibrated.

Examining her surroundings, Margaret led the children outside to the street, carrying Elly on her arm and holding Jaap's hand, as Hendrik stayed close to her, his hand grabbing her skirt. They involuntarily crinkled their noses at the harsh fumes of explosives and burnt things, and the dust from pulverized bricks hung heavy in the air.

The first thing they saw was an endless queue of Canadian military equipment on the main highway moving in the direction of Zwolle. The large tanks were leading, followed by many jeeps with artillery guns, and a lot of armored vehicles and trucks full of soldiers and guns. No horse to be seen. Only then did they believe the Germans were really gone.

Margaret and the other families excitedly talked and hugged in front of the brigade. Most were teary-eyed. Even the men let emotion overcome them for the briefest second, embracing one another tightly. Jacob kissed Margaret on her mouth as he lifted Elly from her arms. He shook hands, slapped shoulders, handed out cigarette packages, and hugged the women and children. Then he dug out of his pockets his sweet treasures and handed out the chocolate bars, first to Hendrik and Jaap, and then to the children of his crew members. The children didn't know what this brown, unattractive-looking stuff was, but once they tasted the chocolate, their delight with the sweet and buttery sensation in their mouths was apparent. They gobbled up right then whatever they were given.

***

Everywhere in the streets, citizens gathered and cheered, sang the national anthem, and embraced one another. Some kept singing: others uncorked the hidden bottles of

Dutch gin and made toasts to the liberators. Overdam's main streets changed into an instant open-air café, where people sat and danced among the rubble and the scattered diamonds of broken glass.

During the following days, Canadian and Polish soldiers granted a rest, were welcomed into Overdam homes, finding easy billeting and warm meals. The farms of the area accommodated many men in their hay lofts and friendly stables. Craven A and Chesterfields aplenty were handy cash in exchange for food and other comforts. The soldiers readily shared their beer and whiskey rations with the civilians on their first party in five long years.

Chapter 108

In the first hour of the liberation, chaos ruled at the brigade. Peters and Dijk had disappeared the previous day, and Van Houten and De Wit had left five days earlier for their jobs with the BS. The brigade's windows had all been blown out and the place was a mess. After the celebratory toast with the men, Jacob directed Van Hardenberg to stay behind as watch commander, start cleaning up, and lock away any weapons and ammunition the Canadians or the BS crew might drop off. He instructed four crew members, Leversma, Dikkers, Van den Berg, and Van der Gulik to follow him to report to BS Commander Postema, alias Simon at the former Wehrmacht HQ.

On arrival at the former Nazi HQ, Jacob told two of his men to check the exterior for damage while joining the BS leadership inside. He asked Henk about having checked for boobytraps.

"Van Noorden, the Air Defense crew already checked for booby traps, and we've declared the facility safe," said Henk, "Postema will establish the head office of the new local government right here, in the hotel."

Jacob stuck his head through the pane-less window and called his men inside.

"Men, sorry to be in such a rush, but I'll have to move on to the next town. You'll all be fine. Good work, men, and thanks so much. We'll talk later." Henk Zondervan shook more hands and then left the building.

Nothing of value was left in the rooms, not even a typewriter, although the Wehrmacht obligingly had abandoned some bottles in a locked cabinet. "Maybe Heusden hadn't wanted his men to become desperate and drunk," suggested Jacob to Simon. After Commander Postema alias Simon put a couple of bottles away for later, he gave the extras to one of the men who went outside and distributed those extra bottles among the jubilant civilians in the street.

In Heusden's old office, Jacob found the white cat. As the animal high-tailed it out of the room Commander Postema approved the space as the conference room.

"This will be our room for investigations," he said. "It'll have to do, until we find a better place. Can you bring your men in here, Van Noorden?"

The crew arranged a pair of tables into one long conference table and placed four chairs behind it and one chair in front. They all sat down, relishing the moment of taking possession of the hated Nazi HQ.

"Thank God. I thought this day would never come," Jacob sighed.

"I know," Postema quietly said. "Every day I yearned for this, and now it's finally here. Let's never forget this moment."

The cat walked back in through the open door and jumped on Van Houten's knees, rubbing its cheek against his chest.

"What the heck!" The tender-hearted sergeant couldn't resist stroking the Nazi cat and evoked loud purring in the little predator.

"Let's get the other rooms ready," said the commander in a bright tone of voice. "Jan, you can stay seated with that sore leg of yours, and take the little hunter home with you today." Van Houten didn't object and put the friendly animal on the floor but got up from his chair anyway.

The commander produced a list of enemies and suspected collaborators. "Prince Bernhard's HQ forwarded lists to all regional BS commanders. I just got mine from Zondervan. The Military Authority prepared this in consult with local input. Let's start by arresting the dangerous elements. Yeah!" Several voices joined in.

"This is the process: we have selected trustworthy policemen and BS members of the Combat Troops division for this work, which could be dangerous. The Military Authority selected the members of the commission, made up of three members from the community under the leadership of Mr. Firm, a solicitor. After an arrest, this commission will investigate all cases in a preliminary assessment of their danger. Van Noorden, you're in charge of the arresting teams.

"Simon, what's going to happen with the arrested?" Leversma wanted to know.

"You can call me Postema now. The commission determines who'll be set free and who need to be locked up for further investigation by Justice. Thanks to Van Houten we'll have a place to put them: Star Camp is now Camp Overdam and the Allies have already turned it over to us. We assigned the guarding jobs here and at the camp to the Non-Combat troops. Van Noorden, here's your list of candidates for arrest. It has known SS officers and Dutch NSB Nazis, so be careful, and good luck. Alright, go to it, men."

When Jacob saw the names of Peters and Dijk on the master list, he swallowed hard. He hoped they would get a fair shake and get off lightly. Being a nuisance was no criminal offense under the law, but joining the SS unfortunately was.

***

None of the BS crew went home to participate in the street celebrations. The new government had other things to do. A few men designated the available rooms without windows and with decent locks as temporary holding cells and numbered them. Others made sure the arrest teams had enough weapons. A truck needed to be hustled for transport to the camp.

Jacob divided the eight men under him into four teams of two, led by Van Houten, De Wit, Piet Koster, and himself. He made sure Piet Koster's team got Peters and Dijk. They each took several names from the long list and got going. By the end of the first day, the teams had arrested forty suspects, secured in the HQ holding cells or the camp.

Jacob arrived home late, satisfied, and spent on that evening of April 10, 1945. Disappointed, he saw that Margaret was asleep, but he didn't want to wake her — she'd been through a few sleepless nights and deserved her rest. He went to the children's room and looked at the sleeping beauties, kissed each child gently on the head, and snuck out of the room, closing the door quietly. Curled up against Margaret with an arm around her waist, he was off into the deep sleep of the virtuous before he could form a thought.

***

Canadian soldiers dropped off more weapons and ammunition with duty officer Van Hardenberg at the brigade building. The healthy-looking and friendly young Canadians took time to visit with the children in the yard, freely handing out chewing gum and more chocolate. To the children, they were like Angels from Heaven dressed in uniforms. It consolidated in Hendrik the desire to become a military man.

One of the soldiers was a black man who impressed the children to no end. Jaap wasn't sure what to make of the man with a face that was obviously not covered with the blackface make-up, like the usual helpers of Bishop Saint Nicholas — the impersonators of Moorish slaves. The whole caravan of *Sinterklaas* on his annual visit to

Amsterdam would arrive by ship from his city of Myra. From there, the Saint brought candies and gifts to children all over the country on his birthday, December 5.

After the Allied soldiers had left, Jaap asked his mom in a quiet voice: "Was that man *Zwarte Piet* [Black Pete]?" In his short life, he'd never seen Black Pete.

Margaret gave the six-year-old a quick hug, smiling. "Oh no, Jaap, that's a negro, son. He's born with that skin color, just as you're born with yours. He's from the country called Canada."

"He was nice, he mama?" Jaap asked.

"Sure was, my boy. He was a big man, right?" She caressed his head and smiled.

"*Ja, ik was een beetje bang* [I was a bit scared]," the boy slowly said.

"No need, love. He was one of the good soldiers."

All evening she expected Jacob to walk in, but he didn't. After the kids were asleep, Margaret went to sleep in an empty bed, exhausted.

***

During the following two days, Jacob's crews kept busy, bringing in the arrested at the same steady pace. After the commission had determined to hold them longer, men of the combat division transported the suspects to Camp Overdam. He had the system running like a soccer player's dream, and his list was shrinking rapidly.

The White Swan Hotel was filled with the noise and commotion of relatives appealing an arrest — wailing wives pleading with the commander for their innocent husbands' release. The rooms at HQ were buzzing. The mayor's couriers came and went, and a host of civilians collected signatures on the paperwork for delivering goods, required for payment. A new post-war provisional government was rapidly taking shape.

Each day, a crowd of curious bystanders gathered in front of The White Swan hotel. Some yelled nasty slurs at the arrested, their frustration and anger from five long years of intense fear and insecurity evident in their faces. A hurray would go up with the arrival of each suspect. The crowd's shouting could be clearly heard inside the building, and it bothered Jacob, although he understood the sentiment. He wanted to return to the law as it used to be, where every accused is innocent until proven guilty and deserves dignified treatment. The emotional drive to take revenge on any random person was wrong but stopping this crowd would cause a riot, so he had to put up with it.

Chapter 109

Camp Overdam went through its own process of chaos and reorganization after the change of power. Jacob met with Simon face-to-face for the very first time, to negotiate to put the freed northern policemen to guard the camp, at least until the Allies would arrive. Most of those men had stayed around town. After locking the gates, Jacob and his crew armed the northern policemen with British Stenguns to keep the camp safe from marauders. One of them, Van Angeren, volunteered to organize the camp's clean-up and the sorting, safekeeping, and distribution of the goods from the storage section.

***

On the day of the liberation, Van Houten's men brought in the first ten prisoners, the former guards of Star Camp who had stayed behind to "wrap up" the camp. BS-member Paske Kort volunteered as the first camp manager. Paske had become acquainted with the prisoners during their six-day hole-up in the forest and knew what he got himself in for.

Under Van Angeren, the would-be guards/policemen had made a terrible mess of the camp within a week, especially the storage section, and it needed to be sorted out. Paske sent Van Angeren out on his ear the same day he took over.

Commander Postema assigned additional guards from the BS-Combat and Non-Combat divisions. He also hired the wife of the KP-pilot rescue Wim Smit to manage the female prisoners housed in a separate cabin on the grounds.

More prisoners arrived in the borrowed army truck. Besides, the Canadian military and Dutch authorities from elsewhere sent their prisoners to the new-old Camp Overdam. By the third day, the number of prisoners had reached 500. That number demanded more guards. The unemployed, returning to life from hiding, solicited for a job at the gate. If they looked suitable, Paske Kort hired them on the spot to help get the gardens and the farm back in order, feed the starving cattle and pigs, do repairs and clean up the indescribable disorder.

On day three, April 13, Commander Postema assigned Mr. Van Loon, as the new warden, the former principal of the international Quaker school on Castle Eerde. Van Loon began to grapple with the prisoners' care and the staff, a nearly impossible job, as supplies were only haphazardly becoming available. Under the new government, the prison was in chaos too, although nobody missed the Nazi discipline.

***

At the end of day three, Jacob arrived at the camp for the first time since the liberation to deliver a group of fifteen fresh suspects. He saw a group of prisoners crowded around the gate on the inside. Somebody shouted his name. "Van Noorden, I need to speak to you." The former warden in his prison getup was surrounded by his henchmen, all of them pushing hard against the gate.

Seeing Charles Nauwaard for the first time since the evacuation stopped him in his tracks. He had forgotten all about him in these last, frenzied days. As the guards tried to open the gate to let the newcomers in, the prisoners inside swarmed them and blocked Jacob, his men, and the new prisoners, causing a deadlock. Inside on the other side of the fence, the new guards roughly pushed and shoved the hated Nauwaard and his traitors forward while forming a barrier with their bodies. Some of the guards shouted degrading epithets, and other guards used the butts of their rifles on the resisting prisoners' heads and shoulders. The guards managed to keep Nauwaard and his mates at bay, leaving bruises and cuts behind on faces, and the new delivery finally entered through the gate.

One of the guards in front of Jacob shouted at him. "Just get out of here, you, *Moffenhoer* [Nazi whore]. We don't need you here."

As blind anger seared hot through his veins, Jacob charged forward and grabbed the guard by the throat with both hands, but he couldn't get close enough to apply real pressure. The guards grabbed him and wrestled his arms behind his back, while a third guard had an arm around his neck. He couldn't move. He couldn't breathe. Looking up, he saw Nauwaard standing to the side, watching him. The bastard smiled.

Deflated, he gave up the struggle. The arm disappeared from his neck. Completely out of breath and panting, he slowly recovered as two guards held him tightly by his upper arms. Somebody warned the new warden. When Van Loon arrived on the scene, Jacob was breathing normally again. When the warden saw him subdued, he told the guards to release their hold on the chief.

Jacob turned to the new warden and demanded, "Van Loon, let them…"

But Van Loon cut him off, and shouted at him, "Shut up. Shut up."

Jacob couldn't believe what he heard and stayed silent.

Van Loon continued speaking in a normal tone but with force.

"No. Van Noorden, my men don't want you here. You're not doing anyone any good. Get out of here and don't come back. Guards, open the gate."

Jacob yelled: "No. You have no right."

Van Loon had already turned his back and walked away.

The guards grabbed him and pushed him through the gate as he was vehemently resisting his eviction. Standing outside de gate, hot and red-faced, he pulled his clothes straight and wondered what had just happened.

Chapter 110

After a twenty-minute wait beside the army truck, Jacob's men rejoined him. The team left the camp in silence. Jacob rode beside the driver, the rest of the team in the back. His brain didn't function well, and he could only focus on Van Loon, who should've let him speak to Charles Nauwaard. He was unable to grasp the fact that the new warden banned him from the camp. Van Loon had made a fool out of him.

To hear a few days ago that Nauwaard was on the list for urgent transport to Almelo to be tried as a war criminal had not surprised him. Was he trying to use their friendship to get a better deal? He resented Charles for putting him in this compromised position, but the new guards' rough treatment of the prisoners was even more disturbing. These new authorities were as ruthless as the Nazis. They were supposed to show respect for the laws that protect prisoners. He had promised Nauwaard as much.

On arrival at HQ, he noticed two of the BS men staying close to him. He was just about to ask if they hadn't anything better to do when Commander Postema came out of his office, walked up to him, and took him formally by the arm. "Chief Van Noorden, a word? Please step into my office."

Postema guided him into the office. Numb and not grasping what happened, he searched Simon's face, looking for a sign of a joke.

Judging by the expression of sorrow on his face, the commander clearly had much trouble proceeding. The man could hardly look him in the eye and was breathed hard. Finally, he spoke again.

"I hate to do this to you, Opper, but I'm acting on the order of the Military Authority. He'll arrive here today or tomorrow and then you may ask him yourself. In line with the direction from the brass to include complaints from the community, we added new names to the list of suspects. I'm sorry to say one of those names was yours." Postema/Simon stopped speaking and took a deep breath.

Jacob stared at him.

The commander finally looked at Jacob when he continued speaking.

"We've received two credible allegations against you. The first suggests you collaborated with Charles Nauwaard, Star Camp commander and employee of the German Security Services. The second charge is for collaboration with SD commander, SS officer Schwier. Beyond these two, we've received a variety of accusations from community members about your actions that involve minor allegations."

Jacob's breathing became irregular, and pain spread as if a fist punched, tore open his chest, grabbed his heart, and squeezed hard. He was struck wordless, his brain refusing to operate. A sudden whiff of something hit his nose — a brand of German cigarettes — mixed with a hint of beer.

Commander Postema continued speaking and the words reached Jacob's brain slowly: "… overall charge is you failed to conduct yourself in a manner expected from a policeman, possibly put the lives of Dutch citizens in danger by collaboration with the enemy. You are under investigation and are discontinued in your function as Chief of Overdam Police, with the continuation of your salary and your rank until proven guilty. I'll make sure the security commission hears you as soon as possible."

Jacob didn't move, still processing the sentences.

Postema cleared his throat. "Jacob. Please, surrender your weapon."

His eyes had trouble focusing, and his ears were ringing. He felt for his gun, slowly removed it from its holster with his right hand, and held it out by its barrel. Commander Postema took it and said, "Please, follow the guards to the holding room. No need for shackles."

The words reverberated: collaboration with the enemy, traitor, a Nazi whore. He stumbled a few paces forward until somebody grabbed his upper arm. Another BS guard grabbed his other arm. Outwardly calm, he followed.

He saw a BS guard hold the mayor's upper arm at the other end of the corridor, leading him into one of the rooms. Did he imagine things in his confusion? The mayor was a compassionate leader, always going out on a limb to get citizens released, on duty day and night, walking the same tightrope as he had. Was the mayor arrested? He wondered who had made these accusations. First himself, now Mayor Van Voorst. The world had gone completely crazy.

***

The guards locked him into a small room. He turned around as the door closed behind him, and in that second, he saw Van Houten standing in the doorframe of the HQ entrance, some distance away, looking at his chief in disbelief, his mouth open. Jacob's face turned hot as the door was locked and bolted. He couldn't see and stumbled another step into the room, fell down on the only chair, and covered his face with his hands. Wetness fell from between his fingers onto the hardwood floor.

Chapter 111

At home with the children, Margaret hadn't been concerned about her husband until Sergeant Van Houten arrived to inform her of the arrest. She stood silently in the entrance of her house, a hand to her mouth, and stared at the sergeant.

"I don't know what to say," he said. "They think he was playing two sides. It must be a mistake. The chief is the most law-abiding man I know, and a great boss." He stood twirling his cap in his hands, sorrow on his face.

All Margaret could whisper was, "Thank you, Jan," before she softly closed the door. She always liked Van Houten and not only because he had her husband's name. He was everything her husband wasn't and that could be interesting. But today, she was numb; even Jan at her door couldn't lift her mood.

She went about her day in a state of suspended emotion, her thoughts a jumble while she completed her chores. Like everybody else, she knew Juergen was an NSB member, but her husband a traitor? Margaret couldn't imagine him secretly admiring the Dutch Nazi Party, or the SS. It wouldn't fit his straight-forward mind or his political views, his austere character.

Although his emotions were a closed chapter to her, she knew he couldn't pretend well. It wasn't in his nature. He'd rather be beaten up by his brothers than submitting to them. Jacob abhorred settling and a compromise, he wanted to be correct, a proud man who would die of shame right now in his cell. After all his struggles to stay on the right side, in the end, accused of being a traitor. She grieved for him. Van Houten was right, and Jacob's arrest was incomprehensible and had to be a mistake.

Granted, a couple of years into the occupation, Jacob had become somewhat friendly with Johanna and Juergen, which had confused her at the time, but she'd always trusted him and thought he must have been thinking of her feelings for this change in attitude. She'd loved him for it as the conflicts in the family hurt her and the children too and made her sad.

When Jacob worked as a border agent before their marriage, he told her he had joined the NSB as an undercover ruse. His spying had led to discovering a significant weapons cache — all above board, and he had received praise and the promotion.

Maybe his past NSB membership from that case had surfaced now, but no doubt the investigators would find out the circumstances, and that would be the end of that suspicion. A sliver of doubt lingered; had there been more to it?

She didn't know what to think. Life was suddenly a nightmare, right when they should be happy together and celebrate the end of the troubles. She wasn't wrong to trust him, no, of course not. In the end, he would be found to be the man she knew: trustworthy and responsible, a staunch loyalist.

Jacob had never been unfaithful to her. He had openly dated Elfriede, and although she was hurt to her core back then, she couldn't blame him. Elfriede was so much more exciting and attractive. Ultimately, it was his choice whom to choose for his wife. Deeds speak louder than words. Even if he had difficulty saying it to her, she was sure he loved her. She would soon see him coming through the door, smiling. Then she could tell him of her own secrets.

She'd kept the kids in the yard to protect them from the roughness happening in the streets. They could hear the crowds celebrating outside. She knew they also knocked on doors, yelled insults in front of the homes of people suspected of collaboration with the enemy, or even resented for stupid reasons, hell-bent for revenge. This happened in other places in the south, liberated before the winter.

She was aware from glances and hateful comments that many people held a grudge against Jacob, a cop, and by extension, against her as his wife. She'd heard about the mobs and the treatment of Dutch girlfriends who had been friendly to German soldiers. The angry people had grabbed these ordinary girls from their homes, shaved their heads bald, and in some cases, drove them around town on carts, like witches during the middle ages. The yelling outside caused her heart palpitations, and she pushed her hands against her chest to force her breathing to slow down, stave off anxiety overwhelming her.

She couldn't stop herself from nagging the children. She'd told them several times: "Go tidy up your room."

Hendrik protested loudly, "Our room is already tidy."

"Then go play with your Mechano, make me a tank."

It didn't work. After days and nights in the cellar, Jaap and Hendrik were desperate for fun, pushing her relentlessly. "We want to play outside. Where is Papa? Why doesn't he come home? We want to cheer and sing outside with the others."

"Just wait, he'll be home soon. He's still at work. The brigade has to help the Canadian soldiers."

"I don't believe you," cheeky Jaap said.

"I don't care, just go play in the back yard then," she admonished.

That first day, they had waited and waited. She'd kept thinking he'd come home any minute now. But he was so late, too late to celebrate in town with the kids, and the next day too. She'd known of other marechaussee wives and children going out in the streets, but she didn't want to risk it without Jacob.

He'd been frantically busy since the Canadian troops' arrival. He'd been stern about waiting for him to celebrate and to stay home until then. She didn't want to disappoint him, or worse, make him angry. He could be fierce, reducing her to tears sometimes.

She walked from the back yard to the front, into the street looking both sides, then again to the back yard, to the boys. She had to use the bathroom each hour. She combed her hair several times. She'd done dishes and had all the food prepared she would need the next day for lunch and supper. Luckily, Elly had a long morning nap after all the exciting nights with little sleep. Although she was near exhaustion, she knew she couldn't sleep now. Jacob had to return home first. She forgot to feed the boys their supper until Jaap finally complained he was hungry.

Chapter 112

The charges had come like a blow to the side of his head during a boxing practice, dizzying him and temporarily knocking out all rational thought. After a few minutes, his faintness withdrew. They must've made a mistake. Commander Simon gave the order to detain him, the same Postema who had given him his spying assignment in September 1943, who had designed and approved his strategy to cultivate a relaxed relation with the Nazis. He carefully groomed his friendships with Heusden and Nauwaard over the last two years, which had proven productive. So why the arrest?

Jacob formulated sentences in his head to convince the security commission he wasn't one of the traitors, that he was clean, his conscience clear — well, mostly clear. Yes, he hadn't minded Heusden, had thought he was a decent man, just a soldier on the other side thrown into a war without any choice, much like him.

Charles Nauwaard was a more complex case. He shivered, thinking about their conversations and the Star Camp's evacuation. The man must've known Jacob's interest had just been business, a job. He wondered if it was payback time for indirectly having prevented Nauwaard's escape. No doubt Nauwaard would be no less subdued as a prisoner than as the camp boss, and he might have wanted to take him down with him. He assumed Van Houten and his men hadn't abused the prisoners during those hairy six days in the woods. But, now he had seen the new guards treat the arrested not so differently from the Nazis — he couldn't be sure of that assumption anymore either.

He reconsidered the rumors going around about him since the liberation. Apparently, from day one camp leader Kort had faced a rebellion from the newbie guards, many of them former prisoners of Star Camp, citing Jacob's friendship with Nauwaard and the Nazis. De Wit confided in him and told him the new guards didn't think he should still remain the police chief and definitively not be in charge of the collaborators' arrests. They had called him the fox in the henhouse. Friend of Nauwaard. My God. He had no doubts he had made plenty of enemies in town during these last years on the job. He hoped that whoever would conduct the investigation wouldn't be someone who had a grudge against him.

The shouting from the crowd outside hurt his brain as if somebody was holding a megaphone to his head. It aggravated his throbbing headache. Locked into a damn storage room, for goodness sakes. His uniform cap was cutting off circulation to his head, so he took it off, laid it on the bench beside him, and took off his jacket, and waited.

The fear of running out of air in the room made him breathe with shallow intakes. He laid down on the floor and stretched his arms out wide. He tried slowly inhaling and exhaling equal quantities of air, in and out, as he wondered what time it was. He had no watch, no belt, no weapon, but they'd let him keep his handkerchief.

He got up and walked the small space, back and forth, as he prayed: Lord, do justice and spare my family. A prayer repeated, each word a step, seven steps to cross the room, seven back, back, and forth.

**

He estimated at least three hours had passed by the time the guards led him into the interrogation room and stood him before the long table he and his crew had set up the first day. Three men in civilian clothes were seated behind the table, and four high-ranking BS members stood to the side, where he should have been standing. Next to the main table sat an army radio with a telephone earpiece hanging from its own pedestal. A uniformed marechaussee officer spoke as Jacob stood to attention. He recognized the voice of his Resistance liaison, his RVV Trustee, Tinkerbell.

"At ease. Take a seat, Van Noorden. How are you? I'm Warrant Officer Jansen charged with collecting evidence on your alleged collaboration with the Nazi regime. Colonel Elbow of the Military Authority ordered the investigation, and a written report with the result will be submitted to the commission, as per protocol. Until cleared, you are removed from your duties. Is everything clear so far?"

"Commander Jansen. Nice to meet you. Understood."

Jansen asked if he would like some water. He could only nod. One of the civilians poured a glass from the water jar at the table's center.

"You were detained on the reports of possible collaboration with the Nazis and putting citizens at risk. As you'll understand, we must investigate all credible reports. Our preliminary investigation has determined you remained on your post as police chief, while you did other, covert work benefiting the local Resistance, the Interior

Forces, and the Allies. You were never an active NSB or WA member, did not side publicly with the Nazis, and have tried to maintain the standards of conduct worthy of a policeman. You accomplished all of that under the most difficult circumstances. Congratulations to you, Opper Van Noorden."

Jacob wanted to nod but, confused, cleared his throat to object and said instead, "Thank you."

Commander Jansen continued. "But, as per the usual procedures after a complaint, you'll have an open dossier. The government has decided that a newly appointed Special Court would adjudicate any complaints about the conduct of public servants during the occupation. You may face a criminal investigation and a trial in this special court, or the case will be dismissed. We did not have the language for this type of offense, but a new category is in development and will be submitted to the courts. It might be possible that other consequences could result from this process, such as paying restitution to society, in some form. In other words, if you made serious mistakes demanding such measures. Any questions?"

Jacob shook his head to clear his mind. He stood up. "Sir, am I still under investigation?"

"Yes, but after what we've heard, I'm sure the formal investigation will undoubtedly result in your exoneration. The information we have collected in the preliminary investigation made it abundantly clear that any reports from the public were based on ignorance of your real role under the Nazi occupation, and particularly your undercover work as an informant to the Illegality. We're aware you've been of tremendous assistance to the Dutch Interior Forces and to the Canadian Forces. The information you were able to collect through your relationships with the Krauts in this town and with the Star Camp command has saved lives."

"Thank you, sir." He sat down again as his knees were giving out.

"The security commission and the Military Authority must do justice but also appear to have done justice. Van Noorden, would you please stand up for the committee's decision?"

Jacob shot up from his straight-backed wooden chair and stood at attention.

"The committee has decided to maintain you in your rank as *Opperwachtmeester* [Warrant Officer], pending the final verdict. Your work here in Overdam is done, and you'll receive a new assignment in Delden as a group commander. I sincerely apologize on behalf of the Military Authority for discontinuing you temporarily, and for the transfer." Chief Jansen took a deep breath and reached out his hand. "You are free to go."

Dazed, he took the hand. "Thank you, Commander."

"You're to take some time off. Your new job in Delden will start in a week or so. By the way, you'd probably like to know that two of your brigade members, Corporal Peters and Constable Dijk, were arrested for having been members of an enemy organization."

Jacob exhaled slowly. "Yes, Sir. Understood. Thank you."

A wave of relief edged with anger overtook him when Jansen returned his gun. He accepted his other personal items as tears of fury burned in his eyes and the urge to hit Jansen, or somebody, almost took over. He straightened his back, saluted, and quickly walked towards the door, then turned around and asked the question that had been on his mind for the last few minutes. "Who will be my new commander?"

"Yes, of course. You'll report to me, until a new authority is assigned. I don't expect you on the job until a week from now. Van Noorden, you need a break. Enjoy it. Just wait a minute, I'll come outside with you. They sound pretty bloodthirsty out there. Ha-hah, who could blame them, right?"

"Right." Jacob forced a small smile. He was hungry, and his shirt was giving off an unpleasant odor. He needed a wash.

Chapter 113

When the two uniformed officers stood side by side on the hotel's front porch, the crowd went quiet. Commander Jansen spoke clearly and slowly as he enunciated each word.

"Citizens of Overdam. Opper Van Noorden has been assigned a new police position elsewhere. The commission wishes to state that his job as an informant for the Illegality during the occupation was appreciated. He's been a valuable member of the community and was an active member of the local Resistance during the Nazi siege."

A voice in the crowd yelled out: "What has he done for us then?"

Commander Jansen replied immediately. "Opper Van Noorden collected and passed on valuable information about strategic movements of the enemy. He was able to cross the front line and provide vital information to the Allies. He fooled the Kraut leadership in town into believing he was a collaborator, and possibly a few of you as well. This led to false reports and as-of-yet unsubstantiated complaints. On behalf of the Military Authority, I have offered my apologies to Opper Van Noorden, and he has graciously accepted them. He'll resume his duties in a new placement, elsewhere. Thank you all for your cooperation."

Jansen slapped Jacob on the shoulder, grabbed his right hand again, shook it warmly, and put his other hand on top. They made eye contact and held it for another two seconds, then Jansen let go of his hand.

"One of the men can give you a quick ride home. We still need you, Van Noorden. Before you go, you might want to say a few words to the crowd."

"Thank you, Sir."

Commander Jansen walked quickly to the entrance and disappeared inside HQ.

Jacob's brain floated a few sentences to its surface. He looked at the crowd and the people looked back at him; he heard their mumbling. He let the words inside him rise to his reluctant lips, and to his surprise, he found his voice. In his usual, strident manner, he loudly propelled his words into the street.

"Dear fellow citizens. We are free! Finally, the Nazis are gone, thanks to the Allied forces and the brave men and women of the Resistance. This is also a difficult time when we remember the people, who have died leaving us in their debt forever. Please allow the BS and the security commission to complete the job they're assigned to do. In our nation, a person is only guilty after conviction in a court of law. Let's not take revenge and stoop to the same criminal level as the Nazis. I request you report only credible suspicions and forward any evidence you may have to the commission and the BS Commander Postema. We must go through the proper channels of justice. That's all I have to say. Long live the Queen." He stepped back into the shade of the porch.

Most of the listeners responded, shouting Long Live the Queen, and some started singing *Oranje Boven*. Others mumbled their dissatisfaction, and someone yelled: "They can't get away with it." Jacob walked to the steps and waited until satisfied the crowd had begun to leave, then stepped off the porch.

Van Houten hobbled toward him on crutches. "My leg is infected, but I'll live. I told your wife this morning. She's probably eager to see you. Sorry about all this. You didn't deserve it, Opper, I told them that. We're all angry this happened." They shook hands without a need for more words.

***

"Need a drink?"

Jacob nodded. He rode shotgun in an army jeep beside the Canadian driver who offered him a cigarette. He replied: "*Een sigaar* [A cigar]?" The lieutenant fished a somewhat crumpled cigar from his breast pocket, then offered him a flask and smiled when Jacob took a long swig.

He said more to himself than the driver: "*Goddank, heerlijk* [Thank God]. This feels good!" He looked around him and only now saw the crushed walls and collapsed roofs and the piles of rubble in the streets. Windows had shattered and the roads were covered with glass shards, crunching under the jeep's tires. People were milling about in groups, celebrating, singing, and cheering loudly. Some had started with the clean-up and were shoveling the mess into wheelbarrows.

Jacob exhaled and inhaled deeply and slowly several times, savoring the fragrances of rubble, wet cement, blooming lilacs, burnt wood, and diesel. Everything smelled intense, and the setting sun had never been so colorful and gorgeous before. He was transported back to that fateful first day of the war, such a lovely day as well. It had been such a different world five years ago.

Chapter 114

After those horrible sleepless nights in the basement with the racket of war overhead, Margaret was still tired by the end of the day, but the stress of waiting the rest of the day to find out what had happened to Jacob had utterly exhausted her. She was in her sixth month of pregnancy, and she shifted her weight on the divan, which wasn't able to comfort her anymore. The hours of waiting seemed like days.

She had tucked the children into bed a while ago, and they were asleep when she heard the sound of a vehicle. She ran to the window and saw a jeep with Jacob next to the uniformed driver. She was already by the door, threw it open, and waited for her husband to step inside. When he embraced her and held her tight, she broke down in tears.

"There, there. It's all good now. How are you feeling, dear wife?" Jacob said, letting Margaret go from his embrace. Putting his arm around her shoulders, he led her to the living room. "It's is all over now."

Margaret dabbed her eyes with a tiny handkerchief. She straightened her back, and with a clear voice, she replied. "Yes, it's fine now, but I want to know why the army kept you. What did you do? I was so afraid for you. Was it awful? Are you alright, *lieve man* [dear husband]?"

He realized she hadn't wanted to use the word arrest. He had no idea what Margaret really thought, just like she wouldn't know what he thought. "I am fine, I want to see the children. Then let's have a talk."

***

Jacob and Margaret went upstairs together hand in hand and watched the children sleeping. Then they kissed each child. Jacob had a quick wash and changed his clothes as Margaret stretched out on the divan.

On returning to the living room, he sat down close to her in his armchair, smoking another precious, real cigar donated by a Canadian soldier.

"Somebody reported me to the Military Authority as a Nazi collaborator," he began. "I appeared too close to the Nazis. What do you think about me? Can you please be straight with me, Margaret? Did you ever think I was a collaborator?"

Margaret took a moment before she answered and cautiously, word by word, spoke her mind. "I was never sure what you were up to, Jacob. It was not for me to judge or ask questions, especially about you being friendly with him, Nauwaard, but I knew you were visiting him often. I knew you took Hendrik for visits to his private residence, and he came here to visit you at the brigade after the air raid. It was all a bit strange. You're not social with people. Yeah, to be honest, I can see why others thought something of it."

He knew not to speak yet.

Margaret pushed on. "I know you have your reasons for whatever you do. I take it as police business and trust you to know what's right. About the Wehrmacht, yes, they were friendly to me because of being German. They knew my mother, and knew Juergen, too, did business with them. Well, you know. I'm not exactly sure what business but it didn't hurt us. So, what's the difference between you and them then?" She sat frozen-still on the divan, looking at him.

He shrugged his shoulders. "Yeah, but what did you think? Say it. Did you think I had gone over to the Nazi side?"

"Honestly! Jacob, I don't know what you want me to say. I don't really think too much about it. We just had to try to get through this time. If you were kind and made friends, it's allowed, right? Even guards, Dutch Nazis, and Wehrmacht, they're people too. I'm sure you didn't betray anybody or arrest somebody who didn't break a Dutch law. And the terrible thing with our neighbors. You couldn't have known those husbands would never come back. And when Ruth and her children were taken away, you were as upset as I was. Those were dark days, dear. We were all trying our best. Can we let it rest now, please?"

"Dear Margaret, I'm pleased you trusted me, but sometimes you're naive. I made plenty of mistakes. I should've refused right off the bat to even be present on any of those raids. I should've protected our Jewish citizens, but couldn't. And bringing in Wouters and Friesema was just dumb."

She looked surprised, for some reason and said, "Wouters from the distribution office?"

"Yes, that Wouters, the supervisor. He and his employee spent time in an SD jail. I had him brought in on request of that Nazi liaison, for an interrogation about a robbery. It could've ended badly. And all my spying on Nauwaard and Heusden could've cost me my job, or worse, sent me to jail. I was lucky enough people in the Illegality knew what I did. Henk saved my neck, and I'm grateful to him, and to Simon too. I owe both of them big time. I know I have dirty hands, because I let things happen when I should've resisted. Like our minister said in his sermon: even if that might lead to bad consequences for me."

"Oh, Jacob, let it go." She shifted, ready to get up.

He frowned. "I can't let it go. My reputation is tarnished, probably for good. Some will always think I was a collaborator. They heckled me with *Moffenhoer*. I haven't told you everything, to protect you. To be honest, to protect myself too. I didn't trust you. The less you knew, the better, especially close to Juergen, a Dutch Nazi — not all that active, but nevertheless. I do thank you for not having been more curious or inquisitive about my work. I would've had to lie more often to you."

She looked more surprised than hurt. "You lied to me?"

He grabbed her hand and held it in both of his, kisses it, and then went on with an apologetic smile. "Not telling something is not the same as telling a lie. I really wanted to go underground into the Illegality and become more active, like Henk, but you wouldn't agree for me to go into hiding. I resented you for it. I guess we all had to make decisions and I made mine, so can't blame you for it."

Her face looked tired, and her mouth quivered. "Oh Jacob, I didn't have any idea you wanted it that badly, but I did get the sense you were mad at me. I suffered from your coldness, and I felt so alone. I thought you'd had enough of me and maybe had another woman somewhere." She was about to cry, and Jacob squeezed her hand.

She bit her lip, then admitted: "Had I known what you were doing, I might've felt better… or maybe not. I would've probably been more scared."

He patted her arm. "I didn't do that much, helping out with little bits and pieces coming my way, nothing major, and there was relatively little risk for us involved. When I was away the whole night at the end — the only real dangerous time — I crossed the front lines and passed on information."

She looked at him sideways, not believing him, and was lost in her own thoughts for a few moments before she realized what crossing the front lines meant. "Good heavens. I'm thankful you didn't tell me." She sat upright, holding on to his hand, squeezing it hard, breathing quickly.

Ignoring her signs of distress, Jacob went on. "I was angry at you for siding with Johanna and Juergen."

"I know," she breathed, then recovered and with a strong voice, said: "But think about this: if it weren't for them, we might've had a difficult time surviving the last winter."

He nodded. "That's true. Maybe I was a little envious as well, you being so close to them, especially with Juergen. I'm not close to anybody, least of all to my family in the west. I have decided I will look up my brothers and make up with them. They were young too, once. It's not their fault Father was so hard on us. You're hurting my hand, dear."

She let his hand go. "Sorry. You know, when you grow up with a twin, that person is like you, but different. Juergen was timid and Mutter made me look after him. I had to tell him what to do, and not to be afraid. Yes, we were close. We are close."

He let her hand go, and got up from his chair. "Would you like me to make you a cup of tea, dear? Or shall I open the bottle I kept for a special occasion?"

A practical woman, she got back to reality: "Yes, why not? I want to tell you about my work with Elfriede, but do open that bottle and give yourself a nice drink. You deserve it, dear man. I'd better not drink anything, with the new baby. When she arrives, the world will be safe, a much better place. I'm sure it will be a girl."

He went to the kitchen to put the kettle on and make himself a sandwich. Pouring himself a snifter of the precious gift of Remy-Martin, he kept thinking on the theme of confidentiality. How much would he have to divulge in the future investigation, and what should he keep hidden? On his return to the living room, Margaret was pacing the room.

"Here is your tea, girl. What's up? What do you mean with your work?" He sat down and looked up at her.

Margaret sat back down on the divan, faced him, and told him of Elfriede's bi-weekly trips as a courier, transporting paperwork and funds, and her near-bust, when she took Elfriede's place just that one time and Van Houten saved her.

"Elfriede did all the other trips. We felt often hopeless, thinking the war would never end. I was ashamed of being German, the reason why I felt I had to do something, and this was easy for us. Elfriede was the strong one. I just went along for the organization of it and did the paperwork. I know Wouters too: he was the receiver."

Jacob grabbed her shoulders with his hands, looked at her, then kissed her on the mouth, and exclaimed, "Margaret, I'm so proud of you. I had no idea."

Margaret blushed and looked simply radiant as he let her go. "It was only once," she said. "I wished you were always this happy with me, or you should tell me more often when you are, lieve man — dear husband."

Jacob rubbed his head, then said, "I agree, I should tell you more often that I am proud of you and love you." He recalled a specific day and added, "I did sense something, when you came back with Van Houten, on Elfriede's bike — shopping for meat, you said. Good thing you didn't tell me. I would've made you both stop altogether."

Margaret had calmed down, and she wistfully said, "Will we ever get over this all? I can't believe what the Nazis have done to the world, especially to the Jewish people."

With her hand in his, Jacob felt his mind and body unwind. Mirroring her mood, he replied, "I agree with you. They're monsters. We don't know the half of it. Wait till it becomes public what all went on in the country, what our deputy ministers and the civil service leadership allowed to happen — despicable. If it ever sees the light of day, heads will roll. In the police force too. In any case, we'll have to move to Delden. Some people in Overdam object to me as chief. I guess I know too much."

She let out a deep sigh, and her face fell.

He quickly put an arm around her and pulled her closer. "Margaret, we won't talk about it now. We'll be alright."

She resisted his pull. "I have to ask you something, dear."

"One second, love." He got up, got his sandwich waiting for him on the table, and returned to the chair. After finishing his sandwich in three bites, he slowly sipped the brown liquid, anticipating the pleasant burn on its way down. "Tell, Margaret, I'm listening. Whoa, this is good stuff." He was not paying much attention to what she had to say, though her tone was different.

"I'd like for us to visit Mutter together soon, and for you to shake hands with her, so she knows you don't hold a grudge. She was blind about Hitler, but it's hard for her to acknowledge having been on the wrong side. She's ashamed but can't say it. She's a proud, old woman, please forgive her, Jacob."

The Remy-Martin relaxed him. "Of course, dear, I can do that. But there's one thing I'll never do again: kowtow to anybody. No matter who, your mother or a boss, anybody who tries to lord it over me. I've done enough brown-nosing to last me a lifetime. It made me feel dirty. From now on I'll say what I think, straight up. Yes, I'll shake hands with Mother, if only to thank her again for having fed us through these times. Alright with you?"

Her face virtually beamed. "Yes, of course, dear, that's fair. Thanks, husband, I appreciate your grace. You have changed."

He sighed. "Well, you'd think I was a monster before now. Like I said, I had my comeuppance; that changes someone. Let's hope the farmers will soon produce enough food because the west is still suffering under a famine."

Margaret got up, kissed him on his balding head, and sat down beside him on the armrest.

He was utterly relaxed now and put his arm around her. "To think I wanted the war to start and fight for the country's honor. What a fool — a child — I was. I won't forget Ruth's eyes. And her children. I'll never forget the dead flyers, and the Star prisoners, their beaten-up faces with broken noses, not more than skeletons, and then the dead. I stood by, helpless. Wim Smith and his Illegals, beaten to a pulp and carted off to a concentration camp. Probably dead too."

"I won't forget Ruth either," Margaret said softly.

They sat in silence, reflecting on the short years that embodied a lifetime of experiences nobody could have predicted.

"The two-faced traitor Nauwaard," he said.

"I thought you might've become friends of a sort." She hesitantly said and looked at him.

"It sometimes looked like friendship, but it wasn't. The man scared me to my core, the unpredictable bastard. Sorry, that slipped out."

He took a deep breath. The bit of brandy had lit his brain instantly, and he kept on talking.

"But I know now what's important. It doesn't matter what religion or what class you belong to. Having to declare what you stand for, and following through, makes you see what's really important. I hope this feeling of unity, the feeling of peace we've got now, will continue. Above all, I now know that my family, you, the children, are the most important for me. I hope our children will grow up in a better world. We're all equal, now that we're liberated from that monstrous regime. We held the fort against the barbarians. We can be proud of it."

"Yes dear. I'm proud of you. I never doubted you." She snuggled up to him.

He squeezed his arm around her waist a little tighter. "I didn't feel so good about myself earlier today. I'm afraid I'll face lots of anger and revenge. It's making me nervous."

Margaret caressed his head. "What could they say about you? You've tried your best."

He took a good swallow of his Remy-Martin, realizing he hadn't talked this much in ages. A sensation of warmth engulfed him like under a cozy blanket on a cold night. His heart was beating strong, and Margaret glowed. She looked so radiant and feminine with her pregnant figure.

"Juergen made some money off the Wehrmacht," Margaret said tentatively. "That's all, I think. He's not a bad man — actually he's a sweet man, just weak. He shouldn't go to jail for it."

Blood ties were more potent than any other, but he didn't have to worry about any Nazis or any of Margaret's relatives anymore. He could be generous.

"If you say so. Juergen's always been a mama's boy, you said so yourself. But I think I will avoid him for a while. Margaret, we're free. Isn't that wonderful? Free! Am I your compass, Margaret, and will you follow this ugly little man to Delden?"

They both laughed. He put his brandy glass down on the side table and pulled her onto his lap. With much giggling and many squeals, they finally celebrated their liberation.

Epilogue

On April 10, 1945, the Canadian troops liberated Overdam. The battle went on elsewhere in the country and around the world. On April 30, Hitler committed suicide. On May 7, 1945, Germany surrendered to the Allied forces.

On the third day after the liberation, April 13, the MG (*Militaire Gezant*) relieved Chief Van Noorden from his job against the BS's advice. This measure halted the arrests and further investigations of other suspected collaborators in Overdam. That same day, the MG also removed the mayor from his position and appointed a substitute, A.J. Immink — one of the aldermen — as temporary mayor. After this action, the MG officer left Overdam.

Since the capture of suspects had stalled and the security of Overdam was at risk with the departure of Van Noorden, the local BS leader, Postema, urged the MG to return and deal with the issue. A new MG officer arrived from Zwolle and promised the BS Commander Postema that a new body of investigation — the *Politieke Opsporings Dienst* (POD) [Political Investigations Department] would be established soon. The selection of its members would be based on consultations with the BS. The POD would carry out further investigations.

None of this happened. No MG, or a representative of the Military Authority arrived. Commander Postema made another request to the MG, this time for the establishment of a local POD unit, to take over the BS responsibilities. This request, and several others after that, also went unanswered. Two months later, nothing had happened.

In his official function as the Commander of the BS, Postema then transferred the guarding role of the Interior Forces' to the Camp Overdam authority, which had established its own administration by that time. Angry and frustrated with the MG, Commander Postema was able to disband his BS unit two months after the liberation. He cited his reasons for this speedy transfer of responsibilities in writing: the MG's lack of cooperation and the sense the MG did not fully appreciate the BS's functions or its legitimacy. After June 1945, with the Interior Forces/BS out of the picture, it fell to the military authority MG to fill the political investigation positions.

The MG assigned H.C.J. Mulder as the POD unit's leader for Overdam. Mulder appointed several local applicants to fill the investigator jobs, such as pilot helper Wim Smit (who had returned from a camp in Germany) and a couple of Van Noorden's former crew members.

Several POD investigators lodged new complaints against Van Noorden: Wim Smit of the former KP, was a victim of SS Schwier and the KK, who had not forgiven Van Noorden for not releasing him when caught. Another POD investigator was a former member of Van Noorden's crew, who carried a grudge against his former chief over a disciplinary measure.

The substitute mayor, Immink, started pushing for the prosecution of Van Noorden. He contacted the new Police Commissioner in Zwolle. The old commissioner, Major Feenstra, was incarcerated, awaiting trial.

The new Police Commissioner was a lawyer, Mr. Breukelaar, eager to pursue Van Noorden's prosecution as well. Mr. Breukelaar had a run-in with Van Noorden during the occupation years in his defense attorney's function for one of his clients — a black market dealer in textiles. In June 1945, Mulder and Breukelaar started a targeted campaign together against Van Noorden with the support of adjunct-mayor Immink.

The POD unit's leader, Mulder, and his investigators gathered witness statements from one another, and from other witnesses, among which where prisoners under investigation and held prisoner in Camp Overdam.

As Postema pointed out in his rebuttal letter to the security commission on behalf of Van Noorden, these witnesses predominantly were local citizens and prisoners of Camp Overdam whose reasons for cooperation with the POD investigators were suspect: they had a negative opinion of Van Noorden for various reasons, not based on criminal facts.

In January 1946, Police Commissioner Breukelaar, POD Leader Mulder, and six other POD members arrived at Van Noorden's home in Delden, armed with Stenguns, to arrest him just as his family was arriving from Overdam with a newborn baby girl.

Van Noorden had lived separated from his wife and children for nine months, due to lack of housing in his new assignment of Delden. His former crew members frisked Van Noorden in front of his wife and children. The Overdam crew took him the forty-five kilometers to the Overdam police station, where POD Leader Mulder in person conducted another interview of Van Noorden.

Van Noorden suggested a number of individuals as witnesses, but the POD investigators did not interview any of them. Several of the originators of the new charges indicated their reason for the new complaints: their dissatisfaction that Van Noorden had been restored in his job as police chief elsewhere. They judged him unsuitable for the role, as he had allegedly collaborated with the enemy.

The new complaints consisted of claims that Van Noorden took unacceptable risks that endangered people's lives, he had reported people to the SD, that he had been an NSB member and a collaborator in cahoots with Charles Nauwaard and SS officer Schwier of Camp Star. The case of a certain German man was mentioned who had been in hiding until Van Noorden reported him to the SD. Van Noorden had claimed that this German individual had committed a child molestation offense against a Dutch youth.

The biased and sloppy investigation that followed was based on innuendo and gossip. It could not come up with concrete evidence of wrong-doing. The leaders of the former Illegality, Henk Zondervan and Romme Postema, expressed their dismay with the treatment of Van Noorden in another letter on his behalf, stating in no uncertain terms that Van Noorden had been a valued member of their Resistance group and that the POD investigators held an unfair bias against the former police commander. The following day, Van Noorden was released again, but his credibility had been damaged in the eyes of the general public.

***

In September 1948, a week before the deadline for filing complaints of collaboration by public servants, Mr. J.v.d. Berg, member of the security commission wrote to the prosecutor of the Special Court, pointing out that Van Noorden had not yet been prosecuted. He expressed his fear the man would get off for lack of evidence if the case went to trial before the Special Court, and he advised Van Noorden should be removed from the police force immediately.

In response, former BS Commander Postema wrote another letter, this time on behalf of the whole former Overdam BS crew, making it clear he saw the complaints and the action of the POD as a revenge action against Van Noorden, in fact, harassment by a few local people who held a grudge.

On 5 October 1948, three and a half years after the liberation by the Allies, Mr. W.L. de Walle, Public Prosecutor-Fiscal with the Special Court in Arnhem, dismissed the case against Van Noorden. This ended the criminal process against Van Noorden.

***

Van Noorden's reputation was never fully restored during his life. Rumors persisted in Overdam and his new domicile, Delden. He refused to discuss the war years with his family and asked his wife to do the same. His children were unaware of his battles during the war years, or his post-war struggles with the Overdam authorities. His rehabilitation had to wait more than seventy years after the events, when his dossier in the National Archives in The Hague finally revealed the facts thirty years after his death.

Author's Notes

This story is a fictionalized account based on actual information from those days. The character of Jacob van Noorden is based on the author's father. Overdam was modeled on the village of Ommen — where my father was group commander with the Royal Marechaussee Corps from September 1943 to his re-assignment in April 1945, when the police force reverted back to its previous separate branches, undoing the Nazi centralization of the force. My father became a group commander in the Rijkspolitie in Delden.

The war was a non-subject within my family. My father answered every question with "*Ach*, that's such a long time ago, I don't remember." I've had to find alternative ways to get at the truth. Through research on the internet and by scrutinizing other works about these war years I found the National Archives in The Hague, and found my father's name. My imagination and help from editors were instrumental in making a story out of this all that would be suitable for sharing with others.

In this story, some the scenes deviated from the historical facts, e.g., the arrest of Van Noorden's Jewish neighbors did not take place this way and is to be considered literary license: to create to tell the truth. My father's statements in the archives explicitly refers to Major Feenstra's orders to conduct searches for Jews, from which my father's crew always returned empty-handed. He never arrested any Jews or had his men arrest any Jews on his orders. Such arrests could have happened, and in many towns the scenes as those described in the novel, did happen in all their horrible reality.

The character of Margaret is based on my mother. The scene in which she is taking over from her sister that one time, did not happen, although many "ordinary" Dutch women like her were couriers, or hid people.

Camp Star was modeled on Camp Erika, located 3 kilometers from the village of Ommen, named by the Germans for the heather surrounding it. Once a Krishnamurti retreat named Star Camp, it was built by the anthroposophical movement in his honor, and the philosopher Krishnamurti stayed there frequently. One former prisoner, who also experienced the infamous camps in Poland and Germany, said of

Erika: "Nowhere was I so systematically physically abused on each and every day like in Erika."

About 170 men died at Erika and another 150 died in its satellite-camps. On April, 10, 1945, the Canadian Allied forces moved into Camp Erika and it became a holding camp for newly arrested collaborators and captured enemies, and renamed Erica (in Latin spelling). In the post-war documentation it was called Camp Ommen. The camp was closed on December 31, 1946.

***

Warden Charles Nauwaard's character was taken from the information available on Erika's *Lagerführer* — camp leader, Karel Diepgrond. He was sentenced to 20 years and incarcerated but ended up serving eight years in jail and was released after being granted clemency. After his release, Diepgrond returned to Ommen, where he lived for some time. He died in1985 in the village of Soest by Utrecht at age 89.

The character kapo Norbert Bakker is an interpretation of Herbertus Bikker, known as 'the butcher of Ommen'. He was convicted to the death penalty, which was later commuted to a life sentence. In 1952, Bikker escaped from the prison in Breda to Germany. In 1993, the Dutch TV program Reporter tracked him down and revealed his identity. He was arrested there, but not extradited to The Netherlands. Germany decided as a Dutch member of the Waffen-SS, he was entitled to German citizenship. Bikker then stood trial in Germany for the murder of resistance fighter Jan Houtman; his trial was suspended due to his health. He died in November 2008.

The Illegality character of Wim Smit was modeled after a real person, Jan Seigers, who was the main force in establishing an escape route of downed Allied pilots, and led the KP group in Ommen from its inception in 1943 until his arrest in 1944. In May, 1945, after the liberation, he returned to Ommen from his imprisonment in Oranienburg, Germany. He was the only survivor of the three men captured together. He was surprised to hear the police chief had been active in the Resistance, and he maintained to his death the man had been a collaborator. Seigers received honor awards after the war from the pilots' various countries on a job well-done.

The Illegality characters Henk Zondervan ("Johan" alias for Frederik ten Broeke) — and Simon Postema ("Simon" Romme Bosma) were modeled on real people. The novel reflects the author's interpretation of their work as described in Aan De

424   Johanna van Zanten

Bronnen Van Het Verzet, a publication of the group, redacted by Jef Last. They conducted their resistance work under the auspices of another resistance organization, the Raad Van Verzet RVV.

Police Commissioner, director Major J.E. Feenstra, Van Noorden's regional boss in Zwolle, and Den Toom, his department head in Hardenberg, were arrested as war criminals. The death sentence had been restored for the purpose of adjudicating war criminals after the war. The Special Court sentenced Feenstra to death and he was executed on August, 29, 1946 for collaboration with the occupying forces and causing the imprisonment or death of his countrymen. The fact that he was a decommissioned military man was a factor in the sentencing. He had been Van Noorden's military commander before the German invasion as well, when both were attached to the VI army.

The reputation of the State Police Corps was severely tarnished. During the occupation, criminal gangs formed within police units pretty much unhindered and had operated freely during the war years. These gangs were fanatically anti-Semitic, and besides rounding up Jews, they robbed Jewish houses and gathered black market goods. Many questions have been raised how this was possible. Reverberations of this history plagued the Dutch police force for years after the war, and its rumblings continue into the present.

Many more policemen and community members must have resisted the Nazis in various covert ways to escape the Nazis wrath. Kudos to those who still knew what was right and what was wrong, when many other Dutch compromised their morals without so much as batting an eye.

***

Religion was an essential factor in the pre- and post-war Netherlands: it ruled all of Dutch society including the politicians. The initial Reformation from the 16th century that had started in Germany with Luther, diversified over time, and other reformers arose independently (Zwingli and Calvin in Switzerland). A counter-reformation swept up Europe with expulsions and executions. The result was that some areas stayed Roman Catholic and in other areas, (Holland) radical protestant denominations arose, some of which still exist today.

The importance of religion and the protection of the religious freedoms led to a variety of political parties, with every church or political stream establishing its own party. Thus, the Dutch coalition-style multi-party government arose. A number of winning parties form a government, led by the leader of the biggest winner. Compromise and negotiation to represent all of the electorate are hallmarks of this style of government.

After centuries of struggle for religious freedoms and for the country's independence from foreign rulers, for the Dutch the concept of choice is an essential factor. The populations' level of participation in the political process has traditionally been high. Successive Dutch governments are typically formed of religion-based political parties together with social-democratic and/or liberal/conservative parties. After an election, the head of state (king or queen) assigned the party leader with the most votes to form the next government.

Although religion was an essential part of society, the separation of church and state is strictly enforced. This is expressed in many rules and customs. For example, a couple who wanted to marry must report to the state office with the proper documentation after which they were married by a public servant. If a couple wanted confirmation of the marriage in a church ceremony, they were on their own and had to arrange that separately afterwards.

Parliament had decided to fund all schools equally, so most town had a protestant school, a catholic, and a public, non-denominational school regardless of the size of the town. Jacob and his siblings attended the small, protestant school. It was not unusual that the children of different schools became embroiled in taunts and chases, as if the Reformation had never ended. A number of special schools exist in the current educational system, such as the Montessori school.

***

This background of the Dutch democracy based on religion's supremacy may come as a surprise to the readers who know the Netherlands as a tolerant and open society. The baby-boom generation (of which I am a member) found its voice in the sixties, when our (mostly urban) youth resisted the conservative post-war attitudes and its battle against a fractionized, repressed society.

Although all over Europe the voices of intolerance with hateful messages are increasing, I hope that the lessons of the occupation years and the war will prevail. Only when growing older have I begun to realize what my parents went through. When I received the first document about my father in my hands, five years ago, I knew I had to write the story.

Acknowledgments

Many thanks go to author Gail Anderson-Dargatz for her generosity and wisdom in her comprehensive evaluation in the early stages of the novel's development.

Thanks to Michael C. Kanyon for his professional editing, whipping the manuscript in shape and providing mental support during the first stages.

Thanks to Sandi Gellis-Cole for her excellent feedback and her assistance in getting the characters more "novelized" and the story away from self-imposed restrictions.

Thanks to my friends for their feedback: Kim Gucho, Ria van Zanten, Don Mitchell, Lisa Purcell Wade, Diane Steinke, Dave Hugelshaffer — brave souls who wrestled with the early drafts.

Thanks to Sir Schokkenbroek, retired policeman in Ommen, who went out of his way and traveled to The Hague twice for my research in the National Archives, and for sharing his knowledge of police matters during war times and of Ommen's history.

Thanks to my brothers, sisters, and cousins for sharing their experiences, especially cousin Henk ten Broeke for inspiring the idea of the story. I gave his name to the character inspired by his father.

I am indebted to the works of Dr. Lou de Jong, Ian Buruma, Willem Stappenbelt, and Guusta Veldman, and the authors of Nederland Gedenk; a memorial record of Camp Erika. I relied on documentation in the care of The National Archives and The Dutch Institute for War Documentation.

I dedicate this novel to my parents, who survived an ordeal that they didn't want to burden their children with.

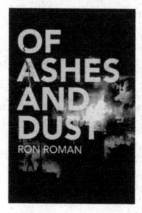